QUEEN

S. MASSERY

Edited by Studio ENP

Proofread by Paige Sayer Proofreading

Cover photo by Wander Aguiar

Cover design by Qamber Design

introduction & warning

Dear reader,

Thank you for joining me! If you are unfamiliar with my work, fair warning: my stories run dark (violence, explicit content, etc.). Sterling Falls is no different.
Reader discretion is advised.
xoxo,
Sara

Prequel: THRILL
(download at smassery.com/thrill)
#1: THIEF
#2: FIGHTER
#3: REBEL
#4: QUEEN

gods

Hades – God of the underworld
Persephone – Goddess of spring, queen of the underworld
Apollo – God of sun and light, twin of Artemis
Ares – God of war
Artemis – Apollo's twin, goddess of the hunt
Nyx – Personification of the night (technically a primordial deity that preceded the Gods and Titans, although she is referred to as a goddess in this series)
Hermes – the Messenger God, the soul-bearer, god of thieves

Cerberus – the three-headed dog that guards the underworld
Chiron – a centaur famous for his wisdom and knowledge (especially of medicine)
Kronos – Titan of time
Deicide – the killing or killer of a god

deicide

de·i·cide | \ ˈdē-ə-ˌsīd , ˈdā-ə- \
    1: the act of killing a divine being or a symbolic substitute of such a being
    2: the killer or destroyer of a god

K orinne Sterling survived—and she's been right under my nose this whole time.

    Unacceptable.

I stride through the wide doors of Olympus, surrounded by people who don't know how to respond to their abrupt dismissal. They flow around me like water, heading to their cars. Returning to their lives. They might only have a hint of what her true identity will do to this town... but I know. She could take what is hers by birthright.

Word will spread.

The deaths of the Sterlings was all anyone could talk about fifteen years ago—and now that fear will be reignited.

In a way, it's poetic. The challenge to get to Korinne will make my victory that much sweeter.

I climb into my car and speed away from Olympus.

Tonight was most illuminating.

Except, now I have a whole new set of problems. Namely, the men who surround her. Cerberus should be dealt with, too.

All in good time.

After all... I've spent the better part of twenty years planning. Moving pieces across the board like this town is a game of chess. I thought I had already won, but I was wrong.

Checkmate is still in my sights.

But first, I need to figure out how she escaped me.

kora

Everyone has left me.

Good.

I can't remember the last time I was voluntarily alone.

I spend the night cleaning Olympus. It's completely silent other than my breathing and the scuff of the broom against the marble. This work could be outsourced, but I don't want someone else to clean up my mess. It wouldn't feel like I earned it.

By the time the sun comes up, shining in through the massive double doors that I've left open, I've cleared away the sand circle, Jace's and Parker's blood, and knocked all the larger pieces of the statue into a pile.

That, I'll get someone else to handle.

With the sun comes my courage, and I venture farther into Olympus.

I stick to the first floor, going down one of the two hallways that frame the staircase. I pass the door to the utility closet under the stairs. It provided me with the broom, then later with the mop and bucket. It has a sink, a bunch of other gadgets, and the electrical panel.

All things that I catalog in my head before moving on.

The main room is shrouded in shadows. Even the sunlight streaming in through the high windows doesn't fully eradicate them. There's a large table off to one side covered in a map of Sterling Falls, and little pieces strewn across it.

Cerberus' version of a war room, perhaps.

I study it for a moment, then move past. It doesn't matter anyway. The Titans are gone with the death of Kronos. I ignore the way that makes me feel—guilt and shame squirming in my stomach. They were destroying Sterling Falls... we had to destroy them in turn.

"Kora?"

I spin around.

One of the last people I expect to see enters the room. The front of his shirt is soaked in blood, and he walks toward me with a limp. He drags a black rifle along with him, the tip scraping the floor.

"What are you doing here, Ben?"

I plant my hands on my hips, trying to come off as nonchalant as I can. Kind of hard when I just witnessed Saint murder his father. The way Ben screamed... I hit him in the back of the head with the butt of my gun. Knocked him out.

Another thing to feel guilty about.

We left him to wake up next to his dead father.

A chill runs up my spine.

"Now you're getting it." He pauses beside the table and touches one of the marks in North Falls. It could've very well been the Titan safe house. "Where is Saint, Kora?"

"Why do you want to find Saint?"

He shoots me an exasperated look. "I think you know why."

"I don't know where he is." I put my hands behind my back, if only to stop myself from fidgeting. I'm alone. Unarmed.

Ben seems much more upset than someone who hasn't seen his father in years might be.

"Do you want to talk about it?"

Ben sighs. In one swift motion, he sweeps his hands across the table. The map, all the loose pieces, everything falls to the floor. He hops up on it, grimacing slightly. He lifts the rifle and points it in my direction. There's a cruel new light in his eyes that he hid when he first came in here.

I stiffen.

"Do I want to *talk* about it?" His laugh is filled with hate. "Sure. Let's talk about how, for *years*, I resented the man who raised me. He killed my mother, you know. He found her in bed with another man and dragged her back to our house. He wanted me to know what happened when people went against him."

Holy shit. He's still pointing the gun at me, the muzzle wavering slightly in the air.

One wrong move, one wrong twitch of his finger, and I'm a goner.

"You never forget what it sounds like," he says softly. "That was just the beginning of my trauma. I witnessed him do countless, unforgivable things. So much so that when I turned eighteen, I ran away."

I edge closer. "To the island?"

He rolls his eyes. "No. That island was a more recent solution to a long-standing problem. The fact that he could find me wherever I went meant that I was never safe. But slowly, the more time I spent away from him, the more I understood his choices. I learned how the world worked, and how it shaped him... and me."

"Ben—"

"Stop trying to get the jump on me, Kora." He sighs, setting the rifle down. "I don't want to shoot you. I just want you to understand."

"I'm trying." I grind my teeth. "But how do you go from understanding him to..." I motion to him as he is.

Bloody, emotional. Almost wild with it.

"Dinner."

I raise my eyebrows. "Dinner?"

"We had dinner." He slides back to his feet, leaving the rifle behind as he approaches me. "He told me that this whole fucking city could be mine if I wanted it. It was my inheritance, there for the taking."

"Did you know you had a brother?"

"*Half* brother," he corrects, his eyes going wide. "Kind of ironic, don't you think? To fuck a married woman while he killed his own wife for stepping out on him."

"Ben—"

"Shut. Up." He's within arm's reach.

I don't know whether to back away or let him approach, so I end up staying stock-still. I ignore the muted fear running through me and the alarm bells trying to urge me to get the fuck away from him.

There's still a piece of me that doesn't believe he'll hurt me.

"To think," he whispers, his hand lifting between us. "All this time, you were right under my nose."

"I'm nobody," I answer.

His fingers curl in the collar of my shirt, and he reels me in. I know I could break away from his hold. Put some more distance between us. But I'm curious, in the most perverse way, to see how far my friend has fallen.

"You were all I had on the Isle of Paradise." I keep my voice pitched low, almost a whisper. Throatier. Hoarser. "What are you doing?"

His eyes find mine. "I think I'm going to take what my father couldn't."

He brings my wrist up between us with his other hand. The hourglass brand is right there, shiny silver. "You kept this hidden."

I raise my chin. I'm not embarrassed by it—not anymore. I've accepted what Kronos did to me, made my peace that no one *owns* me. And it's not my fault Ben didn't notice. I hid nothing.

He runs his thumb over it, and a new light enters his expression.

A man possessed.

His father's death may have very well unleashed a madman.

My stomach turns, and I try to step back.

His fist on my collar tightens, and so does his grip on my wrist. He leans down and kisses the hourglass. My skin crawls. I tense and try not to yank away too quickly. I'm doing what many women have done before me—slipping into aversion, into pleasing. If I don't react negatively, maybe he'll let me go.

I should've learned my lesson with Parker.

No amount of pleading or begging saved me from that monster... and now I'm faced with Ben. Is he a monster? Is he a madman?

Please don't be.

"I'm going to take what's mine." His gaze burns into

me. "Then I'm going to show you what happens to the people you love."

Revulsion sweeps through me.

I yank harder, and he releases my wrist. But he steps with me, his hand still tangled in my shirt, and uses my momentum against me.

His lips land on mine.

A deluge of ice pours down my spine.

I jerk back, shoving his chest. Fuck being meek, fuck letting him walk all over me.

He releases me with a predator's smile.

I stumble away, righting my clothes and trying to find a weapon. What do I have? A forgotten broom lying in the corner? War game pieces scattered on the floor? The gun, if I could get to it...

I wipe my mouth. "What the hell was that?"

He spreads his arms. "I was struck with passion. Can you blame me?"

"Yes," I say. "Yes, I can blame you. For months, you were nothing but kind—"

"Kind? Where was *your* kindness when your friend shot my father in the fucking face like an *animal*? You left me there." He lunges for me.

I dodge back, my steps quick. My heart feels so fucking heavy, though. I'm seeing two versions of the guy I knew.

In a perverted version of how we used to spar, he comes at me again. Except this time, it's so much less of a game than it used to be. There's danger humming in the air between us.

"Come on, Kora. You've got to put your back into it." He smirks. "If only I had known who you were on that island... I might've taken what I wanted from you. No matter... we're here now."

A bitter taste fills my mouth as I try to keep out of his reach. "And what's that?"

The glint in his eyes—how could I have so thoroughly misjudged him? Trusted him? I don't in this moment. Whatever control he has is gone.

He moves faster than I anticipate, crashing into me. We go down, and the back of my head smacks against the marble. White spots flicker in my vision, but it's not enough to dull my senses. His body on top of mine, pinning me to the floor. He grabs my wrists and slides his hand roughly up my side, palming my breast.

I struggle and try to remember how to throw someone off. We didn't grapple like this—and the self-defense class on the island was more about demonstrations than having us practice.

Shake me off, Jace whispers in my ear. *Where's your leverage?*

I dig my heels into the floor, going against my instincts of trying to get away. I shove my hips up and to the side.

To my shock, it works. I scramble up on my hands and knees, but he's on me again. He shoves my face to the floor and straddles me. My arms are ripped up behind me, wrists locked at the small of my back. He drags my shirt over my head. The fabric slides down my arms, and he twists it viciously. Immobilizing my hands.

I make a noise in the back of my throat. The whimper comes out before I can stop it.

He leans down and grabs my hair, angling my head. His face is right there. His lips at my ear. "I think about you and your boyfriends, and it makes me sick." He shifts.

My breathing stalls. His erection is pressing into my ass, and he grinds it harder between us. Making sure I don't miss it—or what's about to happen.

He's fucking turned on by this.

I'm going to be sick.

My stomach knots, nausea heaving through me.

"How dare you," I spit, struggling to throw him off again.

He slams my face into the floor harder than before. My teeth cut into my cheek, and the metallic taste of blood blooms over my tongue. It drags me back into my memories.

Letting Parker walk all over me, use me, hurt me.

I promised myself never again.

But then Kronos branded me. Sold me like a slave. Left me to die.

If this is the man who Ben is inspired by...

"How dare I?" His laugh is dark. "How. Dare. *You*?"

In one rough move, he rises and rolls me onto my back. My arms are still trapped behind me, my shirt working against me. My bra is exposed, my stomach. He settles back on top of me, his weight on my ribcage. My feet slide on the floor without purchase. He's higher up than before, my leverage gone. Panic seizes me when I can't take a full breath.

He pulls at my bra, then finally leans down and bites it.

I shudder as his nose brushes my chest, but it's done. The fabric tears away—and some of my dignity goes with it. He keeps pulling until the straps snap, and the whole thing comes away in his hand. He doesn't care about that, though. He stares down at my bare chest.

I struggle against my shirt, and it untwists. He must notice it's not going to hold for long, because he sucks in a breath. His eyes are dark.

"I should've brought rope," he says. "Unlike me to be

unprepared, but I didn't know where this was going until I saw you all alone..."

I spit in his face. It's tinted pink with blood, and by some miracle, it lands in his eye.

His face contorts, and I use the distraction to throw my head forward.

My forehead collides with his nose.

He yells and falls backward. I roll free of his legs, keep rolling until I can sit up and shake my arms. My legs propel me away from him, sliding on the floor. The shirt finally untwists. I rip it off and pick myself back up.

Cold air assaults my bare chest, but I don't let the flash of horror dissuade me.

I should run.

I should get as far away from him as possible.

That's what those self-defense classes taught, after all. Get in a good hit, then get away. To safety.

But if I leave, I'll never be safe. He'll slip away and find the shadows. He'll come back. Harder.

Better prepared.

He laughs at me and staggers to his feet. He touches his nose and winces, then runs the back of his hand under it. A steady stream of blood drips down. "I think you broke my fucking nose."

"You're actively trying to assault me." I sidestep when he comes at me again, my lungs tight. It isn't fear of *him*. It's old fear that has resurfaced. Memories that have haunted me for a lifetime.

I grit my teeth against the onslaught.

My birth parents were murdered.

I've been kicked around, abused, stepped on. Branded.

That fear loosens an inch because another memory has bubbled to the forefront. Not one, but three.

My parents—the Sinclairs—sitting in the audience of one of my last cello recitals. The hushed hall, the burning lights. I played a piece I had memorized, the one my teacher and I worked tirelessly on to get right. But the piece shifted halfway through. My fingers found notes that I had never played before but somehow knew. My instructor was furious. My parents were confused.

Jace playing that same melody on the piano as I sat in the dark hallway.

And a woman humming it in the depths of my mind. Just an echo, but perhaps the loudest of all.

I bump into the table and refocus on Ben. He's glowering at me, his expression calculated. I've seen versions of it when we practiced, the way he tries to think of the best way to come at me. But never with this much at stake.

My heart is slamming against my ribs.

I feel along the table edge, and my fingers brush the rifle that Ben had abandoned. I touch the muzzle, feeling down the barrel. I don't know if it's loaded or if he just brought it in here to scare me.

His gaze ticks down to my chest. I feel nothing but a desperate recklessness to end this. To see who wins and suffer the consequences.

He twists his lips in a cruel smirk. "There's nothing you can do. I know you, Kora Sinclair. You aren't strong enough to best me."

I am.

I tighten my grip on the gun behind my back. And when he comes at me, I swing it at him with every ounce of strength I have.

It takes him by surprise. The butt smashes into his cheekbone, glancing off his swollen nose, and he screams. This time *I* go for *him*. I drop the gun and tackle him, burying my shoulder into his stomach. The air is driven from his lungs. We hit the floor and roll, and I throw a desperate punch at his nose. It lands, blood spurting out.

His eyes roll back.

I get the upper hand.

The only thing in my mind is a burning anger.

I wrap my hands around his throat.

He chokes and grasps at my wrists, but I lean my weight on my arms. And I squeeze. So tight that I think my nails might break into his skin. So tight that his mouth opens and closes, and his face turns beet red.

"Kora," he mouths.

I squeeze harder. Olympus was born of violence—but so was I.

"I am a fucking Sterling," I tell him. "And you can join your daddy in Hell."

apollo

I stride back into Olympus and look around. It's quiet in the atrium, although the wall sconces are all still lit. Jace's blood has been cleaned from the floor, along with the sand and glass, and there's a pile of marble from the broken statue in the corner.

I let out a breath. It's been a while since Olympus didn't have such a darkness pressing down on it. But with Cerberus gone, it's like I can breathe again.

The throne where the statue once sat had been replaced with Hades' chair, although I doubt he noticed when he was here tonight. He might want to burn it after he learns what Wolfe's father did in it.

I wrinkle my nose and try not to think about *that* scene I walked in on once.

It was lucky that Cerberus was, uh, *occupied*. Otherwise, he might've shot me himself for witnessing it.

But where is Kora?

I go down the hall on the right, slipping into the few shadows that remain.

Even mid-morning, there are still cozy corners to tuck

oneself away in. And that makes me smile, remembering the way Kora leaned on me as we snuck her out of here. How she felt on my arm.

I arrive at the large room we used to hold fights in and stop dead. The table is the first thing I notice. It's crooked, like someone fell into it. Everything has been swept off it.

And then my gaze slips to the body.

I draw my gun. I approach quietly and kneel next to Ben's head, pressing two fingers into his throat to check for a pulse.

"Is he dead?"

I rise and whirl around, my gun already lowering.

Kora is off to the side. By the doors the fighters used. Her back is pressed to the wall, a rifle across her knees. She eyes me and frowns.

"What happened?"

Her hair is loose, wild around her shoulders. It doesn't hide the bruise on her cheekbone, though. I look back down at Ben. His nose is crooked. There's a ring of bruises around his throat. And almost under him...

I reach down and tug the lace free, holding it up.

My mind turns, and I struggle to make sense of why Kora's torn bra is in my hand.

I set my jaw when she doesn't answer me. I drop her bra and kneel back down beside him, checking his pulse again. Just to be damn sure.

Nothing. His skin is lukewarm, his eyes flat and open. Like he died staring right at her.

I want to drive my knife into his eyes. A certain sort of madness washes over me, and my knife, my trusty knife, is in my hand in an instant.

But then Kora is there, and her fingers are closing around mine. She tugs at the hem of her shirt with her other hand. "He didn't win." Her gaze hardens, and it falls to Ben. "I did."

I shiver.

I can't fucking help it.

I drop the knife next to Ben and cup her neck. She doesn't balk when I rise back up to my full height. Her head tips back, keeping her attention locked on me. I'm so fucking angry, it's practically vibrating under my skin.

My hand moves up of its own accord, my thumb brushing her bruised cheekbone.

She flinches. Just a little. Pain flashes across her eyes.

"He hurt you," I state.

"I hurt him back."

It's not enough. I have to touch her—but I won't do it over a damn corpse. I lift her into my arms. Her legs automatically come around my hips, her arms circling my neck. I stride out of the room. Past the Hell Hound-tainted atrium. Out of Olympus entirely.

The sun bathes us in a golden glow.

Sunsets are pretty—but on the cliffs, the sunrises are magic.

It's too late for that. The sun is already up, the pink streaks that might've tinted the sky burned away. She shivers, even though the air is warm. May is slipping into June, and soon those chilled nights will be gone entirely.

I stop a few feet from the cliff edge and set her down, but I don't release her.

"He tried to rape me," she whispers.

Her voice is fucking broken, and the anger spikes through me all over again.

"His hands on me—" She closes her eyes for a second, then opens them. They flash at me, her blue eyes like a storm. Sometimes she's an open book, and right now, she lets me see all of it. Her pain, her hope. "Please, I need you to erase it."

I kiss her softly. My lips touch hers, and I savor her softness.

I should've known that's not what she wants.

Her nails dig into my shoulders, tugging at my shirt. She catches my lower lip in her mouth and sucks.

I groan. My control is fragile, but it seems like she doesn't want me to be in control. Not by the way she's tugging at my shirt, her hands roaming all over my chest. I lick the seam of her lips, and it's like a secret password. She opens for me. I tilt her face and taste her mouth.

Blood.

It's faint. Her tongue tangles with mine, taking my taste for herself. I pull her shirt up, and we break away long enough for me to pull it off her. She raises her arms and allows the black fabric to leave her body easily.

The shock of her not wearing a bra shouldn't register. I saw it, after all, abandoned in Olympus. But her nipples pebble, and I let out a growl.

She gasps when I bend down and suck one into my mouth. My teeth graze it, and her back arches against me. She's got the buttons of my shirt undone and roughly pushes it off my shoulders. I haul her closer, impossibly tight.

We're going to burn to ash.

The pads of her fingers sweep just above the waistband of my jeans, and I nearly combust on the spot. But that doesn't compare to when she dips her hand inside my pants.

She grips my rock-hard dick, her hand sliding up and down. Her fingers go lower, cupping my balls, and my breath hitches.

I need to be inside her.

Now.

I bring us to the ground. I don't think she cares that the dirt and grass bite into her bare back. My mouth is trailing down between her breasts, pressing kisses along the way. Bites that make her shiver. I undo the gold chain belt that no doubt came from my sister. The button on her white pants, then the zipper.

Her breathing is ragged, matching mine. It makes me wonder if our heartbeats are aligned, too.

She lifts her hips to assist me in dragging her pants and underwear down. I take her shoes off, too, tossing them away.

"You're a fucking goddess," I say.

Her red hair is spread around her, her makeup still strong. The bruise on her cheek is getting darker by the minute. Her body, though, is open for me. Her legs part, and she sucks in a breath when I take her ankle.

She watches me as I run my nail up the bottom of her foot, and she jolts. A rare smile flickers across her lips. I cock my head and keep touching her. Sliding my hand up. Her calf, the back of her knee. Her thigh.

I run my nose up her leg, then turn my mouth to her pretty, sensitive skin.

I bite.

She jerks again, but it's followed by a groan. Her fingers dig into the dirt as she tries to ground herself. I finally reach her pussy, and I take a moment to just look. She's perfect, every single fucking inch of her.

And if he had touched her, if he had managed to hurt her worse than the visible bruises—

"Apollo," she whimpers.

I smile and lean forward. Her flavor is like the fucking

fountain of youth. I don't think anyone's pussy should be *this* delicious, but I think it might make me immortal. She's sunshine and smoke, bottled just for me.

My hand wanders higher, pressing on her stomach as I enjoy her clit. Her breathing is erratic at this point, her thighs trembling. My hand inches higher, and I touch her breast.

She goes still.

I glance up at her to find her eyes screwed shut.

No.

I rise quickly, my body hovering over her, and I wrap my hand around her throat. "Look at me," I order.

"I—"

"Open your eyes, baby," I say again, no less harsh. I'm not an idiot. He touched her breast, maybe her nipple, and when *I* did it, it took her right back into that room with *him.*

But I'm going to eradicate him from her memory one way or another.

Pleasure.

Pain.

Both, maybe.

I squeeze, just enough, and her eyes open. They're brimming with tears on the cusp of falling, but I ignore them. If I give in, she'll get the soft version of me—and that won't help either of us.

Because I'm mad at *her,* too. A deep, simmering anger that's a little too close to betrayal for my comfort.

She married Jace.

I heard Cerberus.

I heard his whole spiel while I focused on trying to keep my best friend from bleeding out—while I fought the urge to stab him, myself.

I shove my pants down just enough to release my cock

from its confines, and I don't wait for her go ahead. I ram into her as hard as I can. Her body slides, but my grip on her throat, pushing her into the ground, keeps her from going too far.

Her eyes widen. Her pupils fucking dilate.

I pull out and push back into her, letting out a possessive noise. I don't know where it comes from. I just know that she's *mine*, and I'll be damned if I let that bastard try to take any piece of her from me.

Not her body.

Not her mind.

And definitely not her fucking soul.

I flick her nipple again. Harder. "This is mine." I bite her breast, and she shudders. She's so wet, her muscles clenching around me as I rock in and out of her. I go slow to keep my composure. Losing myself to this feeling would be too easy—on both of us. I move to her other side. "And this," I say to her skin.

My other hand is still on her throat, and I feel her sharp swallow.

I rise back up and claim her mouth.

This kiss is greedy. Hungry. She's coming back alive. I almost lost her for a minute. I tear my lips away and suck on her neck, silently claiming everything I touch. *Mine, mine, mine.*

Her skin is fire.

She arches under me, finally—fucking *finally*—touching me back. Fighting back. Her nails carve paths down my back, my biceps, and each prick of pain is ecstasy. My hand moves between us, down to her core, and she trembles when I touch her clit. I pinch it, and she lets out a moan that goes straight to my dick.

Goddamn.

I fuck her harder, rising on my knees and widening her legs. I look down at our connection. The way her pussy takes me, stretching around my cock. There's a sensation at the base of my spine. My balls tighten.

I press on her clit again, urging her to come first. And she does, writhing beneath me. But she never looks away, and pure joy explodes in my chest.

I roar my climax, yelling for the world to hear. Because if anyone is close enough to hear me out here—fuck them right to Hell. I go still, my cock pulsing.

She pulls me back down on top of her and wraps her arms around my neck. She kisses my jaw. Then my cheek—

I turn and catch her lips with mine.

This kiss is softer. Slower. We taste each other again, and I stroke her hair. I drop more of my weight onto her, and she just seems to melt with it. Her nails dig into my shoulder blades, her grip tight. Keeping me with her.

But we can't stay here forever.

I push back up onto my forearms, regretting the moment I slip away from her. She stays where she is for a moment, then takes my offered hands. I pull her to her feet, and she shivers.

And then I curse myself for forgetting why I was here in the first place.

"What?" she asks, eyeing me.

I shake my head, my expression going dark. "We need to talk."

N o good thing has ever started with *we need to talk*.

My stomach swoops. Apollo and I gather our clothes and pull them on silently, all while I'm trying to figure out *what* he needs to talk to me about.

Oh, shit.

Maybe he can't do this anymore. He's tapping out. We freed him—too little, too late—and now he's taking his freedom seriously.

Was that a goodbye fuck?

"You're spiraling," Apollo comments.

I bite back my retort. He's right. I *am* spiraling.

When we're fully dressed, he takes my hand. I don't question him.

Do I only question Jace's every move?

I ponder that as he leads me back down the hill, past Olympus. He had parked his bike at the corner, in the shade. Two helmets sit on the back of it, waiting for us, and he looks from me to them. And lets out a sigh.

He drops his hand and scrubs it over his face.

27

"What?" I finally ask. "Can you just..." I wave my hand.

He frowns. "Right now?"

"Well, I don't want to wait until next fucking Tuesday."

He smiles, a glimmer, and then it's gone. Sweat rolls down my back, and I'm distinctly aware of the wetness between my legs. I like the feel of him there, but I *don't* like the butterflies fluttering in my stomach. I'm hot and itchy and I'm going to burst out of my skin if I don't get some words moving past his pretty, full lips.

I catch myself staring at those lips. Especially when they curve back up into a smirk. I jerk away, casting my gaze around the room. Literally anywhere else.

"Korinne Sterling," he says, and my heart turns to ice.

I say nothing.

I don't know what *to* say.

"What do you remember?" He steps closer. "Did you know your par—"

"My parents are Ken and Rachel Sinclair," I hiss. "My birth parents—"

"They didn't abandon you," he replies, his tone so fucking even it makes me want to scream. "They didn't give you away. They're not out here living a life without you, or whatever messed-up thoughts you used to keep yourself cold at night."

I push him, but he just captures my wrists and reels me in. He kisses me hard, his teeth scoring my lip.

I bite him harder.

He chuckles when he withdraws, touching his lip. There's a drop of blood there, smearing on the pad of his thumb. "Save some of that fire for Jace, baby."

The husband.

I shake my head and exhale. "How could we get married without me knowing?"

"You sign anything with him?" He cracks a smile. "You've got a bad habit of signing things without reading the fine print."

He touches the brand on my wrist.

"Asshole," I whisper.

He shrugs and hands me a helmet. I take it. There was just one thing I signed in the vicinity of Jace King... in the Hell Hounds club. Cerberus' office.

What had he said to me?

Don't you trust me, Sinclair?

Baiting me. Always fucking baiting me. And I took it like an idiot.

The wash of horror I felt when he signed under my name is renewed, opening like a geyser inside me. The rest of it comes back to me.

"Let's make your freedom official," Jace said in my ear.

I signed.

But... then Jace signed.

And I realized that I wasn't making my freedom official—I was just giving my leash to someone new.

Cerberus took a seat behind his desk and leaned back, grinning at me. "Happy now, girl? You're out from under my thumb."

"Out of the pan and into the fire." I couldn't look at Jace.

He didn't seem to have a problem looking at me, though. He leaned in and whispered, "Let's go."

I swallowed. "Is that an order?"

Jace paused and faced me. He ran his fingers down my jaw and pushed my hair off my shoulder. It was oddly menacing, even though my stupid heart took comfort in it. Like a silent threat and apology rolled into one.

He trailed his fingers through my hair and nodded slowly. "Yes, Kora, that's an order."

How could I have forgotten that?

The separation, the island, the fucking war.

I was happy to see him, the relief of him not being fucking murdered so damn light in my body that I just forgot who he truly was.

My heart is hardening. Inch by inch.

I jam the helmet on and flip the visor up. Apollo has done the same, his dark-brown eyes steady on mine.

"Did you know what Jace was going to do?"

He tips his head to the side. Not a yes or a no. He's angry about it, too, though. It's festering in his eyes. But he had to know *something*. And perhaps he did. The whisper of a plan to keep me bound to them, only solidifying moments before all hell broke loose.

I approach the bike and swing my leg over. He watches me for a moment, then climbs on behind me. His hands slide down my hips, resting on my thighs.

"For the record," he says, his face almost next to mine. "If he hadn't been stabbed, I would've beat the shit out of him for what he did to us."

Us. Not me.

I flip my visor down and start the bike. The motor comes alive with a deadly roar, and I grip the handles.

Apollo lifts the kickstand, keeping us steady. He doesn't bother to point out instructions. I've been on the backs of their bikes plenty of times—if I didn't pick up a thing or two by now, what good am I?

We shoot out onto the street. He reaches up occasionally, correcting something. My speed, how I've shifted gears with my foot. He doesn't mind when we wobble, or when I slip too far to one side of the road. The vibrations of the bike are going straight to my head.

I don't know where I'm going until we get there.

The Sterling Falls Library.

Now that I know more about Sterling Falls, this building makes sense.

It carries the signature Ancient Greece feel, as if it was transported from an older time like Olympus and the SFU Administration building. The wide marble steps lead up to impressive columns. The carvings at the top of each show beasts from myths. The three-headed dog, a demigod with a bow, another with a sword. Beautiful, angelic faces fighting their fates.

Apollo follows me, a hulking shadow, through the entrance and into the cool, quiet library. The inside has been renovated, and I'm surprised how much that disappoints me.

A woman at the front desk raises her hand for us to stop, but Apollo bares his teeth at her. She goes silent and lets us pass with a wide-eyed expression.

I raise my eyebrows at him, and he offers a brief smirk. Still, we don't speak as I wander to the help desk in the back.

"What can I do for you?" The librarian, a man in his forties, smiles at me.

Apollo coughs, and the man pales. He swallows, his Adam's apple bobbing.

"Archives," I say, pulling his focus back to me. "I'm looking for reports on the Sterling family murders."

The librarian tugs at the collar of his button-up shirt. He glances at Apollo again, then nods briskly. "Of course. We usually require that people reserve spaces, but, uh, it's fine. We have an empty booth."

He circles out from behind the desk with a key, and we follow him down a hall next to the desk. He unlocks a room with rows of wire shelving. They're stacked with magazines and newspapers. Against the left wall are five booths. Two are occupied. We take a middle one, Apollo dragging one of the chairs over and sprawling beside me.

My heart beats loudly while we wait for the librarian to return. This room is silent except for the occasional *whoosh* of a slide being turned.

I meet Apollo's gaze. He seems to be contemplating something, then he abruptly stands.

One of the two people, a woman, glances up at him.

She blanches and slowly pulls her headphones off.

"Out," he says simply.

She nods once, retrieving her notes and bag. She doesn't even take the time to stuff everything *in* her bag. She rushes out without a backward glance.

He turns his attention to the last person. A college-aged kid, from the look of him. Maybe a little older. The kid ignores us, even though he has to feel the weight of Apollo's stare. He's got earbuds in, and his foot taps in time to his music.

Apollo scowls and grabs the kid by the back of his shirt.

The kid yelps and tries to shove Apollo off—it's point-less, though. He sets the kid on his feet and rips one of the earbuds out.

"Leave," Apollo barks in his face.

I press my fist to my mouth, trying to hide my smile. When the door clicks shut behind the kid, who was so rushed he forgot his phone, Apollo raises an eyebrow at me.

"What?" he asks.

I rise, letting my full smile show. Damn. It feels good to smile for once. Since everything that happened... I shake it off and shrug, reaching out and hooking two fingers in his jeans.

I tug him closer and rise on my toes, kissing his cheek.

At least, that was the aim.

He turns his head at the last second, and our lips touch.

"I like it when you go a little caveman on people," I say, my lips still on his. Just a small confession. "Growling, looking like you'd rip their heads off..."

"I would," he retorts, leaning back slightly to meet my eyes. "We don't want people overhearing. In fact, I would say it's damn risky coming here at all, asking for that inform—"

"Here it is," the librarian says, coming in with a stack of reels. He stops short and glances around. "Oh. Where did they go?"

Apollo shrugs, expression blank.

The librarian coughs. Or chokes. Either way, he loads the film into the machine in the center. He shows me how to go between slides, then backs up. He clears his throat. *Phlegmy guy.*

"Well, just holler if you have any questions..."

"Thanks." I'm already lowering myself back into my chair and scooting closer to the screen.

My attention goes to Apollo, who returns to me after he's locked the door behind us and put a chair under the handle.

"Not that I'm at all interested," I say, "but what happened to Jace?"

Seeing as how my lunatic ex stabbed him.

I should feel worry. I should be more concerned.

But I'm feeling sort of numb to Jace King right about now.

Betrayal runs deep.

Apollo kisses my shoulder. "I was wondering when you were going to ask."

I raise my eyebrow.

"He's with Antonio. We drugged him and took him to the emergency department. They did a few scans to make sure nothing was stuck in him, like the tip of the knife. They ended up doing surgery to repair the internal injuries, stitched him up, and we got him the fuck out of there before anyone figured us out." Apollo rolls his eyes. "Don't look at me like that. He's fine."

I press my lips together and refocus on the screen.

He's fine. I'm not worried about Jace King. Although the idea of him lying in a hospital bed—as I and Apollo have experienced—is unsettling.

I shift, then lean closer to the monitor. It doesn't take me long to find the slide I need—just a button push, and suddenly it's there. A Sterling death isn't page six news.

The family is splashed across the front page headline.

October first. Eighteen years ago. I was... *three years old.*

STERLING FALLS MOURNS with Founding Family

WILMA STERLING WAS FOUND SLAIN in her home on Monday, September 29th. Authorities are investigating the case. Ms. Sterling was discovered by her fifteen-year-old daughter at approximately eleven p.m., and a 911 call alerted police. Deputies were dispatched.

So far, there are no suspects.

The Sterling family has called for immediate action, led by Wilma's older brothers, Brendon and Mason Sterling. They are spearheading a campaign to bring justice for their fallen sister...

I LEAN BACK in my chair. "How did she die, though?"

Apollo drums his fingers on the table. "I don't know. I doubt that information was ever made public." He eyes me. "Would you have wanted the details slipping out?"

I shudder. "No."

Wilma.

Was she my mother? Someone would've mentioned if I had a sister, right? Not that Cerberus was very forthcoming.

My stomach cramps. I didn't entertain the thought that I had siblings. I mean, I guess I did when I was daydreaming about the life I might've had, but I didn't linger. So I could have a sibling. Or more than one.

I flip through the slides, looking for anything with my... my *real* name on it.

What's real anyway? Is Kora real? Or Korinne?

Apollo switches out the reel for me, and we jump forward in time by six months. April, and I'd be four at this point. Another death that I scan. The paper is light on the details. Mason Sterling and his wife died in a fire, leaving their son behind.

"Alex?" I guess.

Apollo grunts a confirmation.

How horrible.

I study the faces in this photograph. Mason Sterling is tall, towering over his wife, but there's no doubting that they love each other. Their bodies are tipped toward each other like flowers reaching for the sun. They both wear small smiles, holding secrets the camera would never guess, and formal wear.

It's hard to tell if we'd look alike in the grainy black-and-white photo.

"Last one," Apollo says, standing to replace it.

· · ·

LAST OF THE Sterling Family Falls Violently

CHAIR of the City Council and last remaining Sterling was killed last night. He and his wife died from gunshot wounds to their head. Brendon and Leisl Sterling leave behind a daughter, Korinne—

MY BREATH CATCHES.

Brendon.

Leisl.

KORINNE IS FIVE YEARS OLD. She is currently missing. Police are doing everything in their power to locate her. If the public has any information on these horrific deaths, or the whereabouts of Korinne Sterling, please call...

I PUSH AWAY from the table.

My stomach rolls, and I wonder if I'm going to throw up.

Shot in the head?

"It's clear that your father was the one suppressing the media coverage on his siblings' deaths," Apollo says quietly. "That's much more detail than they'd printed—"

I lunge for the trash can in the corner.

Apollo is at my side in an instant as my stomach heaves. He gathers my hair at the nape of my neck and strokes my back until I stop shuddering.

I spit and rock back on my heels. "Sorry."

"What are you sorry for?" He traces my jaw with his knuckle. "This is foreign to you—"

"I know."

The doorknob rattles, and we both jump up. "Mr. Madden," the librarian calls. "This is most inappropriate—"

"Time to go," I breathe.

Apollo nods and takes my hand. He doesn't let go as he shoves the chair aside and unlocks the door, dragging it open quickly.

The librarian is flushed, glaring at us. "You cannot lock this door," he sputters.

"It's okay, we're done." Apollo pulls me past, and I avoid eye contact with the indignant man stuttering behind us. He leads me through the stacks, and I peek up at him.

He's smiling.

I think he likes this sort of thing. Breaking the rules. Or maybe just holding my hand, because his grip tightens when I try to slip free.

We get to his bike, and I let him get on first, quickly sliding behind him and wrapping my arms around his waist.

Easy.

Like we've been doing this our whole lives.

A glass shatters next to me. I ball my fists and hold back my reaction, not moving. I can't remember the last time my father struck me—not since I was old enough to hit back. But right now, anything seems possible.

He's in a rage.

He's flipped a table, and he roars at whoever looks at him the wrong way.

Because of that, most of the Hell Hounds have cleared out of the clubhouse. It was rebuilt over the last six months. Staying at Olympus was just something he did to get under my skin. But Kora firmly knocked him on his ass with her request, and now we're here.

There's still a new-paint smell. The bar is fully stocked, all new furniture. There are more rooms in the back for the guys, and upstairs, too. It was smart to expand and upgrade with the rebuild, even if the main layout is still the same.

I don't know where he was going to put Apollo and me, and I'm not in a hurry to find out.

Knowing him, right now I'd be locked in the basement.

But I turn over what my father told her *after* he granted her request. Or maybe he told her during it, and his admission is what prompted our evacuation of Olympus...

She's a Sterling.

And I'd bet my life that Jace has known who she was from the beginning.

The pieces are all sliding into place, and it makes too much sense. How Jace wanted to chain her to us, how he couldn't seem to let her go. He's never fucking acted like that about a girl before.

I glower at the floorboards.

He should've been honest with us. He should've told *Kora* who she was the second he knew. And now I'm mad enough to join my father in throwing things around the room. But it isn't just anger. He felt the need to hide it from his best friends. It takes me a moment to realize the stabbing pain in my chest is *hurt*.

We share everything. No secrets, no lies. Hell—we even share *her*.

I grip the edge of my stool harder.

Dad is only pissed because now two valuable things have slid through his fingers, no better than fucking sand, and he couldn't stop it.

Kora.

Olympus.

Not me, though. I take a breath through my nose and remind myself that I *needed* Jace to pick Apollo. I can't be mad that the bastard actually went ahead and did it.

Malik enters and slips along the wall to me. He eyes the broken glass to my left and takes the stool on my other side. He watches my father with a more critical eye than most, and I can't help but hate that Malik has more favor than me in my father's eyes.

"You know you're his second," Malik says, perhaps reading my thoughts—or just my scowl. "He declared it."

"He said I was his heir," I say under my breath. "That's not the same thing."

He grunts. "It is. He wants you to take over if anything happens to him. That's what a second does." He nudges me. "And no one is going to follow you if you don't step up."

I eye Malik, silently balking at the idea.

But my father *was* pretty adamant... and that doesn't happen often. He lost me once. It would seem to be pure madness to insert myself deeper into the Hell Hounds.

What if I can't untangle myself from them again?

"Go on," Malik urges. "Show us what you're made of."

He used to say that to rile us up. Jace, Apollo, me. When we were teenagers under his wing, learning to fight, to ride motorcycles, to become shadows. We learned how to steal and kill from him, too. Circles dug by our heels in the dirt, wrestling matches to test our mettle.

I look around the room. A few more Hell Hounds have entered, but even more are outside on the sprawling front porch. The porch will be the last thing to be completed. It needs a coat of stain, then to be sealed. Right now, the wood is too new for the likes of us. Too bright, especially in the rising sun.

I hop off my stool and approach my father. My blood pressure is spiking just from entertaining the idea of getting close to him, but he stops yelling at one of the new recruits when I'm right behind him.

He whirls around, and his eyes gleam.

"You're making a scene," I tell him.

"You knew Kora was special," he accuses, pointing at me.

He's drunk. The bitter smell of vodka assaults my nose. We shouldn't have left him to his own devices when we returned from Olympus, the Hell Hounds that were at the fight spreading out to claim their rooms and make them their own. While my father went and drank himself into oblivion.

"I didn't," I say evenly. "And I sure as hell didn't know Jace married her."

Those words sit strangely on my tongue.

I wanted to marry her, and I'm not sure what to do with that ache in my chest. Did I deserve her? Probably not. Did that stop me from wanting her with every fiber of my being? No.

And now...

My father laughs in my face. "Well, you fucked up, son. If you had stayed with me in the first place, I would've tied *you* to her. As it was, Jace had a more tempting offer..." He waves his hand, dispelling whatever he sees floating in front of his face. "I should've realized it wasn't so simple."

Wait. Jace and him arranged it? Together?

I grit my teeth. "When did you realize she was a Sterling?"

He pokes my chest. Hard. "Not *a* Sterling. *The* Sterling."

I scoff. "Yeah, okay, when did you realize she was *the* Sterling?"

My father hooks his arm around my neck and pulls me down to his level. He moves deceptively fast for an old drunk guy, but I make no noise of protest. No noise at all, just like he taught me.

"Her scholarship was when I first suspected it, you know? I set it up as a way to lure in the heir."

What?

"It didn't hit me at first, because she was removed from receiving the scholarship." He snaps his fingers. "Poof, like she never had it in the first place." He weaves toward the bar, dragging me with him. "I thought the school fucked up. But the girl they did give it to was all wrong. All wrong."

"How...?"

Then it fucking hits me.

Jace knew about the scholarship. Hell. *We* were responsible for the school taking it away from her after that first night in the woods.

Will his laundry list of deceit ever end?

A memory of sitting in the den, contemplating the gravity of our situation—that a girl had witnessed Apollo stab a rat in the Hell Hounds, and we didn't do shit about it —when Daniel called. He had done a brief background of the girl, given us a short overview. Lived in an apartment, was starting Sterling Falls University in the fall on scholarship...

I can't remember if Jace acted weird at that bit of information. But he did suggest ruining her life however possible in order to drive her back to her parents.

Fuck.

"And then she spilled the story after I won her in the auction," my father continues, ignoring the way I'm bent under his arm. "And that was the best money ever spent. Because Kronos was a fucking sucker. There was nothing sweeter than rubbing in his face that he let the *Sterling* heir slip through his fingers."

I try not to glance at him. The way he's talking about Kora with such reverence is unsettling. And I can't help but point out, "You still let her go, though."

His expression hardens. "It was bad intel that threw me

off her scent. She mentioned parents, and I assumed her time in that group home was because they were bad parents. You know, like Jace's."

I am sick of playing catch-up. "Excuse me?"

Dad finally releases me and reaches over the bar for another bottle of vodka. He snags it in his fingertips and twists the top off. "You think I plucked him out of obscurity for his own good?" A disgusted expression crosses his face as he contemplates performing any act of charity. Especially for a kid. He tips his head back and laughs, and it's a hyena's laugh. Out. Of. Control. "He was supposed to give us a fucking angle to find her."

One minute it was just me. Then there were two of us... and then three. I didn't ask my father why, or where Apollo and Jace came from. They told me about their parents in their own damn time, but Jace never mentioned spending time in a group home.

I'm so fucking confused.

"Maybe you should go to bed, Dad," I finally say. "It's been a long night."

"That it has," he mumbles.

Suddenly, he doesn't look like the strong Hell Hound leader I know. He seems tired. There are new wrinkles around his eyes, more gray and silver flecks in his hair. He shakes off my hand, glaring at me, and meanders toward the rooms. He manages his way upstairs, and the large room is drenched in silence.

I spot one of our new recruits in the corner. He's white as a sheet. I point at him. "What are you waiting for, recruit? Clean up this goddamn mess." I storm outside. "And someone figure out what the police know about the Titans."

"Yes, sir," a handful of voices echo.

It doesn't matter. I thunder down the porch and stop on the freshly grated gravel, tipping my head back. The sun hits my face and warms my skin. It burns through my eyelids, but I like the brightness.

After so long in the dark, I'm finally going to get Kora and I some answers.

FIVE

Apollo takes me to a neighborhood in East Falls. It's tucked out of the way, with quiet streets and small but manicured homes lining the way. It feels like an older part of the city.

I've noticed that with Kronos' death, there's been a lack of patrolling cops. At least, during the day. I don't feel the heavy oppressiveness of the gang war either—although that could be all in my head. People still have to function in Sterling Falls. They still have to get to and from work, still have to grocery shop and exercise and see their friends.

Maybe I imagined the weight of the war.

Or... maybe this neighborhood is just extra untouchable.

We coast up a small inclined driveway. The house is teal with black trim. A gemstone color, dark and eye-catching. The lawn is exactly the same as everyone else's on this street: a large tree in the front, short grass, a line of shrubs up against the house and lining the walkway to the sidewalk.

I climb off and remove my helmet, my brow raised.

"Antonio's house," Apollo says, immediately taking my hand. We leave our helmets behind and enter through the door beside the garage. "He still has two of his three kids at home, but they're well-behaved."

"And you're bringing *me* into their lives?"

Apollo lets out a huff, and his grip tightens on my fingers for a second. "If you think for one second that they'd be unlucky or ungrateful to meet you, or that you're somehow this monster—"

"I'm pretty sure I'm cursed." My voice is dry.

"Well, maybe," he concedes. His lips curl into a smirk. "You sure do like to attract danger."

I dig my heels in. "This is exactly why I should stay far away from kids."

He cocks his head. "But don't you want to give Jace a piece of your mind?"

Well, shoot. He knows he has me there, judging from the smile he's aiming in my direction. I rub my chin like I need to think about it, and feign indifference when I say, "Oh. He's in there?"

"He's worse luck than you, arguably."

I lift Apollo's hand and kiss his knuckles. "Thank you," I whisper.

He eyes me. "For what?"

"Making me feel..." I shrug, casting a glance around the street. "Not so alone, I guess."

I just killed someone, after all. A friend.

And that doesn't even begin to cover the hole in my heart that Nyx left.

Just as we've started moving again, I pull him to a stop. "Where's Saint?"

The last thing he needs is to be alone. I mean, maybe he'd *want* to be alone, but...

"Inside. With Tem, too." He comes closer and cups the side of my neck. His fingers skim into my hair, and his thumb ghosts along my jaw. He leans down and presses a kiss to my lips, and I close my eyes. He's gone too fast, straightening up. "Antonio didn't want to bring us all back here with the war, but since there's a good chance it's all over..."

I nod once. I wouldn't want to bring a bunch of gun-wielding, gang-affiliated crazies into my home either.

Apollo leads me into a mudroom. We toe off our shoes, and he doesn't release my hand when we enter the house. There's a murmur of conversation down the narrow hall. I stay half hidden behind him, suddenly struck by a thought.

I tug him back. "Apollo," I whisper. "What are we going to do about Ben...?"

"I'll take care of it when the sun goes down." He squeezes my hand. "It's okay."

I let out a breath and nod. I mean, it's not like he's condoning murder or anything crazy like that... He's done worse. *I know he has.* That thought is comforting in its own way.

We continue into a kitchen and dining room area. Antonio stands at the kitchen island with his wife. They're speaking in Italian, and they don't immediately notice us arrive through the side door. Antonio is just a few inches taller than me, but his wife is positively tiny. Beautiful, too, with long dark hair braided into a rope that swings down the center of her back. It's flecked with silver strands. Her face is absolutely clear, her eyes bright as she talks to her husband.

My heart lurches when he reaches across the island and takes her hand in his.

They notice us, and Antonio smiles his relief. He comes

forward and wraps his arms around Apollo first, pulling him down, and then hugs me.

When he withdraws, he introduces us. "Kora, this is my wife, Vittoria. Vittoria, Kora. Apollo, Jace, and Wolfe's... friend." He gives me a look, like he doesn't know how else to categorize me. I'm certainly not going to be introduced as Jace's wife, that's for sure.

She comes forward, and I smile. She shakes my hand, nodding her pleasantries, then hugs Apollo. Who still hasn't released my other hand.

"Where is everyone?" he asks.

"Jace and Saint are in the basement. Tem is finally getting some rest upstairs in Anna's room," Vittoria says. "It's been a hard night for everyone."

I swallow. Hard doesn't begin to cover it.

"We're arranging Elora's funeral," she continues, her eyes steady on me.

My stomach heaves, and I press my palm to it. I don't know if I can go to a funeral. I made... I made the decision to put Nyx at the front of the house. And I should've known that she'd come face-to-face with Kronos if he tried to escape.

Saint was injured.

She had virtually no backup.

"Hey." Apollo bumps me with his shoulder. "Don't fall down the guilt hole. You'll never get back out."

I'm already there.

Apollo says something to them, then guides me to a door around the corner. It's cracked open, revealing a darkened stairwell.

Basements.

I balk again, and tears prick the backs of my eyes. My feet just won't move. Ice and fire are warring under my flesh, and I don't know if I'm going to freeze over or combust.

"It's okay," he whispers to me. "Kronos is gone. You're safe."

"I'm so far from safe," I whisper back. "Someone killed the Sterlings, and Cerberus just announced to a room full of strangers who I am. Kronos tried to kill me by tying me up in a basement, and some stranger rescued me. So he's still out there, too. Not to mention the Titans who now don't have a leader..."

His dark eyes travel my face, and he nods once. "You're right. But here, in *this* house, no one will get to you without going through me."

That's the problem.

I don't want them to go through *anyone* to get to me.

Either way, I can't let fear rule my life. If there was one thing those stupid therapy sessions helped with, it's that. Little lessons that burrowed into my brain.

I take a deep breath and release Apollo's hand. He stands back as I open the basement door, eyeing the carpeted steps. It seems finished down there, but I can't tell at this angle. It's not like Apollo is going to slam the door behind me and lock me in.

"Is this another fear we need to work through?" he says in my ear, his hands sliding across my hips.

I shiver, cracking a small smile. "Maybe."

He chuckles, and the sound curls in my brain.

It's okay. I've got this.

Twelve steps, and I'm down. It's more like a big family room than a dingy basement. I was expecting the latter. It's set up with couches and a television, a game console under it. I imagine that Antonio's children entertained their friends down here. On the other side of the stairs is a bar and stools, with a music system beside it.

My attention goes back to the couches. Jace is flat on one of them, shirtless, with a bandage wrapped around his torso. The white gauze doesn't hide the dark bruises that mottle his skin, and my heart gives an uneven thump.

Saint sits on the other couch. He stands when he sees us, keeping a hand to his side. A grimace of pain flashes across his face, then it's gone. He doesn't look like he's doing so great. There are dark circles under his bloodshot eyes. He's changed out of his bloodstained clothes, but it seems to still be haunting him. And why wouldn't it?

"He's been sleeping," Saint says in a low voice, stopping in front of us. "I'm going to head upstairs and try to sleep myself."

We nod. There's a lump in my throat, and I don't know what to say to Saint. An apology...? It doesn't seem like enough.

There's nothing in the world that will bring Nyx back.

I approach Jace, stopping just a foot shy of the edge of the couch.

Husband.

Married.

The notion is absurd.

His eyes flash open, and he reaches for me before I have a chance to get away. His fingers lock around my wrist.

"Kora," he breathes. "You're okay."

I jerk free. "Don't you mean *Korinne*?"

He pales and pushes himself up. It takes him way too long to get into a sitting position, but Apollo and I are silent while he struggles. He leans back against the cushions with an exhale. Sweat dots his brow. But that's not good enough for him, I guess. He stands, grunting in pain.

"You fought—"

"I wanted *Wolfe*." I glare at him. "You know, your best friend that you left with the Hell Hounds?"

Apollo touches my back. Just a little pressure, his finger running along the gap between my pants and shirt. Maybe he's getting ready to haul me backward. Because I'm sure feeling the desire to hit Jace in his pretty, bruised face right about now.

"How could you?" I whisper at Jace.

Except... I don't know what I'm asking him. My head hurts with all the questions. He *knew* we were married before I was carted out of the Hell Hounds' clubhouse by the mystery man. And then he admitted to not wanting to come look for me. Didn't want me back in Sterling Falls.

That was his goal all along, wasn't it?

To get me to leave.

So why bind me to him?

Because I'm a Sterling?

I shake my head when he doesn't answer, backing away from him. Apollo reaches for me, but I dodge him, too. This was just a massive power grab for him.

There's an iron weight in my stomach as the truth of it settles for me. Jace did this for one reason, and one reason only: to reclaim Sterling Falls for himself. To get leverage on the gangs, to shove his foot into the door of the city council and the mayor's office...

I want answers, but I'm not sure I want to hear Jace lie to me again.

"Come on, Apollo." I leave Jace standing there. "I can't do this with him."

Not right now. Maybe not ever.

"Stop," Jace calls.

I don't. Being in the basement is making me itch, and

being around *him* is going to make me lose control. After all that's happened in the last twenty-four hours—

"Apollo," Jace says. "Please—"

"Fuck off, man." Apollo is quick on my heels.

We climb the stairs, and I bypass Vittoria. I don't want to stay here. I'd rather go literally anywhere else than stay in this house. Apollo follows me outside, and I gesture to his bike. I open my mouth to beg him to take me away, but I stop short at the sound of another motorcycle roaring down the street.

I watch, a little disbelieving, as the rider turns into Antonio's driveway. They park next to Apollo's bike and flip the kickstand down, then remove their helmet.

My heart leaps into my throat, and I run forward.

Wolfe barely has time to stand, and then I'm on him. He catches me and swings me around, burying his nose in my hair. My eyes are burning, but I inhale his scent and let it ground me. My lips touch his neck.

He groans and sets me on my feet. His hands don't leave me. They're coasting up and down my sides, and he narrows his eyes at something on my face.

He touches my cheekbone, and I jerk at the painful sensation. From when Ben slammed my face into the floor? Or from the fight?

"The asshole you fought hit your other side." Wolfe reads my mind. "What happened?"

"You noticed that?"

He eyes me, completely serious. "I notice everything about you."

Oh. Butterflies take off in my chest—but that doesn't answer Wolfe's question. I glance at Apollo, then back to Wolfe. "Um..."

"Ben," Apollo says, crossing his arms.

Wolfe goes rigid. "What?"

"Ben attacked me," I whisper. I inch closer, so I don't have to have Wolfe trying to peer into my soul. He's good at that, and I'd rather not share my pain with him. He has enough for himself.

Seems he doesn't think the same, though, because he tips my chin up. "Ben attacked you. And he's still breathing?"

"No, actually." I exhale. "I—"

"Did a damn fine job defending herself," Apollo finishes. "His body is at Olympus."

Wolfe's eyes darken. He pulls me into his chest again, locking his arms around me. Something loosens inside me. A dam breaking, maybe. Because the next second, I'm crying. Ugly, loud sobs rack through me.

I didn't cry when Apollo found me.

I didn't cry after it happened, after Ben went slack beneath me.

I didn't shed a single fucking tear until right now—and *now* I can't stop.

"Shh," Wolfe whispers, his hand tangling in my hair. "If you think for a goddamn second that any of us wouldn't have murdered him for even thinking about touching you, you're delusional. You just beat us to the punch."

I relish his touch. I curl my fingers in his leather jacket, holding tight until I can breathe again. He wipes under my eyes and offers me a small smile.

"There she is," he says.

"Korinne Sterling?" So, so bitter.

His smile fades. "No. *You.* The girl I fell in love with. I don't give a shit what name is on your birth certificate. Korinne, Kora. Persephone."

My heart hammers.

He just...

Apollo sighs. "She wanted to get out of here," he says to Wolfe. "Maybe you'd like to do the honors."

I release Wolfe and look at Apollo. He's not exactly hurt, I think, but he's sure as hell not happy. Maybe he thinks this is a winner-takes-all situation, but he should know that I have no desire to choose between either of them.

"Come with us," I say to Apollo.

It's what I have to offer right now.

And it's enough. His eyes light up, and he nods.

I take the extra helmet and slip on Wolfe's bike. He gets on behind me, flush to my back. His thighs bracket mine. I let him take control, keeping my hands on the handlebars just inside his. He frames me in and taps his helmet to mine. One hand drops to my hip, squeezing once.

Our bike roars to life, followed quickly by Apollo's.

I let them sweep me away.

jace

I limp upstairs and make it to the window in time to see Kora get on Wolfe's bike. Apollo is with them as their engines roar, and they burst back out onto the quiet street.

Anger like I've never known descends on me, and I clench my fists to keep from doing something fucking rash. If I threw a temper tantrum and broke something of Antonio's, his well-natured spirit would vanish.

Family first, for him. Always.

Their safety, their happiness.

It comes before us, most definitely. Right now, harboring injured fugitives in his house is pushing it, even if the danger has lessened a few degrees with the death of Kronos.

I'm so pissed I can hardly see straight. The agony that blazes in my side where Parker stabbed me takes over my vision. I blink away the black spots and grit my teeth. This pain will pass like any other injury.

I yank a chair out and drop into it, exhaling sharply. My

chest hurts, the pain layered on top of the stab wound. I don't remember much of last night. I laid on the floor and watched Kora fight, and I thought if I didn't bleed to death, surely *that* would kill me. Her opponent was a big Hell Hound, one who liked to dive headfirst into a bloodlust. Insatiable monster. Apollo kept pushing on my side, the towel in his hand soaking through, but I couldn't take my eyes off her.

And then she fucking won.

The girl I first met, who was so scared in the forest in her cheap gold mask and secondhand black dress, was gone. In her place was someone strong. A warrior. And I was proud at the same time that I was guilty.

Until she asked for Olympus, and Cerberus got that look in his eyes. The one that said he finally believed the truth. That Kora is the Sterling heir. *Korinne Sterling.*

It's a bit fuzzy after that. Apollo got me to the hospital. I had surgery that left my throat raw, and stitches are holding me together. When I was discharged, I came here. But I didn't ask where Kora was, or Wolfe. I just let myself wallow in the pain.

When she came down those steps...

I don't know what I thought would happen.

That she'd forgive me? That she'd doubt Cerberus?

The night I kissed her outside of Bow & Arrow blazes into my mind. Later that night, I was in our office with the taste of her still on my lips, my heart a wreck. My head was a mess. Apollo entered, and he asked what I was going to do. *I'm going to let her think she's free,* I said. *And then it'll be too late.* I was already deciding on her fate and mine, already pushing the wheel into motion.

Now it is too late. She's bound to us. To *me*. And I'm not

a good enough person to let her go. I can't release her as easily as Kronos and Cerberus did. I won't do that.

Saint lowers himself into the chair across from me with two mugs. He slides one to me, and I peer into it for a moment before wrapping my fingers around the warm ceramic.

Coffee.

"I'm surprised Kora didn't stick around," he says, voice mild.

I grunt. I'm not about to admit my own fuck-ups—of which there are several. And seeing as how she just rode off with my two best friends, she's pissed.

That makes two of us.

"Elora's aunt called," Saint continues. "She wanted to come back to Sterling Falls and help with the preparation…"

Nyx's parents and Nyx never saw eye to eye. It's not a huge surprise that only her aunt has reached out to Saint. In the last few years, it's just been the two of them on their own.

And us.

I let a glimmer of guilt touch through my armor. "Whatever you need, man, you know we'll get it done."

He nods, his expression tight. But then he seems to mentally set it aside and refocuses on me. "So, what's the real reason Kora and Apollo shot out of here like their asses were on fire?"

I rub my hand over my face and groan. "Because I'm an idiot."

"What did you do?"

I drop my hand and hold on to the mug again. What did I do? What I've continually done for weeks—*months*—to them. Not just Kora. I've kept secrets from Apollo and

Wolfe, too. My best friends in the world, and I hid major pieces of the puzzle from them.

This isn't a conversation I should have with Saint, though.

Kora, Wolfe, and Apollo deserve to hear the truth from me before anyone else.

kora

I lean back against Wolfe's chest, my body relaxing ever so slightly. It feels good to not be in charge or think about where we're going. He's stretched forward, his arms on either side of me gripping the handles. Apollo rides next to us when the roads allow.

When Wolfe takes a side road, Apollo follows. We climb, going in and out of the trees, and then crest the hill. Wolfe and Apollo both automatically brake, and I flip my tinted visor up. From here, we have a clear view of the southeastern part of Sterling Falls. The cliffs that peter down and give way to the edge of the harbor. Jace's hiding place is down there somewhere, tucked into the marina. A few large ships are docked—nothing huge, not by international shipping standards. There are more empty spaces on the docks than not.

It must be impacting the city. The resources, the economy.

I'm not an expert, but this gang war has caused more damage than I first would've guessed.

"Where are we going?" I ask.

Wolfe drops his hand again, resting it on my thigh. Heat blooms through me, and I fight the urge to squirm. He chuckles. His chest rumbles with it, a mirror of his bike, and he strokes my leg softly. "It's a surprise. I just wanted you to enjoy the view."

I lean back more and try not to pant. I don't know how he manages to make my body light up like a Christmas tree with just a few touches, but... here we are.

"Get on with it, then," I finally say.

He laughs.

Apollo watches us, eyes dark, but he doesn't speak up. Wolfe pushes my visor back down, then does the same to his. Without a word, we take off again. Down the sloping hill. We must be in the vicinity of the Hell Hounds' club-house—their old one, their newly rebuilt one—but I don't see a sign of it. Or any gang members on bikes.

The road dips back down into the trees. Wolfe takes a turn down a long driveway, Apollo on our heels. We slow and coast around a corner, and a house comes into view.

A house that has no business being as gorgeous as it is.

I gape up at it. It's white, but there are a million windows. Two levels. A wraparound porch on the first floor. There are pale-pink and yellow flowers blooming along the walkway.

Wolfe flips the kickstand down and climbs off, then offers his hand. I take it, letting him help me off. I barely notice that he unbuckles my helmet from under my chin and removes it.

"What is this place?" I finally ask, tearing my gaze away to focus on Wolfe and Apollo.

Wolfe smiles sheepishly. "Um... a backup plan?"

I eye them. "What does that mean?"

"Well, it's not like we could predict that a crazy woman

would burn down our house," Apollo murmurs. He steps up and takes my hand. "But we wanted something more fitting for... us."

My heart does this erratic beat for a minute, going crazy, and I stare up at the house.

"Us," I repeat. "Like... you and me..."

"The four of us," Apollo says, and then he winces. "Maybe three of us."

I laugh, if only to mask the spike of pain that lances me at the thought of Jace. If only to stop the knowledge that he hurt all of us with his selfishness.

"Come on," Wolfe says. He takes my other hand and pulls me down the walkway.

There's a detached garage off to the side with three bay doors between the trees. We go up the steps onto the porch, and he guides me to the front door. He unlocks it quickly, one-handed, and then stops short.

Apollo seems to read his mind. He ducks down and scoops me up easily, an arm at my back and the other under my knees. I let out a little yell and hug his neck, but he just laughs at me. His dark eyes gleam as he carries me over the threshold.

That's the sort of thing that married couples do—and I can't marry either one of them.

Because that privilege was stolen from me.

Tears blur my vision, and Apollo presses a kiss to the outer corner of my eye. His tongue flicks out, catching a teardrop that rolls down my cheek.

"Don't be sad, baby," he whispers. "We've got you."

I swallow. It doesn't stop the fact that Wolfe is still a Hell Hound, at his father's beck and call. It doesn't stop the fact that Jace took something from us.

He puts me back on my feet, and they both reclaim my

hands. I let out a small smile, forcing away the twinge of sadness. They lead me through the first floor, and when we get to the large living room at the back of the house, my heart skips.

It's all windows, with privacy shades rolled up at the top of them. It gives me a view of the water.

I hadn't realized we were so close. But there it is, just below a ridgeline. Trust them to pick a house that has cliffs behind it.

Wolfe follows me to the windows, stepping up behind me. He moves my hair off my shoulder and kisses my neck.

I close my eyes and tip my head to the side, giving him better access. His teeth graze my skin, and goosebumps rise down my arms. I shiver, and he laughs under his breath. His hands find my hips. He pulls me back against him, and I don't need more encouragement to grind my ass against his groin. He's hard, and I bite back my smirk.

He groans. "You don't know what you do to me."

I turn slowly in his arms, looping mine around his neck. "You could show me..." I bite my lip.

Across the room, Apollo leans on the kitchen island. His hands are in his pockets, and I let my gaze travel the length of him. His position does nothing to hide the fact that he's turned on, too.

"Did you bring me here to fuck me?"

Wolfe shakes his head. His thumb runs along my waist, the exposed flesh where my shirt has ridden up, and it's doing disastrous things to my nerves. And my heart.

"No," he admits. "I just wanted you to see that this could be a haven... if you wanted it."

"But you wouldn't be opposed to fucking me." I run my hand down his chest, all the way down to where his dick is straining against his jeans. I cup him through the fabric.

"I'd never turn you down," he says. "What better way to christen this place as ours?"

I grin and step back. "And you, Apollo?"

My golden man straightens. "You want us both?"

I bite my lip again, then nod. Because the thought of choosing between the two of them is too much to bear, and I've wanted both of them for... well, far too long.

A hungry expression crosses his face. His gaze flicks to Wolfe, and some silent exchange passes between them. I shiver, my heart pounding harder. Apollo gestures to me, and I go to him without hesitation. His palm skims my jaw, tilting my head back. He kisses me hard—harder than I expect. It bends me back a little, but suddenly Wolfe is there. His hands once more grip my waist, his fingers dancing lower. He traces the edge of my panties, and Apollo's tongue slips into my mouth. I can't help my soft whimper.

Apollo's hands slide into my hair, moving my head, while Wolfe holds me hostage against him. I'm walking on the razor's edge between safety and danger.

I push Apollo's shirt up, and he releases me long enough to tear it off. I toss it to the floor and smile wickedly. I brush my fingers across his scar, the pain of it like an echo inside me. He got that trying to save me from Kronos' death grip.

He shudders and steps into my space. Wolfe strips my shirt off, then unbuttons my pants. He drags them down. Apollo watches, his eyes hooded.

I love this. That I don't feel like I'm invisible, or forgotten, or just something for them to use to get their kicks.

Apollo takes my jaw and turns my head to the side. My lips meet Wolfe's, and sparks shoot through me at Apollo's touch. His wordless direction. His hand moves lower, to my throat, and I moan into Wolfe's mouth.

Wolfe swallows my noises greedily. One of them undoes my bra, tugging it away from my body, and Wolfe cups my breasts. His fingers run over my stiff nipples, then just one as Apollo's hot mouth envelops the other.

Heat rushes to my core, and I barely stop myself from grinding back on Wolfe's erection, which jabs into my ass cheek. But Apollo is already going lower, kissing his way between my breasts and down my stomach. He rips my panties down my legs and licks just above my sex.

I tear my lips away from Wolfe to watch Apollo lean forward and continue licking south. He runs his hand up my leg and lifts it suddenly, hooking it over his shoulder. Cool air assaults my soaked center, but only for a moment. Then his mouth is on me, and I nearly combust right then and there.

Wolfe holds me up, his lips trailing down from behind my ear to my shoulder, then back up. He bites my neck. The pain mixes with pleasure, and I gasp louder.

My orgasm comes out of nowhere. My muscles tighten, and I cry out at the sensation of both men touching me. Wolfe keeps me steady, and Apollo gently presses a last kiss to my inner thigh. When my eyes open again, Apollo is standing. My gaze drops down to his cock, straining against his pants, and then I look over my shoulder.

"My turn," Wolfe growls, spinning me around. He walks me backward until my butt hits the kitchen island, then he lifts me onto it. He shoves his pants down just far enough to free his dick, and he spreads my thighs with a glint in his eye.

"Do you want to taste yourself, flower?" he asks.

I suck my lower lip into my mouth, then nod.

Apollo cups my cheek, drawing my face toward his. His lips touch mine, and then his tongue slips into my mouth. I do taste myself—but I also taste the mint on his breath, and it's a heady combination.

Wolfe thrusts into me without warning. The feeling of fullness obliterates my other senses, and my back arches. Apollo swallows my helpless moan.

"Fuck, Kora," Wolfe breathes.

I flinch.

Both guys automatically tighten their grip on me, and Apollo pulls away from kissing me to look into my eyes.

"You are Kora Sinclair," Apollo says to me. "If you want to be someone else, you can. But you can't get rid of the person you *are*."

Wolfe still thrusts into me, but it's slower. Like he's annunciating what Apollo is saying, agreeing with it. The slow speed is enough to drive me crazy, but I can't tear my gaze away from Apollo's eyes.

And I'm trying desperately to believe him, but there are some things I just... I can't unknow it.

The floor has shifted beneath my feet, and I don't know if I'm floating or falling.

"Kora," Wolfe says again. "Or would you rather us call you Persephone?"

I choke on a laugh, but it's quickly cut off by Apollo's hand sliding down my front. He touches my clit, rubbing a little circle.

"Persephone," Apollo agrees. "Fitting."

"Always has been," Wolfe says in a low voice. "But more so now that you're not ours."

"Fuck." I tip my head back, and my eyes close. "I *am* yours."

Both guys growl at my words, and a lightness I was

missing arcs through my chest. It cuts through the misery that's been holding me hostage. The insecurities, the mistrust.

"I'm yours," I say again.

Apollo's finger moves faster. His other cups the back of my neck, keeping me upright. Making sure I can see both him and Wolfe.

The combination of Apollo's hand and the way Wolfe's dick is thrusting into me is almost too much to bear. Wolfe pinches my nipple, his other hand holding my hip as his speed increases.

"I can't come again," I pant.

Wolfe meets my eyes with a smirk. "You can and you will, flower. A few more times, I think."

Fucking hell.

He gets his way, and I come for the second time. My limbs tremble. He stills inside me, pausing as my muscles clench around his length. And then he's gesturing to Apollo and slipping out of me.

I inhale sharply when Wolfe scoops me up into his arms, carrying me across the room to the couch.

"You want both of us?" he asks in my ear, repeating his earlier question. "Together?"

His husky voice is laced with lust, and I wrap my arms around his neck tightly. I kiss his jaw, sliding my hands through his hair. I don't answer, but I do reach out a hand for Apollo. I want them so badly it hurts.

Wolfe sits, taking me with him so I straddle his lap. His wet cock is trapped between us, pressed against his abdomen and my stomach.

Apollo steps up behind us, between Wolfe's legs, and he thrusts into me.

"Fuck," I breathe.

He feels different than Wolfe. He pumps in and out of me a few times, then draws back. An ache forms between my legs. I brace against the back of the couch and watch Wolfe's face. He smiles at me with a lightness in his expression that I haven't seen since I returned to Sterling Falls.

This is a reprieve for all of us.

Apollo runs his finger through my center, dipping into my pussy. Then higher... and I pause when he pushes his finger into my asshole. My eyes go wide.

"Relax," Wolfe whispers, nipping my earlobe.

Apollo works his finger in, and my legs are trembling by the time he's done. He moves it in and out, fucking me with his finger, slicking the hole with my arousal.

Wolfe holds me steady when Apollo presses the tip of his dick there, replacing it with his finger. I breathe out slowly. He inches in, and my head falls forward. I touch my forehead to Wolfe's until Apollo is fully seated inside me.

"You're such a good girl." Apollo strokes my hip. "Fuck, you're beautiful."

My heart swells.

He lifts me just a little, then something cool hits my ass crack.

Spit.

I don't know why that turns me on, but I grip the back of the couch tighter. Wolfe shifts, and suddenly he's sliding back into me. God, the fullness of both of them makes me moan louder. His eyes flutter, then lock on me.

"You're perfect," he says. "And tight like this. Fuck me twice."

Apollo chuckles. "Ready, baby?"

"Yeah," I manage on an exhale.

They start to move. Apollo pulls almost all the way out and thrusts back in, sending me rocking against Wolfe. We all groan. It takes them no time to find a rhythm, and I whimper at the sensations of being so full. I can barely stand it—in the best way.

Apollo wraps his hand around my throat and hauls me upright. My back is curved, my breasts sticking out in Wolfe's face. He takes full advantage, running his hands all over my front. He leans down and latches on to my nipple, and I combust.

"Oh my god," I murmur, chasing my high.

I push against them, slamming down on Wolfe's erection and grinding back on Apollo. I've lost my mind in the sweetest way possible, and I lose myself to another orgasm. My cunt pulses, my muscles tensing around Wolfe and Apollo. It sends them over the edge, too. Apollo thrusts inside me and goes still. He comes with a groan, his fingers biting my skin. I relish the feel of him inside me.

Wolfe groans, too, jerking up underneath me. I writhe as he continues his assault, finally stilling inside me and coming with a sharp groan of my name.

Apollo pulls out of me first. Then Wolfe. The latter rolls me to the side, and Apollo joins us on the couch. I reach out and take both of their hands, my eyes closing. I focus on trying to breathe and keeping out all the other thoughts.

Like the fact that Wolfe might be here, but he's still not free.

And now I know I'm not either.

A tear rolls down my cheek.

Wolfe leans into me and captures it with his tongue, pressing a kiss to the corner of my mouth. "We'll get through this together," he promises.

I want to believe him, but...

W e eventually pick ourselves up off the couch and move to the shower. It's a standing shower large enough for five people, with three shower heads. Kora gets a look in her eye when she sees it and doesn't bother closing the door behind her.

An open invitation that Wolfe and I immediately accept.

I could stay here forever.

That was the goal when we bought this place. I knew in the back of my mind that our old house was ruined the second Richard Jacobs moved into it. That it would never feel like our safe haven again. But this place feels like home, and we haven't even finished fully exploring it with her.

Not that I missed the intrigued look she cast at the extra-large bed in the spacious bedroom we passed through to get here. *Not that Wolfe and I were daydreaming about certain... activities... when we purchased it.*

When we're thoroughly clean, I turn off the water. Wolfe wraps Kora in a fuzzy robe and bear hugs her from behind, trailing kisses up her shoulder and finding a spot just behind her ear that makes her knees go weak. My cock twitches again under my towel.

All we're missing is Jace, even if I want to punch him in the throat right about now.

Kora giggles, finally pushing Wolfe away from her, and we follow her into the bedroom. Wolfe nods to the closet door. She raises an eyebrow.

She opens it, and her mouth drops open.

We hired someone to stock it with new clothes for us, using a lot of the money Cerberus has been giving us as a stipend. Our other businesses have dried up in the past few months, which meant that sinking money into this place has been more of an investment than anything else.

We'll bounce back, though. Especially with Kora beside us.

She picks out a comfortable outfit. Gray sweat shorts and a white graphic t-shirt with a popular band's logo across the chest. Wolfe and I go to our dressers in the large closet, silently pulling on sweatpants and t-shirts to match her.

"I discovered something," Wolfe says to us. "I was going to confront Jace about it directly, but you two should know."

Kora's lips purse, but she finally nods.

"No more secrets between us," I say.

Wolfe punches my arm. "Exactly."

"Okay, well..." I lead the way downstairs and slip my hand into my pocket. My fingers curl around the folded blade that I put there automatically. I resist the urge to take it out and flip it in my hands. Nervous energy.

What the fuck could Wolfe have discovered about Jace?

We sit back on the couch, Kora curling into my side. Wolfe grabs her legs and pulls her feet into his lap. He mindlessly runs his finger up the bottom of her foot until she jerks.

He grins. "Ticklish?"

"We're waiting in suspense here," I snap.

He loses the smile. Fast.

My stomach knots. Maybe I don't want to know.

But it's too late to stop him, because he lets out a breath and says, "I think Jace knew Kora's real identity from the beginning."

She gasps. Her hand lands on my thigh, and I cover it with mine. Her breathing is coming faster, but she doesn't react other than that.

Wolfe explains that the scholarship she received was set up by Cerberus to find the Sterling heir. That Wolfe's father had managed to conclude that Korinne was brought to that specific group home, and by targeting it, he was hoping the real heir would reveal herself.

By chance, it worked.

And by *chance*, Jace managed to take it away from Kora a few months before school started.

I rub my jaw. How could he have kept that from us? Even if we were in the dark about the whole ploy...

"It gets worse," Wolfe whispers. "Jace came to us because my father thought Jace would be able to find her."

Kora flinches. "How?" she demands. "Wasn't he ten, eleven years old?"

"I think..." Wolfe looks down at her feet. "Maybe he was at the group home."

I choke. "What?"

"He never mentioned being in the foster system," Kora protests. "He's talked about his dad—"

"His deadbeat dad, who wasn't actually his father, you

mean?" Wolfe glowers straight ahead. "Who may have given Jace up when his mother died?"

"Shit," she breathes. "That's…"

"Twisted," I finish. I'm ready to race back to Antonio's house and rain hell down on Jace. What the fuck was he thinking? How many more lies are there between us? Secrets?

Kora sighs. "I'm famished."

I perk up. If there's one thing my family instilled in me since I was a baby—feeding your family is an act of love. That, and I'm perpetually hungry. I haven't eaten since the piece of buttered toast Vittoria shoved at me before I walked out the door this morning. For Kora, it's probably been a lot longer.

Guilt hits me.

We don't have any food here either.

I take her hands and pull her up. "We'll get something," I promise her. My gaze goes to Wolfe, who remains on the couch. "You okay?"

He grimaces. "You're going to go back to Antonio's, right? I've got to head back to the clubhouse. I've already been away for too long."

Kora drops back down and throws her arms around Wolfe's neck. He stiffens for a moment, then hugs her back. He's got a ways to go before he's able to be completely vulnerable in front of us. For years, when he was hurt, he'd lash out with anger. It's admirable, in a way, that he's showing some other emotions.

It's her doing.

"It'll be okay," she murmurs in his ear. "We'll get you free of them."

Something twists in my gut, and I meet Wolfe's eyes. I

nod, affirming Kora's words, even if I don't know if something like that can be done.

We have no leverage against Cerberus.

And without Kronos... who's to say he won't try to take over the whole city?

Kora leads the way to the front door. We let her go, and I put my hand on Wolfe's shoulder. "She's right," I say. "One way or another..."

Wolfe shakes his head. "I know what would have to be done, and I'm not ready for that."

To kill his father, he means.

I bite back any words of encouragement, because... My own father was a coward. He sold me to the Hell Hounds to pay off a debt—and then he did something far worse to Tem a few years later. He got what he deserved.

Cerberus is different.

Not quite fully evil. Not quite good. So firmly in the gray area, it will cost us our own morals to take him down.

Kora screams.

Wolfe and I bolt toward the sound. I get there first, sliding to a halt beside her next to the open door.

A black snake has been nailed to the front door. It twitches limply, still half alive, and dark blood rolls down the wood. I gape at it, then at the paper nailed just above the snake.

You should've stayed away.

A shiver racks Kora's body, and I grab her swiftly, pulling her around so she can't see the damn snake—or the words. They're for her, that much is clear. Whoever did this was probably the culprit behind putting the beheaded snake in her bed while I was drugged out of my mind.

She grips my t-shirt and buries her face in my neck. Her breathing is harsh.

I force my attention up and away, scanning the trees.

Wolfe swears and moves closer to the door. I hand him my knife, and he quietly kills the snake. He doesn't take it down, though. He just steps out on the porch and gestures for us to come with him.

He's unarmed.

Me, too.

I want to curse again, angry at having been so wrapped up in Kora that we forgot about security measures. But the danger should've passed. Kronos is dead, Cerberus doesn't want anything to do with her—

"Sheriff," Wolfe says into his phone.

Kora flinches against me.

I hadn't realized he'd even dialed.

"We've got a situation I wouldn't mind getting another set of eyes... oh, fuck off." Wolfe rolls his eyes and gives Nathan Bradshaw the address. Then he hangs up and stuffs his phone back in his pocket. For all of two seconds. Then it rings again.

Wolfe sighs. "Yeah," he answers. There's a gravelly voice on the other end, just low enough to hear the tone but not the words. "Okay, I'll be there soon."

He ends the call without another word.

"Who summoned you?" Kora asks. She leaves my side to go to Wolfe, tipping her head back and sliding her arms around his waist. "And do you have to go?"

Wolfe sighs. "It was Malik. My father wants me back at the clubhouse."

She rests her forehead on his chest. His hand automatically comes up and cups the back of her neck, his fingers sifting through her hair, but he doesn't try anything else. They just stand there like that for a moment, and then she releases him.

"Apollo and I will wait for Nate," she says. "And we'll fill you in."

Wolfe eyes her, then glares at me. "Keep her safe."

I stride to my bike and take out my gun, already in a thigh holster. I strap it on, then raise my hands. As if to say, *Good enough for you, asshole?*

Wolfe just shakes his head. He kisses Kora's forehead, swiping his thumb across her lower lip, and his expression slowly fades. All of it. The joy, the calm, the relief. I watch it recede like a tide, leaving a blank mask. He pulls his helmet on and climbs onto his bike. It starts with a roar, and we back up as he spins it around.

When he shoots away from us, I feel the loss of him as keenly as Kora must.

She takes my hand. "At least you're not drugged this time," she says lightly.

Fucking hell.

Waiting for Nate to show is agony. We don't want to leave the front yard in case whoever's out there tries to remove the evidence. I don't feel another presence—which seems like some sort of voodoo nonsense, but Apollo tells me it's a gut instinct.

Still, those can be wrong.

Whoever left the message for us did it while we were preoccupied, and they had to have timed it perfectly. The nails drilling into the door wouldn't have been quiet. Then again, Wolfe and Apollo drilling into *me* wasn't quiet... Still, the bedroom door was closed. It's at the back of the house, too. Maybe that would've been enough. Or whoever did it knew they had time to be quiet.

Damn.

Apollo stares off into the trees, lost to his own thoughts. I run my fingers through my damp hair, working out the tangles. Washing it without a hairbrush was my first mistake, but I would do it again to feel their fingers scrubbing shampoo against my scalp.

But even that isn't enough to distract me for very long.

We've got problems.

First and foremost, the whole Korinne Sterling thing. I'm not sure if my sudden identity reveal *actually* means anything. What are they going to do, give an alderman seat to a twenty-one-year-old? DNA test me? Put a freaking crown on my head?

That's not even taking into account that someone murdered my biological family.

Second, I clearly have someone who wants me to stay far away from Sterling Falls. I try to think back, picking out the warnings. The snake here on the door, the snake in my bed. The photo edited to make it look like I was dead.

I wrap my arms around myself.

Parker is dead.

Jace is a liar—*and my husband.*

If Wolfe is right, then Jace knew me as a kid. And everything that happened after that interaction changed his whole life.

Did I steal the chance of a normal family from him? Cerberus swooped in and plucked him out of obscurity because he thought Jace might know me.

But... he didn't find me. So either a ten-year-old knew and kept my secret, or... Or we're just *wrong*, and we never knew each other.

This is fucked up. All of it. I've got a headache starting behind my eyes, the pressure growing until it's all I can focus on. That and my hunger, which gnaws at my stomach like a demon.

I cast a glance at Apollo, biting my lip. I don't want to ask about the last thing on my mind. I want assurance that Parker is dead. That he's not going to claw out of the water and try to kill me for what we did to him.

Wolfe broke his leg, I think. Messed up his knee at any

rate. Even if Parker's body isn't found, we still killed a DEA agent. And that could come back to bite us.

"Kora," Apollo calls, pulling me from my speculation—and worry. He gestures to the driveway, where the sheriff's car is coming down the lane.

My attention goes back to the snake.

It reminds me of the snake mask in the most unnerving way. The man who kidnapped me and brought me back to my adoptive parents—who then abandoned me on Isle of Paradise.

At some point, I'll have to face them, too.

Do they know who I am? Did they hide me on purpose, or...?

I touch the necklace. *KS*. I pull it out from where it usually hides under my shirt. It feels better when the cool silver backing sits against my skin.

Nate climbs out, leaving his dark-green hat behind. He's in uniform, his belt filled with tools. His firearm, handcuffs, a taser, flashlight. Radio.

"You okay?" he asks me.

I nod.

He exchanges a look with Apollo, but Nate still comes to me first.

"Wolfe made it sound urgent." His tone isn't exactly accusing, but...

I hook my thumb to the door. "Someone left me a message. Not for the first time."

Nate spots the snake and blanches.

I stare at him, not quite sure why that invoked such a reaction. But then he's moving past me, bounding up the stairs and stopping in front of the door. The snake is only held up by a few nails now, the paper fluttering above it in the breeze. I'm glad Wolfe put it out of its misery.

"You look like you've seen a ghost, Brad," Apollo says.

Nate jerks, then scowls over his shoulder. "Don't call me that."

Apollo sneers. "Sure thing."

I go to Apollo while the sheriff examines the snake. He wraps his arm around my shoulders, tucking me into his side, and I lean into him. It's not that I need the support, it's that I crave his touch like a drug addict.

"There was the snake in your bed," the sheriff comments. "A few months ago, correct?"

I nod, biting the inside of my cheek to keep from saying more. Like pointing out he probably only saw it because Wolfe and Apollo were arrested. Or asking questions for which he probably doesn't have answers.

He sighs, going to his car and retrieving gloves and evidence bags. He snaps a few photos, then carefully removes the snake and note. He tucks each in a bag with his gloved hands, pausing at the wound that killed the snake.

"It was alive," I say. "Wolfe ended its suffering."

The sheriff nods once, his throat working. "Okay."

"Okay?" Apollo echoes. "That's it?"

Nate tips his head toward his car. "Can I talk to you for a moment, Kora?"

I don't know why I hesitate. Probably because everything the sheriff might say, he could tell me in front of Apollo. But he doesn't seem exactly happy that I'm under Apollo's arm... and I'm curious about what he needs to get off his chest.

So I motion for Apollo to stay put and follow Nate to the back of his car. He pops the trunk and puts the evidence bags into a locked box, then leans against the bumper.

"Word is out about you," he says in a low voice. "Your identity."

My heartbeat picks up speed. Outwardly, though, I scoff. "Alleged identity? At the word of an arguably insane man."

The sheriff nods slowly, eyeing me. "Right. So you didn't go to the library and look up old archives of the Sterlings' deaths?"

I swallow.

That's answer enough, I guess, because his eyes gleam with a *gotcha* expression.

"I can answer whatever questions you want to know about your family," he says. "And..."

"And?"

"Maybe you should call your parents?"

My stomach swoops, and I grab on to the car. I had just theorized that they might know something, hadn't I? But... "They sent me to a fucking island prison camp to keep me from coming back here," I say quietly. "And you want me to just call them up and—and see if they'll be honest with me?"

He doesn't look away from me. "This is important."

"It's not," I argue, stepping back. "It doesn't really change a thing in this city."

He appraises me, but he doesn't stop me from retreating to Apollo. He doesn't say anything else at all, he just salutes us and climbs into his car. We watch him turn his car around and zoom back down the driveway.

I let out a breath.

"Food," Apollo says suddenly. "Then maybe we'll go bitch-slap Jace and get some answers from him."

A grand idea. Better him than my parents.

wolfe

I stare up at the body. Someone cut into it pretty well, leaving a pool of blood beneath it. The guy's feet dangle above the sidewalk.

He's been nailed to the side of Descend.

Which, now that the Titans have all but abandoned ship, makes it my problem.

Also... he's missing his head.

The rough cuts in his neck make me think it wasn't an easy decapitation. My nausea is increasing the longer I stare, so I finally blink and force myself to scan the neighborhood.

It's strange to be in West Falls in the daylight, without much fear of an attack. Malik has the Hell Hounds fanned out around the block, keeping watch for the inevitable arrival of the police. But he wanted us to get a look at it first, so here we are.

Six months ago, three Hell Hounds were found decapitated. We had no idea who committed the crime or why. Nothing ever came of that investigation. Not that the police care about murdered gangsters—that's life on the rough side of town, right there. If an answer doesn't immediately present itself, it becomes a cold case before the ink has dried in the file.

This guy, though, seems familiar.

"Check this out," Malik says. "This was on the other bodies, too."

My throat closes. Cut into the man's wrist is a twisted *K*... and an *S*.

"Destroy that," I order.

Malik eyes me like I'm fucking nuts. But they were on the other bodies, too?

First the decapitated snake in Kora's bed, then decapitated Hell Hounds... and now a fourth one?

What the fuck is going on?

"Malik," I say evenly. "Cut the fucking flesh off his wrist."

He does it. He pulls a blade and grasps the guy's wrist, turning it at an angle. He slices through like he's cutting a piece of cheese from the block, and he doesn't say a word when I hold out a handkerchief for him to put it on.

I fold the soft white fabric over and keep it in my grasp. It's fucking disgusting—but Malik should've mentioned this. He should've said something about Kora's initials being on the other bodies.

I try to recall what was special about those guys, then I snap my fingers. They were with Cerberus and Kora when they did the press conference with the mayor. After the fire.

And this guy...

I grab his hands and flip them over. He's got bruises on his knuckles—a classic sign of a fighter. Which, as a Hell Hound, isn't too surprising. But there's only one fighter who would've been close to Kora in the last week.

The one she fought.

It's not unusual for guys to survive the fall over the cliff.

But... the more I think on it, I don't think we *did* toss him. There was chaos in the room after Kora asked for Olympus. A mad rush for everyone to get the fuck out.

I look at Malik again, considering.

All four Hell Hounds have had unpleasant interactions with Kora—but it clearly ended worse for them than it did her.

Kronos is dead, or else I'd be sorely tempted to ask if anything remotely similar happened to his crew. If they've been attacked...

A sharp whistle comes from one of our guys, and Malik drags me toward my bike. He shoves me on it, climbing on his own.

We're gone in a heartbeat, but I can't stop the sick feeling from creeping through me. Something that says Kora has her own dark guardian angel... or she's in serious trouble.

Maybe both.

It takes too much willpower to go straight back to my father. Willpower that, frankly, I don't have. So before Malik can block me, I take a turn down a tight alley. I hit the throttle and shoot forward, swerving onto a new street. A few more, and I'm heading back to North Falls.

To Antonio's house.

Because fuck my father, and fuck not getting answers from Jace.

When I arrive, Apollo and Kora aren't here. At least, his bike isn't in the open garage, and I doubt Antonio would be pleased if they rode around back. Tearing up his grass would be a strike against us in Vittoria's eyes, for sure.

I hop off and storm up to the front door.

It's opened before I can get there, and Tem throws her arms around me.

I'll admit... it surprises me for a split second. I let her hug me and pat her shoulder awkwardly until she releases me. Her eyes are glassy with unshed tears, and a prickle of discomfort holds me hostage.

She's clearly suffering from everything going on. Nyx's death, first and foremost. But I refuse to think about that, and I move past her. Hunting for my best friend, who I may or may not strangle.

I'll base my decision on what sorry excuses he comes up with.

Jace and Saint are in the living room. I don't know where Antonio is, but Vittoria steps into the room from the other doorway. One look at my expression has her backing out again.

"Get up," I growl at Jace.

He raises his eyebrows for a moment, and his jaw tics. After a second, he climbs to his feet. His face contorts with pain.

Good. I hope it fucking sucks to stand and move and cough and breathe.

Fucker.

"You've been lying to us." I stride forward and stop just shy of touching him. "You have one shot to set the record straight."

He exhales. "Maybe we should wait for Kora—"

I see red.

I punch him, my fist moving faster than my brain. My knuckles catch him across the mouth, and his head whips to the side. I straighten. The pain in my hand wakes me up a bit, but I don't hit him again. Or move an inch. I just *wait* for another lie and try not to feel like the floor is crumbling beneath my feet.

"Wolfe," Jace mutters, touching his lip. "I had to—"

I hit him again. This time, he isn't as prepared. He stumbles back, and I shake out my hand. "I can do this all fucking day."

A bike roars outside, and we both spot through the window Apollo and Kora coast into the driveway. She hops off first, shaking out her hair, and her gaze goes to my bike. Her lips press together. She and Apollo hurry inside.

In seconds, they're standing behind me. Probably taking in the sight of the blood on Jace's face and my stiff posture.

"Go on," I goad Jace. "They're here now. No more excuses."

He makes a noise in the back of his throat. "Kora—"

I slap him. Hard. The noise resounds through the room, and he glowers at me.

"Yeah, you're dealing with me," I snap. "Don't talk to her. Don't even fucking look at her."

Traitor, a voice in my mind whispers.

Jace winces, then nods. He focuses on Saint, who has been sitting motionless on the couch. "Can you give us the room?"

Saint hops to his feet. He grabs Tem's hand—she must've followed Kora and Apollo in—and tugs her away before she can voice a complaint. Then it's just the four of us. Apollo closes the French doors, and Kora circles around Jace to peer down the hallway leading from the other entrance. There's no door to close that side off, but she seems satisfied no one is lurking.

"Explain yourself." Apollo folds his arms over his chest.

Jace moves to the window and leans his shoulder

against the side of it. He touches his jaw, his lip, and for a moment, I think he might just ignore us.

But then he sighs, and his shoulders sag.

"I'm sorry."

We're silent, waiting for him to continue. A simple sorry isn't good enough, and he knows it.

"After my mom died, my father got rougher with me. Beating me in private didn't get him the satisfaction anymore—he would do it anywhere he deemed fit. In the car, in an alleyway outside the grocery store, behind the school." He gets a distant look in his eyes. "Eventually, someone saw and reported it."

"You were taken away," Kora guesses.

She's circled back around, and she takes my hand. The pads of her fingers brush over my knuckles. I don't want her talking to him—he doesn't deserve to be in the same fucking room as her. But *she* deserves answers. So I take comfort in the fact that she's holding my hand, not his.

"St. Theresa's," Jace answers bitterly. "Because no one wants a boy who fights to solve his problems."

I narrow my eyes, recognizing the name of the group home that Kora came from. I remember it vividly, pulling the story out of her when we were first getting to know her. Back when I thought she just lied to get the scholarship. She had those fancy parents, after all. That doesn't happen to every foster kid.

"I lived there for six months before I met Kora." He faces her. "You and I..."

She squeezes her eyes shut. "Don't."

"You didn't answer to Kora at first. That was the name you were brought in under. It's what they introduced you as, but you said yourself that it wasn't your real name."

She shakes her head violently. "Stop."

"Kora—"

"I said *stop*." She holds her hand up. "I don't give a fuck about what shared past you think we have, Jace. I want to know why you thought it was okay to force me to marry you—and you didn't even have the balls to tell me? Or, I don't know, *ask*?"

He comes at her, and I practically shove her behind me.

"Don't," I warn.

Jace stops short. "I wouldn't hurt her."

"You're lucky she's allowing you to even look at her," Apollo growls.

"Fine," Jace grits out. "Cerberus had the contract. He was getting close to figuring out who she was. Her parents coming into town had thrown him off temporarily, but..."

"But what?" Kora whispers from behind me. "But you wanted to tie me to you anyway? But you didn't want to set me free, you just wanted to put me in a cage of *your* making?"

My heart thunders, and I reach back and run my hand along her hip. Just to make sure she's still with me. Her forehead touches my back, and I stand strong between them. I know she can fight this battle—but I'm still willing to throttle him for this.

"I didn't want you to come back to Sterling Falls," Jace finally says.

Kora picks up a glass from the coffee table, left behind by Jace or Saint, and chucks it at him. He manages to catch it, but the liquid splashes over him.

I hide my smirk, remembering a similar instance happening to me. Although our fight ended in sex, and somehow I don't think Kora's as keen to spread her legs for Jace this time around.

Good.

This is the first time Jace and I have been at odds. Judging from Apollo's uncomfortable expression, he's thinking the same. It's always been the three of us versus the world since we were kids.

Jace stares at her in shock, his nostrils flaring. In a quick move—against his better judgment—he lunges forward and grabs her shoulders. He walks her backward until she hits the wall, and I go to follow.

"Don't," Jace snaps over his shoulder at me, the tables suddenly turned.

I narrow my eyes.

He focuses his attention on her. She leans against the wall, letting her head tip back, too. Her expression is mild, although her eyes tell a different story. If looks could kill.

We're either going to all leave this room with our problem fixed, or...

"You already tried that bullshit with me, Jace King," she breathes. "I know there's some twisted ideology in that brain of yours—but all I want is the true reason *why*. Why couldn't you fight for my freedom? Why did you have to bind me to you instead?"

He hesitates.

Apollo growls, and it takes everything in me not to rip Jace's hands off her.

"Jace," she says in a low voice. "It's my fault that I didn't read the contract. But you..."

"He what?" I demand.

She doesn't tear her eyes away from him. "You told me to trust you. And I did."

Fuck.

Jace grunts, releasing her like she burned him. "Doesn't mean you should've."

"I did, though." She follows him. This is her fight, and

she's committed to it. "So tell me, *husband*, what made you want to marry me? Was it because you knew I had a claim to..." She waves her hand around, maybe to encompass Sterling Falls in general. Or an inheritance.

We have no idea what her being a Sterling means. Well —Apollo and I don't. Jace might.

Jace doesn't answer, and I can't handle it anymore. I tug Kora away from him, urging her out of the room. She comes with me willingly, and Apollo follows behind.

I'm glad we didn't tell Jace about the snake, the threatening note. Fuck *everything* he's done since we met her.

"When you get your story straight in your head, let us know," Apollo says to him.

I scoff. "That'll be the day."

jace

FIFTEEN YEARS AGO

I'm sitting on the floor beside my bed, unpacking for what feels like the hundredth time. Another foster family that didn't want to deal with me. St. Theresa's Group Home is a spot for troubled and wayward kids—that's what a plaque on the wall says anyway. Whatever *wayward* means.

I've got no issue figuring out that I'm the definition of *troubled*.

The door opens, and Ms. Wilcox sticks her head in the room. It's not a terribly large space, especially with four bunk beds and dressers. We're each allowed two drawers to put our belongings in. If we have that much stuff.

"Jace," she says when she spots me. "This is..."

I focus on the girl she's shoving into the room and miss her name. She's got orange-red hair and an explosion of freckles across her face, and she's younger than me. By a *lot*.

I open my mouth to tell Ms. Wilcox that kids and I don't

get along, but she's already walking away. Leaving the door wide open, and the kid looking lost just a few steps in.

Great.

I motion her to join me. She's stick-thin. I eye her overalls curiously. The white t-shirt under it has ladybugs and flowers on it. She's barefoot. She has a white bag, the kind you put your groceries in at the market, clutched in her fist.

"What's your name?" I ask, still slowly taking stuff out of the black trash bag.

She runs her fingers along one of the rails of the bunk bed and sucks her lower lip between her teeth. She gets close enough that I wonder if she's going to knock right into me, but then she touches a bruise on my neck.

I jerk back. "Hands to yourself," I yell.

She falls backward and lands on her butt. Her eyes fill with tears, and we stare at each other for a moment.

See? This is why I don't hang out with kids.

"I'm not supposed to tell people my name," she whispers, brushing furiously at her cheeks. She hooks her thumb under the chain around her neck, pulling out a black stone pendant. She runs her finger over the back, then shoves it back under her shirt.

That's... weird. I shrug, pretending her situation is normal. "Okay. So what do you want to be called?"

She doesn't answer me.

I sigh and grab the last thing out of my bag, then crumple it in my hands. I appraise my meager belongings. Some things the foster parents bought me this last time, some from others. Nothing from my old life.

It's better that way. I don't want to think about my mom.

I shove everything in one of the drawers and rise, then

slowly offer my hand to her. Breaking my own rules already.

She hesitates, and something twinges in my chest.

Have I already become a jerk like my dad?

Then she takes it, and I pull her to her feet.

"Boys sleep in here." I lead the way to the next room over. "Girls in here." I spot an empty bunk, one of the high ones, and point to it. "Everyone's out on a field trip, so it's just us and Wilcox right now."

And why our art therapy lady didn't show the girl to her room is beyond me.

I cross my arms and wait for her to scale the ladder. She doesn't bother unpacking her bag, she just leaves it at the foot of the bed and climbs back down. She eyes me, then crosses her arms over her chest.

A mimic.

Lovely.

"How old are you?" I ask.

"Five and three-quarters."

A whopping five years younger than me. Literally half my age. I shake my head and leave her there.

Well, I try to... until I realize she's followed me back into the hallway.

"What did Wilcox say your name was?" I'm full of questions, but I think I like this mystery. It takes my mind off my own shitty situation.

"I don't remember." She frowns. "It's..."

"It's what?"

She lifts one shoulder. "Similar."

"To your real—"

"Jace," Wilcox barks, a second before I slam into her. She catches my shoulders and keeps me at arms distance. "You should be more careful."

I clear my throat. "Sorry, Ms. Wilcox."

She appraises me for a moment, then nods. "It's lunchtime. Are you hungry, Kora?"

Kora. I turn the name over in my head. The girl nods at her, sucking her lower lip between her teeth again. She takes Wilcox's hand, and I step away.

"Not joining us, Jace?"

"I'm not," I lie.

They go one way, and I go another. Which is for the best. Connections—especially in a place like this—will only hurt me in the end.

KORA HAS FOUND her way to my side in the long rows of pews in the chapel. I can't say I hate it, because she's the only one who's remotely friendly to me. Although I don't know if she knows she's being friendly or if she thinks of me as an anchor.

The girls pick on her when I'm not around. They tug her bright-red hair, they mock her pouty lips and freckles. They pull at her clothes like they've never seen someone wear overalls before. Certainly not every day for two months.

Ms. Pearson tried to get her to wear something else on laundry day, and I've never heard someone scream louder. She had to give Kora a shot, some sort of sedative, and the girl slept for the rest of the day.

The next, Kora acted like it hadn't happened. No tears, no fear.

Still, I think she's wary of Ms. Pearson. Pearson is the director of St. Theresa's. She has final say on adoptions, at least before the applications get passed up the chain. Still—

she has the power to stop them or push them through, and that's *everything* to kids like us.

"Do you believe in God?" she whispers to me.

Whisper is a bit of a stretch. Her question is almost spoken at normal volume, and I eye the back of Pearson's head. Waiting for her to turn around and accuse us of not paying attention to the sermon.

St. Theresa's Group Home—where the kids spend two hours every Sunday in chapel, listening to an old, half-deaf priest rant about some specific lesson in the Bible, praying aloud, praying silently. Kneeling, sitting, standing.

It's ridiculous.

"No," I whisper back. "Keep your voice down."

She frowns. "Who do you believe in?"

I think about that for a minute, then settle on an answer. Because *I don't know* rarely cuts it with an almost six-year-old. "Myself," I settle on.

Kora told me a little about herself over the past few weeks. She opened up the tiniest bit before clamming up again. Something worse than fear keeps her thoughts to herself—but she did tell me her parents were gone.

Gone. Dead.

I told her my mom was gone, too, and she hugged me. The good kind of physical contact. Not like when my dad would lay into me, or the foster parents who thought pinching me was a good way to discourage certain behaviors.

Now, she giggles, and Pearson whips around. She drills Kora with a glare hot enough to scald, and Kora slouches into me.

My jaw tics, but I manage to keep a straight face when Pearson glowers at me. She does turn back around fairly quickly, and she doesn't threaten to separate us. So... that's nice.

Behind us, the pews are unusually full.

Because it's Family Day.

Also known as: mass marketing a child for adoption.

I let out a sigh as the priest says something about salvation. Not entirely sure what he thinks he's going to impart on a bunch of kids. That our souls can be saved if we pray?

Unlikely.

"I don't believe in God either," she whisper-yells back after another few minutes. "But I like the Greek ones."

I raise my eyebrow. "What?"

"Zeus and Hades and Poison."

"Kora," Pearson snaps. "Quiet."

The girl lets out a whimper and slides even lower, until she's practically flat. I shake my head and pull her hand. She brightens as I drag her out of the pew and up the aisle to the door in the back. Some of the adults scowl at us, but no one stops me.

I've nearly perfected my untouchable look. The expression that says, *touch me and die.* Well, maybe not die. But touch me and get seriously hurt. As hurt as I can manage to get someone. The only one who doesn't fall for it is Pearson.

We go through the vestibule and burst out into the sun. Across the lawn is the group home. There's a parking lot to our left, filled with cars, and someone hung up a large *Welcome Families!* sign over the main house doors.

Kora lets out a sigh of relief, tipping her head back and closing her eyes. She doesn't stop coming with me, though, her steps sure. Like she trusts me not to lead her over the edge of a cliff or something.

Weird.

"Poseidon," I say suddenly.

She opens her eyes when the sun leaves her skin. We're in the shade under a tree, and I drop down to the grass. She flops down beside me and doesn't react.

"Not Poison. *Poseidon*." I chuckle. "What do you know about them?"

"Zeus has lightning." She leans forward and rips handfuls of grass up, then lets the breeze take them from her open palms. "Poison has the water."

"And Hades?"

"He's a king of the underworld. You know, he harbors lost souls." She smiles. "I think he's my favorite."

"The Devil is your favorite." I don't understand her sometimes.

Scratch that. I never understand her.

She lifts a shoulder, adjusting the strap of her overalls. Even today, Pearson tried to get her into something a little nicer. One of the dresses she came with, or a shirt without a stain on it. Not that there's a stain on the overalls. She's freakishly neat.

Unlike laundry day, though, Pearson didn't want to drug her. So she let Kora win this battle. Never the war, though.

"He's not the *Devil*," Kora says, frowning and drawing my attention back down to her. "He's like, the defender of the dead."

I stare at her, trying to figure out why a five-year-old—almost six-year-old—knows so much about Greek Gods.

But I don't have a chance to find out, because suddenly, someone grabs my ear and hauls me up. I barely manage to see Ms. Pearson out of the corner of my eye, but she doesn't bring me back to the church. She drags me toward the house.

"Return to church, Kora," she calls over her shoulder.

The pain in my ear isn't anything new, but it still makes me hunch into her. I grit my teeth and refuse to cry out. Even when she leads me down the hall, which is clear of clutter for once, and to the basement.

I dig my heels in, but there's no use. She guides me down the wooden stairs and releases me with a push.

"No one will want to adopt an unruly, combative boy," she snaps at me. "So you can stay here until everyone has left. And if you make a single noise, I'll make sure you sleep down here for a month. The least you can do is not sabotage Kora's chances."

I almost rush back up after her, but her words burrow into me.

She's right. I'm unadoptable—and I don't want Kora to miss out on a family. I can cut it here, or in the rough foster homes, but Kora is still innocent. She's still... a kid. Unlike half of us who live here, who have grown up way too fast.

So I watch her stride back upstairs and lock the door behind me. The darkness presses in, and I sit heavily. The cold seeps into my skin through the threadbare fabric of my clothes. There's nothing down here except boxes and dust. Bars on the windows to keep people out... or in. Nothing soft, nothing warm.

There are loose pieces of grass clinging to my pants. I brush at them angrily, fighting to keep control of my emotions.

This is hell.

No.

I chew over what Kora told me. The story she wove in my head with just a few words. This isn't hell... *this is the underworld.*

And I just might become its ruler yet.

TWELVE

kora

S tep one: call my parents.

Wolfe hinted that I might be in danger, but then his father called and summoned him away before he could elaborate. So it's just Apollo and me right now. I'm sitting on his bike outside Olympus.

There are ghosts in Olympus, and I'm not so keen to return to its depths. Especially since the sun has set and darkness is falling.

I hold the cell phone we collected from Antonio's, and I finally dial the number. Apollo has wandered away from me, going up the hill to the cliff's edge. He eventually slips into the side entrance of Olympus, and I press *dial*.

"Kora?" My father's voice fills my ear.

I start. "How did you know it was me?"

"Blocked number—I was hopeful." He hesitates. "I... let me get your mother. Hold on."

My chest is tight. I know I'm calling with a purpose. I need answers from them. But... it hurts. A blade is being twisted between my ribs. If they knew...

"Kora?" My mom's voice now. "Are you okay?"

"You mean, am I okay now that I'm not trapped on an island?"

I imagine the wince that accompanies her sharp inhale. "Honey—"

"Save it." I close my eyes. "I just need to ask you something. And it's important that I get the truth."

They're quiet. Waiting for me to continue? They're on shaky ground here. One wrong move, and I'm gone forever.

That's what I tell myself anyway. But another voice in the back of my mind whispers that they're family. That I can't abandon them at the drop of a hat. Even after everything they've put me through...

"Anything you want to know," Dad confirms.

I take a breath. "Did you know who I was when you adopted me?"

Silence.

Then Dad says, "We found out after we started fostering you. And we knew it when we made the adoption official, yes."

"How?" I whisper.

"We had a holiday party." Mom's voice is hollow. "Your father's friend from Sterling Falls came to visit. He... he recognized you." She lets out a low noise. "And you recognized him."

I pull the phone away from my ear. I recognized their friend? And yet, if it was the same man who kidnapped Jace and me... I don't remember him.

"Who is he?" I finally ask.

"Your uncle," Dad admits.

My heart skips. The Sterlings are gone—but I have an uncle?

"What's his name?" One more piece to the puzzle that I'll have...

My phone buzzes against my ear, and I pull it away. *Nathan Bradshaw* flashes across the screen. He would've had my number from... well, I'm not exactly sure how he got this number. That alone sends a creeping doubt through me, and I hit *reject*.

"Honey, you have to understand—"

"I have to understand nothing," I snap. "You lied to me. You put my life in jeopardy—"

"He's only ever watched out for you," Dad explains. "How about you come home and we can sit down..."

"No, Dad. Give me your friend's name."

Mom murmurs something in the background. Too low for me to make out the words.

"Jeremy," he finally says.

I clench my jaw and wait. The name *Jeremy* will get me nowhere.

"Bradshaw," Dad finishes.

The whole fucking world screeches to a halt, and I'm vaguely aware of the phone slipping through my fingers. It bounces off the bike and to the ground, but there's a ringing in my ears. An echo of surprise... and finality.

I eye Olympus and debate getting Apollo. I start the bike and rev the engine, waiting a few seconds. When he doesn't emerge, I lean down and pick up the phone. I text the sheriff: *Where are you?*

He responds immediately. *SFU.*

I swallow and shove the helmet over my head. It feels like second nature at this point. I stow my phone and look up again. Apollo strides toward me with a confused expression, his brows furrowed.

"Get on or I'm leaving without you," I say.

He swings his leg over the bike. He takes the second helmet after a moment, then his hands return to my hips.

I flip the kickstand up and lean forward, and we shoot out onto the street. My blood flows fast through my veins, carrying a recklessness to them. But I don't want to be reckless. I want precision. I need to be at the top of my game.

I wish Nyx was here.

I ease off the throttle at that thought, my chest spasming.

Apollo's hands slide down my thighs. "You okay?"

I force a nod. I need to keep going. All the way back to Antonio's house, where Apollo and I both climb off the bike. I leave my helmet behind, my jaw set. Apollo follows, and his confusion is visible.

Jace won't give me answers... but I need his help. Because there's clearly history between him and Korinne Sterling and maybe all the fucking Sterlings. I don't know.

I'd ask Wolfe, but he's still chained to his father. Indefinitely, I fear.

Jace is in the kitchen, leaning against the counter without a shirt. I stop dead and stare at the row of stitches holding his side together.

Parker really did a number on him, and I *hate* that Parker even got close enough to land those punches.

And then he didn't fight fair.

"Come to take another jab at me?" Jace asks, biting off the backing of a bandage and pressing it over the wound.

"I'll wait till you feel better," I say with a lightness I definitely don't feel. "But I figured out who the man who took us is..."

Apollo makes a noise behind me.

Jace looks up slowly, his guarded expression melting away. "Who is it?"

I tip my head toward the road. "Let's go for a ride."

He narrows his eyes. "You and me?"

"I'm pretty good on a bike these days."

"And you want me to go with you."

I fold my arms. "Is that impossible to believe, asshole? That just because you've sabotaged my life—"

"I didn't sabotage anything," he snaps.

"Yeah, sure. You keep your secrets and lies to yourself, then. I'll go figure this out on my own." I get halfway down the hall before I hear him follow me.

"Fine," he yells. "I'm coming."

I frown at the twinge in my chest. He deserves answers—that's the only reason I'm doing this. Jeremy Bradshaw didn't just fuck with me... he fucked with Jace, too. Made me think he was going to kill him.

I'm not sure of Jeremy's relationship to Nate. Sibling? Father?

I try to picture the man who took me out of Sterling Falls. He called me K. *Like he knew*.

"You okay?"

I ignore Jace and go to the bike. At least we won't have time for conversation. But then Jace grabs my elbow and steers me toward one of the cars in the garage. Not Antonio's, that I'd borrowed before, but a cherry-red sedan.

Great.

He doesn't offer me the keys, and I press my lips together as he slides into the driver's seat.

I'm half tempted to just leave him sitting here. I could probably outpace him on a bike, lose him downtown...

"Come on," he sighs, his door still open. He swings his legs out so he can see me. "You wanted me to join you."

I cross my arms. "I guess I should've expected you to go full asshole mode, huh?"

He blinks at me, then gets out of the car. He tosses me

the keys, and I catch them against my chest. "You drive, then, bossy."

"Me? Bossy?" I glare at his back.

He disappears around the passenger side, the door opening and slamming shut.

I let out a breath. *You can do this.*

I might drive off a bridge first, though.

Jace thankfully doesn't talk the whole way to the university. He doesn't ask questions. It might be the fact that I crank the radio volume as soon as the engine turns over, blasting us with enough music to deafen a horse.

The beat of the music vibrates in my chest.

When we arrive, his brows inch up. But he doesn't say anything else.

I shut off the car and face him. "I brought you because there's some part of me that knows you deserve answers."

He stares out the window. "I know you want an apology, Kora, but... I can't do that."

"Did I ask for an apology?" Anger flares through me, flashing like a strobe. "I asked you *why,* and you didn't say anything. It makes me think the worst."

He meets my eyes. "Maybe you should."

Ouch.

But... I don't believe that. It's a lie. But *why* is he lying to me?

I get out of the car and stride toward the large adminis-tration building. Jace follows a moment later, moving slower. He probably shouldn't be out, but it's now or never. We can take a break after I get this piece of information from the sheriff.

We ride the elevator in silence. I consider texting Nate that we're here, but the element of surprise might work in our favor.

Or not.

We emerge on the second floor, which has been taken over by the sheriff's office. Jace follows me into the offices, a loyal shadow, but I really wish I had thought to bring my gun with me.

Which is ridiculous, because who feels the need to be armed in a police station?

"Ms. Sinclair," the receptionist says, her brows furrowing. "The sheriff is expecting you."

"Oh, is he?" I smile to hide my discomfort. So much for the element of surprise.

"Down the hall, his office is the last door on the left." Her gaze switches to Jace, but she doesn't say anything. No doubt she recognizes him from the wanted posters—the ones that have all but disappeared in the wake of my return.

I lead the way, and Jace finally whispers, "Are you going to give me a clue here?"

"No," I say.

He grunts, keeping pace with me.

I knock on the open door to Nate's office. He lifts his head from the file he was hunched over, then shoots to his feet. "Kora," he greets me. "And... Jace."

"You said I could ask you some questions," I say tentatively, stepping into his office. "Is now an okay time?"

He nods, still watching Jace. "You sure you want him around?"

"I'm pretty sure he's entitled to know, since he married me behind my back."

Nate pauses. His hands ball into fists, but he doesn't move out from behind his desk.

His tone does get icier when he orders Jace, "Shut the door."

Jace shoves the door closed. He flips the lock and pulls the blinds, then drags one of the chairs away from the desk. It reminds me of how he acted in Kronos' house, facing off against him and Ben.

My heart aches at that.

And... I didn't tell Jace what Ben did to me. *His half brother.*

Guess he's not the only one keeping secrets.

I swallow. I can tell him about that another time. When the dust has settled. But right now, I've got my father's words burning in my ears, and I want answers from the sheriff.

"You said you'd help me." I take the last seat.

After a beat, Nate sits, too. "I meant it."

"Did you mean it because we're related?"

Jace hisses.

Shock flickers across the sheriff's expression, but he doesn't deny it.

"I've been trying to piece together some things," I continue. "And my father was helpful enough to supply the name of the person who took me out of Sterling Falls when the Titans attacked the Hell Hounds' clubhouse."

Nate sits rigid. Jace seems to mirror him.

Satisfaction spreads through me that I've managed to surprise both of them.

"Jeremy Bradshaw," I say slowly. I cross my arms. "An old friend of my father... but apparently, the uncle to the long lost Korinne Sterling."

"Kora—" Jace leans toward me.

I hold up my hand, glaring at Nate. "Is he a brother? Or your father?"

"My father," Nate confirms.

"And I don't suppose you'd introduce us?"

He winces. "I could probably do that."

"How long have you known about Kora's true identity?" Jace shifts in his seat, trying to sit up straighter. He's got a sheen of sweat across his brow, but he doesn't comment on the pain he's in.

"I could ask you the same," Nate says.

"Your father has been sending us threatening messages," I say. "How are you okay with that? Whose side are you on?" And then something else occurs to me. "Wait. Was Wilma Sterling your mother?"

Nate rises, a clear indication that while he said he'd help, he didn't really mean he'd be at the wrong end of an interrogation. Desperation claws at my throat as I wait for him to elaborate. Jace and I sit immobile for a handful of seconds.

Finally, the sheriff relents. "My family was kept out of the papers when she died. It was the bit of peace her brothers offered us. To not be hounded by reporters..."

"Nadine discovered her, though," I guess.

"She was never quite the same after that." He lifts one shoulder, never breaking eye contact. "Nevertheless, she's made something of her life. She hasn't let the tragedy slow her down."

There are Sterlings everywhere.

I don't know if I want them for a family. I can't trust any of them. Especially not the sheriff... as much as I want to.

"Set up a meeting with your father," I say, although it definitely sounds more like a plea. "I have so many more questions. About——"

Jace puts his hand on my thigh.

I shove it off without thinking. He doesn't offer me comfort. He doesn't offer me anything except a contract that has bound us together.

Maybe I should inquire about divorces. Or an annulment—like the whole thing never even happened. *Poof*, gone.

Could I do that to us?

The sheriff clears his throat, his gaze on Jace's hand. Which now rests in a fist on his own thigh. "I'll see when he's around and call you."

Not the most decisive answer, but I'll take it. My nerves are crawling under my skin, and for once, I listen to them. I flee to the elevator and ride it down alone.

I have an uncle. Cousins.

I didn't ask Nate how Alex Sterling fits into the equation, but I will. I'll keep coming back until my curiosity is satiated. I've got more questions than I know what to do with. *Is* his father responsible for the threatening messages? Did he do it to keep his daughter on the city council? Or to drive me out of Sterling Falls? Why a black snake—not once, but *twice*? He wore a black snake mask the night he took Jace and me, too.

It has to be significant.

I rub my face and let out a loud groan right before the elevator *dings* and opens.

I go to exit and almost crash headfirst into Alex Sterling.

My mouth dries.

He chuckles, slipping past me. "Probably not your floor," he comments. "Unless you want to walk down four flights of stairs."

Sure enough, there's a *4* placard on the wall just outside the elevator.

Not my floor. How did I not even notice the elevator was going up instead of down?

I reenter the elevator, fighting the blush creeping up my cheeks.

"My bad," I mumble.

His dark hair is swept back, his jaws free of the five o'clock shadow he had the last time I saw him. Granted, that was the middle of the night after an explosion that took out a few buildings in West Falls... His navy-blue suit and white shirt are crisp and wrinkle-free. Overall, he seems in total control of himself.

And I'm related to him.

Not that I'm about to blurt *that* out.

We stand beside each other, and my stomach swoops up into my chest with the fall of the elevator. Or maybe it's just my nerves.

"Enjoying being back in Sterling Falls, Kora?"

I glance at him. "What?"

He keeps his gaze on the digital number counting the floors down to one. "You've certainly made an impact, is all. I heard you had a hand in taking down the Titans."

I snort, then slap my hand over my mouth. "Sorry, um, no." I'm speaking through my fingers like a child. "I wasn't anywhere near that."

He shoots me a knowing smile. "I wasn't trying to incriminate you. And then Olympus... Congratulations, by the way."

"On...?"

"Winning your fight."

"You know a lot."

He shrugs. "It's my job to know a lot." He reaches into the breast pocket of his suit and withdraws a card. "If the sheriff doesn't satisfy your curiosity about your past, please let me know. I'd be happy to help."

I take the card and scan it. *Alex Sterling, Alderman.* His phone number, email address. I swallow and nod, but my heart is hammering that he, too, knows. Of course he does.

It seems like the whole town suddenly knows, thanks to Cerberus' loud proclamation. But he didn't call me Korinne. He, for one, seems to respect that I'm not going to up and change my name because of some rumor.

A rumor that a lot of people are believing.

"Thank you. I will," I answer.

The elevator finally slides to a halt, and the doors open. Alex motions for me to go out first. I tuck his card in my back pocket and walk down the hall. He goes in the opposite direction, and I glance over my shoulder at him. He's moving at an unhurried pace, his hands in his pockets.

Like nothing is wrong.

I frown at that, then shake it off and head back to the car to wait for Jace.

jace

We pull up to an unfamiliar house.

Kora gets out, taking the keys with her, and I sit in silence for a long moment.

I'm not used to being out of control. And while I'm not *literally* out of control in that sense, I'm not in control. So... it's the same thing.

I focus on Kora bounding up the porch steps. She sticks a key in the lock and opens the door, disappearing inside. She leaves it open, probably as a hint for me to follow her. And after another minute, I force myself to move. My side tugs at the stitches. My whole body hurts, but I push it aside.

I should've taken the pain meds Antonio offered me. It was a prescription bottle with my name on it, clearly filled from the hospital, but my stubbornness got in the way. I didn't want my senses to be dulled by meds.

They're dulled by pain instead.

Hand on the rail, I shuffle up and into the house. I close the door behind me, looking around the bright, airy space.

Kora sits on the kitchen island, down a wide-open hall

that ends in a massive living-and-kitchen space. The whole back wall is practically all windows, giving us a view of the water beyond.

"What is this place?" I ask.

She tilts her head, a small frown playing on her features. "You guys and your secrets."

"That doesn't answer anything."

"Wolfe and Apollo bought it," she says. "Apollo is on his way here now."

My throat works at the silent implication. That Wolfe *isn't* on his way, because he's still with the Hell Hounds. But also—they bought this place? When?

I take better stock of the house. I don't see any reason why they'd pick this spot, except with Kora in mind.

But Kora has only been back for a few weeks. Not long enough for them to have managed this... which means, while I was hoping she *wouldn't* come back, they were counting down the days till she returned. Not only that—they were planning for it.

"Do you remember anything from the group home?" I can't focus on how much of an asshole I really am, so I ask that instead.

She bites her lip, then shrugs. "I don't know what's real and what's made up anymore."

"Think." I don't know why I can hold on to those memories so fucking *clearly*, and she can't even remember anything about that place.

Because she was five, you moron.

Her brows come together. "There was a nice woman," she says slowly. Her fingers trace an invisible pattern on the counter. "She did... painting?"

"Wilcox," I supply.

She frowns harder, like I shouldn't know that. *But I do.* I remember it all, as much as I've tried to forget.

I venture closer. "She did art therapy."

Kora nods once. "And another woman. She was strict. I tried to stay out of her way."

"Pearson."

"How do you know that?" she whispers.

I get to the edge of the island, where Kora is still perched, and grip the counter. "What else do you remember?"

"The girls were mean. Jace—"

"You brought me here for a reason," I say, forcing the words out before she can continue. "And it's not just to keep going in circles like we are. You're pissed at me. I want you to understand why."

Kora's gaze lifts, meeting mine. She nods once. "Okay."

"The girls," I prompt.

"I have hazy memories of them not liking me. But I did have one friend."

Me.

I wait. My body is suspended in time as she squeezes her eyes shut and relives those moments through a foggy glass. If it's enough, I can't say. I never shut off my memories from that time. I can live through every goddamn second in my mind like I'm still trapped in the foster system.

"Jace," she finally chokes out. "You were there?"

I exhale, and with it goes some of the tension that's been settled in my bones since the day she got to Sterling Falls. "I was. I knew you." *I still do.*

"Did you know I was Korinne Sterling?"

"Not then."

"When?" She slides off the counter and stops just short

of touching me. "And why does *that* justify everything you've done since then?"

I can't help but reach for her. And she doesn't flinch away when I put two fingers under her chin, lifting her face so she looks at me again. Because I want her to see how dead serious I am when I admit this next part.

"Because I've known you for a lifetime," I growl into her face. "And you're mine. In every fucking way that matters."

"You gave me no choice in the matter," she spits back.

My laugh is hollow. There's no winning with her.

"You can't just apologize, can you," she says suddenly.

I drop my hand. "I could if I was sorry."

"But you're not." A step back. She's retreating, inch by inch.

"I'm not," I agree. "I'd do it again in a fucking heartbeat."

"Why?"

Why? Of all the asinine questions. I stride forward. She goes back. We move around the island until she corners herself, and I keep coming. I press my hands to the counter on either side of her. Her chest rises and falls rapidly, but she's still pissed. From zero to a hundred in a flash.

"I had been kicked out of so many fucking foster homes before I met you. I was drowning. Getting into fights, stealing, running away." I lower my head, touching my forehead to hers. Shock flickers through me when she doesn't headbutt me. "And then Wilcox brought you in and made me show you around the house. But it wasn't enough. You had no friends. But you had me."

I wet my lips. "And then... everything changed."

"What happened?"

"I got out of the basement, and the world had shifted."

That probably doesn't even make sense to her, but it means the world to me. It was the day my life shattered.

I go to pull away, but she wraps her hands around my neck. She keeps her forehead against mine like that will just let the memories come out easier.

And maybe she has a point, because they do.

When Ms. Pearson finally unlocked the basement door, allowing me to go back to my room... Kora was gone.

"Cerberus came for me a month later. Acted like a decent guy—"

Kora snorts.

"Charmed Pearson. Or paid her off, I don't know. Either way, the next thing I knew, I was on my own with him. He showed me your picture." My throat is so dry, it's like I'm right back in the passenger seat of his Cadillac. It smelled like cigar smoke and ash, even though it was pristine. "He asked if I knew you."

"What did you tell him?"

My greatest shame. "I told him I did," I whisper.

Her nails bite into my skin, but she doesn't let go. "Then?"

"Then came the hunt."

She shivers. "But no one found me."

No, they didn't. "They didn't know your new name. I couldn't let that go. It plagued me for years that I could've —that I almost—"

"Stop." She sighs.

The sound moves against my lips, and I try not to live in the agony that I've carried with me since I was ten. I betrayed her. I gave her up. It doesn't matter that Cerberus was unsuccessful—I was too weak.

But then I learned from my mistakes.

"You weren't going to get put in that situation again," I say. "I swore on my life that I would keep you safe."

And I *did*. It's why I pushed her out of Sterling Falls time and again. It's why I risked everything to free her from Kronos, then Cerberus.

"I gave him Olympus." My last confession.

She releases me, surprise parting her lips. "What?"

"The deal. The fucking—I gave him *everything*. In exchange for you."

"Because..."

"Because I fell in love with the idea of you long before I met you as an adult." *Fuck.* We're doing this. Why not? *Just be honest.* "I cherished the idea of you for so fucking long, you were all that kept me sane. And then you came back into my life, just as the sharks are circling us. And you came back again. And again. But it's not *me* that you see. It's Wolfe. It's Apollo." My voice cracks.

"Jace—"

"I'm in Sterling Falls because Cerberus wanted *you*." I fight to keep the desperation out of my voice. The fear. This is everything I've held close to my chest, hiding from *everyone*. Even my two best friends. Hell, I've barely begun to admit these secrets to myself. And yet, I can't seem to shut up now that I've started. "I tried so hard to save you, and every fucking thing I did seemed to be in vain. So when I only had one last move to play, I played it. I won't apologize for that, Kora."

I let out a breath. What she does with that information is on her. But I've laid it all out, and I've never felt so vulnerable.

FOURTEEN

kora

J ace just laid his whole heart out in the open, and I
have no idea what to do. I already feel like I'm being
torn in half by Wolfe and Apollo. No one is making me
choose between them. But adding Jace to the equation,
finding out he's done this all *for* me—it's impossible.

My heart aches at the thought of the ten-year-old boy
left in the wake of Hurricane Kora. I was only five. Almost
six. And yet my presence at the group home seemed to have
changed everything for him.

I close my eyes and try to remember the day I met the
Sinclairs. Someone had led them to me, I think. Pearson or
Wilcox or one of the other staff. I was standing under a tree
while the church service continued, and I was... I was
crying.

Hiccupping for breath.

Because...

They took him away.

All at once, those memories resurface. Sidling closer to
him on the church pew, pressing my shoulder to his arm.
Seeking him out in the boys' room after the girls taunted

129

me about something foolish—my hair, my clothes. Meeting him for the first time, being drawn to the boy with the haunted blue eyes. He was the anchor that kept me from going adrift, and I did my best to forget about him after I left.

I forced him from my mind, because letting him stay there would've hurt too much.

But it hurts now, too.

My eyes burn, and an uncomfortable lump forms in my throat. I'm two seconds away from losing it, because I should've looked into his eyes and immediately recognized him.

Shouldn't I have?

Recognized a boy who, up until right now, I forgot existed?

I shudder.

"Do you hate me?" he rasps, like it's the most painful question he's ever asked.

Maybe it is. Because he's done so much to make me hate him, and so much to unravel it. Sometimes simultaneously.

"I don't know." I'm taking the easy way out, but my emotions are a mess. "I just..."

The front door slams.

I leap back, like being caught within arm's reach of Jace is a bad thing. Pain flashes across Jace's face, a shadow that's there and then gone. I frown at it, at *him*.

Apollo enters the kitchen with bags balanced in each hand. He sets them on the counter wordlessly, but his gaze misses nothing between Jace and me. He doesn't say anything to Jace but turns to me. "I tried to get a variety of favorites."

I inch closer, watching as he pulls out food. A variety,

for sure. Some easy-to-cook meals, like boxed macaroni and cheese, fresh veggies, and fruits. Then more intricate things that might push at our skill level in the kitchen, spices and meats.

"I'm going for a walk," Jace mutters.

He leaves us, and silence reigns for all of two seconds before Apollo comes around the island and wraps me in a hug.

I tip my head up, resting my chin on his shoulder, and exhale.

"You look two seconds away from crying," he says in my ear. "Should I go beat his ass?"

I sigh. "No. No, it's my own doing, I think."

"Okay."

I extract myself from him and smile sheepishly. "Um, is Olympus...?"

"All clear," he says. "I contacted some of our old employees. They're going to start cleaning it up and remove all traces of the Hell Hounds."

All this time, we thought Cerberus had just moved into Olympus because it was there for the taking. But Jace is the one who gave him the key... in exchange for me. My gut twists. But I fought for Olympus, and I'll keep fighting for Wolfe, too.

"You seem exhausted," Apollo says.

I nod at the truth in his words. I'm not sure when I got a decent night's sleep. It hasn't been in the past thirty-six hours, that's for sure. He directs me to the stairs, and I climb them without protest. I strip off my clothes and fall into the bed, curling up in the center.

My eyes close of their own accord, and within moments, I'm asleep.

FIFTEEN YEARS AGO

I flip open the music box and wipe tears from my eyes. It still plays, but the ballerina who once lifted up and spun slowly has snapped off. I can't stop crying, and I hate it.

I hate tears. I hate that I don't know why I'm crying. Just that this music box is *mine*, and Sandra doesn't like when things belong to one person.

We live in a group home, dummy. What's yours is mine. Then she played too rough, and the ballerina snapped off.

"What's that?"

I sniff and look up. Jace doesn't seek me out very often, but now he comes farther into the girls' room closet—my secret hiding place—and sits beside me. He takes the box from my hand, closing it and ending the sad song.

He turns the box over, examining it. "To K," he reads.

I sit up straighter, balling my fists to keep from lunging at him. I'd been tracing the markings on the bottom of the music box for *ages*, but I didn't know what it said.

"Keep going," I urge.

He smirks. "To K. Your heart is stronger than your mind. Love, Mom and Dad."

I wrinkle my nose.

He sets the box down on his lap, tracing the edge of it. He keeps pushing the pad of his finger onto the corner, as if to break his skin. "Not what you were expecting?"

No. Because my parents...

I shake my head violently, my hair swinging around my face. When I think of them, I hear sobs. Screams. The same ones in my nightmares.

The girls tease me about those, too. How I wake up

shivering and wet-eyed, the plea for my parents on the tip of my tongue. Sometimes it chokes me up just how badly I want my parents.

"They're not coming back?" Jace asks.

"No," I whisper. But I'm not allowed to talk about it. Not why I'm here, not my real name. Wilcox asks me about it sometimes, in the art room crouched next to my desk. She runs her hand up my arm and whispers that it's best for me to forget about where I came from, and I don't know why.

My eyes fill with tears again.

Jace takes my hand. His is warm in mine, his grip tight. "It's okay. Mine aren't either."

That night, I jerk awake with another nightmare. Blood-covered walls and an echoing scream, the burn of fire. My throat is full of ash, and I can't catch a breath. I look around sharply, my panic increasing, but only find a room full of empty beds.

"Shh," Jace says, climbing halfway up the ladder to get to my bed. He rests his forearms along the rail and watches me pull myself together.

I hiccup and wipe the back of my hand under my nose. Eventually, I manage to exhale normally. Not like I'm gulping for air without success.

Jace stays propped on the ladder, his face shadowed in the darkness.

There are night lights along the walls, but their faint glow doesn't reach up here. After a moment, he climbs up the rest of the way and sits at the foot of my bed.

He reaches some silent conclusion, because he pats my foot. "It's okay, Kora. I'll keep the nightmares away. You sleep while I keep watch."

PRESENT

I jerk awake. The memory of that music box, of *Jace*, is so loud that it hurts. I sift through my past, trying to figure out what else I'd forgotten. It seems like a bottomless pit lost in the back of my head.

But... I remembered my parents at that point. Of course I did. I probably remembered who took me away from them, too. Somehow, I forgot everything about that time. Pre-Sinclair.

I shiver and push the blankets off my legs, swinging them over the edge of the bed. It's dark out, but I can't tell what time it might be. I fight the urge to get out of bed. I *should* just go back to sleep.

But then a hand wraps around my wrist from behind, and I scream.

The training Ben instilled in me kicks in. I twist my wrist and latch on to the hand that grabbed me. I'm moving before I actively decide to fight, and I have the hand torqued up at an angle before he even knows what hit him.

"Kora," Apollo wheezes, sounding like he's half in pain and half trying not to laugh.

It takes me a long second to realize what happened. That it must be the middle of the night, and Apollo crawled into bed with me. That I'm now straddling his hips, and he's facedown in the mattress with his shoulder at an odd angle.

The door flies open, and the light comes on.

I look over at Jace, then down at Apollo.

I release his hand and scramble off him. My face gets hot. On *fire*. Damn.

"Um..."

Apollo rolls onto his back and grins up at me. "That was kind of hot, baby."

"Are you okay?" Jace asks me. "You screamed..."

I wet my lips and swallow. "Yep, just surprised. Sorry."

I take a closer look at Jace, and another stupid memory smacks me in the face.

"Pack up your stuff, Kora," Ms. Wilcox urges. She's herded me back through the house, ignoring Ms. Pearson's sharp expression as we pass. She waits in the doorway of the girls' room while I shove my belongings in a plastic bag.

I pause at the music box.

When Jace saw it, he seemed sad. So I tuck it under my arm and march past Ms. Wilcox, going to the boys' room. I go to his bed and climb up, hiding it under his pillow. I don't see him—I think Ms. Pearson has him locked away somewhere. The thought makes my skin crawl, but I wasn't able to say anything to her. She studiously ignores me unless she's trying to get someone to take me.

When I'm done, Ms. Wilcox purses her lips. She doesn't say anything, though. She just nods like it was inevitable and shuffles me back downstairs. We stop in front of a man and woman who tried to talk to me earlier.

They didn't seem to mind when I didn't have much to say.

"Hi, Kora," the woman says, crouching to get on my level. "I'm Rachel, and this is my husband, Ken."

I nod and don't respond.

"You're going to come stay with us for a while, if that's okay with you?"

My throat dries. "Okay," I whisper because I don't have a choice. My belongings are in a bag in Ms. Wilcox's hand, and I don't have anyone else.

And... that's that. I'm put in their car. I don't return to St. Theresa's.

I PRESS my hand to my chest and stumble farther away from the bed—and from Jace.

The *song*. The one he'd played on the piano. Well, he played two. One that sounded like a lullaby—one that I might've expected to be in a music box. But that wasn't it. It was the second one that he'd played, the one with the haunting notes that scratched some deep part of my brain.

And it suddenly hits me that he's been honest with me about our past. Today, at least. He's the boy I did my best to forget. He's the boy I *did* forget. But the one who changed absolutely everything.

Tears flood my eyes. I go to Jace and stop in front of him, tipping my head back to glare with my blurry vision. I don't know what I want from him. I don't know what he wants from me.

But damn it if he didn't win back a piece of me today.

He pulls me into his chest. One hand cups the back of my head, and the other arm is banded around my upper back. It takes me a minute to register and lift my arms. I hug him back and let the tears fall.

I don't know what we are, or what we'll become. But I am getting a better sense of what we were as kids.

Lifelines.

Malik sits beside me in the clubhouse. My father is not pacing for once. Or drunk. He's standing at the head of the room with a deadly calm surrounding him, and I get the image of a hunting dog that has caught a scent. He's shed the wild demeanor, and he'll move with deadly accuracy until he has his prey in his reach.

It's his way—but he hasn't had an enemy quite like this one.

An invisible monster.

The Hell Hound who was decapitated... his head was found on a spike in South Falls, outside the docks that Cerberus controls. The one where his drugs are imported. The one that, up until last night, was run under an alias. It wasn't connected to us on paper, but someone discovered it.

The sheriff's office has been all over it. They're presumably more baffled than us, but their presence, coupled with Kronos' death, has effectively loosened Cerberus' hold on the mayor.

No more neutral zone interference. No more policing—coupled with the fact that school's out, there's not a need for extra policing from the Hell Hounds. So Brad is right back up our ass again, like the good old times.

The clubhouse is filling with Hell Hounds. Some of them have been staying away out of self-preservation, but my father made things very clear. If you're not with us tonight, you're against us.

Tensions have been high. And I've got no doubt that blood will be shed tonight—in one way or another.

To make things worse, the decapitated Hell Hound was the one who fought Kora. That was my suspicion, and now it's become a reality. Like the *KS* that was carved into his skin wasn't enough of a fucking hint.

Someone is either trying to protect Kora, and they're sending a clear message to everyone who gets close to her to back the fuck off, or they're trying to scare her.

Maybe both.

"This city is ours," my father says without preamble, and the room falls silent.

Even Malik and I sit up straighter, our gazes cutting around the room. One of the recruits has been hustling drinks out to incoming members, but he goes still, too. The dangerous tension is clear in the air. Impossible to miss.

I imagine it's been this way for years, and I simply forgot about the power that Cerberus holds over his followers. I got a taste of it while we were at Olympus, but he never called full-scale meetings like he does here.

"This city is *OURS*," he roars.

We're immobile. I don't know where he's going with this. I'm not in his confidence. Not entirely. Malik might not be either, judging from the way his brows are furrowed.

"The Titans are gone," he continues in a normal voice—but this is what elicits a cheer from us. Even Malik.

But all I can see is Nyx, and my own damn guilt gets in the way.

"Kronos is dead. The police are spread too thin to stop us." He smirks. "Tomorrow night, we act."

A chill goes up my spine.

"Act?" someone questions.

"We test the will of the city against our own," Cerberus answers. "We make it bleed for us."

Fuck. Fuck. Fuck.

"What is he talking about?" I ask through my teeth, directing my low words toward Malik.

"He's lost it," Malik breathes.

Glad we're on the same page.

"Enjoy your night, my friends." Cerberus spreads his arms. "Because tomorrow, we take what we're due."

The meeting breaks with my father striding down the aisle of chairs and tables to deafening noise. I shouldn't be surprised by this—he's cultivated a bloodthirsty bunch over the years. He culls who doesn't impress him. Even the recruits prove their worth to him before he takes them on. And they'll no doubt have to prove themselves again before the week is over.

I sit still, listening to the chatter around me. My back is pressed to the wall. A recruit speeds by, but I lean forward and catch his arm. He whirls around and is about to snap something when he sees me.

His face pales. "C-can I get you something, sir?"

Malik snorts.

I don't react to that. I'm not partial to the sir, but I'll take it over some other, less fortunate names. "Two beers,"

I say. "And how do you feel about potentially dying tomorrow night?"

He's still pale, and with my hand on his arm, I don't miss the way he tenses, and I don't particularly mind the way my own attention sharpens in response. I want his honest reaction—and fear will either make him truthful or stick to a bland answer.

"I..." His lips flatten, then resolve enters his expression. "I'll be ready."

Bland. *Boring.*

"Good," Malik says.

I release the recruit and shoot Malik a look. "Ruining my fun?"

"You messing with the recruit is like watching you play with food."

"Endearing?"

"Disturbing," he replies.

I sigh. In truth, maybe I wasn't expecting blood tonight so much as craving it. For the last six months, almost seven at this point, I've been holding back in all regards. I didn't want my father to influence me or pull me back. I didn't want to lose myself.

But now that Kora has returned, I'm not afraid of losing my anchor. She'll bring me back.

So my calling for blood has returned with a vengeance, and I fear I'm not doing everything I can to prevent myself from slipping.

I fear I don't want to...

"Come on," I mutter, rising.

The recruit has returned with the beers, and I snatch one from his hand on my way past.

Malik follows, a louder version of a shadow. We weave

between the tables, but I don't have it in me to be pleasant. Instead, I'm burning up on the inside.

On the porch, I take a deep breath. There are the familiar rows of bikes, the smell of gasoline and smoke, the engines rumbling as some guys prepare to ride.

I take a few swallows of my beer, then shove it into a Hell Hound's open hand. I don't bother to wait for him to curl his fingers around it. I hop off the porch and continue to my bike. If I can't get dirty, I'll ride away my aggression at the front of a pack of bikers.

Malik grumbles something behind me, but he's following. As I expected.

He might want to kill me. After all, I took his position.

Another intriguing idea flares to life in my mind, and I imagine how the Hell Hounds would react if I started shit with Malik. Or someone else.

But that's not my place. I'm not fighting for rank. Fuck, I'm not even fighting to *keep* my rank. No one has challenged me—not even Malik. It's surprising in this herd of animals who only have baser instincts: to rise. To grow their own power. To protect themselves.

Animals.

I get on my bike as the leader rolls up to me.

"You want to take this one?" he asks.

I jerk my head in a nod.

He grins.

I yank my helmet on and slide down the clear visor. I wish Kora was on the back of my bike, but that will have to be another time. I can show her that the gang isn't *all* bad. Not when we're united.

Malik's bike roars to life. He's got a distinctive sound, like a truck's engine. Or a plane taking off. His modifications never fucking stop. I think he might be able to fly on his bike if he were to only attach a pair of wings.

Mine rumbles beneath me, and I glance around at the pack of riders. A thrill goes through me when I see them laser-focused on me.

Me.

Unlike my helmet, which encompasses my entire head and protects my eyes from the wind, theirs are just on top of their heads. Their bikes are upright, meant more for cruising and intimidating than anything else.

Mine—and Malik's—are built for speed. If we hit asphalt wrong, leaned forward as we are, we'd go over the handlebars and crack our heads open.

No thanks.

Still, no one seems to mind that I'm different. Or maybe they've long since come to accept it. Either way, they follow me down the drive and out onto the road. Malik sidles up almost next to me. His front tire stays even with my knee.

I glance back and catch a dozen headlights.

Maybe more.

The adrenaline that pumps through my blood is unlike any other. Second only to her.

And I am still so fucking resolved that Kora would enjoy this, that she'd like this midnight tryst, that I pull my phone out and call the number she last had. I clip my phone to its holder in front of me, and the earpiece in my helmet beeps as it connects the call.

It's about time we get her a replacement for her phone, damn it.

"Hello?" Her voice is breathy in my ear, kind of hoarse. It's past midnight, so maybe she was sleeping.

"Hey, flower," I answer. "What are you doing?"

"I'm at our house," she whispers. "Where are you?"

My heart pounds harder at her words. Our house. I could die happy in this minute, with all thoughts of anger and adrenaline left behind. Really—just kill me now, with those words ringing in my ear.

"Wolfe?"

"I'm here," I say. "I'm debating something."

"What's that?"

"How I can steal you away," I admit. "Because I have a feeling you're not hanging out alone."

"And you want an adventure?" Her voice is higher. I've managed to intrigue her. "Right now?"

"Yeah. What are you wearing?"

I swear to God I can feel her smile from here.

She laughs under her breath. "Well... panties," she says slowly. "And a shirt that may have come from your closet..."

I smile, too, and I'm fucking grateful for my helmet. It keeps our conversation private. "What's it look like?"

"Dark green. Like your eyes when you're chasing a high."

"Like now," I counter.

"Is that why you called? You want to chase a high?"

I find myself nodding. "I want to chase a high with you."

We're going toward the center of town when I wave to Malik. I've had enough of them for the moment—we'll meet back up soon. With Kora. He slides into the lead, and I peel off. No one follows me down a side street, and then I pick up speed until I'm flying back toward the house.

My house.

Our house.

"Wear jeans," I say when she doesn't respond. "Boots."

"Anything on top? Or should I go shirtless?"

145

I growl before I can even stop myself. "Wear something fucking conservative. A turtleneck."

"Oh my god," she laughs. "Seriously?"

"You know what? I'll pick it out." I turn onto our road, and in a matter of moments, I'm there. But when my headlight sweeps over the porch, I see the truth.

I'm too late.

I put my feet down and rev the engine, because it's the only thing I can do in this moment.

She's fucking gorgeous.

She listened to me, at least. Dark jeans and boots that are about as similar to her old pair that we could find. But her shirt is... well, fuck, I can see her nipples from here. She's wearing a red satin cropped top. It exposes a slice of her flat, toned stomach, and I immediately bite my tongue to try and stem my hard-on.

Too late, though. My dick rises in my pants, and I have the feral urge to just... strip her down right this moment.

Later, I promise myself. When I can get a true moment alone with her.

She does a little twirl in the spotlight my bike's headlight has created on her, and then I see the jean jacket in her hand. And the phone in her other. She lifts it back to her ear. "So... you think I should change?"

"Fuck," I groan.

She laughs, and it echoes in my skull. It's another sound that I'd like to hold on to forever. I stay where I am as she approaches, still dancing to some beat that only she can hear.

Devilish little monster.

I yank my helmet off and set it in my lap. She smiles wider when she sees my face and ends the call between us.

Her phone is stowed in her back pocket, but she's still out of reach.

I crook my finger at her.

Kora finally gets to me, and I haul her in. Her skin is hot under my palms, which slip from her waist around to her back. I kiss her hard. Almost savagely. She doesn't seem to mind, leaning in and giving it right back to me. Her teeth graze my lower lip, nipping and tugging. I groan into her mouth.

I'm fucking unhinged.

She arches her back, pressing her chest into mine, and it takes all of my willpower to withdraw. We breathe, and I register her hands on my shoulders. She swipes her thumb under my lip, showing that, yeah, I have red lipstick smeared across my face.

I lick my lips and taste what she must taste every time she wets hers. It's not the worst taste... and I like that she looks a little less put together.

Except, we're about to be out in public.

I take her jean jacket and open it. "Put it on."

"Yes, sir," she snips.

My fucking cock jerks again, and I capture her arms in the denim. I hold the wrists hostage, keeping her from freeing herself, and lean in. "Don't call me sir if you don't want me to take charge, flower."

She tips her head to the side. Her eyes burn into mine. "What makes you think I don't want you to take charge?"

I release her, shaking my head and letting out a laugh.

Because she has been into that. And if I slipped my hand down the front of her pants, I think her pussy would tell me she's into it now, too.

"Later," I say. "Come on."

She climbs on behind me with a slight groan—but

mostly in good humor, I think—and puts on the extra helmet I now always carry. Once her arms are wrapped around my waist, I put my helmet on and hit the throttle. With my foot still on the ground, I whip us in a tight circle and shoot back toward the road.

I could've asked her where Apollo was, or if she told him I was sneaking her out. But I like the mystery of it.

In another lifetime, it could've been just us.

And yet... There's something in me that doesn't agree with that. I don't know if I would've been it for her, or if we'd only be *it* with Apollo... and Jace.

We feed different parts of her soul.

Kora's clearly feeling some sort of way, because her hand inches lower. Her movements are miniscule, and I don't realize where it's going until her thumb skates along my bare skin above my jeans.

I let out a breath, knowing she can't hear me.

But her fingers keep going lower, until her whole hand is wrapped around my dick. She squeezes, and I hit the throttle.

I imagine her laugh. Her thighs are tight around mine as she strokes me. She doesn't even seem surprised that I'm hard as a rock.

The bike wobbles, but I just grit my teeth and push us faster.

This is a certain kind of high, certainly.

But not the one I had in mind...

SIXTEEN

"She went with Wolfe?"

My shoulders inch higher, but I don't move from the window. Of course she went with Wolfe. He called, and she went running. It only bothers me because I wanted to wake up beside her. And instead, I woke up to her leaving.

Jace sighs behind me, then moves closer. He sets a mug down on the table beside me. "A peace offering."

I glance over at him. "It's going to take a lot more than coffee for that, dude."

He runs his hand over his face, hiding his scowl. "I know."

I turn toward him, realize that, yeah, I'm fully fucking pissed. The last few days have done nothing to stem that anger. Not even watching him almost die.

In fact, I think I'm *more* angry at him because he's hurt. We can't even fight it out like we normally would. Not that we've ever been on such opposite sides.

"You would've done it, too," Jace swears, like he can

read my fucking mind. "You would've chosen the same if you were in my shoes—"

"But I wasn't," I snap. "Because you boxed us out and tried to do things solo."

Hurt. I'm *hurt.* And I hate it. Hate that feeling that drapes over me like a second skin. I can't seem to shed it.

"Was it because you wanted her to yourself?" The words cut my throat.

Jace flinches, but he doesn't retreat. His expression remains open, and it makes me wonder if he really does want to resolve this. Instead, he lowers himself into one of the chairs and motions for me to do the same.

I sit heavily and gesture to him. "How's the battle wound?"

He grimaces. "It's healing too slowly."

"It's been three days? Two?"

He grunts.

I shake my head and return my focus to the window.

"You look like a lost puppy," Jace comments. "Waiting for his owner to come home."

"Don't make me regret talking to you," I grumble. But... yeah. I can see the correlation.

"I wanted to free her," he says. "And it wasn't working. Not with Cerberus. He needed something big, but he also wanted her chained down. I think he wanted a way to be able to wrangle her back in line if he had to."

I turn that over in my mind.

"I'm sorry, Apollo."

I blink at Jace. "You're apologizing? To *me*?"

He shrugs one shoulder. "I know how much she means to you, and I took away..."

"You didn't take away anything except her right to choose which one of us she wants to marry." I scoff. "Come on, man. She's still mine. And Wolfe's. And maybe she's still yours after what I saw a few hours ago..."

They'd hugged. She'd cried. Then she'd crawled back into bed with me, sniffling and creeping closer until she was pressed to my side. Until Wolfe called and she left with him anyway.

"You're jealous of him," Jace says.

I jerk, then glare. "You're judging *me*?"

"You're preaching about her being with all of us, but when she leaves you to go to him..." Jace laughs. "I get it. I do. I don't want her out there, doing God knows what with him, while we're—"

"Stuck here?"

He goes quiet. "Well, Wolfe is the most stuck one of us all."

Guilt lashes through me, and it tears apart the jealousy. It just rips it to shreds and gives me the clarity I was lacking. "He needs her."

"Yeah."

I nod to myself. I think we've been off since we've been apart. The three—*four*—of us were solid before the Titans attacked the clubhouse and the sheriff's fucking father took Kora and Jace away. Before Wolfe and I were arrested and coerced back into the Hell Hounds.

Being separated... it's hurt us more than anything else.

"We need him," I point out, perhaps unnecessarily. "We need to get him out of there."

Jace sighs. I don't like it when he sighs, like he's already thought of it and dismissed it as impossible. But it can't be. We just need to go and rip Wolfe free from—

"He has to do it himself," Jace mutters. "I tried. Kora tried. We both fucking failed, or do you not remember that?"

I frown harder. "I know we failed."

"So we can't just rip him away from the Hell Hounds," he continues. "Because his father will just keep coming for him. And we'll never be safe."

There's someone out there hunting us already. The snake on the door. And prior to that, drugging me... trying to drug any one of us, I'd imagine. Whoever laced our glasses wasn't aiming for any one of us in particular. Then the decapitated snake in Kora's bed.

"Wait." I narrow my eyes. "There were Hell Hounds being decapitated..." The most recent of which was just on the news today. Everyone important is keeping their mouths shut, though, so no real information has been released. And we haven't had a chance to talk to Wolfe about it.

All I know is that he went there. Saw the body in person.

"And?"

"It's not weird that there's a snake with a severed head in Kora's bed? And then Hell Hounds with severed heads..."

Jace stares across the room. He's thinking it through. Trying to put all the puzzle pieces in order.

"She's had a stalker forever," he finally murmurs. He shoots to his feet. "The photo? And a phone call—"

"What phone call?" I follow him to the front hall, where we left keys for the cars hanging by the door. "Jace."

"She got one telling her to leave Sterling Falls," he says, but he's distracted. Already trying to figure out what to do next. Meanwhile, his hand hasn't left his side, and he can't walk without a limp.

I grab his arm.

He jerks free of me, still moving, and I sigh. I shove him against the wall.

"What the fuck?" He pushes at my hands, but I ignore him. "Get off me."

"You're not leaving this house." I step closer, putting my palm to his chest. "Because your wound is not fucking ready for you to go kicking down doors. And we don't have any idea—"

"Jeremy Bradshaw," Jace growls. "That's who kidnapped us. That's who Kora's parents are close with. He—"

"Will be ready for you." My voice stays so even, I deserve a medal. "We've been over this."

Jace pauses and eyes me, then... he nods. Finally.

I back off.

"When did you become the level-headed one?"

I smirk. "I've always been level-headed."

He snorts and heads away from the front door. "Yeah, fucking right. I'm going to wait for her in bed."

"In her bed, you mean?" I scowl, following him. "What makes you think she wants you and not me?"

His laughter drifts back to me. It's been far too long since I've heard that sound, but I try not to linger on it. "I think she'd want either one of us after having to tear herself away from Wolfe."

I tilt my head. He has a point. But it's definitely not going to be him in her bed when she gets home.

Home. What a miraculous thing. And it really does feel like a piece of each of us.

Funny how things change. After I was so mad at her for burning down our house. But she was right—we needed change. We needed to be able to build something with her, as a unit of four instead of three.

Even still. I might be sharing my girl with my best friends, but that doesn't mean they get to win. I chase after

Jace and flop down on the bed beside him. He has a faint sheen of sweat on his forehead, maybe pain-induced. So I take pity on him and don't shove him to the floor. The bed is extra-large—we don't need to touch.

He stares at me for a second, then rolls his eyes. He probably agrees that this isn't a matter worth fighting over. He just says, "At least get the light."

I get no warning from Wolfe. Just the roar of other bikes on the road ahead of us, slow cruising and sounding like a freight train. He doesn't turn away, doesn't try to avoid them. We join their ranks, and I quickly pull my hand away from his pants. I lock my fingers together around his abs and fight the wicked blush that's taking over my face.

The bikers smile and nod at him. They look at me and only show a flash of confusion, or concern, and then we're moving on. We cut through them... *Wolfe* cuts through them easily. They may see him coming in their mirrors, or maybe his bike just sounds different than theirs.

Some lift their fingers from the handles, giving us subtle acknowledgement.

My heart pounds out of control... and now I get why Wolfe wanted me to dress conservatively. I thought he was *joking*. I thought we'd fuck on the porch, or inside, or go for a ride on our own.

We're surrounded by Hell Hounds.

Then the leader glances over at us, moving to the side,

and Wolfe lifts his fingers in a subtle wave. I mirror it when I recognize Malik.

It's not that I don't like him. I just don't particularly agree with his views. You know, following around like Cerberus' pet dog.

Ironic, right?

Wolfe sits up a little straighter, forcing me up, too. It takes me a moment to admit to myself that we're not in danger, we're not going to die. They're not going to turn on him.

But then I catch sight of a cop car out of the corner of my eye, and I tense all over again.

Wolfe sees it and glances back at me. His eyes crease with a smile, and his hand drops down to squeeze my thigh.

Okay... so, cops aren't a problem?

I guess it makes sense. What cop in their right mind would pull over a dozen bikers? We turn down residential streets that eventually fade into downtown. We coast by the school with its imposing marble administration building, the library farther down. Through the financial district, all metal and glass. Then up to North Falls, along the main drag. Malik stays steady at Wolfe's side, never passing him.

Hierarchy?

Bow & Arrow is dark and quiet. I don't know if Tem has been back since that night...

And then we're past it, and I set my worry aside. We pick up speed as the road inclines, and suddenly the cliffs drop away on our left. We're heading back toward Olympus, having made a loop through Sterling Falls.

Except, Wolfe doesn't keep going. He swings onto the shoulder and motions for Malik to keep going.

When he shuts the bike down, the headlight extinguishing, it takes me a long moment to get my sight to adjust. The moon is high, almost full, and casts the grassy area in pale, faint light.

My heart pounds. All I can do is hold on to him for a moment, trying to rein in my emotions. The adrenaline of riding with a gang of bikers, and now the absolute quiet that envelops Wolfe and me.

I unclip my helmet and pull it off, setting it in the grass. I shake out my hair while he sits immobile. I scoot back but don't get off, and Wolfe puts down the kickstand. His helmet is on the ground next to mine. He looks back and raises his eyebrow.

I'm already unbuttoning my jeans. I don't really give a shit that we're on the side of the road—it's the middle of the night, and I want him so bad it hurts.

He lifts me up and drags me around so I'm sitting in front of him, my legs draped over his thighs. My heart is beating way too fast. He leans into me, and I lean back. My shoulder blades touch the center of the handlebars.

He smirks, then runs his hands up my legs. I almost groan at the contact alone.

"Did Apollo not take care of you tonight, flower?" He seems more bothered by that fact than anything.

I shake my head slowly, biting my lip. "It's been a long night."

"Why?"

"Jace—"

He growls.

I lean forward and cover his mouth with my hand, shaking my head. "I'm starting to remember some stuff," I admit. "And it freaks me out. I wanted to get Jace alone so he would tell me the truth. As much of it as he could manage anyway. And I think he did."

Wolfe just looks at me. For a long moment.

I lower my hand, but he catches my wrist. His thumb brushes over the hourglass, but he doesn't stop there. He brings it up to his lips and bites it.

Hard.

"Ow," I say mildly, tugging back.

He doesn't release me so easily. His teeth are still in my skin—not breaking it, but it's going to bruise—and his tongue darts out. Then he kisses it. He gives my wrist his sole attention, and a flutter starts in my stomach. He's not even looking at my face as he does it.

Maybe he can feel my quick pulse there.

His lips move higher. Inching along my forearm, the crease of my elbow. He pauses only long enough to shove my jean jacket off my shoulders, yanking it off me completely and tossing it aside. Then he's right back where he was, his ministrations shiver-inducing.

When he gets to the strap of my red camisole, he licks under the string and then carefully moves it aside. He pauses on the bite marks on my breast left by Apollo, then kisses over them. My back arches. He slides the other strap down, then tugs my whole top down.

I'm not wearing a bra, and my nipples immediately stiffen in the cool night air. He palms my breasts and bites and sucks at my throat. My lips part, but I don't voice my thoughts. That I'm climbing out of my damn skin.

The last thing I want is to go slow.

"Wolfe, please," I beg. *Please go faster. Please stop torturing me. Please touch me more.*

He chuckles and withdraws entirely, leaving my skin hot. I may combust. I open my mouth to tell him so, and he just kisses me again. His hands lock in my hair, taking full possession of me. I can't move. He controls it all, right down to my pulse.

But then it's over. He leans back and rights my shirt, pulling the straps back into place. He rebuttons my pants. My core aches with need. He puts me on my feet, and I stare at him as he takes my hand.

"Wait." I try to stop him. It occurs to me that we've been here before. With the sound of the ocean so fucking close, and the cliffs... "This—"

He's already kicking off his shoes, then socks. He yanks his jeans down with one hand and steps out of them, still moving toward the ledge.

"Wolfe." More desperation in my voice.

"Face your fear, Kora," he urges.

He stops and balances me. I take my boots off—because the last thing I need is to damage them. I like them. Socks, jeans. I'm left in the red cropped shirt and black panties, but he doesn't get distracted by that—except the slow perusal of his gaze up and down my body, lingering on my bare legs. He smirks, while my skin is so hot, I'm going to burn through it.

He turns and tows me toward the edge, and then he stops.

I peer over the side. The water catches the moonlight and tosses it back, looking like a gleaming, wriggling mass far below us. To our left is the stairs cut into the rock.

Nyx jumped here. Saint, too. And then Wolfe.

I swallow past the lump in my throat at the unexpected grief. If anyone would enjoy this night, it would be Nyx. She'd be urging me to jump.

"I know what you're thinking," Wolfe whispers in my ear. His voice coils there and lingers like smoke. "You're missing your friend."

"I am," I manage. "And…"

"And I think she'd like that we're doing things that remind us of her," he finishes. He steps in behind me and kisses my neck.

I close my eyes and let his hands roam, but he stops again. He presses me closer to the edge, then moves away. "Jump, Kora."

I don't think.

I just do.

The rock bites into my bare feet as I take two huge steps forward and push off. I'm weightless for a moment, my hair lifting around my head. And then I'm falling, and my stomach swoops into my throat. I only have a moment to take a deep breath, and I hit the water feetfirst.

It's shockingly cold. I throw my arms out once I'm under, slowing my speed, and the iciness of it almost steals the air from my lungs.

There's a noise beside me, and then a hand finds my wrist.

Wolfe. I should've known he wouldn't leave me in the water alone for very long.

He pulls me to the surface, and I gasp. I slick my hair out of my face and wipe the salt water from my eyes. His hands find my hips, and he draws me to him. He's keeping us afloat, and this spot is uniquely sheltered from the stronger waves. I loop one arm around his neck, and the other slips between us.

The cold water hasn't had an effect on his erection, and I smirk at the way his lips part when I wrap my hand around him.

Without waiting, I navigate his cock through his boxers and rock my hips against him. I pull my panties aside, holding them out of the way until he surges forward. He pushes into me, and we both gasp. Ocean water rushes over our shoulders. He kicks to keep us afloat, but damn it. I'd drown for this sensation.

I take over, using my legs around his hips and hands on his shoulders as leverage to fuck him. He maneuvers us toward the rock ledge, and before I know it, he's hoisted me off him and up onto the rock. He quickly follows, stripping off my panties and thrusting back into me.

The wet rock is cool on my back. Water rushes up over the lip, soaking us further, but it doesn't matter. I love the fullness of Wolfe inside me. I love the way he's got a grip on my wrists, holding my arms down.

I wrap my legs around him again and lift my hips to meet him. My skin is still hot, burning in comparison to his. I wonder if he can feel it where we're connected. He's turned me into an inferno.

Wolfe leans down and kisses my jaw, evading my lips. I try to kiss him, but he just ducks lower. He's tracing Apollo's bite mark on my breast again.

And then he bites, too, and I let out a scream. He moves my shirt down again and licks my nipple, sucking it into his mouth. And he keeps stroking the deep spot inside me, but we're moving slower.

The cold water rushes over us again, cooling my hot skin.

"Wolfe," I moan. "I need to come."

He withdraws from my nipple and lifts back over me. With one hand, he reaches between us and rubs my clit. It does the trick—after being worked up for the past hour, it doesn't take me long at all for an orgasm to power through me.

"Look at me," Wolfe growls.

I hadn't realized I'd closed my eyes, but I force them

open. I meet his gaze, and ecstasy fills me. I dig my nails into Wolfe's shoulders and hold on. My muscles tremble. His eyes are in shadows—I can barely see his face above me. But I know he's staring at me with as much passion as I feel for him.

"You're perfect," he says.

His thrusts get harder. My back moves along the rock, scratching my skin, but I relish the discomfort. He changes angles, looping my leg around his arm and drilling into me until I'm ready to scream again. Everything is so hypersensitive.

His pace increases. He's chasing his own version of a high, until he slams into me and goes still. He falls forward, coming with a groan. His hands slide under my arms, pressing to my shoulder blades. He hugs me to him, almost bone-crushing with how tight he grips me.

And all at once, the emotion catches up. My throat closes, and I hug him back just as fiercely.

This is our stolen moment.

"I'm afraid for what I'm going to do," Wolfe whispers in my ear. "And I'm so fucking scared I'm going to lose you because of it."

My heart is in my throat now, and I can't breathe for a moment. He shudders when I run my fingertips up his spine. But I take a moment to consider the worst things I can think of him doing... and it isn't enough to dissuade me from him. From us.

"I love you," I reply. "And I don't know if you really understand what that means, because your mom left and your dad sucks. But I know what love is, and I will show you every day for the rest of our lives that I will be here. For you. With you."

His head dips, forehead pressing to my shoulder. His

hips rock slightly, his dick still inside me. I thought my heart might go out of control when I said that, but it's steady. *I'm* steady.

"I can't breathe without you," I continue. "I want your darkness, Wolfe. But I want the light, too. I want every form of you. Wolfe. Ares. *You.*"

Isn't that just a mirror of what Apollo said to me? Those words helped me—and now I'm passing them on to Wolfe.

I grip him tighter. He's hard again—or maybe he never lost it, I don't know—and he fucks me slower this time. We're so close together, I imagine the beating of his heart is the one I feel against my ribcage.

"I'll fucking die if I don't free myself from my father."

I just keep holding him. I just keep holding on while something cracks in my chest.

Because if he dies, then I will, too.

That's a promise.

kora

Wolfe drops me off at the house and gives me one more searing kiss. Our skin is still cold from the water, but heat blooms through my chest at our contact. I don't care that I'm soaked through, that my jeans cling to my legs and my socks are damp inside my boots, that my panties were lost to the ocean.

Tonight was fun. Unconventional, a little bit heart-breaking, but *fun*. I want to go back and jump off the cliff again.

Which is insane.

I shake my head at the smile that won't fade and toe off my boots and socks just inside the door. The house is silent, just a ticking wall clock in the distance. I tilt my head and wait. No one has come running. If Wolfe's bike didn't wake them up when he picked me up, then surely they'd hear it now.

A thread of trepidation twists through me. I walk with light footsteps through the first floor, checking each room

The couch Jace was sleeping on before is empty, the blanket thrown over the back of it.

Same couch that Wolfe, Apollo, and I...

It felt vindictive, in a good way, to not tell Jace what happened on that couch. So I smother my smile and head for the second floor.

I stop short in the doorway to the bedroom.

They're both in bed. Jace and Apollo. They're not quite touching, but... honestly, they're closer than I would've thought. My abdomen clenches. Why does that sight turn me on?

I shimmy out of my jeans, then my shirt. I pull my wet hair up on top of my head and crawl up between them. Jace stirs first, rolling toward the center. His hand grazes my thigh, and I let out a soft breath.

But there's still something that keeps me from going straight to him. Lingering betrayal, even after all the pretty words he threw at me. Even though I know he meant them.

I straddle Apollo and lean over him, running my hands up his chest. Under his shirt.

Goosebumps break out down his skin from my cold contact.

He wakes up with a start, his gaze immediately finding mine in the darkness. He sits up suddenly, and his lips brush mine. "Did you have fun with Wolfe?"

I nod once, then take the kiss he seems to be offering.

"You taste like seawater."

"I jumped off a cliff," I breathe against his lips.

His hands move down my sides, over my bare ass. He takes in a breath when he discovers my lack of panties, and one hand continues to rise up my back while the other slides in front. He presses on my sensitive clit, and I kiss him harder.

Apollo's fingers inch down farther, pushing into my pussy. He tears his lips away and thrusts two fingers deeper inside me. I bite my tongue to suppress my moan, mindful of Jace still sleeping beside us.

Whether he's sleeping or pretending, though, is anyone's guess.

Apollo withdraws and lifts his wet fingers between us. "Wolfe's cum, baby? Still inside your pretty little cunt?"

I nod once. That's the only warning I get before Apollo pushes his fingers into my mouth.

I can't stop my groan now as I taste him and me.

Apollo's erection thickens between us. I want him inside me. I want them all like I've never craved anyone else. For them, I'm insatiable.

And then I'm flipped over. My back hits the mattress beside Jace, but I don't have time to cast a glance in his direction—because Apollo's face is between my legs.

I tip my head back, and my body bows off the bed at his first lick.

He doesn't do it because he has to, or to butter me up. He tastes me—*and Wolfe*—like he's starving and he'll never get another meal again. His hand skates up my belly as he works my clit, palming my breast and rolling my nipple between his fingers.

Another hand touches my other breast, and it takes me a moment to realize that it's Jace. His touch is so different from Apollo's, I'm ashamed that I didn't recognize it right away. He pulls at my nipple until the slightest bit of pain flutters through my chest.

I roll my head to the side and meet his gaze.

Apollo chooses that moment to suck hard on my clit, thrusting three fingers into me. I gasp at the explosion of sensation. Jace leans forward and grips my chin, directing my face to his. He bites at my lips instead of kissing me, his tongue invading my mouth. I'm breathless, flying high, and take it with a deep groan.

Jace keeps a hold of my face as Apollo rises up and rolls me on my side. Facing Jace. Apollo lies behind me, lifting my leg and thrusting back into me in one hard move.

My mouth opens wider, letting Jace in. He tastes like coffee—a peculiar taste for the middle of the night. There are hands all over me. On my breasts. My throat. I know Apollo's grip is there, capturing my pulse. He squeezes once, cutting off my breath, and my heart skips.

I like it too much. The way I crave them doesn't decrease the more they do it. It's turning me into an addict.

Jace grunts, and he shifts closer. He yanks down his shorts and frees his dick, and I pull away from his lips to stare at it for a moment. I remember the feel of it moving in me. It seems to pulse and twitch the more I stare.

"You want to suck his cock, baby?" Apollo asks.

I lick my lips, then glance back at him.

Apollo smirks, reading my expression. He releases my throat and shifts us quickly, barely letting me orient myself, and then I'm on my hands and knees, my head over Jace's lap. He looks pained for a split second, but his gaze heats when my lips part.

I don't think about anything other than this moment. I lower my head over his dick. I lick the bead of precum from the tip and take the base in my fist. He grunts when my mouth closes over him, and his hips thrust up. He hits the back of my throat, choking me for a second, before I bob back up and inhale through my nose.

Apollo holds my hips and slides back into me. I hum at the sensation. Jace's fingers wind into my hair, directing my movements.

In this... I don't mind the lack of control. I give in to them.

Apollo manipulates my body and Jace's dick fills my mouth. I suck and run my tongue along it, teasing him. I cup his balls and squeeze gently, almost smirking at the way his breath hitches. All the while, Apollo yanks my hips back to meet his thrusts. He's hitting a spot deep inside me, building me higher...

And then Jace's fingers find my nipples, and I'm a goner.

I come again, and all I can hear is rushing noise for a moment. Apollo picks up speed and follows a moment later. He jerks, spilling inside me.

Jace pulls my head off his cock a moment later. He and Apollo guide my limbs like I'm a puppet—and at this point, I think I am. My legs are jelly. I straddle Jace, and a second later, he's pushing inside me.

I let out a hiss. He's thicker than Apollo, and he stretches me just a little more.

"You're going to have to help me out, princess," Jace breathes. He touches the weeping bandage.

I nod and lean down, kissing him for real this time. My tongue skates along his lower lip, and I suck it into my mouth before releasing it. I'm careful to keep my weight off his torso. Just my knees pressed to the bed on either side of his hips and my hands framing his head.

Apollo leans against the headboard beside us. He's got his semi-erect dick in his hand, and his gaze is fixed on us.

I lift myself just a little and lower back down. Jace's eyes roll back, and he grips my hips. His nails bite into my skin.

"Fuck, Kora," he whispers.

Part of me wants to torture him. So I move slowly, inching up and down. I swivel my hips and run my hands up my body. I tweak my nipples, then lean back and watch his dick slide in and out of me. Giving him the perfect view of it, too.

"Please," he says. "You're killing me."

I smirk. I never thought I'd hear him beg for anything—but I kind of like the sound of it.

We're suddenly illuminated with light, and I glance at Apollo. He has his phone in one hand, and he winks at me over the top of it.

"Who do you wish was here, baby?" he asks.

I meet his gaze. "Wolfe." It comes out on a sigh.

"Give him a show," he orders.

Jace groans. "She just clenched around me. I think she likes that idea."

"Like she liked riding Wolfe's hand in the backseat of our car," Apollo continues. "So now you're going to show him what he's missing."

I put my hands on Jace's chest and lift. He guides me back down, his hips rising to meet me. Something flutters in my chest, worse than the heartache of the last few months. Something that seems a lot like hope.

Apollo shifts, crawling closer to me. The light of his camera turns my pale skin even whiter. He puts it up, angling down to catch him lean in next to my breast. His breath fans across my skin, and I let out a sigh. His lips brush the bite marks still coloring my chest.

"Bet you liked seeing these," he says, and I get the impression that he isn't talking to me.

Jace is completely controlling my pace now. My breasts bounce with the force of it, but Apollo doesn't seem to mind. He lingers close enough to touch me, but he doesn't. He just lets his hot breath raise goosebumps on my skin.

My head falls back. Apollo winds his fingers through the strands of wet hair that have come loose from the tie.

He snaps the tie free and tosses it aside, letting my hair fall down my back. He grabs a fist of it and turns my head to face him.

And the camera.

"Tell him," Apollo orders.

The same command issued in the car.

I shiver.

Jace's thumb skates over my clit, and I gasp.

"I can't come again," I say honestly.

"You will, baby." Apollo lets out a dark chuckle. "And you'll do it with Wolfe's name on your lips. Maybe that will be incentive enough to stop this nonsense."

Ah. My heart skips again, and my gaze goes to Jace. He watches me sharply, but he doesn't seem to mind that this is more about Wolfe than it is about him. He presses down harder on my clit, and pleasure bursts through me.

"Fuck," I mumble, my back arching. "Wolfe," I pant. "I need to—"

"You need his cock in your ass," Apollo says. "Let me help you with that."

He pushes my head forward, and Jace suddenly goes still. I whimper, my nails digging into Jace's chest. The light from Apollo's camera moves behind me, and then Apollo's fingers are thrusting into my pussy next to Jace's dick.

Holy. Shit.

I fall forward and rest my forehead on Jace's chest. He reaches up and hugs me, keeping me against him, and lets out a pained wheeze of his own. But he doesn't let me pull away or even move an inch.

"I'm fine," he growls in my ear. "More than fucking fine."

I don't know how he can speak. I'm on fire, burning from the inside out.

Apollo finally withdraws his fingers. "One day we'll do this together," he says, more to himself than anything.

I shiver at that. Two in my pussy? Surely not...

He uses his wet fingers to lube my asshole. I try not to clench or tense, but it's nearly impossible when the head of his cock rests there.

"Just do it," I plead.

He spits on me, then pushes in. It burns for a second, but the familiar pain quickly gives way to pleasure. I'm so fucking full, my mouth just opens and closes for a moment as I try to adjust.

"Ready?" Jace manages.

Apollo gives a grunt of acknowledgement, and they move—but it's different than when I did this with Wolfe and Apollo. They were in sync, their thrusts matching. Jace and Apollo seem to trade, so I'm never not filled with a cock. And Jace is still tracing circles on my clit, so gently I almost don't notice it. Until he ramps up the pressure.

"God," I cry. "I'm going to come."

"You've got two gods inside you," Jace says, thrusting upward hard enough that I see stars. "You'll come twice more before we're finished, you filthy girl."

I tighten my grip on him, trying to push back on Apollo and also meet Jace's movements. It's nearly impossible with the way they're holding me. My toes curl with the ecstasy of it. But Apollo pulls my head up by my hair, forcing me to look at Jace again.

His face is completely in shadows.

"Kiss me," I demand.

He meets me halfway, pinching my clit at the same time. I combust instantly, my scream swallowed by his mouth. He devours my noises and cups my jaw. He groans deep in his chest, and his hips spike harder, pounding up into me.

And then he goes still, his orgasm triggered by mine.

"You're so tight with Jace filling you," Apollo grits out, his movements jerkier. "You take us so fucking well, baby."

He pulls out suddenly, and a second later, his hot cum lands on my ass cheeks. My back. Goosebumps race up my spine, but I don't mind the mess. Even when Apollo smears it into my skin, rubbing his palm up between my shoulder blades. I let myself sag against Jace, utterly spent.

"Holy shit," I whisper. "That was awesome."

Jace is still inside me, but he makes no move to let me go. Or to let me clean myself up. Sometime during that, Apollo shut off the camera. He flops beside us and touches my cheek, his smile just visible in the darkness.

"We owe you one," he says.

I shake my head, but his hand is already moving south. Slipping between our bodies. There's no embarrassment. Apollo doesn't even seem to care. I close my eyes, my head on Jace's chest. Apollo pays extra attention to my clit. It's sore, but the pain almost makes it better.

I clench around Jace again, tensing and trembling as I come. I don't have the energy to even say much. My mouth opens on a silent cry, and he only stops once my muscles relax. Jace is half-hard inside my pussy again, but he doesn't act on it.

Apollo licks his fingers. He taps something out on his phone, then tosses it. It's still dark out, for the most part. The sky is just barely starting to lighten. But right now, I don't give a shit what time it is.

My eyes close again.

Within moments, I'm asleep.

jace

I wake up in a tangle of limbs. Kora and I woke up earlier, my dick hard and already inside her—how we managed to sleep like that, I'll never know—and I fucked her until she screamed *my* name. To make up for the fact that last night seemed to be about giving Wolfe the courage to leave the Hell Hounds once and for all.

I know. I saw through Apollo's thinly veiled attempt. And I agree. Wolfe will have to take action eventually, in one way or another.

Apollo didn't contribute much that time, just watching us with his head mashed into his pillow. He seemed to be content to fuck his fist to the chorus of Kora's screams.

We all went back to sleep after that.

The exhaustion of the last few weeks has finally caught up with us. Not to mention the stab wound in my side trying to heal, sucking my energy away.

I stretch and ignore the sharp pull in my ribcage. The damn stitches are driving me nuts, making it impossible to do *anything* without pain. Not that pain stops me. In some cases, it wakes me up like a shot of caffeine into my bloodstream.

Kora shifts, her ass pushing against my thigh. I take a moment to extract my legs from hers, then carefully move from the bed. It does pain me to leave her. But the moment I'm gone, she flips onto her back and takes my spot.

I smile to myself and head to the bathroom. I snag a pair of sweatpants on the way, leaving my torso bare. I need to clean my stitches and rebandage it. It's warm to the touch, which isn't great. The doctors would probably say something about doing too much. But I've barely done anything.

I've just been existing, and this stupid stab wound isn't healing.

After cleaning and covering it again, I tug on my shirt. I leave Kora to her sleep. She needs it, even if she thinks she's invincible.

My heart tugs. I look over at her and Apollo before I get to the door. He's curled around her now, his arm slung over her stomach. Her face has a healthy, relaxed appearance. Her hair is a mess of tangled waves, textured from the salt water she didn't rinse out.

Downstairs, I turn on the coffee pot and rummage through the cabinets for the cereal I saw Apollo buy. When we lived at the other house, we had someone who would deliver groceries and make basic meals to get us through the week. Food wasn't at the forefront of our minds until Apollo saw how much Kora needed it.

Guilt winds through me, and I sit heavily at the breakfast bar.

I put her in that position. And not for the first time, I question if I did the right thing.

My gut instinct is to say *yes*, I did it to protect her. I

knew that scholarship was a trap for Korinne Sterling. And whether or not Kora was her, I didn't want her to be. Her eyes... her gold mask that first night. It was all wrong. But her name. Her *name*.

It's why I kept her ID. Because I wanted to track down every piece of information I could about her. Confirmation number one: she had the name of the girl I knew from the group home. Confirmation number two: she was the right age. Confirmation number three: the Sinclairs' adoption paperwork showed Kora was at the group home.

But I pushed her into Kronos' arms, and it's a miracle she escaped that unscathed.

Almost unscathed, I correct. She has lasting nightmares and a brand on her fucking wrist from him.

And then she fell for my best friends.

I didn't think I'd feel such agony. And *why*? It's not like Kora was mine. Not then. Not even when I knew exactly who she was, and she didn't seem to have a clue about me.

My phone goes off, and I leave my guilt behind. Wolfe's name scrolls across the top, and I frown. I figured he'd be blowing up Apollo's phone, not calling me. Especially with all the tension left between us.

"Hey," I say, because I'm an idiot who suddenly doesn't know how to act around him.

"We need to talk."

I raise my eyebrows. My coffee is ready, and I hold the phone between my shoulder and ear as I fix up the cup. "Okay. About what?"

"My father." Wolfe blows out a breath. He's talking softly, but I hear the distant sound of bikes.

"Where are you?"

"I went for a fucking walk." He chuckles. "Pretty sure anyone would see through it, but I can't be bothered."

I laugh at that. Yeah, I don't know if *taking a walk* is a good excuse in Cerberus' book.

He sobers fast. "He's planning something."

"What sort of something?"

"I think he wants to take over. Like... all of it."

"What the fuck does that mean?" My heart picks up speed until it's pounding. Take over? We knew he wanted power—but does this mean having the underbelly of the city suddenly isn't enough for him?

"He wants legitimate power," Wolfe whispers. "I think he wants to kill the mayor. City council. I don't fucking know, he didn't go into a lot of detail. And he didn't give us time to—"

I tilt my head at the sudden pause, and a prickle of unease slides up my spine. "Are you safe?"

"Yeah, man, you just about bust my balls with the video Apollo sent." His tone has changed. Lightened. Although it sounds fake. He continues, "Next time you plan to double team my girl, send me a fucking invite."

"When is this attack?"

"You want me there tonight?" Wolfe asks, forcing a laugh. "No can do. I have plans."

Of all that's holy. "Do you want us to do anything?"

"Yeah. Give her a kiss for me."

I grit my teeth. "Whatever you do, you come back to us. To *her*. Do you hear me?"

"I don't know if she'll want me after what I'm going to do."

Broken.

So fucking broken.

What happened to us? My heart cracks at that, but I shake it off. I shake off *everything*, because there's only one good outcome of tonight. And it's Wolfe walking through our front door.

Our. See how quickly we adjust?

"She forgave me," I say thickly. "After everything I did. She'll forgive you, too."

"It's not that." Wolfe clears his throat. "It's that I don't think I can come back from this."

I want to reach through the phone and ask him what he has planned—but I don't. Because on some deeper level, I know exactly what he's going to do. And I want him to do it, more than I've ever wanted anything.

"She'll find you," I whisper. Because I know it's what he needs to hear. One act won't lose him to the darkness forever.

He sighs.

The line goes dead.

I stare at my phone for a moment, then set it down. I contemplate warning someone. The sheriff or his sister. Even Alex Sterling. New relatives of Kora, and thorns in my side.

Or...

I trust Wolfe.

"You have a sad look on your face."

I flinch and meet Kora's gaze. She lingers in the doorway for a moment, wearing Apollo's t-shirt. It's large on her, hanging mid-thigh. Her hair is up on top of her head, and she's makeup-free. She seems young. Unguarded.

"Come here," I say, swiveling in my chair. She circles the island and stops between my legs. Her hands land on my thighs.

My dick twitches.

She smirks, her gaze falling to my lap. "Someone wants round three."

I lift one shoulder. "He's not the only one."

Kora laughs. "*He*, huh?"

"What, should I call him *it*?" I chuckle and clutch her hips, pulling her even closer. Maybe I'm just testing her newfound acceptance, to see when she'll cringe away from me. She doesn't object when I press my lips to hers.

Her hands slide higher, and she palms my dick through my sweatpants. I groan into her mouth, and it hardens fully. Her fingers play against the waistband and tug it down on one motion. My stiff cock bobs in the air, and then her hand is wrapped around it. She squeezes, sliding her fist up and down.

I kiss her harder. I want her mouth on me. I want to bury myself in her cunt.

But she seems content to stroke me, and her tongue slips into my mouth. I slide my hand under her shirt, finding her breasts bare. It's her turn to moan as I massage them, brushing my thumbs over her nipples.

Then my hands go lower, and I realize she's not wearing panties. Not only that... she's soaked. I slip my finger through her heat and try not to lose my damn mind.

"Fuck," I growl against her lips. "You came down here with a purpose, didn't you?"

She pulls back slightly and smirks. "You shouldn't have left the bed..."

I push her back a step and stand. I like that I tower over her. I like that she's not intimidated by it—and never has been. God knows I've tried my best to instill that fear in her, but she just doesn't cave. She presses all of my buttons, over and over again. I walk her backward, until she hits a wall. And then I lift her by the backs of her thighs and thrust into her.

It's easy. Like we've done this a million times before.

But at the same time, it's... different. It's better. Each time I touch her is just better and better, and I don't understand how that's possible.

She gasps and rocks into me. Pleasure rushes through me, but I want to be touching all of her. I kiss her lips, then tear my mouth away and slide it down her jaw. To her throat. Apollo and Wolfe left their marks on her skin, but I want to leave my mark on her soul. So deep it hurts.

"Jace," she groans. Her nails dig into my shoulders.

I have scratches from last night down my chest, but that's nothing. I pound into her harder, my teeth catching the skin between her neck and shoulder. Holding her still like a wild fucking animal as I take what's mine.

"What am I to you?" I release her skin for a moment to ask the question. My breath hits her skin. She's a writhing mess against the door, especially when I swivel my hips and change the angle.

"You're—"

I slam into her and stop. She makes a pathetic noise, her pussy clenching against my cock. It's enough to make me blow my load early, but I manage to hold off. I stare into her eyes, absorbing her lust and desire and darkness.

She's one of us in that regard.

"I'm *what*?"

"My husband." Her voice breaks on the word.

Heat flashes through me, and I nod approvingly. "Good girl."

Her head falls back against the wall.

We're Hades and Persephone.

I trapped her in marriage. I followed the myth, hungered for the stories after Kora told me about them for the first time. To fill some sort of void in me that she left behind.

I became exactly who I said I would when Pearson threw me in that basement.

"Do you believe in soul mates?"

She meets my gaze again, sucking her lower lip between her teeth. "Maybe."

I slide out of her and slowly push back in. Her eyes flutter at the sensation. Gone are the quick, hurried moments. I want her to remember every fucking second of this.

"I do. I think my soul knew yours the moment we met fifteen years ago." Push. Pull.

She shivers, staring at me with a new expression. Awe, wonder, confusion.

"Maybe you're meant for all of us," I say. "But I'm only meant for you."

She leans forward and kisses me again. Her lips move against mine, and her arms wind around my neck. I give up my slow pace, the ache in my balls signaling that I'm getting close. I want to chase the rush, but she hasn't been taken care of yet.

I release one of her legs and rub my thumb over her clit. She whimpers in my mouth. Sore, maybe, from last night. From the orgasms that we forced from her body. She doesn't try to pull away, though. She kisses me harder, nipping my lip. Blood blooms across my tongue. I thrust my tongue into her mouth, making her taste it, too.

My savage queen just groans and drags me closer. Her breath comes faster, and I guide her closer to climax. My own is right there, and only a force of will keeps it at bay.

I'll wait for her.

And then it's here, crashing over her, and she comes with my name on her lips. She clenches around me, and I let myself go, too. I press my forehead to hers as my cum spurts inside her. It's ecstasy. Flashes of light pop in front of my eyes. My own fireworks display.

"Oh my god," she finally says, catching her breath. "Wow."

I slowly pull out and drop her thighs. Her feet touch the floor.

But I'm not done. I push her back against the wall with a hand on her chest, and I thrust two fingers inside her.

She gasps, using the wall to keep her upright. But her legs fall open.

"One day, we're going to put a baby in your belly." I drop to my knees and press a kiss to her stomach.

We.

She puts her hands on my shoulders. "No time soon. I have the IUD."

I look up at her. Her pussy is so pretty, leaking my cum down her thigh. Running over my fingers even as I try to contain it. "You won't have it forever."

She shivers, then bites her lip. She does that when she's unsure, when she's turned on...

I rise and kiss her again. It's not a demand. It's just a promise.

T he men rise when I enter the room. I spare them all a glance, fighting to hide my confusion, and motion for them to sit. Them jumping to their feet is the sort of fanfare my father appreciates, not me.

As long as they shut up when I'm speaking, I couldn't care less what they do when I don't need them.

Not that I've ever really needed them.

Malik comes in from the front, and I can't help but notice that he doesn't receive the same attention. Some of the Hell Hounds eye him uneasily, others nod to him. But none rise. And that makes my gut clench.

"You ready?" Malik asks, arriving at my side.

He's ten years my senior, and yet...

"Ready as I'll ever be," I say. "For having been left in the dark on this particular project."

We're expecting the worst with what my father told us last night.

When I was on the phone with Jace this morning, one of the recruits had followed me out. Then blushed mightily, catching pieces of the conversation I wanted him to hear.

He's sporting a black eye now, after I interrogated him on what he heard. Just to make sure he didn't catch anything important.

I'm not fooled. I know my father wants people to watch me, but he's only asking those who he can afford to lose. The recruits, the bottom feeders. The other side of the coin is that they want so badly to rise in the ranks, they'd do anything.

Including rat me out.

It's creeping toward eight o'clock. Earlier today, seven of us rode through West Falls. We wanted to make sure there wasn't still a lingering Titan presence—and they would've made themselves known if they saw us. But the streets were all silent and nearly empty. The most shocking part was the construction zone near the Titan bar, Descend. There was a gaping hole in the street, crumbled asphalt falling down to the abandoned subway tunnel below. It's near where we found the beheaded Hell Hound, but Malik and I didn't go that way then.

I slowed my bike and stared down into it, knowing that Apollo and Artemis were responsible for this. Knowing that, if they hadn't acted, it would've been a lot more devastating. And farther downtown. Under the university, maybe, or in a more populated area.

Not many people hang around outside nowadays. They're still recovering from the war. Or perhaps they don't believe it's over. They're in West Falls, after all. They could be waiting for the Hell Hounds to stake their claim on the Titan territory.

My father has left it alone—for now. Because he has bigger targets in his sights.

Truthfully, I don't know what he meant by taking what

we're due. As far as I'm concerned, we're due nothing but the ground beneath our feet.

We defeated the Titans. Maybe not *we* as in the Hell Hounds. But the Titans met their end all the same.

"Heads up," Malik says.

We seemed to come to a silent agreement that we're temporarily on the same side. He's always been my father's second, but my move to the front of the line hasn't caused any ill will between us. A miracle.

My father enters. He's wearing the suit he's so fond of, light gray with a white collared shirt beneath it. He doesn't look like a biker right now. He looks like he's about to make a speech at town hall or speak with the mayor in front of a row of cameras.

I set my jaw.

The rest of us look like bikers. Leather jackets or vests, jeans, guns on our hips or tucked into the front or backs of our pants. Boots. Angry scowls. There's a restlessness here tonight, everyone on the edge of a precipice waiting for my father to tell us what we're doing. Where we're going. What we're taking.

"You're all here," Cerberus says, smiling at his legion. Then his gaze lands on me. "Ah, Wolfe."

I rise. The Hell Hounds in my way shift aside, letting me pass.

My heart pounds, and it's too quiet in the room. Dad's become a wild card, and I think everyone wants to know what he has planned for tonight. The anticipation is high.

I touch the hilt of the knife at my hip. My gun is on the other, plus a backup strapped to my ankle. It doesn't feel like enough, but it'll have to do.

My father claps me on the shoulder, turning me to face

the crowd. "How many of you have wished to stick a knife in my son's gut?"

Silence. Shock.

He laughs, shaking me a little. "No one. That's a ringing endorsement, my boy. And how many of you have wished to see me dead at your feet?"

No one moves. Pretty sure they're not even breathing.

"You have a loyal gang," Malik calls. "No one wants to see either of you dead."

My father presses his lips together, then nods once. "Of course. I know that. But I do know that loyalty can be a fragile thing, especially when someone stronger comes along."

For a moment, I wonder if my father is afraid of my power. His fingers dig into my shoulder, pulling me into him. I've long since given up on trying to see the good in him. He's done bad things to so many fucking people.

I don't smell alcohol on his breath, and my stomach twists. Whatever happens tonight, he's going into it sober.

"He's been hiding something from us," my father says.

I raise my eyebrow but don't open my mouth. I don't know what he's discovered, and I will not incriminate myself. If it's a confession he's after, he won't get one.

"What's that?" someone calls.

"He'd rather be in bed with his best friends than here with us," Cerberus spits.

I force a smile, but I may throw up. He put me in a position of power when he refused to let Jace and Kora win my freedom at Olympus. He masked it by calling me his heir—but it stuck. And now his men look at me as someone to follow, too.

Still, I need to play the game if I want to survive tonight. I say loudly, "Getting laid and bloodshed are a close first and second in my book, Dad. You may have some misinformation."

His expression hardens. "Are you telling me my sources are wrong?"

I shrug. "I think no one knows my priorities better than myself."

"Were you not on the phone with them just today, lamenting about fucking them—"

I scowl and shove his hand off my shoulder. In a flash, I have him up against the wall with my arm across his throat. "You lost the privilege to so much as fucking think about them," I say in a low voice. "And if you think them knowing I have a girl waiting for me outside the club is going to sway them, I think you're just grasping at straws."

Dad shoves me away from him with a snarl. He carefully rights his suit and clears his throat. "You don't want to learn what I will do to keep you in your place."

I smile again. It's just a show for the bloodthirsty Hell Hounds watching our every move. If they sense weakness in either one of us, it's over. So I let my smile do the talking, and I keep quiet.

After a moment, Dad faces his gang. "We're taking the university."

Murmurs break out, but the talking ceases with a wave of his hand.

"The mayor and city council think it's a stronghold. They operate there, as does the police department." He smirks. "They're all in one place, ripe for the picking."

"It's late," I point out.

"The last time they all gathered after hours, it was for an emergency." The corner of Dad's mouth keeps lifting, until his face is contorted by madness. His sneer is cruel. "We're going to give them one they can't resist."

He barks out orders, dividing his crew into two groups. One helmed by Malik. The other is on their own, with one mission: to create chaos.

I bite the inside of my cheek as that group leaves first, their bikes roaring and then fading from our hearing. Destruction is the name of the game. What and who they'll ravage... I don't know. He picked the worst of them for that group, too. Giving them free rein is dangerous, and I can't do a thing to call them back. Not now.

Malik claps a hand to my back as he moves past me. My father tells him where and when to meet us, and then Malik and his men are gone. My father and I stare at each other for a moment, and I have a feeling I'm playing a bigger part in this than I realized.

"With me," my father orders, striding for the door. He gets into a car, a Hell Hound already waiting in the driver's seat. I hesitate for a moment, then get in the backseat with him.

We ride in silence, alone on the road.

"Do you remember your first mission with me, son?"

I glance at my father and nod once.

It was a test of loyalty. He saw how close Jace, Apollo, and I were getting. He wanted to establish that the first and foremost connection should always be to him. He could make our lives pleasant... or not.

I sit back and let myself remember it. The way the air felt so hot, like it was burning. A summer night without relief, not even the wind slipping past us as we raced our bikes toward West Falls could cool us down.

There was a shipment of drugs that the Titans were expecting, and Dad had ordered us to interfere. Steal it if we could, destroy it if we must. He was in charge that night, riding with us—this was back before he decided the view was better from the backseat.

I was sixteen.

My uncle was there, too. My uncle...

"I don't know why you're bringing this up," I say quietly. I draw my gun and check it, just to give my hands something to do.

"Because I know what's been on your mind, son." He leans in, putting his hand on top of mine. "And I just want you to know that I'm not as easy to kill as my younger brother."

"Why you think I would kill you is beyond me," I answer.

Panic, though. Panic thrums through me like electricity. Because that has been the answer all along, and I've been hiding from it. Ignoring it as an option. Pretending that I can find some other solution when it's the *only* thing that will free me.

I feel the manacles locked around my wrists like physical restraints, dragging me deeper and deeper.

But to do that, I would need to go farther than I have before. Darker than I've gone.

My phone vibrates. I pull it out and check it next to my thigh, then swipe through the message to delete it.

"Who was that?" he asks.

"Kora." I glance at him and stash my phone again.

He waves his hand. "Tell her you're busy."

"I'll just talk to her later," I murmur.

And then we're here. The car draws to a stop, the headlights going out. The driver checks his own weapon, keeping one eye on the road.

It doesn't take long for other cars to arrive. People from the sheriff's office, off-duty patrol, and the city council.

They'll all be rushing here to put emergency protocols into place. They'll vote to lock down the city, send more patrols, take in everyone they can manage. If they can capture any of the Hell Hounds, that is.

I don't want to know what sort of hell they're creating out there.

The sheriff hops out of his personal car and shoves his hat on. He rushes inside. Nadine Bradshaw follows a moment later in an SUV. She barely waits at the entrance for another alderman, lingering in the doorway just long enough for the man to catch it.

The last to arrive is the mayor. But I keep track of the police cars streaming out of the university with their lights and sirens already blaring. They split off in different directions, which leads me to believe that the Hell Hounds have split up, too.

My stomach twists again. All that pent-up rage from the war, the Hell Hounds' hands tied. The senseless deaths of their friends, with Cerberus ordering no such action be taken. It's easy to picture their hatred, their fury. They're going to take it out on the city.

Malik arrives, followed by at least a dozen Hell Hounds. They surround our car, and my father hops out. I follow slower, meeting Malik and my father on his side.

"Your job is to secure the exits," Dad is saying. "Make sure no fucker leaves this building without a Hell Hound escort."

Malik nods.

"You, me, and Wolfe will enter with four men. I want one in the elevator, and the other two in the stairwells. One stays with us." He inclines his chin. "Pick your men. We're moving now."

I follow Dad again. Malik is calling out orders, and then

he's with us. His arm brushes mine, but he doesn't speak. I withdraw my gun, but it isn't necessary. A Hell Hound swoops in front of us and kicks open the main doors.

The first floor is empty. He continues to lead, weapon out. He opens the door to the stairwell, and Malik gestures for one man to stay. We continue, and another calls the elevator down. The last goes to the stairwell at the opposite end of the building.

The one in front heads back to the elevator, joining the Hell Hound who stayed back to call it. The elevator chimes, and the doors open. We're met with two police officers.

The two Hell Hounds fire before the cops have a chance to react. The gunshots are muffled—suppressors screwed onto their weapons—and they both hit center mass. The officers fall back, no doubt the Kevlar under their uniforms catching those bullets. The Hell Hounds step into the elevator and shoot them in the head.

I force myself to watch the light go out of the cops' eyes.

The Hell Hounds haul them out of the elevator and step in. Malik, my father, and I go in after them, and the five of us ride the elevator up to the sixth floor.

This... is not going to end well.

"Stay here," Dad orders one.

The other comes with us.

Malik and I follow my father down the hall. The police station is on the second floor. We're on the top, the sixth, where the city council has convened. I vaguely remember Kora telling us that the city council met when the subway car exploded. So they're probably here, in a conference room, considering the same scenarios.

Different gang, new day. Same solutions.

Dad leads the way to that conference room. We're alone in the hall, until someone steps out of a side room. We know all their faces. The seven aldermen, the mayor. She's not one of them, and Dad shoots her without hesitation.

Don't you fucking flinch.

She falls back, letting out a choked cry. Her hands come up to her chest, her shirt quickly soaking through with blood. We stride past her, and my father motions for us to stay back for a moment.

Then he kicks the door in.

And he waltzes in like he owns the place.

My mom keeps calling.

Mom feels like a funny word, seeing as how I once had a real mother, and now she's dead. She may have been dead before I ever left Sterling Falls. That part of the timeline is frustratingly hazy.

Apollo sits beside me on the couch, a movie playing. But his gaze keeps going down to the rattling phone on the coffee table.

It was a present from him and Jace. They reactivated my old number, got everything that had been synced to the cloud redownloaded. It must've alerted my parents, who began to call... immediately.

And they haven't stopped.

I have unread texts from Marley, including a litany of apologies. Even a few from holier-than-thou Janet, which I immediately deleted. That bitch can fuck off to the bottom of the ocean.

My phone goes still, then lights right back up.

"You should answer it," Apollo finally says. He nudges

me, then snags it from the table. He holds it out, offering it to me.

And I just watch it buzz on his palm, lit up with a picture of my mom and me. Our cheeks are pressed together, wide smiles on our faces. My red hair and pale skin versus her gold-bronze skin and dark hair. We never looked alike, but I always loved that photo. How happy we seemed. The crinkle in our eyes was the same. How we tilted our heads together.

Nostalgia and longing and homesickness rear their ugly heads.

I sigh and take it from him. "Fine." I swipe to accept the call. "Hello?"

"Kora? Oh, thank God—"

"You've got to stop calling me," I interrupt. "Please."

Mom pauses, shocked into a momentary silence. "I... I'm sorry. We got an alert that your service had resumed, and we were worried. We're still... we're still your parents."

I close my eyes. Apollo's arm winds around my shoulders, drawing me into his side.

"I know you're worried, but don't you see how what you did to me hurt me?" My voice cracks. I've wanted family for as long as I could remember. I've wanted the truth of it. And now it's all staring me in the face, and I miss the people who lied to me for fourteen years.

"I'm so sorry," Mom whispers. "Are you safe?"

"For now," I say.

"Kora—"

"Please stop calling me," I whisper. "I'll reach out when I want to talk. But forcing yourself in my face isn't going to work."

"Okay," she says. "I love y—"

I hang up before she can finish her sentence. I crawl into

Apollo's lap and throw my arms around his neck, burying my face in his shirt. My eyes burn with unshed tears. He hugs me tightly as I try to regain control over my emotions.

Jace enters the room and sits beside us. He picks up my legs and puts them across his lap, rubbing my calf.

"She talked to her mom," Apollo explains in a low voice.

Jace sighs. "You can't shut them out, Kora. They're family."

I lift my head and glare at him. "You're family." I hate to admit it, but it's true. Marriage certificate or not, they're mine. I'm theirs. "You and Apollo and Wolfe. I don't need—"

"You may not *need* other people, baby, but sometimes forgiveness is its own form of peace." Apollo kisses my cheek. "It doesn't have to be today, or even next week. We can hide out here until you're ready to face it."

Jace nods his agreement, but his eyes are shining with a newfound emotion.

Did he think I was going to reject him? After this morning?

I reach out and lace my fingers with his, then rest my head on Apollo's shoulder. He hits *play* on the movie, turning the volume back up.

The only person I wish was here and isn't, is Wolfe.

But I'm hoping that won't be the case forever.

wolfe

He's going to kill them all.

Everything is moving in slow motion. The way he strides into the room and lets his cruel gaze sweep around. The screams that come from some of the aldermen. The way Alex Sterling rises in his chair, glowering at my father.

The last Hell Hound stays just outside the conference room at my dark look. I don't need another wild card in the room with us. My father is enough of one as it is.

Dad pulls a gun and points it at Sterling. "Sit," he orders.

Sterling stares at him for a long moment, then does as he asks. Malik and I are still in the doorway, blocking their escape. I count the seven aldermen that make up the city council, the mayor, and Nathan Bradshaw.

I grit my teeth and curse their stupidity. Did they really think themselves so infallible that they'd gather together without protection?

"This is a coup," my father tells them.

One of the women opens her mouth to object, but my

father doesn't let her. He strides around the table and grips her hair, yanking her head back. Exposing her throat. Her mouth gapes in surprise, and he pushes the muzzle of his gun past her lips.

She makes a gurgling noise, fighting against him.

"Waste of space," he says.

He pulls the trigger.

Blood and brain matter spatter the wall behind the dead woman. She slumps in the chair, then topples off it to the floor. Someone screams, and it echoes in my head.

The same thought repeats: *he's going to kill them all.*

Silence reigns after that.

Dad takes a handkerchief from his pocket and dabs at the spatter on his face. He sheds his suit jacket, tossing it over the back of the dead woman's chair, and moves down the line.

The sheriff is glaring holes in my head.

"Dad," I try. "Killing them isn't necessary—"

He rounds on me, shoving his gun at me. The muzzle burns my throat, hot from use. I grit my teeth and take it, locking eyes with him.

This is so wrong.

"Stop," I say in a low voice. "You can't—"

"You will not tell me what I can and cannot do." He shoves me against the wall and steps back up to the foot of the table. Straight across from him is the mayor. There's a pale sheen of sweat on his brow, and he's gripping the arms of his chair like he's watching a horror movie.

"Stand."

The mayor casts a glance at Alex Sterling, then the sheriff. Neither has made a move, but it's clear that their lives are on the line. They'll act eventually, when the gun shifts in their direction.

Malik is furious, his jaw tight. His hands are balled in fists at his sides. But he won't act. He's never acted against my father.

The mayor rises on shaky legs.

"Will you give me your city?" Cerberus asks.

Because he's no father of mine. The separation in my mind becomes sharper. A ravine splitting open in my body, pushing me farther away from the man who raised me. The nonsensical, manic man who craves power over everything else.

The mayor throws his shoulders back. "No."

The word hardly has time to settle in the air when the *bang* of the gun goes off. A bullet between the eyes. The mayor falls backwards. There's blood on the glass wall behind him, cracks branching out from where the bullet went clean through it.

"Wolfe," Bradshaw mouths, his voice barely audible. "Do something."

I jerk.

Dad moves to the sheriff with lethal speed. Like the first woman, he wrenches his head back and presses the gun to the underside of his jaw. It must burn like a bitch, but Bradshaw doesn't so much as flinch.

This is Kora's cousin.

This is one of the only people who can connect her to her past as a Sterling.

Before I know what I'm doing, I lunge forward and knock my father's gun from his grip. It skitters across the table and ends up in the center. I punch him in the face before I lose my nerve.

Dad roars and stumbles backward.

"Malik," he snaps. "Hold him."

Malik doesn't move.

The one act of defiance I need.

I go at my father again, my heart breaking. It doesn't matter that he's a monster. None of it matters. But in order to hit him again, I have to shove all that down. So deep, I'm not sure I'll be able to retrieve it again.

He swings at me, and his fists connect with my jaw.

The sharp stab of pain wakes me up.

Wakes up the monster that hides under *my* skin.

I rush him, my shoulder catching his stomach, and we smash into the wall. He hammers blows down on my back, uncaring that the room behind us has fallen to chaos. Chairs tip in the aldermen's rush to get away from us. He manages to get me off him and throws me into the wall, and then he's on me.

His fists slam into my face. "You ungrateful"—*punch*—"little"—*punch*—"shit—"

I twist out of his hold and elbow him in the throat. He chokes, and I reach for my gun.

Only to find it on the floor, out of reach.

"Missed that trick?" Dad asks, wiping his bloody mouth. He spits a glob on the floor, then shakes his head. "I had such high hopes for you. But you're just as fucking soft-hearted as your mother—"

I yell and charge again. We hit the floor, and I wrap my hands around his throat. I stare into his eyes and let him see how much I fucking *hate* him.

For driving everyone away from us.

For trying to turn me into him.

He scrambles at my arms. His nails dig at my skin, ripping at me. Blood drips down in lines, landing on my hands. His throat. I push harder, squeeze tighter.

His face gets red. He can't talk.

It would be easier to shoot him—but neither of us

deserve easy. This is as messy as we can get, and I hate every fucking second of it. I loathe that he's making me do this.

That I had a choice between him and a room full of people who have only tried to make this city function.

I fucking hate him so much, I don't even realize that I'm lifting his head and smashing it back to the floor until Malik hauls me off him. His head thumps down, already a red ring around his throat.

But he doesn't move. I watch his chest, wait for the sudden inhale.

Nothing comes.

"Thank you," Alex Sterling says. "You saved us."

I ignore him and grapple with my warring emotions. Horror and rage snake through me, and I pretend I don't see his outstretched hand. I turn to Malik.

All the heat has been sucked from the room, leaving me colder than ice.

"Call off the Hell Hounds. I want everyone back at the clubhouse immediately."

I spare a glance for Cerberus, then away. He hasn't moved, but the sheriff leans down and checks his pulse anyway. He gives me a look that says he's gone, and I nod stiffly.

"Take his body back with you," I add.

"Yes, sir," Malik says quietly.

He's serious.

He's going to listen to me.

I take that in stride and retrieve the gun from the center of the table. I unload it, dropping the unused cartridges to the floor one at a time. It doesn't take me long to dismantle it entirely. The pieces fall from my hands.

I spare a glance for the sheriff. Who texted me when we

were on our way. Who told me that there was only one feasible option for all of us.

But I acted too slow, and now I'm going to face consequences of my own making.

I storm outside. The Hell Hound at the door goes in with Malik to assist him. The elevator doors are still open, the second Hell Hound leaning against it to keep it from closing. He squints at me, confused until I growl at him, and then his spine snaps straight. He moves out of the way.

I get in the elevator. I don't feel like myself.

I don't feel like anything at all.

Especially when the elevator begins to descend, and all that anger in my chest builds and builds and builds until I can't take it anymore. I'm going to explode.

I turn to the Hell Hound riding the elevator with me, and I shove him.

He hits the wall, eyes wide. "Boss?"

"Knock me out." Because it's either that, or I start screaming and I don't stop.

He hesitates.

"For fuck's sake," I growl. I punch him in the gut, and he finally swings back. With the butt of his gun. I don't flinch back from it, even though I see it coming. I stare right at the approaching object, and it nails me in the temple.

Lights out.

deicide

I sort through the photographs on my table. Still shots of Korinne and her... *cohorts*. My lip curls in disgust, and I brush my fingers over one photo. I draw it closer to the light.

Korinne is reckless. She rode on the back of the Hell Hound heir's bike a night ago. She laughed when he pulled off to the side and goaded her into jumping off the cliff.

There are more photos. Of them in the water. Of him *fucking* her. I keep those buried in the pile. It's the only way my anger stays under control.

To kill one would be to tumble the whole house of cards that Korinne has built around herself.

Jace King is her husband. There's a copy of their marriage license on my wall, at eye-level. Reminding me that they both need to die if I want the Sterling line to end. Her medical files from Emerald Cove are in the corner, tabbed with notes. Nothing of use, except the intrauterine device that keeps her from getting pregnant.

I have information on Apollo Madden and Wolfe James,

too. Their histories, their records. Arrests and injuries and every fucking physical since they were ten years old.

Cerberus is dead. That, at least, is a victory. Another target wiped clean.

And I didn't even have to get my hands dirty.

I leave the table and go into my kitchen. On the counter is a chessboard, a game only just started. When I returned from Olympus after Korinne took back her throne, I knocked every piece to the floor. I threw the board against the wall. My rage was insufferable, loud.

But then I regrouped, and I began again.

A new plan.

The doorbell rings, and I nod to myself as I move a pawn forward. I let in my guest, who takes a look first at the photos, then at the chessboard. We're of the same opinion, I think. That Korinne is better off dead with her men bled dry along with her.

My guest sets a sack on the table, over the photos.

A black snake slides out, immediately curling over the edge and wrapping around the leg of it. I pick it up and let it wind around my hand. It's long, almost three feet, and thick-bodied. It climbs farther up my forearm, its tongue flicking out.

It's a beautiful snake, like the ones before it. Non-venomous.

Not a threat.

But fear-inducing...

I smile. Ending the Sterlings isn't enough anymore—I want to terrorize her first.

saint

"Hey." Tem knocks on my door and pushes it open before I can respond.

I sit up from my position on the floor and raise an eyebrow.

"Oops." She blushes. The color blooms on her cheeks, a sweet pink that spreads to her ears.

"It's okay."

I hop to my feet and grab a hand towel, rubbing it down the center of my chest. Exercise seems to be the only way I can cope these days, even if it hurts like a son of a bitch. The stab wound from Kronos is healing, but *slowly*. I can relate to Jace's pain. He's just a few weeks behind me. The burn is doing a shit job healing, too.

"What's up?" I ask her.

Her hair and makeup are done, and she's wearing a short gold dress. It complements her olive skin and dark eyes, but I don't focus on that. I don't focus on any of it except to remind myself that she's the opposite of Elora. Shorter and curvier and warmer, where my girl is—*was*—tall, thin, pale. Covered in my tattoos and strong as hell.

Not that Tem isn't strong—

"I'm going to Bow & Arrow," she says. "Antonio wanted inventory for our reopening next week, and I can't stay here. I'm going stir crazy."

"That doesn't explain the dress," I mutter. My neck is heating the longer I'm in the same room with her. And the more I have this inane reaction, the more anger spikes my blood pressure. "Why would you go out in that anyway?"

"Because I like it," she says slowly, eyeing me in a new way. Hurt, maybe, judging by her furrowed brows. "And the last time I checked, you get absolutely zero say in what I wear."

I turn away. "I think I'll stay here."

"And I think if you stay in this room any longer, you're going to grow mold."

I shake my head. "I won't go back there."

Because of Elora. It's the last fucking place I saw her.

The funeral home is finishing the preparations. Her parents have checked out, more shocked at her death than anything. But they've long since accepted the gang life in Sterling Falls. They knew exactly who she was involved with, and as such...

I think they care, but they're forcing themselves to keep away. To protect themselves.

I'd never. I don't want to protect myself. I want to kiss her forehead one last time and squeeze her hand, even though I won't get the soft breath of laughter that always preceded my lips touching her skin. Even though her fingers won't curl around mine in response.

Fuck.

I hurl the towel down and shut my eyes as tightly as I can.

"Go away." My voice is so fucking sharp, I hope it cuts

Artemis. I hope she stops trying to heal me, or fix me, or whatever the fuck she's trying to do by always barging in my room.

She comes around and steps in front of me. Her gaze falls to the hourglass scar on my chest, the one that ruined good ink when Kronos pressed the branding metal there. It missed the tattoo I got for Nyx—barely. If it hadn't, and then I lost her...

She presses her finger to my raised flesh, and chills skate up my spine. My muscles lock down, and I stop breathing.

"You can't hide forever," she says. "I'm hurting, too."

"Good." I lean in, getting right in her face. "I hope it hurts forever."

Because then we won't forget her.

She drops her hand and steps back. Her eyes don't fill with tears, but they widen with shock. That I could be so heartless? That I could be so cruel?

She hasn't seen the worst of it.

But if she sticks around, she will.

"Go do your stupid fucking inventory, Artemis. Go be good at something, because you're certainly not good at cheering me up."

"Dick," she murmurs, stepping past me. "Forget I asked."

The door slams shut in her wake, and I drop back down to the floor. I brace my feet under the edge of the dresser and resume my crunches. I'll continue until I can't breathe.

And then maybe I'll be able to sleep.

TWENTY-FIVE

NINE YEARS AGO

I follow my father through South Falls. The city is different at night. It takes on almost a new shape. The shadows feel bigger, the danger louder. My blood races through my veins, mixed with a heady boost of adrenaline. It's one thing to ride with my friends, but it's another thing entirely to be riding with purpose.

And knowing that getting caught isn't an option. Not when we're going into enemy territory.

Jace and Apollo will get their missions soon. My father promised them as much. With it comes the reward: bikes of our own.

I've been riding bikes almost since before I could walk. But it never came with the privilege of owning it outright. Of caring for it, maintaining it, riding whenever I damn well pleased.

Dad said sixteen was a good age to become a man. Contribute to the family—what he called the gang. They're the only family I know. Jace and Apollo are both younger than me. Not by much for Jace. A full year for Apollo. But my sixteenth birthday was just last week, and now I'm here. Trying to prove myself.

Malik rides beside me. He took us under his wing at my father's direction. Trained us on how to fight, how to use weapons. Anything is a weapon if you wield it in the right way. Guns, knives—they're easy. It's when you lose those that you have to get creative.

We've all got our strengths, I'm quickly learning.

But Malik's job is to make sure we can survive anything. I've got more than a few scars to prove his teaching methods are unorthodox.

He glances at me, and I offer him a tight smile. Training or not, I'm *nervous*. The thrum of my blood under my skin wakes me up in a way I've never felt before, until I'm practically buzzing.

We slip through the quiet streets until we find the truck. Someone had marked it earlier in the day with a red X on the back corner. We track it through South Falls, almost to the edge of Titan territory. My heart thunders.

Finally, we're on the isolated road that heads straight into East Falls. Dad signals us, and four Hell Hounds shoot out around us. They cruise up in front of the truck, sailing past it. Two stop. They park their bikes across the street and pull guns.

The truck slams on its brakes. The red lights illuminate Malik, Dad, and me. We swerve around the truck and stop next to the driver's door.

Malik hops up and wrenches the door open. In a matter of seconds, he has the driver on the ground between his legs, the gun aimed at his head.

Another Hell Hound comes and takes over for him, allowing Malik and Dad the freedom to go around back.

Another Hell Hound is already there, up on the truck with the door's handle firmly in his grip.

He waits for Dad's go-ahead, then yanks it open.

The door makes a rattling noise as it rolls upward.

The stench hits us first. I rear back and fall on my ass, immediately covering my nose and mouth. In the trailer isn't a shipment of drugs, like I had expected—you know, the crates with false bottoms, the drugs hidden inside.

Nope.

There are girls.

Women.

Malik grabs a flashlight and shines it inside, and they flinch away from it.

There are at least ten of them, wearing threadbare clothes that hang off their bodies. I glance at my father, whose jaw is working. One of the Hell Hounds rushes to the side of the road and pukes.

The retching noise, coupled with the smell, is giving me the urge to vomit, too. My stomach rolls. I suppress it and stand again, then gesture to them.

Above all else, they need to get out.

They don't move, so I hop up. Dad doesn't say anything as I enter, my feet sliding on the wet, grated metal floor. I motion for one of the girls to come to me, but they all skitter backward.

There's a tipped-over bucket toward the back that the smell seems to be emanating from.

The bastards who put these girls in here gave them a single bucket to defecate in.

Anger spikes through me. I snag the closest girl's wrist and pull her toward the opening. She might be my age. Or younger. I pass her down to Malik. More girls come with me. It seems to have broken their frozen terror, because suddenly they're all clamoring to get out.

I finally hop down and wipe my hands on my pants. That smell is imbedded in my nose, and I go around the corner to take a few deep breaths. Then I round back on my father, that anger getting wilder inside me.

"You said drugs," I hiss.

He shakes his head. I think he's surprised, too, but he'd never admit it. "That's what the intel said."

"Your rat in the Titans got it wrong."

Dad shoves me. "Get out of my face, kid," he growls. "Come with me."

I follow him past the girls, around to the driver. Dad kicks the driver over onto his back, then steps on the man's throat. Not hard, I don't think. It's more of an interrogation than an outright murder.

"Did you know what you were transporting?" Dad asks.

Malik steps up beside me, watching with arms folded over his chest.

"N-no," the man stammers. "I just pick up the container from the shipyard like they t-tell me to."

"The Titans?"

The man shakes his head. "This was going to North Falls. Special order."

The intel was *really* wrong. Unless we got the wrong truck? I glance at Malik, but his expression is stoic.

Dad leans in closer. "Who were you meeting?"

"The guy who owns the club, Terror—"

Dad puts more weight on his foot on the driver's throat. The man squawks, pushing at his foot, but he's got no leverage. His face goes red, then darker. He struggles while my father presses even fucking harder, and finally there's a noise. Like a crack, or a snap.

The man goes still.

"Crushed his windpipe," Malik says in my ear. As if I needed someone to tell me what I just saw and heard for myself.

"Wolfe. With me." Dad steps over the driver and climbs up into the truck. "Someone shut that back. Get the girls to the clubhouse."

A chill goes down my spine. Malik eyes us for a moment, but I don't hesitate to circle around and climb up into the passenger seat. I have a feeling our mission has changed.

Terror is a sex club in North Falls. It operates in the basement of one of the regular nightclubs.

Even worse... we know who runs it.

I watch the girls, our bikes, the rest of the Hell Hounds disappear out of view. We ride through West Falls and up into North Falls without incident. We don't speak. I don't fidget. Now's not the time for it, although my heart is still going crazy. No matter how many long, slow breaths I take, it won't ease up.

We drive around the back of the club, to the hidden entrance for Terror. The truck hisses as Dad hits the brakes, and we wait in the dark cab. Finally, the door to the club opens, and my heart sinks.

My uncle steps out, eyeing the door for a moment. "You're fucking late."

Dad shoves the door open and leaps down. He has his gun in his younger brother's face before the latter can react, and I scramble out of the truck, too.

"Cerberus—"

"Explain yourself."

My uncle pushes Dad's gun away, straightening his suit. Of the two, he's the businessman. The one who runs

the clubs—both Terror and the legal nightclub above it—
and keeps cash flowing into our gang above board.

This isn't the mission my father envisioned for me. I can
still smell the bile, so sharp I can almost taste it, and my
stomach turns again. I've never been so horrified, and my
father is willing to let his brother explain.

I spin away, pinching the bridge of my nose. How? Why
is he allowing his brother to give him weak excuses? I've
seen him kill men for less.

"It's for us," Uncle says. "We needed new blood. We pay
well, these girls wanted a better life. They knew what they
were signing up for—"

"Where did they come from?" I ask.

Dad looks at me, but he doesn't tell me to be quiet. His
gaze is appraising.

"You're getting the wrong idea, kid," Uncle snaps. "This
is grown-up business."

I puff my chest. "I am adult enough to ride with
them—"

"Oh, your maiden voyage?" He sneers, considering.
Maybe he's thinking about his first ride with my father,
when he turned sixteen. After a moment, he shrugs. "I'll
teach you. Come with me."

He heads inside, and I follow him. Because I'm still
pissed and confused and I don't know why Dad isn't
putting a stop to this. Why would he allow his brother to
bring girls into our city, to work at Terror? To be subjected
to the sexual desires of paying customers? That's what the
club is. Pay the price to make your wild fantasies come true.

We go down a set of stairs, into a dark corridor. Uncle
glances back at me, gesturing for me to come up beside
him. We pass closed doors, painted black to match the
walls. A steady bass thumps from speakers somewhere

above us, and it almost drowns out the noises coming from behind each of the doors.

"Have you fucked a girl, Wolfe?"

My brows furrow. "Yes."

A girl from Sterling Falls Academy. I met her at a party that Jace, Apollo, and I snuck to in North Falls. It was... fine. Uninspired. She got herself off, and I lasted a shameful minute or two longer. Not exactly the sexual prowess I want to be known for.

"A lot of people fuck girls," he continues. "And they get off just fine. But there are some who need more... stimulating prey."

Prey?

We continue down another hall, and then he opens a door that's marked *Private*. We enter into another hallway... but this has glass windows on each side, giving us a view of the rooms.

I don't want to be here, but I can't look away from the girls... and the men. Some are completely naked, thrusting into tied-up, gagged girls splayed out on tables. Others have whips in their hands or knives. In those rooms, there are welts and streaks of blood dripping down the girls' thighs, asses.

Most of the girls have dull, glazed expressions, and I grit my teeth.

"We don't just snatch girls off the street." Uncle stops in front of one of the windows.

The girl is crawling toward the man, who sits on a gilded throne. She kisses his feet, and he kicks her in the face. She sprawls backward, her chest heaving, before she slowly rolls over and tries again.

"They're paid," he reminds me. "But our turnover... you can imagine how this line of work burns a girl out."

I can imagine how this line of work *crushes* a girl.

"This isn't legal," I say softly. I've learned to get quiet when I'm angry, not louder. Because people expect loud. They expect yelling and slamming and fists.

I don't want to be what anyone expects.

"No, it isn't," Uncle agrees. "But it is profitable."

There's a roaring in my ears. He finally leads us out into a room where there are half a dozen girls and no men. One has a band tied around her bicep, a syringe caught between her teeth, filled with a dark liquid. She taps at her vein, then quickly injects herself.

She's not the only one high on heroin. The others are in various states of zoned out, half-dressed. They sport bruises, welts, burns.

"You can't be serious," I whisper. "You don't just snatch them off the street—where do they come from?"

"From their parents."

I stare at my uncle.

"We have a few of these clubs around the city," he continues. "This one is specialized, of course. But when they need to recover, they're sent to the brothel in East Falls. Near the old pantheon building." He chuckles, opening another door with the twist of his key and allowing us to exit back into the first corridor. "You'd be surprised at how many men give up their daughters to absolve their debts."

My mouth opens and closes.

What I just saw...

"Whose idea was this?" I ask him.

"Take it easy, kid," Dad says, stepping forward.

There's no easy.

"Mine," Uncle says.

And that's that.

My gun is out before I can stop myself, but time slows down. The miniscule widening of his eyes, my father's alarmed shout. The way my finger finds the trigger, and the effort it takes to squeeze it.

The sound.

The goddamn sound of it firing.

The bullet hits my uncle in the chest, and he staggers backward. I fire again, and again, until the sound is etched in my brain along with his bloody body.

Silence.

My father looks at me, then sighs. He seems resigned but not surprised. Not anymore.

Maybe this was the christening that he had planned all along.

Or maybe he just realizes what I won't learn until later.

That I'm destined to end our line.

kora

T'm getting sick of my phone ringing.

But when I see the caller ID, I find Malik's name.

"Hello?" I answer, hating that I sound so freaking breathless. I don't want to give him the impression that I've been sitting by the phone, but...

The Hell Hounds rained *literal* hell down on Sterling Falls last night. Apollo stood out on the porch with his gun, waiting for trouble to find us after the sheriff gave us a heads-up. And sure enough, two bikers had turned down our driveway.

Jace and I waited inside, in the dark. Apollo strode out to meet them.

He didn't kill them, but whatever conversation they had made the two Hell Hounds speed away.

"Hey," Malik says on an exhale. "How are you?"

"How am I?" I furrow my brows. "I'm fine. How are you? How's Wolfe?"

We heard about Cerberus' death. The sheriff called. Then Nadine. Then Alex freaking Sterling.

Then the news started in the morning, *Breaking News*

scrolling across the bottom of the screen. Jace, Apollo, and I just... stared. I didn't know what else to do as the reporter talked about everything that had happened last night. And neither did they. We watched it all, the montage of destruction throughout the downtown districts, the robberies, and finally the deaths. An Alderman, an assistant, the mayor. Cerberus.

They didn't show their deaths. That might've been a touch over the line. But the reporter said Alex Sterling, who has taken up the position of interim mayor, will be making a statement later today.

"We need to get Wolfe out of the clubhouse," Malik says. "He's drunk."

I check the time. "It's not even noon."

"Exactly."

Fuck.

"Okay," I say. "We'll be there soon."

I rush around the room, pulling on jeans, checking my gun and sliding it into the new shoulder holster Jace and Apollo got for me. I put on a jean jacket over it, hiding the weapon from sight, and then zip on my boots.

Jace and Apollo are in the living room. They look over when I skid to a halt in front of them.

"We need to go to the clubhouse."

Apollo groans and nods. "I better not get the shit kicked out of me again."

Jace snickers and follows us out the door. We pile into the car—borrowed from Antonio, which we should definitely think about returning. Apollo drives. Jace sits in the backseat, silent. Glowering at his kneecaps.

"What?" I ask, turning around.

He sighs. "I'm just worried."

"About..."

"He killed his father, Kora." His blue eyes slam into mine. "Are you going to forgive him for that?"

Wow. I sit back and cross my arms, facing forward. I don't bother answering. Apollo eventually turns on a radio station, scrolling through them until he finds one that's playing music. He hums along to one of the songs.

I mouth some of the words, but it's not enough to pull me out of the dread that's threatening to suck me underwater.

We arrive at the clubhouse. There are far fewer bikes here now, but they had a busy night. Can't blame them for sleeping in... right? I choke on my laughter, earning a curious look from Apollo.

Before the engine can fully quiet, Malik is slipping through the main doors. He waits for us on the porch with a sad glint in his eye.

I mean... he just watched his boss die. That's got to be a little sad, right? But it isn't like his eyes are red-rimmed, unless he plans on saving his tears for solo time.

I join Malik on the porch, Apollo and Jace moving a bit slower.

Malik takes turns shaking our hands. "Thanks for coming. I know he did this for all of you as much as himself."

I bite my lip. "Hopefully he doesn't hold it against us."

There's a crash from inside, and Malik winces. "Who wants to go in? He's alone in there. There's a few guys repairing the fence in the back that Wolfe shot up, but other than that, I sent everyone away."

My eyes go wide. I look from him to Apollo, then Jace.

They're both watching me.

But honestly? I don't know if I have the ability to pull him back from this edge.

223

"You can do it," Apollo whispers. He cups my cheek. "He needs your help, baby."

I swallow and nod, then move past Malik. I open the heavy door enough to slip inside, and it makes a dull crashing noise as it closes on my heels.

They did a good job rebuilding the clubhouse. It has a likeness to the old one, but better. This space here, with the bar in the corner and tables scattered around, seems bigger. The ceilings are taller, too. There's a set of stairs in the corner, leading up to rooms. There's still the lingering scent of new construction, fresh-cut wood and sawdust.

And Wolfe is perched on top of the bar, his feet swinging. He has his gun beside him and a bottle of Jack Daniel's dangling from his fingertips, and there's shattered glass around him. His face is a patchwork collection of bruises. A black eye, a darkened cheek, his lip and forehead split. There are scabbed-over scratches on his forearms.

He didn't kill his father the easy way, that's for sure.

He mumbles to himself as he reaches down and snags a tall glass from behind the bar. He eyes it, then hurls it at the wall. It smashes, the sound reverberating around us, but he doesn't even react.

It's nonsensical.

Wolfe doesn't notice me until I'm five feet away, picking my path through the shards of glass.

The Jack Daniel's bottle falls from his grip. It explodes when it slams into the floor, glass and liquor going everywhere. It sprays on my boots, my shins.

"I'm dreaming." he stares hard at me. "You're not here."

"Want me to pinch you?" I offer, getting up to him. The glass crunches under my boots.

"No." He leans forward and touches his forehead to

mine. "I don't want to go back to reality. Not when we can just push everything bad out right now."

My heart cracks, and I shake my head. I put my hands on his thighs, spreading them so I can get closer. "You can't do that."

"Can't do what?"

"Bury your head in the sand." I hold on to his legs tightly. "Come back to me, Wolfe."

He straightens. He's quite a bit taller than me in this position, sitting at the bar. My eyes are level with his stomach. And since he's not making a move to get down... I guess I'm going up.

I grab one of the stools and drag it closer, hoisting myself up to kneel on it. Then I crawl forward, forcing Wolfe back. I push the gun out of his reach. Not that I'm worried. I just don't really want it near us.

He doesn't object when I straddle him and push his chest, until he's lying flat on the bar. His legs still hang over it.

I lean with him. My breasts push into his chest, and my forearms frame his face.

"Am I real?" I ask him. I shift my hips slightly.

He groans and grasps at my waist. "No."

"Why not?"

"Because you'd never be here," he whispers. "You'd never come back for me after what I did."

"And what did you do, my love?" I kiss the corner of his lips.

He huffs, his eyes fluttering shut. I can't smell whiskey on his breath. Just his own scent.

I kiss him again, inching down his jaw, inhaling.

Some part of me says that he's not drunk... he's just hurting. And so fucking numb.

"How can you love a monster?"

I rise back up until I can meet his green eyes. They've cracked open again, and he seems more grounded in reality this time. The haze momentarily clear. But he looks so heartbroken that I can't do anything but press my lips to his ear and admit my truth.

"Because I'm a monster, too. And you loved me first."

His fingers slide into my hair, and he directs my mouth to his. He doesn't hold back, taking every inch of me as his. He draws blood from my lip, and the gasp of pain only serves to wake him up more. He sits up, taking me with him. He cradles the back of my head and the small of my back and kisses me deeper.

A groan vibrates in his throat.

"Come with me," I say, tearing my lips away.

I move to get off him, but he has a different idea. He keeps me against him as he slides to his feet, walking us out of the circle of shattered glass. Only when we're out of the range of glass does he let my legs slide through his grip, and my toes touch down.

He pulls my jean jacket away from my body, eyeing the gun. His smile is faint and gone before it has a chance to stick.

I take his hand, squeezing firmly, and lead him outside. He flinches at the brightness, then quickly looks away from Jace and Apollo. His shame is loud.

Malik is gone.

We put Wolfe in the backseat, and I join him. Neither of us say anything about how he's supposedly drunk, and I hold his hand the whole way back to our house.

He stares up at it when we get out of the car, his shoulders hitching.

"I can't go in there," he says. "I—"

"I need you," I blurt out.

He goes still. He can't meet my eyes. That happened halfway here, his gaze sliding away and staying fixated on the window. Although he hasn't had the nerve to pull his hand away.

There's still hope.

"I need you here," I whisper, softer. I trace my free hand up his chest, but he captures it and moves it away. "Please."

Finally, *finally*, he nods. He follows me in, up the stairs. I guide him into the bathroom and turn on the water in the walk-in shower, then go back to him. He stands like a statue as I remove his shirt, then unbuckle his pants. I push them down with his boxers, and he kicks them off with his shoes and socks.

I strip, too. I let my hair down and unclasp my bra, tossing it on top of his clothes. I bend over, drag my panties down, and give him a show of my ass.

He doesn't verbally react, but when I glance back, he's hard.

His eyes are angry.

Good. Another emotion besides sadness.

I pull him by his wrist into the shower, gasping at the cold water that sluices over us. It pours out of three shower heads. I move to turn up the temperature, but Wolfe stops me.

"I can't be with you anymore." His voice is rough. "You should go. I'll get dressed and head back to the clubhouse. You, Jace, and Apollo can live your life and be happy."

I can't be with you anymore.

The words bounce around my head for a full minute. I gape at him, trying to make those words make sense. He's fucking crazy. Batshit insane. Totally, completely bonkers.

I laugh at him. It takes too long for the sound to

227

subside, and I shake my head. My abs hurt, and the water pounding into my side is numbing my skin. But I relish the dark look in his eyes.

"You're not getting rid of me that easy," I scoff.

He growls. "Kora. I—"

"I don't care that you killed your father," I shout.

I push him, and his back hits the tile. He eyes me warily, but I'm going to lose my shit on him, and he's just going to have to deal with it.

"Do you think I'm not attracted to you anymore?" I step forward.

He doesn't answer.

"Do you think I can't possibly love someone who would kill for me?"

"Listen—"

"*Shut up*," I hiss. I drop to my knees in front of him, not caring that the water now hits the back of my head. It plasters my hair to my scalp, brings goosebumps up on my arms. All that is secondary to the sight before my eyes.

His cock bobs in front of me, and I reach out and stroke it. It's warm, silk-wrapped steel under my fingers. And now he's the one who lets out a hiss when I part my lips and slide him into my mouth.

Fuck his insecurities.

Fuck the fact that someone made him think he was damaged for protecting what's his. For doing exactly as his father taught him to do—to fight for power, to take it without remorse.

He's stiff as I take him farther. The tip of his dick hits the back of my throat, and I pull back slightly. Then I suck him deeper, swirling my tongue and hollowing my cheeks. My wet hands move up the front of his thighs, and I cup his balls. I moan at the taste of his precum on my tongue.

Wolfe exhales sharply, but he doesn't take control. He seems almost afraid to touch me at all, and that hurts. Just a little.

But it's not nearly as painful as what must be going on in his head and his heart.

He lets out a choked noise, and I squeeze his balls. They tighten in my hand, rising, and suddenly his cum spills down my throat. I force myself to keep my fingers away from my pussy. I'm soaked between my legs, I'm sure. The need to orgasm is growing.

I swallow around his head, then lick him clean. I rock back on my heels and meet his gaze, only to find the darkness replaced with white-hot lust.

"You still want me." He's in awe? He's *surprised*?

"I fucking love you," I answer, wiping my lower lip. "I want you now. I would want you even if I witnessed it. Even if his blood was on your hands. I know you're dark, Wolfe. You chose to become Ares for a reason. But I love Ares as much as I love Wolfe." I hesitate. "I may have even loved him first."

He shakes his head and helps me to my feet. Without a word, he snatches my hips and swings me around. He pins me to the wall and catches my wrists, holding them above my head. He kisses me like I'm his oxygen, and I arch my back into him. My nipples brush his chest, getting harder, and the need pulsing between my legs is almost unbearable.

His tongue sweeps through my mouth, and I whimper. Still no taste of alcohol. He holds my crossed wrists with one hand, and his other goes to my breast. He rolls my nipple between his fingers, tugging slightly. I'm a gasping mess by the time he pulls away.

"You remember what happens when you break the

rules?" His voice is husky.

Rules.

I shiver.

Those rules were so long ago, but they immediately resurface.

You come first.

We haven't played that game in a while. But I can see why he's brought it up. Rules give us order. Order soothes chaos. And if his mind is chaotic, if he's drowning in too many emotions, then we can restore it with order. With rules.

"I broke it," I say lightly.

He shuts off the water, and I take my chance to slip out of the shower. I grab a towel, wrapping it around me.

He follows without one, his expression the sharpest I've seen since we found him in the clubhouse.

I get the distinct impression of being stalked, and a shiver racks through me.

Can't say I'm opposed...

So I do the sensible thing. I turn and sprint out the door.

There are acres and acres of forest surrounding the house. We own some of it. The city owns the rest. It spreads in every direction—except east, but that's a steep drop into the ocean—and continues north until the edge of Olympus.

I find Kora's towel on the floor next to the open front door, and my pulse kicks up.

Finally, some other emotion besides horror.

Jace comes around the corner and stops dead when he sees me. His eyes drop to my junk, then back up. "Why are you naked? And wet?"

"Shower gone wrong." I look out the front door again. There are dainty wet footprints heading down the stairs. "Did you see Kora?"

"Nope."

I smile. The little flower wants to make me work for it, then.

I wave Jace off and step outside, taking a moment to scan the tree line.

There's a flash of red between the trees off to my right,

and I don't hesitate. I leap off the porch and run for it. The bite of rocks into my feet wake me up, the pain as refreshing as that cold shower... especially if my reward is Kora.

Like my mouth on her sweet cunt.

Fucking hell.

She's fast. I hear her laugh ahead of me, and I find the trail that she must've already discovered. It cuts through the foliage, around brush that would've otherwise slowed us down. Pine needles stick to the soles of my feet, dirt flicks up behind me and collects on my calves.

My lungs ache.

But above all, I'm turned on. The chase is an adrenaline rush.

I take a corner, and she's suddenly right there. Almost within my grasp. I reach out and touch her hair, but it slips through my fingers.

She gives a nervous yelp and pours on a burst of speed, but I match it. My arms pump, my muscles scream.

I take a chance and dive for her.

We go down in a tangle of limbs. I push her to the earth beneath me, but I'm not prepared for her to fight me. She bucks her hips, sending me rolling, and then she's up again. Dirt and mud smear her porcelain skin, and I hop to my feet after her.

"You can't run forever," I call.

My voice reverberates in my skull. More like, *I* can't run forever. I didn't realize she was this quick, had this much endurance. I burst into a small clearing and find her waiting for me. But she's not laughing anymore.

"You're right," she says. "We can't run forever."

I lower into a crouch. Akin to a fighting stance. "Do you concede?"

"No."

"If I win, I'm taking what I want from you," I warn. "Last chance, flower."

She just smiles. I don't miss the shiver she tries to hide. I bet her pretty little cunt is soaked. She turns to face me as I edge to the side. I saw her defeat the giant Hell Hound at Olympus. I have no doubt she thinks she can take me, too.

But then she slides her hand up her side and touches her breast.

My dick twitches. It's already rock-hard at the idea of what's about to happen, but now the pressure gets more pronounced. She brushes her thumb over her nipple, and her lips part.

I lunge for her when I'm close enough, and she evades me. I go at her again, before she can recover, and my arms lock around her waist. We hit the ground hard. The breath is forced out of her, and she's still for a moment.

Then she comes alive like a demon, kicking and pushing at me. I push her down, but there's a desperation in her movements, wild panic. Her knee connects with my thigh, but it isn't enough to stop me.

Ben did it like this. That thought hits me with sudden clarity—and I loathe him all the more for it. I grit my teeth and catch her wrists. She's stretched out beneath me, and I drop my full weight on her. Pinning her into place.

"I'm not him," I growl in her ear.

She goes still. Her breathing is ragged, and her eyes are screwed shut.

I change my hold on her wrists to one hand, and the other goes down between her legs. I grip her thigh and part it roughly, barely giving either of us time before I thrust into her.

Her back arches. I hold her inner thigh as I fuck her, keeping her open for me. I put distance between us, looking down to see how her pussy accepts my dick. Her body trembles, but she's stopped fighting. And she's so fucking strong, she doesn't even know it.

She's a weapon of her own making.

Fierce and beautiful and so utterly perfect.

I stroke deep inside her, relishing the movements. Every time I twist my hips, hitting a new angle, her thighs shake. So I do it again and again until she comes apart just from that. Until she's shattering around me, writhing and trying to get free again.

"Stop," I order. I'm still inside her, still absorbing her shockwaves. And so fucking hard, I might explode at any second. Her wriggling isn't helping matters.

Her eyes flash, and she rips her wrists free. She puts her palms on my chest.

I pull out of her and quickly flip her around. Her nails dig into the grass and dirt.

I spread her ass cheeks and run the tip of my cock up her slit. I pause at her asshole, and she stops moving.

"Apollo's had your ass," I say, leaning over her and biting her shoulder.

She flinches, and her breath comes out in a sharp exhale.

"He filmed it like *I* was the one fucking your sweet little asshole." I lick the bite, then do it again a little farther down her shoulder.

Kora squirms beneath me, but she doesn't say anything else. Doesn't even object. Which makes me think she wants it, too.

I pull at her hips until they're slightly raised, then I slide my cock back into her pussy. The motion elicits a moan from her lips. It feeds the beast inside me—but not enough.

I spank her ass. The noise surprises her, and she

clenches around me and lets out a hiss of pain. There's a red mark on her pale ass cheek. I do it again, in the same place, and she bucks.

I drill forward with my hips, pushing deeper inside her.

Her low groan fills my ears. She doesn't fight me.

When I don't move for a long moment, she turns her head and peeks at me through the curtain of damp hair. I can only see one of her eyes.

I don't like that.

I pull out just as quickly as before and put her on her back. She stares up at me, breathless, and slowly reaches for me. She cups the back of my neck with both hands and tugs me down on top of her.

I brace on my forearms, resisting the urge to kiss her again. Resisting the urge to push my dick back inside her. Instead, I ask, "How did you kill Ben?"

Her nails dig into my neck, and her blue eyes widen. "I don't want to talk about that."

I tease her slit, shifting just enough to cause those pretty eyes of hers to flutter. "I think you're forgetting whose punishment this is."

Both of ours.

"Do you want me to show you?" Her husky voice scratches an itch in my soul.

I find myself nodding, transfixed, and barely notice her leg coming around mine. Her foot slides up my calf, sending little shivers up my spine.

"He was on top of me," she says. "He had my arms locked in my shirt behind my back, and he ripped off my bra."

I clench my jaw.

"I headbutted him." She lifts, aiming her forehead to my nose.

I move faster, kissing that beautiful, strong forehead of hers.

Her smile is faint. "Broke it, I think. Then scrambled away and got free. He came after me, and I smashed him in the face with his rifle."

This was a bad idea. I'm getting angrier by the second that this asshole had his hands on her. Doesn't matter that he's dead. Doesn't matter that Apollo had our guys take care of it. If I had the power to resurrect him, just to torture him to death, I'd do it.

"I lunged for him," she continues, her fingers digging into my skin. Urging me down until my weight is flattening her to the ground. The grass tickles our bare skin, but she was pressed into marble by him. "We rolled, and I made sure to come out on top."

She moves quickly, flipping us, and I let out a huff when she lands astride me. Her hands on the back of my neck move forward, around my throat. She leans down, until her lips are hovering just over mine. "And then I squeezed until he stopped moving."

We're more alike than she knows.

I crush her body down to mine and lean up at the same time, stealing a kiss. My heart is going a million miles a minute, because she *knows*. The feeling. The anger. I kiss her until I can't breathe, and it's only then that I realize she was tightening her grip on my throat.

My head falls back to the ground, and I stare up at her while my lungs burn.

She moves lower, and suddenly she's got my dick lined up. She pushes down, and my mouth opens. Nothing comes out. My lungs are aching, but I don't make her stop.

I let her fuck me and use me and take her pleasure as I hold her thighs. My depraved pleasure is increasing.

There's an ache in my balls that demands that I just let go.

She kisses me and releases my throat at the same time, and I inhale her scent. My hips jack up into her harder. I come suddenly, damn near violently. I groan out her name, my throat scratchy.

She grips my hand and moves it to her clit. Her tongue strokes my mouth, and I rub her clit hard, taking my cum and her wetness to lubricate it. My other hand goes to her asshole, and I push one finger in. She gasps, and then her climax rocks through her. Her holes squeeze at my dick and my finger, but I don't stop with her clit.

I flip her onto her back and pull out, but I'm fixated on the hot little button between her legs.

"I can't," she says, squirming away.

I shake my head. "Punishment." But I add, "At least I'm not making you count."

She scoffs, still trying to inch away from me. "You wouldn't."

"It's either this, or I make you count as I spank the life out of your ass."

Her cheeks turn red.

I file that away for later.

Her lips part when she comes again. Her hips lift off the ground, and I smile my triumph. I duck down to kiss her again, then hop to my feet and pull her up with me.

She sways, resting her hand on my forearm.

My dick stirs again.

Seriously. She's touching my *arm*. I ignore it and look her up and down. She does the same and covers her mouth with her hand.

"We're filthy," she laughs.

I smile.

I didn't think I'd ever fucking smile again, but here I am, grinning like an idiot. We're covered in streaks of mud and pieces of grass. I flick a bug off my arm, then turn her around and make sure nothing's crawling on her.

She takes a step and winces.

"What happened?" I demand.

She lifts her foot.

There's blood. She brushes at it, and a few bloody stones fall to the ground.

Shit. I did this, didn't I? No—she ran outside without shoes. But it was my idea to punish her, which caused her to run. Well, she blew me, which led to—

"Wolfe." Kora shakes my arm, rolling her eyes. "It's fine. Just a scrape."

"Certainly not." I go down on one knee. "Get on my back."

She only hesitates for a second... and that's how I know it's not just a fucking scrape. Jace and Apollo are going to kill me, if I don't do it first. She climbs on, and I have to use way too much willpower when her center touches my back. There's wetness there—her arousal and my cum. Like, *fuck me twice*, I could easily go again. And again.

Her arms come around my shoulders, and her lips touch my neck, just under my ear.

I lock my arms under her thighs and rise, pitching forward just slightly so she doesn't slide right off.

"I killed my father the same way," I say when we're in the thick of the trees.

Her hand flattens over my heart, but she doesn't speak. Better that she doesn't, so I don't lose my nerve. My face aches, the bruises an abysmal reminder of our fight.

"I got the upper hand, and we went down. It was luck

that I ended up on top and was able to stay there." I sigh. "I strangled him and bashed his head into the floor."

Kora just kisses that spot on my neck again. "Good," she whispers fiercely.

I stop walking. "Good?"

She squirms until I set her down, and she circles around to face me. "*Good*," she repeats. "Because now you can come home to us. You're home, Wolfe."

My eyes burn. The horror that's been plaguing me since last night, the guilt that's been infesting my heart for even longer as I came to terms with what I had to do, ebbs away.

Kora forgives me.

Forgive might be the wrong word.

Maybe she just accepts it because it's what she would've done in my shoes. Maybe she didn't see any other option for freedom.

I catch her hand, bringing her branded wrist up to my lips. She knows all about being entrapped, and I hate that we can share so much darkness.

But at the same time? I wouldn't have it any other way.

I flash the screen of Kora's phone to Jace again. Her dad called. Then the sheriff. His sister, Nadine. Now Alex Sterling.

"Didn't realize our girl was so popular," I joke. I flop down beside Jace.

He's playing a video game, driving a car around a course and trying to avoid the shells that keep getting tossed his way. I watch him for a moment, letting her phone keep vibrating on my thigh as he gets taken out by a rogue banana.

Another player scoots past him into first, crossing the finish line inches before him.

He hits pause and tosses the controller on the cushion beside him, then snatches up the phone. He answers it before I can stop him. But at least he puts it on speaker.

"Kora Sinclair's phone," Jace says smoothly, smirking to himself. "Who's calling?"

"Who is this?" Alex Sterling demands.

I snicker.

"Her assistant, of course. She's getting so many calls these days..."

Alex huffs. "Of course. One of her boyfriends, then? Apollo, perhaps?"

Rude to think Jace and I sound anything alike.

"Close," Jace says. "Starts with a J..."

"Jackass?"

I choke.

"Wouldn't be the first time someone called me that. But you're not really endearing me to pass along your message." Jace presses his knuckles to his mouth.

He's enjoying this about as much as I am. After the week we've had, we need the entertainment. Still, it's pretty hard to keep quiet while Alex sputters on the other end of the line. After all, isn't he technically family?

The line goes silent for a moment, and Jace checks the screen to make sure Sterling didn't just hang up on us. Which I kind of think he would, just to avoid talking to Jace any more.

"Fine," Alex says. "Hello, *Jace*."

My best friend smirks.

"Could you please let Kora know that I'd like to meet with her?"

I raise my eyebrow. Is it safe? And I can tell Jace has the same line of thinking, because he seems to be weighing the options.

"I'll pass it along," Jace finally says. "No promises."

"Thank—"

Jace hits the *end* button and sets her phone aside. He glances at me. "What?"

"I didn't say anything."

"Do you think she should meet with him?"

I shrug. "I don't know."

"Me neither."

Her being a Sterling is... well, I suppose Jace always knew. I'm not sure when I'll be able to let that go. He kept secrets from us. Well. One secret. One huge fucking secret. So she should get to know her cousins if she wants. And if she doesn't want to, then she doesn't have to do it.

Simple.

But when is anything ever simple?

I glance toward the front door. Her and Wolfe ran out of the house butt naked and wet, and they still haven't returned. It takes a lot of effort to set aside that jealousy, too, and to try not to picture what they're doing.

Mainly because I know what they're doing.

Jace wordlessly hands me the second controller, and I grunt my thanks. He restarts the game in multiplayer mode, and we focus on the screen until the front door swings inward.

I hop up, Jace following a second behind. They come down the hall, and we both stare. She's on his back, her legs wrapped around his waist and her hands clutching his shoulders. They've got dirt and grass stains everywhere.

Blood drips from her foot onto the floor.

"What the fuck, Wolfe?"

He ignores me and backs up to the kitchen island, letting her slide off on the counter. He glances at Jace, who also seems like he's ready to punch Wolfe's face in for injuring our girl.

"Guys."

My attention snaps to Kora.

"I'm fine." She gives me a soft smile. "It was my idea, and I cut my foot on a rock. No big deal."

"Where's the first-aid kit?" Wolfe grumbles. He yanks open random drawers.

I roll my eyes and snag it from the pantry. I move to help, but he blocks me.

Naked Wolfe in my space... Hmm. I scowl and hand over the bag, then circle around and step up on Kora's left side. "Can you at least put on some pants?"

He rolls his eyes.

Jace returns—I hadn't even noticed that fucker leave—and throws a pair of sweatpants at Wolfe. The latter smirks and tugs them on, then lifts Kora's leg. He examines the bottom of her foot carefully, then releases her and motions for her to scoot backward.

She does, and I watch her move with a lump in my throat. She lies back and crosses her arms over her stomach.

"Does it hurt?" Jace steps closer on her other side.

"Now that I'm thinking about it," she admits. "But it's okay."

"It won't be fine if you need stitches," Wolfe mutters. "I shouldn't have done that."

She sits up suddenly and grabs his wrist. "Don't."

"Kora."

"Wolfe." Her voice is fierce.

He softens. Pretty sure she's the only person on this planet who could do that. Which made her perfect to bring him back from the brink after he'd killed his father.

She lies back, and he carefully picks out the pieces of stones that embedded in her skin. Then he rinses her feet and holds up a bandage. "I'll wrap them after we're clean," he says.

That done... my gaze goes to her pert breasts. Wolfe finishes his ministrations, and her breathing is rapid. Her chest rises and falls too fast. I reach out and run my finger up her arm, enjoying the way she shivers. On her other side, Jace leans down and kisses her temple.

"Guys," she whispers. "I'm fine."

"You're better than fine," I say. I inch closer and wrap her arm around my shoulders. She doesn't object when I scoop her up and carry her away.

Jace and Wolfe trail us upstairs, and I don't set her down until we're in the bathroom. Even then, I don't let her feet touch the floor. She gets set on the counter, and before I can move away, she grabs my neck and pulls my face down.

Her first kiss is soft. But then all that jealousy sneaks back inside my chest, demanding that I take more from her. I press harder, the kiss becoming a war between our lips. She spreads her legs and tugs me closer, and her hand slides into my pants. Under my boxers.

She grips my dick and pumps. I groan into her mouth. The corner of her lips tilt up, but she doesn't pull away. Or stop.

Insatiable little monster.

And I love it.

Jace moves Kora's hair off her shoulder and leans into her. He inhales her scent.

I grip her jaw and turn her mouth toward Jace's. Her fingers tighten on my dick as she meets his lips. His teeth immediately catch her lower lip. My hand lingers on her throat, catching her pulse.

Her thighs spread wider, and I look down to find Jace pushing two fingers into her pussy. I add my own two fingers, and she shudders. Her back arches forward. I press my thumb on her clit, rubbing quick circles while Jace and I thrust our fingers in and out of her. He snags her lower lip again and pulls just as her climax hits.

Her eyes flutter, and she reaches out for Jace's and my shoulders. Jace tears his mouth free, licking her lower lip and smiling like he has a secret. Then he takes his fingers out and puts them in her mouth.

I smirk at her shocked expression.

"Suck," he whispers.

Her lips close over his fingers, and I swear to fucking god, I get harder.

"Bath is ready," Wolfe says behind us.

When she releases his fingers, I carry her across the bathroom to the large tub. She wriggles out of my grasp and steps into it, exhaling softly. Wolfe steps in behind her, lowering so she can sit between his legs. Jace grabs a wash-cloth and hands it to him, then takes another and dips it into the warm water.

They must've put some sort of bath soap in it, because there's a layer of bubbles that obscure her lower half.

"Lean on me, flower," Wolfe urges.

She rolls her eyes but doesn't object when he draws her back against him. Jace is taking care of the smudges of dirt on her body, dragging the cloth across it... and other places. I watch with a greedy eye, absorbing her every reaction.

He runs it over her breasts, his eyes fixated on her chest. Her breathing hitches, and she focuses on his face. Wolfe buries his face in her hair, and my attention snags on him for a moment. Worry tugs at me, but... he seems okay right now. He's here with us.

If anyone can save him, it's us. Kora and Jace and me.

He hugs her tightly, ignoring Jace's wandering hands.

Kora's gaze shifts to me. She reaches out and snags my fingers.

I squeeze back.

We've been to literal hell and back. I sit heavily at that, leaning against the wall next to the tub. Jace kneels, too, but he sits back on his heels and slowly stops moving. We all lapse into silence.

"Wolfe," Kora eventually whispers. Minutes or hours later, I couldn't say. We were all lost in our thoughts for a time. She twists in his arms, cupping his cheek and drawing his face up. "Look at me."

His eyes are red-rimmed.

My heart drops, but Kora doesn't flinch away from his tears. She may have felt him crying long before now.

She leans forward and kisses his cheek. Then his other.

Without warning, she lets herself go backward, submerging in the water.

She comes up with her hair plastered to her face. She shifts so she's facing Wolfe, and she shoves his shoulders down. He grips the edge of the tub but isn't fast enough to stop his head from going under.

He comes up sputtering, wiping the water from his eyes. "What was that for?"

Kora just smiles. "We need to wash our hair. Skipped that step earlier..." She reaches for the shampoo and squirts some in her palm, then rises on her knees to get a better angle at reaching his head.

Fuck. Part of me wants to drag Wolfe out of the tub and take his place, because the way her fingers are scrubbing in his light-brown hair looks positively marvelous. By the way he's tipping forward, giving her better access, seems like he's in agreement.

"Is he hard, princess?" Jace asks suddenly.

She glances over her shoulder at him.

"Take him inside you."

Her hand leaves his head and disappears under the water, and Wolfe makes a pained noise. My heart thumps erratically when she does what Jace says.

First time for everything.

She lifts and then lowers herself in Wolfe's lap, letting out a hiss of breath. His eyes flutter for a moment as she adjusts on top of him. As he adjusts to being inside her again. But her gaze is back on Jace, seeming to wait for something else.

"Keep washing his hair," Jace urges.

He brushes his fingertips over her shoulder, and she shivers.

"Make her come," he orders Wolfe. "Unless she stops..."

A wicked gleam enters Wolfe's eye, and he nods. His hands disappear under the water. She gasps, lips parting. Her soapy hands run down the back of his neck, leaving a trail of suds.

I slide my hand into my pants and stroke myself. Because, fuck it, this is too hot not to. Especially when Wolfe gets her to lean back and dives down on her breast, sucking her nipple into his mouth.

"Fuck," Kora moans. Her head falls to the side, her fingers barely moving in Wolfe's hair anymore. She's more holding him to her chest than anything.

"Stop," Jace says.

Wolfe pries his lips away from her skin.

Her brow lowers, and she scoops up a handful of water and pours it over his head.

He shakes it off, smirking at her, and then shifts her onto her back. She lets out a yelp with the movement, and Wolfe follows, leaning over her and pinning her down.

He seems to be done listening to Jace. He thrusts into Kora hard, and her eyes roll back. She grips him so hard, her nails dig into his shoulders. The water sloshes, but neither of them seem to care. Their faces are out of the water —barely.

250

I rise and grab the stopper, letting the water drain so they don't fucking drown. Her hands curl around the edge of the tub, bracing her body and to keep from sliding.

He moves faster, pulling gasps and whimpers from her like he's playing an instrument. I stroke myself harder and then force myself to stop. I don't want to come watching them fuck like my own personal porn movie.

She comes first. Loudly. Screaming his name and leaving red scratches on his back.

He pulls out a second later and comes on her belly, her chest. My skin is hot as he leaves ropes of cum on our girl. Marking her.

"My turn," I say, rising and offering my hand to her. She takes it, and I help her out of the tub—but we don't really make it very far.

I don't *want* to make it far.

I press her against the wall and kiss her again. She tears at my shirt and pants, her wet hands everywhere, and I suck her tongue.

She jolts, but then she's moving faster. More urgent.

I kick my pants away and lift her, only taking a second to line up. Her warmth envelops me, and I let out a sigh.

She locks her legs around my hips, and I let my hands explore her body. Her breasts, her nipples, her throat. I guide her back and break the kiss, meeting her eyes. My hips roll slowly, working in and out of her.

The expression she gives me...

Fuck.

I tighten my grip on her throat. Not enough to stop her breathing, but enough to cause a little fear. And a whole flood of wetness between her legs.

"You like that, baby?" I ask, grinding into her.

She opens and closes her mouth.

"You take us so fucking well. You're a goddamn queen."

And she looks it, even now. With wet hair and running makeup and leftover soap and cum clinging to her skin. But Jace isn't the only one who likes to make demands. I want her on her knees, begging to be able to climax.

Another time.

Right now, I just give her what she wants.

What we all want.

"Touch yourself," I order. "And come for me."

Her eyes heat. She touches her clit, and her hand slips through the cum. She pushes her fingers between us, pushing into her pussy with my cock. It feels too fucking good, I almost come on the spot. She pulls out and touches her clit, rubbing circles while her head falls back on the wall.

"Apollo," she gasps.

"Look at me," I growl.

Her eyes open as the orgasm rocks through her. Her walls clench around my cock, and I let go, too. I still inside her, the bliss sweeping through me. I lean forward and kiss her again, not wanting the moment to end.

kora

Apollo lets my feet touch the floor, and he gives me one last soft kiss before stepping back.

Before I can move, Jace is in my space. Already naked. His cock presses into my belly. He looms over me and grips my chin, directing my face up. It reminds me of when he used to think intimidating or scaring me would work. But then he descends and takes exactly what he wants from me. His lips crash into mine. There's frantic energy there that I hadn't noticed before.

He's showing me now, in his urgent movements. In the way he bites at me, his hands pushing at my skin.

I push back. It feels natural, like we're just giving in to the antagonistic chemistry between us. My palm lands on his bandage, and I put pressure on it.

He groans and fists my hair, yanking my head back and raking his tongue down my throat. Little pops of pain emanate from my scalp, from his vicious hold, but I relish it.

He lifts me and carries me to the counter, sweeping it clear. The soap dispenser and our toothbrushes fall into the sink. He grips my legs and spreads them wide, leaning down and sucking my sore clit into his mouth.

I yelp and shove at his head, but his hold on my thighs just tightens. He swipes his fingers through the wetness at my slit, then pushes a digit into my asshole without warning.

My thighs clamp on his face, and his breath huffs with his quiet chuckle. Then he bites my clit.

Bites it.

And holy shit, I like it.

I shatter, my scream echoing in the tiled bathroom. I see white for a second. My body is electrified, and I lean back on my elbows. My head touches the mirror, and I stare at him.

Jace grins and steps back, allowing me room to stand.

If my legs will hold me... which I'm pretty sure they won't. Not after that.

"Kneel," he says softly.

I stare at him for a moment, contemplating. Over his shoulder, Wolfe and Apollo watch. Waiting to see what I'm going to do.

It's so obvious that this is my choice. That I could say no, and it would be the end of it. It's that, more than anything, that drives my decision.

I slip off the counter and sink to my knees in front of him. A delicious shiver runs up my spine. He strokes the side of my face, brushing hair off my shoulder. Soft movements. I tip my head back to see him better and fight more chills at the dark look in his eye.

The first time the three of them have had me together— something that I didn't really question but also never thought about. It seemed improbable that it would ever happen. Even with Jace injured, it's clear he doesn't let a little pain stop him.

The head of his cock runs over my closed lips.

I keep them closed, even as he smears precum across them. My hands have landed on my thighs, and I tighten my hold. He does it again, then draws back. His thumb skates across my bruised cheekbone, fingers splayed on my neck under my ear.

"Open," he says.

His voice is so quiet. But I think the quiet version of him is more serious than any yelling.

My mouth opens. I just orgasmed, and I already want another release. I clench my abdomen and try not to squirm.

"Tongue."

I put my tongue out.

There's fire under my skin, a burning need mixing sharply with anticipation.

When he finally steps back within reach, his fingers slide into my hair again. He holds my head still and pushes his cock into my mouth.

I taste him for a moment, and then he hits the back of my throat. I choke, but he's unrelenting. He doesn't pull out... he pushes deeper.

"Relax," he grits out.

I close my eyes and do it, and he slides into my throat. My lungs burn, but I don't move while he enjoys the way my throat tenses around him.

He withdraws, and I suck in a gasp through my nose. It's the only reprieve I get, and then he thrusts back into me. He moves slowly, methodically, and his hand never leaves my hair. His thumb draws little circles on my neck.

He's fucking my face.

And I'm okay with it.

I lift my hands from my thighs and grip his ass. He growls when I pull him harder into me.

More.

Harder.

Faster.

He gets my silent message and truly takes my face. Tears flood my eyes, and drool spills out my lips with every thrust. I'm choking, gagging on him, and it only seems fitting.

He owns me, doesn't he?

They all do.

He swears. "I'm going to come, princess," he warns. "Don't you fucking waste a drop."

I hum, and the vibration does it. His cock pulses in my mouth. I swallow quickly, tasting the salty-sweet liquid. He pulls out, and I wipe my mouth. I smile at him, but he yanks me to my feet. His hands are everywhere, brushing over my breasts, my belly, my hips.

"I got carried away," he says, his brow furrowing. "I didn't—"

"I'm good."

"Your lip is bruised." He leans in and kisses me. Gentler. Sweeter.

I miss the whiskey-and-destruction flavor that I'd come to associate with him... but I'm just as into this version, too.

When he finally steps back, I sag against the counter.

Now I really do need a shower.

Or a nap.

Or both.

I eye the three of them, and they trade glances. Apollo is the first to move back to the shower, starting it up and warming the water. I hold my hand out to Wolfe, who comes closer and wraps his arms around me.

"You okay?" I whisper in his ear.

"Kind of want to punch Jace for going so hard on you, but... yeah."

I want to tell him that it's okay to miss his dad and be glad that he's dead. That those two things can exist in him simultaneously. But I don't want to bring it up. He nudges me toward the shower, and I step in.

As I had predicted before, there's enough room—and enough showerheads—for all of us. Wolfe rinses the rest of the soap from his hair. I rinse myself off, then pick up the bodywash and drizzle it all over me.

When I glance up, they're all staring at me.

I blush. "What?"

"You're so fucking sexy," Apollo mutters. He darts in and kisses me.

I laugh into his mouth. "Thanks?"

Wolfe motions for me to keep going. I can't seem to wipe the smile off my face as I grab a shower sponge and scrub my chest.

How do they always make me feel so good about myself? Even when I'm on my knees for them, I'm empowered.

So totally opposite of how I was raised, and who I dated before I came to Sterling Falls.

At that... well, I sober pretty fucking fast.

"What's wrong?" Wolfe asks.

I shake my head.

They narrow their eyes at me. Like, all of them. I give them my back, rinsing off the soap.

Which, in retrospect, is a terrible idea. Like turning your

back on the enemy. Except my enemies have become my lovers...

Anyway. They crowd around me until I face them again, my back hitting the tiled wall. Jace redirects the water spray down, so he's not blasted in the face, and I sigh.

"I was just thinking how lucky I was to have you guys and not still be trapped in a relationship with Parker," I mumble as fast as I can.

Wolfe scoffs. "That fucker didn't deserve you."

I look away and ask what I'm really afraid of. "Do you think he could've lived?"

He hesitates—and that's answer enough for me.

"Do you think he's behind the snakes?" I press on, determined. It's better to just get all of this out in the open anyway. That, and my pussy needs a freaking break. "He works for the Sterling Falls Drug Enforcement Agency, he could've found a way to get drugs into our house, in the Jeep..."

"He's a coward," Jace spits. "And everything we've dealt with so far has been from a coward. Trying to warn you away."

"Except the murdered Hell Hounds," Wolfe says.

I cringe. I had forgotten about them, but now that news report pops back up. Jace, Apollo, and I had speculated that they might be related to me somehow. Apollo fills Wolfe in on their theory about the correlation with the beheaded snake in my bed, and I finish cleaning myself.

I leave them to finish in the shower and wrap a towel around myself. I right the things Jace knocked off the counter.

"There's something I have to tell you guys," Wolfe says.

I turn around and find them in front of me again. "What is it?"

He's the one to wince now. "Those bodies..."

Uh-oh.

"Spit it out, man," Jace snaps.

Wolfe glowers at him. "They were Hell Hounds who had interacted with Kora. And they had her initials carved into them."

I gasp, grabbing Apollo's arm. "You—they—"

"The first three were with you when my father took you on camera," he explains. "They were his security. Then the last who just turned up was the man you fought at Olympus."

"Shit," I breathe.

"Ain't that the truth," Apollo agrees.

Wolfe releases the towel from around his waist and dries his upper half. "It's okay, Kora. No one is going to get to you here."

Kora Sinclair.

Korinne Sterling.

Same initials... so was it someone I knew from my previous life? Like Parker? Or have I attracted an old enemy of my parents'?

THIRTY

jace

I hold the umbrella over Kora's head as we file up the paved sidewalk. She keeps her arm looped through mine, huddled close to avoid the rain.

The weather is sharing in our misery today.

Lightning streaks across the sky, and thunder booms a second later.

Wolfe follows behind us with his own umbrella. Ahead are Apollo and Artemis, then Antonio and his wife, Vittoria. And in front of them strides Saint.

Unlike the rest of us, he doesn't carry an umbrella. His black suit jacket is soaked, his white shirt sticking to his chest. His short hair is plastered to his face, but he doesn't make any move to wipe it away. I watch him through the shifting bodies, tempted to tow Kora around and catch up to him.

But he's walking fast for a reason, and I have to say... I don't think I'd be acting any differently if Kora was taken from me. So I keep my eye on him from a distance.

Finally, we reach the mausoleum.

Nyx chose to be cremated, but her grandparents had

purchased a large family slot in the mausoleum. A black plaque with Nyx's name has been hung on the marble beside theirs. It's on the outer wall, but there's a covered walkway that circles the building. It lends some cover for visitors, although Saint stops just shy of it.

There are flowers at the base of their section, a little stand with her name on it. Elora Whitlock.

Saint wasn't able to give her his last name. Hart. And that hurts worse than anything else. The fact that she'll never take his surname, never walk down the aisle toward him, or sign her name on a marriage certificate.

I swallow sharply, and Kora glances up at me.

The urn is back at Antonio's house. He pointed it out when we arrived this morning, placed on the mantel over the fireplace in the living room.

It's been a long day, and it's not over yet.

Saint wouldn't leave his room. Sat on the floor under the window and stared into nothing, his pressed shirt and suit laid out on the bed. A bed which was freshly made, so neat it didn't even look like he had slept on it.

When asked, he revealed that he didn't sleep on it.

Ever.

Wolfe and Apollo got him up and dressed while I supervised. It's been a week since Wolfe rejoined us at the house. A blissful, fast-paced week. It seemed to come and go faster than any other week in my life.

I got to see Kora breathe the life back into Wolfe.

We reconnected as friends, finally back on solid footing.

But in Antonio's house, Saint was suffering.

And the guilt hits me again, drilling into my chest. I should've kept Nyx and Saint as far from Kronos as possible, and I should've been there for Saint after. Should've spared Saint the sight of seeing Nyx dead...

I visit that night in my head over and over again, replaying it. Trying to make it happen differently. And each time, someone else dies. Sometimes it's Kora. Wolfe. Saint. Other times, we all escape clear only to later realize that Kronos and Ben blew up the subway car and killed Apollo and Artemis.

Dreams that hold me hostage, nightmares that don't shrink away when the sun comes out. And of course, there's the small fact that I'm Kronos' son. Another layer to the guilt added to my growing madness.

"Breathe," Kora says in my ear. She's on her tiptoes to reach, her warm exhale hitting my neck. "You're holding your breath, Jace. *Breathe*."

She presses her hand to my chest, right over my heart. I watch her face and exhale in time with hers. Then inhale.

Exhale.

"I don't know what that was," I mutter.

"Looked like a panic attack," she whispers. "Seemed like how one feels to me anyway. When I don't want anyone to know."

I grimace.

We step under the covered walkway, and I set aside our umbrella. Wolfe joins us, standing just a little behind Kora. She reaches back and threads her fingers with his, holding on tightly.

Apollo and Artemis join us, too. The latter is distraught. Her eyes are red, lined with dark shadows. She has a tissue in her fist, and her chin trembles like she's barely holding it together.

I exchange a look with Apollo, absorbing his guilt, too. Our issues kept him away from his sister when she needed him. We all lost a friend, but Artemis and Nyx were especially close.

The sky cracks open again, the *boom* of thunder nearly on top of a bolt of lightning. Wind whips through our small party, snatching at our hair and our clothes.

A man steps forward and beckons to Saint. He inches forward as if he were stuck in mud, but eventually he gets up beside the man.

"Thank you for joining us," the man says. "My name is Samuel. I'm a teacher at Sterling Falls Academy, which is where I first met the Whitlocks. I knew Elora's family and had the privilege of watching her grow up. She was a marvelous, bright young woman."

Saint stares at the concrete under our feet.

The man continues on about Elora—*Nyx*—until Saint waves him off. He lifts his head and looks around, pausing on each one of us. Taking stock of us, maybe. I hold his gaze, and he nods once. Then he clears his throat.

"What Samuel said is true." Saint clears his throat again. He's hoarse, and the pounding rain threatens to overtake his voice. "Elora was the brightest soul I've ever known." He touches his chest, where the galaxy tattoo is. "She's my best friend."

He stops talking.

Vittoria steps forward and wraps her arms around him, uncaring of his rain-soaked clothes. She hugs him tightly, and he buries his face in her shoulder. He doesn't hug her back, though. His arms stay at his sides.

My heart aches for my friend, and my hold on Kora tightens.

These are our dangers that killed Nyx. Kronos dragged the knife across her throat, but we practically put it in his hand.

If only we had acted sooner.

If only we hadn't involved them.

Kora brings my hand to her mouth, kissing my knuckles. I jerk and stare down at her, but she's still watching Saint. Her lips hover just over the back of my hand.

"I'm sorry," Saint chokes out. He faces the plaque. The shiny new plaque with Nyx's name on it, that commemorates her birth and her death and nothing in between. His jaw works. "I can't do this."

Without another word, he runs into the rain. The storm chases him as he weaves across the rows of gravestones, disappearing over a hill and out of sight.

"Reception at our house," Vittoria says carefully. "Artemis?"

I glance at Apollo's twin. She's staring in the direction Saint went with tears in her eyes. But at Vittoria's call, she flinches away.

I narrow my eyes.

Kora pinches me, then tugs me after Wolfe. I grab the umbrella again, shoving it over her head before she gets drenched.

"I'll be right there," I say suddenly, pushing the umbrella's handle into her hand. I steal a kiss from her lips, warm in the cool spring air, and then prod her forward.

I stick my hands in my pockets and wait for them all to file away. It takes a few minutes for them to disappear down the hill, back toward the parking lot. I step up to the plaque and brush my fingers over the etched letters.

Elora Whitlock
The darkness only makes you shine brighter.

A LUMP FORMS in my throat, and my vision blurs.

Fuck.

I promised myself I wouldn't cry.

I dash away the tears before they can fall and head in the direction Saint went. I break into a jog. Pain slashes through my side, and I wince. But it's good. I deserve this pain. Need it to keep moving.

He sits under a large oak tree, his knees drawn up and his elbows braced on them. He hangs his head, but he looks up when I approach.

I open my mouth and shut it again. Anything I want to say sounds fucking stupid. *You okay? How are you? I'm sorry. So fucking sorry.*

So I don't say anything.

"You remember when we met?" he asks.

"You and me, or…"

"Elora and I."

I nod. It was our opening night of Olympus. I remember being nervous as hell, thinking we had no experience operating a *real* business. But the funds we had saved up were sunk into property—into Olympus—and out of our reach. What was meant to just be our stronghold turned into a last-ditch effort at carving a place for ourselves in Sterling Falls.

"You dragged her off the cliff, didn't you?" I sit beside him, leaning back against the trunk. It doesn't provide much cover from the rain, which has lightened just the slightest bit.

He chuckles. "Yeah. Well, not really. I asked if she wanted to do something crazy with me."

"You probably didn't realize the jump was only just beginning." That night got out of control. *Fast.* But we put an end to it and saved Nyx from having her legs broken, or something like that. Whatever that madman was threatening.

We offered them jobs. Saint designed our masks, but we wanted Nyx to fight for us. It was a double-edged offer that would get her out of her home in West Falls, too. Something she desperately needed.

Because we didn't send invitations to fighters off the cuff. We researched. And stalked. Nyx caught our eye at the gym she used to go to, and we started shadowing her from there. A scrappy underdog, and a pretty girl to boot? A gambler's catnip.

"I appreciate everything you did for us," Saint says quietly. "And I keep replaying it... I don't think I would've got the girl if you guys weren't there."

"You would've," I argue. "You loved her. Even then."

"Even then," he agrees.

He looks away, and his shoulders hitch. His throat works, and tears fill his eyes. It's like a dam breaks, and in seconds, he's sobbing. Ugly, racking sobs move his whole body.

The noise stabs through me, and my throat closes again. I fight the burning in my eyes. We sit, and I watch the dark clouds roll past us, and there's no end in sight to his misery. It stretches out in front of us.

Eventually, he takes a few deep breaths, his face contorting.

"You love her so fucking much," I whisper. I don't touch him, don't try to comfort him any more than being here can. Because while I sympathize, and I think I can imagine the pain he might be feeling... the truth is, I'm fucking clueless. I don't *want* to know what it feels like to have my heart ripped out.

All I can offer him are the facts. I just say the truth and hope that he'll come out on the other side of it.

"I don't know how I can live without her," he admits, his breathing too fast. "I don't want to. I just want to follow her, and I fucking can't. There's not a goddamn thing I can do about it."

Fuck.

I take his hand and squeeze it tight. "You're not alone."

"I'm not even human anymore." He wipes his face with his other hand. His tears are mixing with the rain coming down. He squeezes my hand, then pulls away. "I'm not going to kill myself."

I eye him. "You'd tell me if you were?"

"Probably not."

A dark expression flickers across his face, like he's actually thought about it. That's more worrying than anything. While we've been off in la-la-land having *fun*, he's been miserable. Of course, up until a week ago, I was right there with him. But as soon as Kora took me back... *poof*. Gone.

God, am I the monster?

"I'm so fucking sorry," I blurt out.

He shakes his head. "Don't."

"It's my fault—"

"*Don't.*" He slashes angrily at the air, like he's cutting through my words. "Don't diminish her sacrifice." He scowls at the grass, reaching down and tearing out clumps between his legs. "She knew the risk. She fucking wanted Kronos to be stopped, and she put herself in front of his car. It's not your fault she went after him. It's *his* for slitting her throat—"

"Okay." I hold up my hands in surrender. "You're right."

She did do that. She was brave.

But Saint shouldn't be alone. Not after admitting that he's thought about suicide.

He could come back to our house. There's an extra room—

"I don't want any part of your love fest," he says, preempting my thoughts. "I *might* kill myself if I have to hear you, Apollo, and Wolfe go at it with Kora all night."

I laugh at that. I'd probably feel the same if I had to listen to Saint fucking, too.

So that means I need to find someone else to watch over him. *Fine.* No problem.

I hop to my feet. There's not an inch of me that was saved from the rain, but whatever. This talk was worth it. I hold out my hands and lift Saint to his feet, then pull him into a rough hug.

"You're going to be okay," I tell him. I tighten my hold when he tries to shove me off him. "Listen to me. You are going to be okay… eventually. Not today, not tomorrow, maybe not even a year from now. But someday you're going to smile again. And the grief won't feel so heavy."

He exhales. And unlike with Vittoria, he does hug me back.

I can't help but feel a little accomplished by that.

But I still have the overwhelming urge to lose my shit—and I refuse to do that in front of Saint. Not when he's the one who lost everything.

He rubs his face again, then swipes his hands through his hair. "Just don't assign Vittoria or Antonio to watch over me," he says. "They're worse than helicopter parents."

But that's what you need.

I bite my tongue and nod. "Anyone else is fine?" I confirm. Because I have someone in mind, but I don't think he's going to go for it...

He lifts one shoulder. "Guess so."

"Deal."

I hold out my hand, and he shakes it. I smother my smirk and hook my thumb toward the parking lot. "Let's go eat some food and listen to people tell stories about Nyx. Okay?"

He exhales. "If you say so. But there better be alcohol there."

"I'm sure we can arrange that."

kora

Artemis and I are drunk, because this party is depressing as fuck.

Nyx's aunt showed up to Antonio's house with her parents in tow. They missed the ceremony, of course, and our little gathering at the mausoleum. But now they're in a corner, keeping to themselves and dabbing at their dry eyes with tissues.

Then there were the people who tend to come out of the woodwork at wakes. Men and women who shook Saint's hand and told him they fought Nyx at Olympus, or knew her family, or had watched her fight.

It doesn't really matter if she won or lost against those who claimed to go up against her. But I'd like to think she beat them all.

There's a big, glossy photo of her and Saint on an easel by the fireplace. The neon sign of his tattoo shop—which I've never been to actually, but Artemis pointed it out—is blurry in the background. They're posing for the camera, her arm looped around his waist and his around her shoulders. Her long, dark hair is loose, and she's wearing color for once. A pale-pink shirt covered in daisies. Jean shorts, flip-flops.

It makes me realize how much of her life I missed. Or rather, how much I didn't inquire about.

My eyes go back to the urn on the mantel.

I lift my glass to my lips, disappointed when only a dribble of melted ice falls onto my tongue. Artemis is nursing a beer, her fingers curled around the bottle.

We started with shots of whiskey.

Bad idea.

The room tilts a bit as I stand, but I catch myself and head back toward the bar set up in the front room. I transitioned from the shots to margaritas, while Tem went with something lighter. Not that it stopped her from pounding back two beers in fifteen minutes.

But no one is watching us, so I pour myself another. I go a little too hard on the tequila, leaving room for only a splash of the mixer.

I sigh and stir it, then head back to the couch.

Someone catches my arm.

I whirl around and stare down at the hand until it falls away from me. Then my gaze lifts, and my mouth opens. Closes. Opens again... closes again. No thoughts come up, no idea what to say.

Alex Sterling frowns. He tugs at his cuffs, pulling his starched white sleeves down over his wrists. "Are you drunk?"

"Why?"

"Because you're weaving." He takes my elbow, bringing me farther into the house. Into the kitchen. He pulls out one of the chairs at the table and motions for me to sit.

The drink vanishes from my grip. He sniffs it, then sets it aside. I scowl.

A bottle of water replaces it.

"Drink that," he says.

I raise my eyebrow.

"Kora."

Fine. I unscrew the lid and take a few swallows, watching until he finally rolls his eyes and nods that he's satisfied.

I lower the bottle into my lap. "Why are you here?"

"To pay my respects."

"Did you know her?"

He pulls out the chair next to me, twisting it so he can face me. "No. I came to pay my respects to you."

I blink, and my words disappear again. He came to say his respects to *me*? I didn't know her that well. I... in the grand scheme of things, I got off easy compared to the guys. Tem. The guys. *Saint.* I don't need respects.

He shifts. "I also wanted to see if you're doing okay. After you didn't call me back..."

"You called?"

"Jace didn't pass along that message?" His jaw tics. "He answered your phone sometime last week. I just wanted to get together with you and see if I could help with any puzzle pieces about my family. *Our* family."

My stomach swoops. "The Sterlings?"

"Yes."

"Did you grow up with... them? My parents?"

"I did," he says. He rests his elbow on the back of his chair, reclining slightly. Relaxing, maybe, or settling in for a story.

I want to stop him, because I don't think I'm in any condition to remember details of a story. But I don't speak, don't even move, because there's a larger part of me that's starving for knowledge. More than the newspaper articles can provide.

"Your father, Brendon Sterling, was an alderman. He was also on the board for Sterling Falls University. He did a lot of community work with your mother, Liesl. They were loved in the town, quite honestly." His smile slides off his face. "We were all heartbroken when..."

I reach out and take his hand.

He looks up, surprise parting his lips. I squeeze his fingers.

"Do you remember me, then?" I ask lightly.

"Of course. You had bright-orange hair back then, not like now. The darker color suits you. A lot of freckles in the summer. Your parents doted on you." He smiles. "Nadine and Nate babysat you. I had a job at the time, so I wasn't... around as much."

I nod, swallowing sharply.

"I have some old photos, if you want them?"

"You do?" I hardly breathe the words.

His smile widens into a grin. "Of course. My father loved to document stuff, and I have boxes of photographs and scrapbooks my mom made for us. I'll send you my address, maybe we can connect later this week?"

I nod eagerly. "Thank you."

He rises, glancing behind him. Someone's crying in the other room, the sobs feminine and loud. Maybe Artemis, but I'd bet more on Nyx's mother.

"I'm going to head out," he says. "Give them my best, please."

"Of course." My head is buzzing, and I watch him navigate through the bodies easily. He's swallowed by the crowd, and I take another gulp of water.

"There you are." Wolfe appears around the corner. He

drops into the chair Alex just vacated, but he leans forward and runs his hands up my thighs. His fingers slip under the hem of my dress. "You look too fucking good, flower."

I smack his hands away. "We're at a wake, Wolfe."

He sighs. "Yeah."

He wants a distraction. And I'm just drunk enough to give him one.

I stand and offer my hand. He meets my gaze, and his grows dark. He lets me lead him out the back door. The rain has stopped, the storm fizzled out. The sky is dark, with bright pinpricks of stars. No more clouds, even.

We've been inside longer than I realized. Long enough for the moon to rise. It's just a sliver tonight, lending no extra light.

The stairs are a little tricky, but I don't think he notices my death grip on the damp railing. We get down to the ground, and I search around before landing on a corner of the house that's shrouded in shadows. The raised deck blocks the floodlight from reaching us.

I push him against the house and press my body to his, going up on my toes to reach his mouth. Our lips touch softly. Tasting each other.

"Are you drunk?" he whispers.

I lift one shoulder. "Yeah."

He chuckles and spins us around, switching our positions. "Then you shouldn't do any of the work."

He drops to his knee.

I suck in a breath—then quickly realize that he's not fucking proposing. Not when he runs his hands up my thighs again, raising the skirt of my dress and ducking under it. He picks up one of my legs and places it on his shoulder.

"Wolfe, you can't—" I was thinking about making out,

not getting caught with a man under my skirt. At a wake. "What if someone—?"

He runs his finger down my center, over my panties. The feeling is muted because of the fabric, and he teases me like that for several passes until he dips a finger beneath it. He continues to tease my slit, touching everything except my clit.

"Please," I finally groan. "Wolfe, just—"

His mouth descends.

But *again*, my panties are in the way. My eyes flutter at the sensation of him sucking my clit through the fabric. His nose brushes down my center.

"You smell divine," he says.

He lowers my leg and pulls my panties down my legs. I step out of them, and then my legs are spread again. I have no shame when my hand lands on his head over my dress, pushing him harder into my core.

"I've got you," he says. He kisses my inner thigh, then nips my flesh.

Goosebumps rise on my arms, and heat floods straight to my center.

He continues to explore between my legs, until I'm panting and trying to direct him where I want him.

He just chuckles.

I shut my eyes tight. The guys and I have been adjusting to being in one space again for the past week. The sleeping arrangements have been a little weird. I'm trying to get them all in the same bed, but one or two of them beg off and find separate beds to sleep in. Maybe I snore, or they just don't like sharing.

That's going to change. It's already changed over the course of the past seven, eight months.

Wolfe's tongue flicks my clit, and I cover my mouth to

block my gasp. He pushes two fingers into me, curling and rubbing the spot inside me that makes my legs go weak.

He makes a noise in the back of his throat, a groan of contentment. He sucks and licks and finger-fucks me right to the edge.

And when I think I'm going to topple over, he pulls away.

"Asshole," I groan. "Why—"

But he's rising to his feet fast, his pants already undone. He hooks my knee over his arm, spreading me wide, and thrusts into me.

His lips swallow my scream. I immediately come, my body tingling. He takes his own pleasure from me, and I grip his shoulders. His tongue invades my mouth like his dick invades my pussy, taking what he wants from me.

"You're going to walk back into that house with my cum dripping down your legs." His mouth is still against mine, the words hovering just between us. The way his lips move as he talks is its own form of a filthy kiss. "They'll smell it on you. Jace and Apollo. They'll smell the sex and get so fucking turned on, I bet they'll each try to steal you away. But I was buried inside you first."

I nod.

He licks my lip. Kisses me again. Each thrust has me jolting backward, and he finds his release. All I can do is hold on.

He goes still a moment later, buried in me. His dick throbs as he comes, and I clench around him. I hold his shoulders, not wanting the moment to end.

But he pulls out and tucks himself away, then rights my dress. He puts his fingers under my chin, lifting my face, and swipes his thumb under my lower lip.

"Good thing you didn't wear lipstick tonight," he says. "That would've been a dead giveaway."

I allow a small smile, then look around. "What did you do with my underwear?"

He smirks. "They're in my pocket."

"Wolfe."

He shrugs and heads back inside.

"Wolfe, you can't keep—"

"Let's see how long they can hold out, hmm, flower?" He chuckles and opens the sliding door. He's gone, angling around a group of people who have congregated in the kitchen.

I grit my teeth, but I don't have it in me to be too mad. I pat down my dress and touch my hair, making sure the back isn't crazy from rubbing against the siding of the house. It seems perfectly intact, so I take a breath and head inside.

No one even bats an eye.

I snag my forgotten drink from the counter and gulp it down. It's mostly tequila, and it burns a track down my throat. I relish the warmth that spreads through my limbs, my muscles relaxing.

Artemis and Apollo are in the living room, sitting on the couch. I spot Jace talking to some Olympus fighters across the room. Wolfe isn't around, but he could be out front with some of Antonio's friends.

I smile to myself and head toward Apollo and Artemis.

Apollo's eyes widen when I fall into the space beside him.

"Hey, baby." He leans in and kisses my cheek. He lingers and inhales.

Yep, I fucking smell like sex.

His gaze drops to my lap, and a small frown tugs his lips down.

I knock my shoulder into his and lean around him.

My drinking buddy has a new beer in her hand. Her eyes are half-mast, but she gives me a smile. "You got up to some trouble, huh?"

I laugh. "Did I?"

"My brother looks like he wants to go caveman on you." She shrugs. "I miss sex."

Oh dear.

Apollo shoots to his feet. "I'll be back."

I chuckle and scoot closer to her. I press my thighs together, trying to contain the mess Wolfe left behind. I should've detoured to a bathroom or something, cleaned up a little. Because, sure enough, it's run down my thighs.

"You got a napkin?" I whisper.

She hands me one. She doesn't comment when I shift up on my knee and make a subtle swipe at my thighs. I'm facing her, so no one can really see. Probably. Never mind that we're in the living room, with people around us. Does anyone give a shit that I have my hand up my dress?

"Kora," Tem giggles. "You're bold."

I sigh and flop back down, stuffing the napkin into one of the empty beer bottles. "I feel better, though."

"You've got two guys staring at you," she mumbles.

Great. "I'm not going to look."

"Okay."

"So, nothing romantic happening in your life?" I poke her leg, changing the subject.

She heaves a sigh. "Nope."

"Not... Malik?" I snicker to myself. Because let's be honest, their sexual tension is off the charts every time they're together. Which isn't often, I think in part because Tem likes to play the avoid game.

"He's the worst sort of asshole." she sits up. "Let me set the scene."

I eye her and try not to smile. "Okay."

"Sixteen-year-old Artemis Madden. Fragile. Maybe a bit scarred from some shit that happened the year before. Ready to, err, move past it." She rolls her eyes. "She throws herself at the guy she's been crushing on while staying with her brother. *Malikai Barlow*. Handsome, tattooed, growly—"

"A teenage crush, huh?" Damn it, I'm smiling.

She huffs. "I threw myself at him, Kora, and he flat out rejected me. *Twice*."

"How does he reject you twice?"

"Well, it was complicated. Either way, he's the bane of my existence and a reminder of my stupidity." She sets down her beer and rises. "I think I need to get some fresh air."

She stumbles away. I sit there for a moment, then jump up. I suddenly remember that I have eyes on me, but I refuse to look over and make Jace or Apollo snap.

I sneak upstairs and lock myself in the bathroom.

Wakes are not the place for sex.

Wolfe is just incorrigible.

Fuck, they're all incorrigible.

Which means I'm not particularly surprised when Jace is waiting for me in the hallway. He's leaning against the wall, his arms crossed. He's lost his suit jacket, and the cuffs of his white shirt are rolled up, exposing his muscled, tattooed forearms.

My cheeks heat as his gaze peruses my body.

I step back into the bathroom.

His eyebrow raises, and then his surprise vanishes. He follows me in, closing the door softly behind him and locking us in. His hands find my hips, and he pulls me in.

"Are you being naughty?" he asks in my ear.

I shiver. "I didn't start it."

"I think you did, princess. Did you take your time cleaning away Wolfe's evidence from your pussy?" He pushes my skirt up, his palm ghosting along my thigh. When he reaches my hip, his eyes widen. "No panties."

I lean in and drop my voice. "Someone stole them."

"Did they? As a thief, I thought you would've had some countermeasures."

"Anti-theft devices on my underwear?" I tap my chin. "Sounds barbaric. Especially when I happen to like it when they go missing..."

Jace smiles. His hand is inching closer to the apex of my thighs. But then he pauses.

"You know..." His smile fades.

I search his face.

"What?" I whisper.

"It's selfish of me." He sighs. "But I'm just thinking about how Saint and Nyx never got to live happily ever after. He was going to propose, I think. He kept quiet about it. But I saw a sketch of some rings that he was designing..."

My chest tightens, and I wait for him to continue.

But he doesn't. He just bows his head and kisses me soundly. I don't fight it. He came back with Saint from the cemetery, and they were both quiet. Now I taste his grief and I let him give it to me. I want to tell him that I can carry it for a while, but our lips are stoking a fire between us. A fire that's going to kill us.

Joke's on you, Wolfe. I lose. I can't resist Jace, not when I've got him alone.

I push him back, then spin around. The dress skirt fans out, and I feel like I'm floating for a moment. Still drunk. I bend over, bracing my hands on the counter, and raise my dress over my ass.

I glance behind me, but Jace hasn't moved. He's just watching me like I'm the best fucking thing to ever happen to him.

And I am.

"Fuck me," I beg.

He nods. Undoes his belt, then yanks his pants down enough to free his dick. He's already hard, a bead of precum oozing out the tip. I almost turn back around to taste it, but he steps closer and grips my hips.

He runs the tip through my folds. *Teasing*, like Wolfe. Over my clit, then my slit. I keep waiting for him to thrust inside me, but he doesn't. Back and forth.

He palms my ass cheek, and my face flames.

Jace chuckles. He slides slowly into my pussy, and I groan.

"You're fucking soaked," he says. "But this might be Wolfe, too..."

I don't say anything.

He pumps twice, then pulls out. I almost snarl at him, but then he aims a little higher. Understanding dawns on me as he thrusts into my ass without warning. His hand slams over my mouth at the same time, muffling my yell.

He keeps pushing and pushing until his hips touch my ass, and I breathe out sharply through my nose.

Holy fuck.

He feels giant.

"Ready?" he asks through his teeth.

I wriggle slightly, my mouth open against his palm. I

think I could manage a *yes*, but my voice is just out of reach. I just want him to *move*.

He does. He pulls out and thrusts back into me hard enough that I see stars.

In the best way.

Jace doesn't let up either. He pummels into me, and his balls swing down and slap against my slit. That's its own version of pain and pleasure. His fingers tighten on my face, and he urges me to rise up. I arch my back, whimpering as he hits a new angle. His teeth catch my earlobe.

"You make the most erotic noises," he says in my ear. "And I can't wait to hear every single one of them later."

I groan.

"But right now, I need you to be quiet." He bites my ear again, harder. "If you're quiet, you get to climax."

And if not...

He removes his hand, letting my upper half sink back down to the counter. His thrusts get more brutal. He slides his hand into the top of my dress, and I bite my tongue when he touches my nipple. Just the barest brush, sending tingles shooting through my chest and straight to my empty pussy.

My mind is going haywire. I cover my own mouth again, not trusting my drunk brain to keep myself quiet, and bow my head. He keeps working my ass and my nipples. Both of them, both hands. He tugs and twists, and pain and pleasure wrap together.

We deserve this.

"Look at us," he says suddenly.

I lift my head and meet his gaze in the mirror. I hadn't noticed... but now I suddenly can't stop staring. At the way his hips jack forward, and the corresponding feeling deep inside me. At the lust and desire and love in his eyes, and the way he fights his own verbal responses to this pleasure. His lips tremble, mouth open.

He shudders, still fighting the groan, and slams full-hilt inside me. He leans forward as he comes, releasing my aching nipples and bracing his hands on the counter on either side of me.

He stays inside me. His weight is on my back, on his hand on the counter, and he reaches around to my clit. He plays me like an instrument, and in no time at all, I'm breaking to pieces around him.

When he finally withdraws, I tug my dress back into position and face him.

"I'm sorry."

His eyebrows shoot up. "For what?"

"Messing around at Nyx's wake—" I shake my head, mortification running rampant through me. And regret. Like, *damn*, why can't I just control myself for a few hours?

He pulls me into a hug. Surprising, but so necessary. I wrap my arms around him and hug him back tightly, my ear over his heart. It's thumping a quick, steady beat.

"I needed this," he admits. "A little levity for all the grief in this house."

I close my eyes. "Okay."

"Take a minute," he says. "You've been so fucking strong today, Kora. But it's okay if you break down, too. No one will blame you. She was your friend." He releases me and cleans himself off, then kisses my forehead.

My eyes fill with tears. He looks for a moment like he wants to try and cheer me up, but I wave him off. He's right —I should let myself go through it. The faster I do that, the faster I can accept it.

Jace unlocks the door and slips out, leaving me alone. I let out a breath, then sink to my knees. I let myself miss her.

Something breaks inside me, and the floodgates open. I cry and hiccup and make a mess, and then I clean myself up.

I stare at my reflection and wipe away the smear of makeup under my eyes. This used to be a familiar position for me. Crying in the bathroom, that is. Except my tears were usually caused by Parker screaming at me, or throwing something, or worse.

He's gone.

Maybe.

Probably.

I shake off the bad feeling.

There's one guy who I owe an orgasm. May as well use him for a distraction, too.

artemis

"How're you doing?" Jace asks.

I eye him and don't answer. I'm riding the edge of buzzed and drunk. About two hours ago, I was *drunk*. But I've downed some water, ate some crackers that my brother shoved at me, and now I'm on my way to happy town.

Except Jace has his scheming face on. And if there's something I've learned over the years, it's to never trust *that face*.

"You doing okay?" Same question, framed just slightly different. As if that will make a difference in how I *feel*. Or how I choose to answer.

Because I feel like absolute garbage. I feel *everything*. Loudly. Every inch of grief, every speck of guilt, it's all amplified like my emotions are fireflies in a glass jar. And someone keeps shaking it, over and fucking over again, until they're all lit up and in agony.

I want someone to sedate me.

I want to go to sleep and not fucking dream of my best friend.

I *want* Nyx to be alive.

But apparently, what I want is one hundred percent out of the question.

"Are you still sleeping at your apartment at Bow & Arrow?" Jace asks, changing the subject.

That has me suspicious, but at least he's not asking me how I'm coping anymore. This question is one I can answer.

"Sometimes I sleep here," I admit. "Just to help Vittoria out with..." *Saint.* Although I'm beginning to think he's unhelpable. Unreachable. "But no. I sold my house and bought a condo downtown, and I've been staying there."

He squints at me. "When did that happen?"

"Recently," I hedge. Because I sold my house two days after Nyx died. It was a spur-of-the-moment thing driven by the fact that she used to stay with me. On nights when I got lonely, or when the night terrors became too much.

Yep. Not regular nightmares.

I don't remember most of my night terrors, unless I can't wake up and they bleed back into regular nightmares. But most times, I wake up in a full-blown panic attack and then can't fall back asleep.

Even worse are the times when I wake up and I can't tell if I'm still dreaming.

All said, I wasn't going to step foot back in that house. I hired movers to pack up all my shit and haul it to a storage locker, and from there I sifted through the things I wanted to keep. The condo is good. There are city noises when I open my windows, traffic and sirens and people. I have people above me, below me, beside me.

There, I'm not alone.

But the truth about the *condo* is that I bought it almost a year ago. And then it just sat empty, because I was too afraid of change.

Now, it's laughable. Fate literally said, *fuck your fear, Artemis. Here's some change for you.*

I sit up and face Jace.

Antonio and Vittoria have retired to their room. Their kids, who came back for the funeral and wake, are staying at friends' houses. Last I saw, Kora was disappearing with Apollo into the garage. My stomach twists because I know what they were sneaking off to do, and I really, *really* wish I didn't.

But with Jace in front of me, my curiosity rears up again.

"So, how's your relationship work? Do you take turns? Like assigned nights?"

"Me and Kora?"

I wave my hand for him to continue because he's missing a few key members. But he plays dumb, his expression blank.

"You, Kora, my brother, Wolfe. I mean, that's a lot of..." I wrinkle my nose and abruptly change my mind. "Never mind."

He laughs. "Yeah, thought so."

"You want to ask me something." I push myself to my feet. I sway just a little, my legs unsteady, but Jace knows better than to try and help me. Once my arms are out, and my balance secured, I smile brilliantly. "So...?"

"Come with me." He tips his head toward the hallway.

I shrug and follow him into the office in the back. Antonio likes to say it's his office, but Vittoria spends more time at his large oak desk than he does. She pays the bills, keeps the house organized. Hell, I've even seen her in his restaurants sorting through receipts. He's a genius in the kitchen but not so much at basic accounting.

I step through the doorway, and Jace closes the door behind me.

"What's she doing here?"

I whirl around.

Saint sits on the floor in the corner, with piles of books around him. Every time I see him, he's on the goddamn floor. And he looks... well, fucking miserable, honestly. But it's more than that. He seems tortured.

Not to mention he went through actual torture at the hands of Kronos. Who then killed the love of his life.

I sigh and turn away from Saint. He's made it clear that he doesn't want me around him. I *tried*. He stayed at my apartment right after it happened. Slept on my couch. I cooked him breakfast, which he barely touched, and then he stormed out. And yet, here I am. I still hang around this house, as if he's going to change his mind about me.

"Artemis." Jace takes my hand. "You'd do anything for your friends."

I narrow my eyes at him. I would. But I can't figure out what that has to do with Saint.

"Absolutely not," Saint snaps, reading through Jace's bullshit.

I grind my teeth and wait for him to just get to the point. My glare is a fierce thing, and Jace actually drops my hand when I turn it on him. He rubs the back of his neck, which is beginning to redden.

"Saint threatened to kill himself," he blurts out.

"Fuck you."

"The peanut gallery needs to shut up," I snap at Saint.

Jace glowers at his friend. "You said I could pick. I'm picking Artemis."

Saint leaps to his feet, his fists balled at his sides. His face is getting redder by the second, but he doesn't even deign me with a glance. He stares at Jace. "I didn't really think you'd stoop so low—"

"Whoa, whoa." I hold up my hands. There's a lot to unpack here, so I start with the obvious. I point at Saint. "First of all, him picking me for whatever the fuck he wants isn't *stooping so low*. I'm great. Exceptional, even."

Jace snickers.

I whirl back around and jab him in the chest. "*Second of all*," I hiss. "You need to explain what it is you're *asking* me to do, on the basis that I have the power to say no."

He has the good grace to look ashamed. Or, slightly chagrined. Hard to say.

"You're right," he says to me. "I went about this in the wrong order."

Saint doesn't say anything.

Asshole.

"Saint needs a babysitter," Jace amends. "Because he said he's thought about killing himself, and he also said he wouldn't tell anyone if he did seriously think about doing it."

I... don't know what to say to that.

"I want him to move in with you," he continues. "For a year."

My mouth drops open. A *year*?

"Why would you do that to me?" I ask. "Why a year?"

"Because you'd want to keep him alive, and I don't want either of you thinking a few weeks is going to make him miraculously recover." He steps closer, his palm landing on my shoulder. "Please, Artemis. You're the only person I know who doesn't let him get away with his bullshit. And he already said he didn't want to move in with me."

I scowl. "Of course he doesn't want to move in with you. You guys probably fuck like rabbits all over that house. No one would want to live within a mile of you."

Saint chuckles, then coughs to hide it.

Worse than any emotion I've felt tonight, a sliver of pride blooms in my chest.

Fuck.

"What do I get out of this?" I ask Jace.

He rolls his eyes. "Is keeping him alive not enough?"

I frown, because he and I both know that keeping Saint alive is a bigger—and harder—task than either of us will admit. Still. I'm a businesswoman. "We can discuss my compensation at another time."

I face Saint again. No matter what Jace and I agree to, I have a feeling I don't have a choice... and Saint doesn't either. My stomach is in knots. The most unanticipated reaction? *Butterflies.*

I cross my arms. "Well? I'll pretend you weren't brutish and rude the first time Jace tried to ask. What's your opinion on this?"

He shakes his head, stalking past me to the door. "I think this is the worst fucking idea on the planet." He pauses, hand on the doorknob. "But I'll do it."

Relief.

Anger.

He yanks the door open and strides away. I watch his back, and one thought remains.

I'm so fucking screwed.

kora

The Bradshaws are at my door.

All three of them.

I squint at Nate, trying to kickstart my brain. It's early. Jace went out for a run with Apollo. Wolfe had to spend the night at the clubhouse and try to sort out... I don't know. But I can imagine that it's been chaotic there. He comes home after his time away always looking exhausted.

In the past few weeks, we've gotten into a routine. Wolfe will go see to the Hell Hounds, and Jace, Apollo, and I will head to Olympus. We've been systematically ridding the halls of any trace of other people. What I cleaned that first night was just the tip of the iceberg.

Wolfe sent Hell Hounds to pick up stuff they wanted to keep, but it wasn't much. Clothes and knickknacks. It was kind of sad to see how few possessions they had with them.

We hired help, too. Men and women who worked faithfully for the Gods of Olympus for years, who now seem a bit shocked to be seeing our bare faces. The first wave showed up wearing plain black masks. They were hesitant to remove them—as if we didn't know who they were.

Still. I learned all their names and thanked them each day they left.

We're paying out of the business savings account. But once we open again...

We'll be okay.

Olympus will be okay.

Anyway, that doesn't really explain why the Bradshaws are on the porch with... coffee?

And a bag that smells like breakfast sandwiches.

My stomach growls. But I'm distracted by the third Bradshaw.

Jeremy. Their father.

My kidnapper.

I thought, for a long time, that he had killed Jace. Hoped against it, of course, but there's only so much hope on the Isle of Paradise. The more I stare at him, the more questions I have. About the Sterlings, sure, but also about the Sinclairs.

"Good morning," Nadine greets me after a moment of silence. "How are you?"

"I..." I clear my throat. "Just fine. What are you doing here?"

"You haven't been answering your cell."

My incessant cell phone. It goes off *all the time*. Mom backed off for a week or two, but apparently that's the only time she allowed me to wrap my head around the mindfuck of my life. She's started back up, once or twice a day. Dad tries, too. Alex Sterling. Random numbers with the Sterling Falls and Emerald Cove area code, so I have no idea who they are. Nate. Nadine.

Jace took my phone out of my hand one day and gently ended the call. Then he shut it off and put it on one of the bookshelves in the living room.

"It'll be here when you want to talk," he said, shrugging.

He was right.

I didn't want to talk. Especially after the funeral.

"Can we come in?" Nate asks. "Um, you had mentioned wanting to meet my father. This is Jeremy—"

"I don't need an introduction," I interrupt. "I said I wanted to meet *with* your father. Not that I wanted to be ambushed at my house by him."

Still. There aren't alarm bells going off in my head. As much as I might be freaked out by them here, my body isn't on high alert. Weird as that may be, I don't think I'm in danger.

"We do need to talk, K," Jeremy says.

I cringe.

His gaze is steady on me, and I eventually step aside.

They file in past me, going to the kitchen. Nadine sets down the bag of food, and Nate spreads out the coffees. I take up one of the shorter sides of the island and peel off the lid from my coffee. It's exactly the way I drink it.

I look up at him sharply, and he points to his father.

"Your mom used to drink it that way," Jeremy explains. "I don't know much about you, but I figured that was a good guess."

"It was." Still, I'm unsettled by it. "So..."

"I owe you an apology," he continues. "I'm sorry for frightening you. For acting the way I did. But we have our reasons in this family that sometimes don't come across as... normal."

I can see the family resemblance. Nate and Nadine have reddish hair—hers lighter, his cut too short—but they share the same square jaw and lips with their father. I can see it in Nate's eyes, too. The shape, not the color. And his nose. Nadine got more of the delicate looks, maybe from her mother.

Nate isn't in his sheriff's uniform today. He wears a button-up blue shirt, the cuffs rolled up, and dark jeans. His beard is trimmed close to his face. I eye him for a moment, wondering what reasons he had for conspiring with Kronos. For keeping me locked up and not just breaking me out.

Jeremy pulls something out of his back pocket, sliding it across the island to me.

I wrap my fingers around the metal object.

It's the folding knife, but the edges have been warped by heat. It's singed, ash stuck in the grooves. I pry it open and set it back down, my gaze on the sharp point. I know immediately that this is the knife that Nate gave me the day Kronos tried to kill me.

"My son tipped me off after the end of the auction that Cerberus had won, and Kronos was probably planning something to interfere with the transfer," Jeremy says. "Once you were in the house, he sent me the address. I got there as fast as I could..."

I thought I was going to die that day. I had given up. The stairs were on fire, the door to my freedom was locked.

"I may have gotten you out of that house, but you fought for your survival." He reaches out and taps the knife. It rattles against the counter. "*You* wanted to live. You made it possible for me to get you out."

My eyes are burning. I'd stopped dreaming about fire,

that horror replaced with far worse things. But the rush of heat and searing smoke comes back to me. Then what happened after.

I shake my head and wipe away a tear. "You saved me, sure. But then you put me right in the arms of Cerberus James."

He has the good grace to seem embarrassed. "You're right. I told your parents where I had brought you, but they were too late."

"My parents," I repeat. I pick up my coffee and gesture for them to follow me outside. I don't want to stand. I want to curl up on one of the rocking chairs on the porch and wait for Jace and Apollo to come back.

"The Sinclairs." Jeremy walks next to me, his kids trailing us. "I met your father when he was a journalist."

"He mentioned that." I glance up at him. "Didn't say who you were, but..."

"Ken is good at protecting his sources. And his friends."

We take seats, and I gulp down a few swallows of coffee. The air is cool, but the day is going to be warm. We're in the thick of June weather. Still, I wish I had something other than shorts and a sweatshirt. Something I could hide my head in, maybe.

Sand? If I could turn into an ostrich...

Unfortunately, I just have to suck it up and ask the hard questions. And yet, I chicken out and ask a question I already know the answer to. "Your wife was related to my parents?"

He nods. "Wilma. Her older brother was your father, Brendon. She was the youngest. The middle child was Mason."

Alex's dad, then.

"How..." How what? How did my parents meet? How did they die? How were they as people?

My stupid eyes are burning again.

I look out over the driveway, into the tree line, and try to spot movement. Jace and Apollo were taking one of the trails along the water, so they should be emerging from there. The same opening that I had spotted when I was being hunted by Wolfe...

Nadine leans forward and takes my hand. Her skin is cool and dry. "I used to babysit you."

Alex mentioned that.

"Your parents liked to do date night," she says. "And in the summer, Nate and I would stay at your house while they worked. You were the cutest little kid."

Jeez.

"Your parents loved you," she adds, her voice firm. "You were their whole world."

"Thanks." I pull away. To cover the obvious, I draw my legs up and wrap my arms around them. "No one knew where I went?"

They exchange a look.

I sit up straighter. "What?"

"You have to understand, Kora," Nate says hesitantly, "this was a chaotic time. The gangs were just coming into power, and your parents were fighting them. Hard. There were no rules. Even daytime was dangerous to be out alone if you had Sterling blood."

"Okay..."

"A year prior, my brother and his wife were killed in a fire," Jeremy says. "Arson, the police suspected. But arson is notoriously difficult to prove—and even harder to convict. So whoever set that fire got away with it. It was then that we began to suspect Mason's death was connected to Wilma's."

I nod slowly. "And my... birth parents?"

They were shot in the head. That's what the article said in the library archives anyway.

"We found them when Brendon missed an appointment." Jeremy seems pained. His brows furrow, his lips tip down. "It had been more than twenty-four hours. And you were gone."

"Did they..." I clear my throat. "Did they send me away? Did they see it coming?"

"Your parents played things close to the vest. They might've done any number of things to keep you safe."

"And we will, too," Nadine adds.

I glance at her, my brows drawing together. "What do you mean?"

"It's not safe," she says softly. "You're a Sterling."

"You are, too," I point out.

She shakes her head. "Not a recognized one. It's just the way of things. I'm a Bradshaw. I have Sterling blood, but that's not good enough. This whole town has been built on the Sterling *name*."

Movement draws my attention to the edge of the driveway.

Jace bursts through the tree line first, his furious sprint dying away to a jog. A second later, Apollo follows. They're both covered in sweat, their t-shirts off and tucked into the waistbands of their shorts. They're grinning, relaxed.

I try not to ogle them. Because *damn*, their abs are glorious. It makes me want to lick the sweat from them... or get up to more exciting endeavors.

Jace's head snaps up, and he jerks to a halt.

His stitches were removed last week. The doctor said he was healing quite well and commended him on taking it easy. That drew a snort from me, because *easy* isn't exactly how he's been doing. But whatever. It's still a healing wound, the line where the stitches were, pink and warm to the touch. He's been cleared for more physically demanding exercises. Like running.

And sex.

I almost snorted at that one since a stab wound hadn't done much to slow him down. But neither I nor Jace seemed inclined to inform the doctor of that.

"You," Jace growls, coming up the porch steps and striding toward Jeremy. His brows lower, his eyes flashing with fury. "Get the fuck away from Kora."

Jeremy stands. "We came to talk, not fight."

"Fuck off," he snaps. Jace gets right in his face, practically chest to chest. "You lost your right to talk when you let her psychopath parents ship her off to Isle of Paradise."

Jeremy's gaze snaps to me. "They what?"

Apollo joins us, his gaze bouncing around between the five of us. Jace reminds me of a live bomb, ready to go off at the slightest jostle. I stand and go to him, threading my hand through his. He finally tears his scowl away from Jeremy and focuses on me.

"Go clean up. We'll talk when you're back." I rise on my toes and kiss him.

He leans into it, making it a little more than the peck I had planned. When he pulls away, he sighs. "Just don't go anywhere with them. Don't *trust* them."

I nod once, then push him toward the door.

Apollo swats my ass on his way by. My face heats, a blush I'm sure rising swiftly to my cheeks. I don't acknowledge it, or the fact that I have three boyfriends.

Some things are just... hard to explain. Especially since these people are technically family. There are boundaries, right? Lines drawn.

Nate changes the subject, telling a few stories from childhood. Nothing too heavy. We eat the breakfast sandwiches, and I sip my coffee. I find myself drawn into the way Nate weaves a tale.

Another fascinating side to him.

Jace and Apollo return with wet hair and fresh clothes. They're positively delicious in tight-fitting t-shirts and jeans, and I *really* need to stop salivating over them. There's a space on the couch beside me, plus another chair. Jace drops down beside me and pulls me into his lap, and Apollo takes my seat.

I narrow my eyes at both of them.

Conspirators, I think, about getting close to me.

Jeremy shifts. If he's uncomfortable with our new seating arrangement, he doesn't voice it. Instead, he says, "I owe you an apology, too, Jace."

Jace tenses under me. His arm is draped around me, keeping me against him, and I run my fingers up and down his forearm.

"I believed the Sinclairs when they shared their concerns about... *Kora*." Jeremy hesitates to even call me that. "I had heard of your reputation, along with your friends'. I agreed with them that they should get her out of Sterling Falls immediately, and they asked me to make it happen."

"I don't hear an apology in that," Jace responds.

I let out a groan under my breath.

"I was wrong for judging your situation with Kora," Jeremy says. "And I am sorry for it. And everything that transpired after."

Jace is silent for a moment.

Too long, maybe, because Jeremy continues, "I see how much you care about each other. I saw it that night, too."

I close my eyes and fight against the images of being dragged away from Jace in the burning clubhouse. I almost lost my mind.

It's a miracle that I didn't lose my mind on that island.

My breath hitches.

"Did you know where the Sinclairs were going to send her?" Apollo asks Jeremy.

"No," he says honestly. "As far as I knew, they just wanted to get her home."

"I was home," I whisper. "For a while. A month, I think. I wasn't..." My mouth is cotton. I barely remember the month I was home. It's a blur of tears and yelling and retreating so far into my head, I was hoping I wouldn't find my way out again. "I wasn't functioning. So I don't blame them for taking action. But—" *Breathe, Kora.* "I do blame them for leaving me there. Far longer than I should've been." *Five months.*

That kind of kills the mood. Not that it was particularly happy to begin with, but...

"I have one more question." I focus on Jeremy. My uncle. It's weird to even consider that he's *that*, but here we are. "What does it mean that I'm a Sterling? What's the expectation?"

I've been wondering this for a while now.

Jace shifts, and I sense him and Apollo's attention both sharpening, too.

Jeremy glances at his children, then back at me. "Your options are open," he eventually says. "And I think you may have to prove your identity with a DNA test, which we can arrange. But as the daughter of the eldest Sterling sibling, you could hold a spot on the city council. You'd receive your parents' inheritance. Their land, their money, their businesses. To do with what you wanted." He pauses. "In my ideal world, I'd like to see you do all those things and become the woman your parents would've wanted you to be. A strong Sterling in this town. It's your birthright."

A chill sweeps up my back.

"But with that comes danger," Nadine interjects. "Someone was willing to commit multiple murders to end the Sterling line fifteen years ago."

"Kora has been getting threatening messages," Jace says.

Jeremy narrows his eyes. "What kind of threatening messages?"

"Snakes," I say simply. "And warnings to leave town. *Again*."

Nate nods. "I have that documentation." He glances at me. "Unfortunately, it didn't lead anywhere yet. We're still on it, though."

The first time I met him, he was called to the school for Apollo's bike exploding. Which very nearly killed us. He confiscated my backpack and later returned it with a listening device.

"I would like to see that, son." Jeremy waits for Nate's nod, then focuses on us. "I'll look into it. I have some strings I can pull..."

"Thank you," Apollo says. "We appreciate your help in the matter."

Jace grunts.

The Bradshaws stand, and Jace puts me on my feet, too. I shake their hands and watch them all file down into the nondescript blue SUV. It pulls away, and I try to decide if I feel better or worse after that meeting.

"Can I trust them?" My voice is small.

Jace sighs. "I don't know."

"Until we know, let's go with no," Apollo suggests. "Trusting people has only bit us in the ass."

I chuckle and head inside. Ain't that the truth.

wolfe

"They want to follow you," Malik says, practically chasing me outside. "Why won't you just give them that?"

I shake my head. It was another long night of trying to make sense of the shambles my father left behind. I barely slept.

The Hell Hounds need a strong hand to lead them. And they've shown that they'll listen to me. The murder of my father scared them off the idea that my position could be easily ripped from me, which means it was the best thing I could've done.

But it also kills me because I watched my father die at my hands. Under my hands.

And that guilt keeps eating at me.

It lessens when I'm with Kora. When her scent is wrapped around me, or her legs, or her pussy...

I've been away from her for too long, and the guilt is going to destroy me if I stay here longer. For now, the Hell Hounds have been put to pasture. My orders were: ride, have fun, but don't do anything stupid.

Maybe I'm an idiot for thinking they won't do anything stupid. But they'll find out what happens if they disobey me.

"You can handle it," I snap at Malik, who still hovers beside me. "I don't know what you want from me."

"I want you to lead," he growls. "I'm not taking over. Not if it means fighting you. And you know that the only way they'd respect *me* is if we both got bloody, and I came out on top."

He knows as well as I do that there's no fighting me. My father created a monster in that regard. A deep, vicious monster that comes out when I'm fighting. The red haze that descends... it makes me lose control.

I almost killed Jace in front of an entire Olympus crowd because of it.

"Stop," I say quietly. "You're my second. Okay? Lead in my stead, with my blessing. Call me if there's any problems, but I'll be back tomorrow." I swing my leg over the bike, then pause. "Oh, Malik."

"What?"

"What's happening with the restaurant?"

He narrows his eyes. "Still operational, as far as I can tell."

I grunt. That restaurant fuels a lot of our business, especially since it's located downtown. The *deluxe* aspect is a convenient way to sell drugs in the city. Although it's been a little quiet since there's a reduced population in the summer months. And the Hell Hound's head was found outside our docks. The cops swarming that area has made us divert our shipments, and it's put us behind.

As much as I hate to say it, we need *something* to keep our lights on. So...

"Tourist season is beginning," I say. "Look at our funds and see if we can purchase any property in North Falls."

Malik's eyes light up. "Done and done."

I grin and fire up my bike, then slide my helmet over my head. The extra helmet I keep with me, ever hopeful that I'll have Kora on the back, is strapped down behind me. Maybe she'll take a ride with me when I get back.

My phone rings, and my smile only gets bigger when I see her name on the caller ID.

Speak of the devil.

"Hey, flower," I answer.

"Hi."

Her voice is husky, and I immediately picture her in bed. Naked. Touching herself.

"What're you wearing?" I ask.

She laughs. "Get your mind out of the gutter. We're going to the beach. Do you want to come?"

I perk up. "I do."

The last time we were in the ocean, it ended in us getting freaky. So therefore, salt water gets me hard.

Sorry, I don't make the rules.

"See you there," she says.

The line disconnects.

Fuck, I love that girl. I ignore my boner and race toward North Falls. The road I take leads me past Olympus, and I cast a glance at it. In the morning sunlight, it seems like something straight out of a myth.

I wonder if that was the point when it was built.

Probably.

The guys and Kora have been working hard to clean up Olympus after the Hell Hounds left it, and I know I need to contribute. Or else I'll walk in and it won't feel like mine. It's the work that creates the bond.

I nod to myself and promise to carve out time in the coming week. The road angles downward, and I spot the main road of North Falls in the distance. The wind whips at me, invigorating and refreshing. I pass the spot Kora and I cliff jumped.

Soon enough, I'm coasting down past the boardwalk. I spot Kora's red hair first, then Jace and Apollo's tall figures. They have their two bikes, which makes me smile. If riding with the Hell Hounds is a thrill, it's nothing compared to racing along with my best friends for nothing but the pleasure of it.

I park and hop off. "Good day for a ride," I say to them.

Kora rushes me, throwing her arms around my neck and kissing me soundly.

My heart pumps harder as I wind my arms around her and tip her back. My tongue slips into her mouth.

"Okay, okay," Apollo grumbles.

I straighten her back up, but she doesn't seem in any hurry to release me. I bury my face in her neck, inhaling her scent. Fuck, she smells good. Floral. My dick is getting hard again just having her near me.

But finally, I release her, and she steps back. Her cheeks are pink, though.

She's changed out her septum ring for one with a black stone in the center. Much fancier, and I have to wonder about the change. Before, it was just a nondescript silver ring that kind of flew under the radar.

"How are you?" I ask her, pulling her into my side again.

Her smile wobbles.

Uh-oh.

"What happened?" My gaze shoots to Jace and Apollo, who don't seem *too* distressed. Which is annoying that I've been left out of the loop again. *Stupid Hell Hounds.*

"I met Jeremy Bradshaw." She quickly explains the whole thing.

I grind my teeth together. "Maybe you don't have to take the DNA test," I say. "You can just keep being Kora Sinclair, if you want."

She's already shaking her head. "People know, Wolfe. I think the people who matter—the ones who want me gone —have known for a while."

Fuck.

She laces her fingers with mine. "Today's not about that, though. We're going to have a good day, and eat hot dogs and ice cream, and swim..."

I allow myself to let go of the tension in my shoulders. If she wants a day to pretend that everything is fine, I'm good with that. She pulls a beach bag out of the compartment under Apollo's bike's seat. Jace unloads a big blanket. We trek across the sand, making quick work of spreading the blanket and anchoring it down with the stuff they brought.

I'm actually impressed with how empty this section of the beach is. The closest people parked on the sand are at least a football field away. Maybe more than that. The point is, we have privacy.

Kora straightens from rummaging through the bag and peels her shirt off.

I'm unprepared for the fucking perfect bikini she's wearing.

It's dark red, pretty much the same color as her hair, and strappy. Like BDSM tie-you-up strappy. The whole thing is intricately connected and crisscrossed over her chest, her back, to the bottom of her ribcage. I'm not sure how her nipples are staying covered. One wrong move and they'll slip out. Which is fine in the bedroom, but in public?

She wriggles out of her jean shorts and reveals

matching bottoms—although not so fragile-looking, luckily.

It must've taken her forever to put that top on.

And I'm betting it won't take us any time at all to remove it.

She wears the black stone pendant around her neck, dangling between her breasts. It takes me a moment to realize she's matched her nose ring to the silver and black of that necklace.

She smirks at us and heads for the water. Her hips sway, her hair swishing with the movement. Her body is perfect. *Divine.* And all I want to do is sink my teeth into her skin.

Then sink something else into her...

I scramble up and lose my jeans and shirt fast. I don't give a fuck that my black boxer briefs are about to be soaked. Beside me, Apollo and Jace are shedding their clothes, too. They planned ahead with actual swim trunks, but what-fucking-ever.

"Last one in has to watch," I yell.

I sprint for the water and catch Kora around the waist. She screams as I toss her over my shoulder and bomb through the waves.

It's fucking cold—but no worse than the last time. Kora shrieks when a massive wave slams into us, soaking us from head to toe. I dig my feet into the sand and set her down, then take her hand and pull her out deeper. Past the break.

She latches on to me, her hot skin searing mine.

"This feels familiar," she whispers.

I kiss her hard, licking the seam of her lips. She parts her mouth and lets me in. My hard-on presses into her, and she moves her hips to rub against me. I take what I want from her lips, from her tongue. Her fingers slide through my hair, scratching at my scalp.

Hands wrap around her hips, guiding her back into another body.

I crack my eye open and see Apollo. His hands run up her sides to cup her breasts.

She gasps into my mouth.

She reaches out blindly, and then Jace is there, too.

Guess he doesn't care about our bet.

"I've watched enough," he says under his breath.

Well, that's true. He lasted a few months just watching us, actually. So I tear my lips from hers and direct her face toward him.

I kiss her shoulder, her neck, while Jace's tongue slips into her mouth. Her thighs tighten around my hips, and I groan. My teeth graze her shoulder. Apollo's hands are still everywhere, frantic, and my hips jack involuntarily when his knuckles graze my cock on his way to her pussy.

Not that I'm *that* opposed...

I think he might be reading my mind, because he pushes the flap of my briefs aside. The water rushes around my cock, and I fight my groan when he wraps his hand around me and guides me to Kora's slit. He's even moved aside her bikini bottoms.

He keeps his fist on me as I push into her, and my mind almost shatters.

I'm fucking his hand *and her pussy*, and I've never felt such a fucking sensation.

"Oh my god," Kora breathes, meeting my gaze. Her head falls back on Apollo's shoulder. She grinds her hips on his hand. "You two feel perfect."

"Good," Apollo growls in her ear.

I'm going to explode.

Apollo releases me on my thrust, and I suddenly slam all the way inside her.

I lose control. He holds her steady as the waves push at us, and my hips jack forward over and over. Breaking my own rules, chasing my high.

His fingers are on her clit, bringing her to the edge fast. Her breath comes in mad pants, her eyes glazed. Apollo brings her to climax at the same time I reach my own. She cries out. I come, too, stilling inside her. My heart pounds like I just ran a marathon.

She floats back down to earth slower, and she locks eyes with me. Then over her shoulder at Apollo. Back to me, although I think her words are for both of us.

"That was the hottest thing I've ever felt," she confesses. "Are you okay with that?"

Apollo and I definitely just broke some wall that had been between us, and I'm not mad about it. I nod at him, and he smiles. His relief is apparent.

"Kora," Jace says.

She breaks free of us and drifts to him. I rub her leg as she goes by. She wraps her arms around his shoulders and hooks her legs around his hips. We've drifted a little bit, the water up to our chests. He hoists her higher and leans down, biting her breast through the red bikini.

She moans. His fingers dig into her ass under the suit bottoms, and I don't miss that he slips one hand farther in to touch her asshole. Apollo moves forward and pulls the fabric down, giving us a view through the water. He thrusts his finger in and keeps working her breast, her nipple. Her hands clutch at his head.

"Apollo," Jace finally says, dropping her back down. "You want Apollo to fuck your ass, princess?"

Kora bites her lip and nods.

"Hold tight," Apollo says. He grabs her hips again, and my hand goes back to my cock. He first slides his dick through her pussy lips, slick from me. I stroke myself at the sight. He doesn't even fucking wait. He just pushes into her.

She arches her back, and her lips pop open. She takes him like a fucking rockstar.

And my dick stiffens, begging to go again. Doesn't matter that the water should be cold enough to retract my balls up. Seems like we're impervious when it comes to her.

"Beg for both of us," Jace orders.

"Please fuck me." The words are out of Kora's mouth like she couldn't say it fast enough. "Please, I want both of you. Right now."

Jace chuckles. He strokes between her legs, and I inch closer. I brush her hair aside and lean in to claim a kiss, and she gives it to me at the same time that Jace plunges into her.

She yelps into my mouth. I swallow the sound hungrily, pressing my body to the side of hers. Her hand comes down and strokes my dick, and I groan. We're all making indecent noises, gasping and moaning our pleasure, and it's just turning me on more.

This is my family. All three of them.

Her hand squeezes. Apollo and Jace are fucking her with vigor, jolting her body with every move. I slip my hand under the straps of the bikini and roll her nipple between my fingers. Her breathing is erratic. I free her nipple from the fabric and tear my lips from hers, leaning between Jace's chest and hers to suck it into my mouth. I nip it, teasing the puckered flesh, and flatten my tongue over it.

"I'm going to come," she pants. Her hand is on the back of my head, her other looped around Apollo's neck behind her.

"Wait," Jace demands.

I slow. Her hand that was on Apollo's neck goes back to my dick, and she jacks me off with quick, sure movements. Their motions slow, too, stroking her and eliciting delicious trembles from her muscles.

I kiss up her collarbone, to her throat. Her head falls to the side, and I nip her earlobe. She keeps pumping me, and my balls tighten. The familiar feeling comes on again, and I meet Jace's eyes. I give a frantic nod.

They pick up their pace. Kora groans, shifting and trying to meet both of their thrusts, but they're totally invading her. Jace plays with her clit. Her eyes flutter with every move, and her body tenses.

"Now," Jace orders. "Come for us, princess."

She does. She cries out and orgasms, and I thrust my hips into her fist. The sound alone gets me off, and I come into her hand.

Apollo and Jace follow quickly after, each stilling inside her. We're all so close. She kisses Jace. Then me. Then twists back and lets Apollo ravage her mouth.

We drift like that, as a unit. The waves rock us forward and back, and it's actually pretty fucking soothing.

A break I knew I needed but wasn't expecting.

Finally, they pull out and straighten her swimsuit. She smiles shyly, further adjusting it. We tuck our dicks away, and I splash Jace.

"First one back to the blanket wins," I call.

He shouts after me as I swim furiously for the shore.

I grin.

kora

When we grow tired of the beach—well, when we get hungry—we re-dress and head back to the bikes. I'm on Apollo's back, his hands under my thighs and my hands on his shoulders. Wolfe and Jace are on either side of us.

I'm content. Wet, tired, satiated. We played in the sand, in the waves, for what felt like hours. We needed the break, and I'm glad I didn't resist when Jace suggested it. The funeral took its toll on all of us, and then everything that's happened to us before that...

We deserved a day off.

We almost reach the bikes when Apollo tenses.

"What—"

"Fuck. *Stop*," he yells at Wolfe and Jace, a few paces ahead of us.

His warning does no good. I spot the device attached to the side of one of the bikes a split second before it goes off. The bike erupts in flames, exploding outward. I shield my face as the heat pushes into us, immediately followed by the force. Apollo stumbles back, dropping me and turning in the air. He lands on top of me and somehow manages to stop me from cracking my head on the sidewalk.

Déjà vu.

My ears are ringing. I shove at him until he rolls to the side and lets me stand. Somehow, that didn't fucking kill us. I find Wolfe and Jace lying on the boardwalk and rush to them. The front of Wolfe's t-shirt is singed, and Jace touches the back of his head, which comes away wet with blood.

But they're conscious, and okay as far as I can tell.

The bikes, on the other hand...

Apollo drags me up, then helps Jace to his feet. I tug at Wolfe's arm and steady him when he sways.

"Fuck," he curses. Loudly. His ears are probably ringing worse than mine.

"We need to get out of here," Apollo urges.

I nod, and the four of us rush away from the burning bikes.

Someone tried to kill us.

Apollo pulls us down an alley, emerging on a quieter side street, and then farther down. I catch sight of the dark-sided Bow & Arrow.

Sure enough, that's our destination. Apollo unlocks the door and holds it open for us. We bypass the empty club and go to his sister's apartment. Also empty.

We fan out, Jace and Wolfe checking the small space while Apollo locks the door and thumbs a message out on his phone. I stand awkwardly in the living room and pat down my pockets.

Jace stops in front of me. "Are you okay?"

He doesn't wait for me to respond. He runs his hands up my arms, down my back, Turning me around and checking to see if I even have a scratch on me.

Bruises, maybe, from Apollo falling into me. But otherwise—lucky.

Too lucky.

"Are *you*?" I whisper. I drag a chair out from the kitchen table and shove him down into it, then circle behind him. The back of his head isn't too bad. There's a cut there, which is seeping blood into his dark hair. I grab a towel and wet it, then return and apply pressure.

He growls.

"Shh," I mutter. "You're bleeding."

"Who the fuck is trying to kill us?" Wolfe asks.

He sits, too, and tears his shirt off. He holds it up, the front ruined. I don't know how the blast didn't singe off more—like his eyebrows. My gaze runs over him, trying to put together that he's okay, too.

"My arm hair is gone," he adds.

I choke on a laugh. "That's what you're focused on?"

He shrugs, then tilts his head. "You worried about us, flower?"

I drop the towel on Jace's shoulder and round the table. "Are you serious?"

He lifts a shoulder again, leaning back in the chair. "We're in one piece."

Ugh. I want to smack him—until I see the hint of strain in his eyes, too. I step closer, grinding my teeth together. He wants me to yell at him, because that will feel better than fear. He wants me to prove that I'm okay.

"I see through you," I whisper.

His eyebrows raise. "Oh, yeah?"

I nudge his legs wider, stepping between them. I bend forward, until my face is right in front of his. Hands on his shoulders. His hands find my hips.

"You'd like to hide your fear behind some witty banter."

"Kora," he protests.

I smile. "It's okay to be scared, Wolfe. But if you'd like to see for yourself that I'm okay..."

I step back and peel my shirt off. The bikini top, which was a confusing mess to put on, comes off easily, too. I drop both at his feet, then shimmy out of my shorts and bottoms.

All eyes are on me as I turn in a slow circle, completely naked.

And man, is it thrilling. After the adrenaline rush we just had?

Jace catches my wrist and pulls me into his lap. I squeak, but he only runs his hand up my back and fists in my hair. He tugs my head back, exposing my throat and forcing me to lean farther back. My shoulder blades touch the table, then my head, until it's supporting the upper half of my torso.

"You'd rather distract us with your gorgeous body than think about the alternative," he says. With his free hand, he traces patterns across my stomach. Not going down to where I suddenly ache for him, or higher.

"Let's talk about the alternative," he continues.

My abdomen clenches. "I'd rather not."

He leans forward and kisses my collarbone. I let my head roll to the side, eyeing Wolfe at the other side of the table, and Apollo by the door. They both are motionless, their eyes dark. Content to watch—for now.

"Option one," Jace says. "Apollo doesn't see the device. We get closer. *Boom.*"

His teeth score where he was just kissing, and I flinch.

"You'd have to say goodbye to Wolfe and me, princess."

I stare at the ceiling and refuse to let that scenario play out in my head.

"Option two. Apollo doesn't see the device. The fucker who planted it waits until we're *all* closer. *Boom*."

This time, I'm ready for the bite. But not the location, on my breast. My lips part.

"We'd all be gone, and then… perhaps their mission would be accomplished. No more Korinne Sterling. No more arrogant jackasses who take down gangs." His smirk is evident in his tone.

He's still tracing my stomach, my abdomen, but now he goes lower. Over my hip and along the outer edge of my thigh.

My legs part, and he chuckles.

"Option three."

I close my eyes.

"This wasn't about killing us." His fingers inch back up on my inner thigh. His breath is hot on my breast, and his grip tight in my hair.

"But…"

He nips me again, closer to my nipple, and the breath in my lungs sputters out on an exhale. Desire builds between my legs at this sweet torture.

"If Wolfe and I had been paying attention, we would've seen it, too," he says. "It went off when we were twenty feet away. Whoever planted it knew it wouldn't kill us—so therefore, it's a message."

"And it's why we're here," Apollo adds. "Instead of waiting for the sheriff to show up and take notes."

I swallow and force my gaze to Jace.

"Distracting yourself with sex…" He smiles. "Well, I don't think you'll ever be without a willing partner or two."

He releases my hair, and I jackknife upright. I grab his face and pull him to me. *Hard*.

Our lips slam together.

He's been driving me nuts for the last few minutes, and I don't really care that he's right. That I'm totally using sex to distract us. It's just another version of Wolfe's angle.

But Jace is right about another thing, too. The timing was off.

Something tugs at my memory, but it disappears when Jace forces his tongue into my mouth. He pushes my legs wider, and I gasp when someone kisses the inside of my knee. I moan into Jace's mouth, but I don't release his face. If anything, I hold him tighter.

His hand roams my back, and the other squeezes the thigh closest to his torso. He holds me open while his erection presses between my hip and his stomach.

I glance down and find Apollo kneeling there, his mouth ascending toward my pussy.

"Look at me, flower," Wolfe commands.

I tear my lips away from Jace and turn to stare at Wolfe. Jace's lips move roughly to my throat, sucking and nipping. I already carry marks from them all over my body, but the thrill of them marking me further sends a chill up my spine.

Wolfe locks eyes with me and rises. He pushes his pants down and climbs on the table.

My eyes widen when he crawls forward, sinking to his knees at the edge. His cock bobs in my face, and Jace nudges my back. I lean forward, opening my mouth. He thrusts his hips forward slowly and inches inside. I groan around him, working my tongue around his shaft and tip each time he draws out.

I relax my throat and take him deeper, my body vibrating. Apollo's mouth finally lands on my center, his tongue swiping over my slit and up to my clit. He nibbles and sucks, and my hips move along with the motion. I grip the back of Apollo's head and pull him closer with one hand.

My other grips Wolfe's ass, urging him to go faster.

Jace's hands are back on me, running all over my skin. He palms my breast, his thumb skating over my nipple. Between his attention, Wolfe's dick in my mouth, and Apollo, I'm going to combust.

"She likes that," Apollo groans. He thrusts two fingers inside me, curling them and rubbing my G-spot. He sucks my clit into his mouth.

I arch my back and gag on Wolfe's shaft as I come. He pinches my chin, keeping my mouth open as he chases his release.

He's not fast enough, though, because suddenly Apollo has risen and is sliding his cock into me.

Jace lets out a groan, and his fingers land on my clit. He rubs fast, already working me up again. "You're so fucking perfect."

I moan.

Wolfe growls, and his fingers tighten on my jaw. A rush of adrenaline sweeps me, and he pounds in earnest. He hits the back of my throat, then down, and I can't do anything except keep my mouth open.

"Get ready," Wolfe bites out.

He stills, and I swallow him down.

When he pulls out, I still have some of his cum on my tongue. The taste is musky and unique to him, and I don't think. I grab Apollo's neck and yank him forward. I give him an open-mouthed kiss.

He freezes, tasting what I taste.

And I wonder, for the briefest moment, if I misread him.

But then he's growling into my mouth, his tongue tangling with mine, and his hips jack harder. I cling to his shoulders, but I can't ignore that Jace is still playing with my body, too. His fingers lazily circling my clit and my nipple almost in the same speed, same pressure.

Apollo yanks out of me before he comes, giving me a look, then shoving me off Jace's lap and to my knees. I hit the floor hard, but I just part my lips for Apollo to slide inside. He's only in my mouth for a moment, as I swirl my tongue around his shaft and taste my juices on him.

He stills. His dick pulses, and cum spurts into my mouth.

I keep my mouth open when he withdraws, and I see the approval in his eye that my tongue is still coated in white.

"Kiss Wolfe, baby," Apollo says.

Wolfe straightens. His jeans are fastened again, and he comes around off the table to look down at me.

"Fuck," Wolfe mutters. He drags me up and presses his lips to mine.

Them tasting each other through me is one of the single most erotic things I've ever witnessed. Or been a part of...

I push my tongue into Wolfe's mouth, and he sucks at me. The kiss is screaming hot, sending tingles all the way down to my toes. Amplified by Apollo's and Jace's eyes on us.

Eventually, my heart stops hammering. I break away and lick my lips. But Jace pulls me back to him and turns me to face him. He guides me back down to straddle his lap. I lean into him and kiss the corner of his mouth. I drag my lips over the stubble on his jaw, down to his neck.

I want my marks on *him*. All of them, really. But I'll start with him.

His fingers tighten on my hips when I bite his neck. He tilts his head, giving me room as I suck and lick at the same spot. His fingers push into me. First two, then three. I moan and rock my hips forward. I unbutton his pants and pull them open. He lifts and helps me shove his jeans farther down, freeing his cock. It stretches tall between us. I eye it and lean my forehead on his shoulder.

I curl my fingers around it and stroke him, trying not to breathe too hard. Even though they have me in pieces.

"Wife," Jace says in my ear. "Ride me."

My pussy clenches at that thought, and I shift closer to him. The distance between our chests vanishes, and I rise. The tip of his cock runs over my clit. I shiver, tempted to do it again. It notches in my slit, just the tip inside me.

"Ride me," he says again, more of a demand. "Take me inside you, princess."

I lower myself, biting my lip. He feels like heaven in this position.

Any position, but especially this one. I settle and wriggle, enjoying the fullness. I could just stay here forever, as weird as that sounds. I don't know what it is about Jace's cock.

He touches my chin, making me look at him. "You like this?"

He knows I do. He can see it in my expression.

Until he lifts his hips, and my expression must turn hungry.

"There she is," he says, kissing me.

He ravages my mouth, this kiss hot enough to scald me. I wrap my arms around his neck, trying to get closer to him. We're already close. A million contact points.

But there's that worry again, edging through the lust. My fear is as real, and as avoidable, as Wolfe's.

His hand disappears from my hip—only to connect with a *slap* against my ass.

I jolt, wet heat flooding down between my legs. I move,

rising and lowering myself on him. I roll my hips and ride him as demanded—in a completely selfish, feral way.

He's still kissing me like it's his only source of oxygen. Our lips are glued together, our teeth and tongues clashing.

He's my air, too.

He thrusts up into me, going deeper and hitting a new spot that leaves me gasping. I climax, screaming into his mouth. He swallows my sound, then lifts me and sets me on the edge of the table.

He braces his hand beside me, his other banding around my waist, and he picks up speed. It's animalistic, and he looms over me. We're slick with sweat, our bodies pressed together. I close my eyes and hold on until he finally goes still.

"God," I finally say. "That went well."

We break apart, and my feet touch the floor again.

I smile. "Now let's tackle the little issue of someone trying to kill-slash-warn us."

THIRTY-SIX

I follow Wolfe down the road. Jace and Kora went the other way. We're circling back toward the bikes with as much subtlety as we can manage.

My sister had some of my clothes in her closet, so we were able to change. My chest feels weird, like there's some weight sitting on my ribs, pressing inward. Maybe it's a newfound, invisible awkwardness between Wolfe and me. The way he's walking a little stiffer, his mouth set in a thin line.

I still taste him. Or the memory of him. And Kora. They're intertwined on my tastebuds and in my mind, and I need to separate them.

There has only been Kora.

But now there's Kora-and-Wolfe.

And I'm finding that I don't mind.

I reach out and almost grab his arm, but I fall short. There's a line I will have to shove myself over, and I need to work up my courage. I'm not one to usually run, emotional or otherwise. But then he's disappearing around the corner, and I lose my chance.

And maybe my nerve.

I blow out a breath and follow.

The boardwalk is now amassed with people. Police cars. Yellow tape and flickering red and blue lights. The bikes are destroyed globs of metal and plastic in the center of the hellstorm. I catch up to Wolfe, and we try to fly under the radar walking past it.

No one gives us a second look.

I'm not sure what we're going to find, though.

Then Wolfe ducks under the tape.

I grit my teeth and glance around. He's making a beeline for one of the cops. I shake my head when I recognize the asshole Wolfe is heading toward. I bite back a groan and force my legs to keep moving.

"Ballen," Wolfe greets the man.

The cop is older, with thick silver hair and cold blue eyes. He's got a little pouch on his belly. Other than that, not much gives away the fact that he's trying to retire within the next few years… with a sizably bigger bank account than what the Sterling Falls Sheriff's Office would pay out in a pension.

Long story short, this guy would do anything for cash. As such, he's been under anyone and everyone's thumb. He's worse than a prostitute—and just as unreliable.

Max Ballen goes white for a second. He nods abruptly and shakes Wolfe's hand. "Congratulations are in order, my boy? For, ah, assuming the leadership position of the Hell Hounds?"

Wolfe's grip tightens on his hand, and he yanks the cop closer. "Now, where'd you hear something as ridiculous as that?"

Ballen smiles, his eyes flicking from Wolfe to me. "Well. Word gets around. If you ever need anything—"

"You know how this works," Wolfe growls.

The cop stops talking.

There are a few pressure points Max Ballen has, and Wolfe uses them. He's already got his phone out, flashing the incriminating video stored in an encrypted file. Ballen starts mumbling some excuses about whores and drug dealers and being undercover, but Wolfe just laughs.

"This is why we work so well together, Ballen," Wolfe says. "I see through your bullshit. You help me, I help you. In more ways than one. Isn't that generous? I keep your precious little secret *and* grease your palm... if you provide useful information." He lets the threat hang clear in the air.

"Why do we have to do this here?" Ballen whispers. "My colleagues..."

I roll my eyes. Pretty sure half the force knows he's dirty, because they're right there along with him.

"Who in this town could construct something like this?" Wolfe asks, gesturing to the bikes. "It was remote activated."

Ballen's eyes widen, and then he nods frantically. "Your bikes, then? Right. Well, there's a short list. I'll have to check with our tech department..."

"You do that." Wolfe tucks his phone back in his pocket and pats Ballen on the shoulder. "We'll be in touch. Say hello to your darling wife for us."

He smirks as he passes me, and I waste another second glowering at the cop before spinning and following Wolfe. Always fucking following lately.

At least we'll get some answers. Whether they're helpful or not.

We take a different path back toward Bow & Arrow, and my courage picks up again.

"Wait," I call. We're in a curving alley, hidden from view on either side.

He stops and looks back at me, pushing his hair off his forehead. "What?"

"We need to talk." My heart picks up speed.

"Okay." He faces me, his hands in his pockets. His expression is guarded. "About?"

"Us." I step closer. "And what happened."

He shifts. "You're my best friend."

"And we just crossed a few lines," I add, my voice wry.

It doesn't surprise me that he *doesn't* want to talk about it. That he might be playing at whatever happened between us as just some part of sex with Kora. And that's brilliant... but I think there's more. Another level of caring between us.

Just because I've always loved him as a brother doesn't mean feelings can't change.

"Stop me if you don't feel it," I order, stepping farther into him.

Sometimes action is just... better.

He doesn't resist when I shove him against the wall of the alley. He sucks in a breath when my eyes drop to his lips, and I feel his rapid heartbeat under my palm. He doesn't fucking move when I slide my hand up and wrap it around his throat. My fingers tighten just the slightest bit.

I lean forward and press my lips to his.

I'm kissing my best friend.

Doubt and unsurety surge in me when he doesn't react. He's a statue for a second, and I pull away. Because I'm pretty sure I just fucked up our friendship. Ruined absolutely everything. And now I'm going to have to go back and admit to Kora that I have more feelings than I can contain, and I don't know what to do with it.

But then... *Fuck,* he comes to life. He drags me back into

him by the front of my shirt and kisses me harder. I groan into his mouth as my dick wakes up, stiffening in my pants. His pulse is positively erratic, and he lets out a noise when I squeeze his throat harder.

I shove him back to the wall. Our lips clash.

It's different than kissing Kora. His lips are no less soft, but there's an edge to him. A wildness and scent and just a fucking difference, I don't know. His taste, the way he moves. Our mouths open, and his tongue slides against mine.

Our bodies press together. His arousal is clear from the evidence digging into my hip, the same as mine into his.

I nip his lower lip, then pull away. My hand drops from his throat.

Holy shit.

We're both gulping for air, and I don't want to see whatever expression is on his face. Because that kiss was pretty fucking awesome. Ruining it with the aftermath...

No thanks.

Okay, so maybe I lied when I said I didn't run from things. Because I'm running now, if only to preserve it in my head.

I lead the way back to Bow & Arrow and will my hard-on to subside. Wolfe is just behind me, his breathing still ragged. That, at least, makes me feel a little better. That he was just as caught up in it as me.

I'm cranky by the fourth building. Most of the shops are open on the first floor. Apartments on the upper levels. A rooftop. But no freaking elevators.

Jace takes my hand and kisses my knuckles, and he points. "Just one more."

I sigh. "They could've just been on the street," I complain. "You know, watching us from one of the shop windows? Couldn't it have been as small as a garage opener?"

He nods. "Yeah, but let's assume the person wanted to make sure they didn't draw attention."

Great.

We head back down. Six flights of stairs. On one of the landings, I pull Jace to a halt and loop my arms around his neck. "What do I have to give you for a piggyback ride?"

I smile my best, most alluring smile. He chuckles. "That bad, huh?"

"I'm just tired." I pout. "You guys barely let me sleep anymore."

"Poor Kora," he mocks, leaning in and pressing his lips

339

to the corner of my mouth. "All those orgasms really wear a girl out."

"Exactly!"

He picks me up and balances my ass on the railing. His fingers play with the hem of the shirt I stole from Tem's closet. "Maybe we're doing you a favor."

My breath hitches. "Oh, yeah?"

"Because what about those pesky nightmares?" His hot palms are now under my shirt, sliding up my sides. "You haven't had them in a while..."

I shiver. "That's true."

He grins, triumphant. "So there must be a correlation. And I'd rather have you exhausted from coming on our cocks than scared in a dream world where I can't reach you."

My heart thumps harder. I meet his gaze, then drag him in to kiss me. His lips graze mine.

Barely enough for anything, and he's pulling away. Well, not so much pulling away as turning around between my legs.

"Climb on, princess," he says.

I smile and wriggle forward. He grips the backs of my thighs and hoists me higher, and I lock my arms around his shoulders. I duck down and lick his ear, delighted when *he* shivers.

"Is that your secret, Jace King?" I ask in his ear. "My tongue..."

I lick his ear again, and he jolts.

He pinches my thigh. "Stop that."

I chuckle darkly. There's no way I'm going to stop. My mouth stays right by his ear as I whisper, "It's just like when you hit that spot deep inside me, and my legs tremble..."

"Fuck," he exhales. "Can we focus?"

"Sure." I adjust myself on his back. "Let's go find the lair of the person who's trying to kill us. Sounds like a good plan."

———

No such luck on the killer front. We catch a ride with Daniel, who pulls up looking horrified and intrigued by the story we told him on the phone. I'm in the back between Wolfe and Jace. Apollo claimed the front, and he sits with his arms folded over his chest. There's a new scowl that hasn't left his face since we joined back up.

I glance at Wolfe, who is back to tracing lines on my thigh. I squint at the patterns, trying to see if he's drawing letters, but it's all indistinguishable.

Daniel brings us back to our house. He grabs his laptop and follows us inside.

Jace pours us drinks, and we settle on the couches. I eye Wolfe. Then Apollo. Daniel is chatting away with them, his laptop open and fingers flying. I don't know what he's doing—I was a little distracted when they talked about it. Because I'm focused on my guys.

My senses are telling me something is up, and I tap my fingers on my thigh until Jace's hand covers it.

"You okay?" he whispers in my ear.

I nod, then turn to put my lips to his. "Do they seem off to you?"

He glances from Apollo to Wolfe, then shrugs.

I shake my head and stand, drawing all their eyes.

"You're going to hang out, right?" I ask Daniel. "We'd love to have you for dinner."

Truth is, I actually really do like Daniel. He seems like a

pretty chill dude, and my guys trust him. Which means I can sort of trust him, too. Not far enough to throw him, or whatever that saying is. Either way.

"Sure," he says easily. "Thanks, Kora."

"Cool. Now, I need to talk to both of you." I gesture at Apollo and Wolfe.

Wolfe narrows his eyes at me.

Apollo looks... *suspicious.*

I swallow my nerves and head upstairs. They'll either follow me, or I'll have to go back and drag them by their ears. *What an image.*

Sure enough, they both enter the bedroom a few seconds behind me.

I close the door and plant my hands on my hips. "Someone tell me why you're both acting weird."

Apollo opens and closes his mouth.

Wolfe rubs the back of his neck.

It hits me suddenly.

This is my fault.

I focus on the floor, the sudden stab of guilt piercing my chest. "Is this about what we did? I'm sorry. I should've asked—"

"No, baby." Apollo comes forward and takes one of my hands. "It wasn't you."

"It was us," Wolfe adds, his voice gruff.

I look back and forth between the two of them. "Huh?"

"I..." Apollo pauses. His hand tightens on mine, like he's preemptively trying to hold me with him. "We kissed."

Oh.

Oh.

See? I knew there was something there. A smile splits my face, and I have to stop myself from bouncing on my heels. And I can't tell them, *I told you so*... because I definitely didn't *tell* them anything about my new suspicions.

But there were definitely signs. The level of comfort they have around each other and me, especially when it pertains to sex. The way they look at each other sometimes. Rare glances that they might not have even noticed.

And I didn't notice either, until recently. Then the pieces added up.

"You're not upset?" Wolfe asks.

I shake my head. "No. Why would I be?" I take a breath, and it's clear they want a little more from me. Like... honesty. The full truth. I sit on the bed, scootching back and crossing my legs. And I really think about it. About them kissing. I can almost see it in front of me, and I'm not shocked by the surge of wetness between my thighs. "The thought of you kissing turns me on. If you went further—"

"No one's saying we go further," Apollo grumbles.

Wolfe nods.

I hold up my hands, frowning at them. "I'm just saying, *if* you want to go further... I want to be there."

They both stare at me.

I shrug. "It's hot. Okay? It turns me on, I'm wet just thinking about it, and if you decide you wanted to fuck or blow each other or whatever, I'd like to be... a small part of it."

"Flower," Wolfe whispers. "You couldn't be the small part of anything. You're the main attraction."

I roll my eyes.

But Apollo is nodding his agreement. "He's right. Our pleasure... it would come after yours. Or during... But not without."

"Okay," I agree.

They're inching closer to me, and I shake my head. My

body is too sore for any of their foolishness. And I have no doubt that once we get up here later, they'll all want another piece of me.

Wait.

"You two have been avoiding sleeping in the same bed with me," I accuse. "With Jace. The four of us."

Because it would've put them beside each other?

Wolfe's cheeks pinken. "Um..."

"Oh my god." I jump up and grab their hands. "We can all finally sleep in the same bed? Now that this is out in the open?"

I kiss Wolfe on the mouth, then quickly repeat with Apollo.

That might make me happier than anything else.

But then I leave them there, lest they try to get up to any funny business. If we do that, I'll never be awake enough for this dinner party.

"Let's invite Artemis," I suggest when we're back downstairs, flopping down next to Jace. "And Saint. And whoever else."

"For dinner?" Jace asks. "Do we have enough food for that?"

Apollo scoffs. "Of course."

I grin. "Well, let's call them."

Three hours later, Apollo and I are manning the food, although he's definitely the boss. He's got a green-and-red apron that says, *Eat, drink, and be merry* on it. Definitely a Christmas apron, but I don't dare point that out. I just chop what he puts in front of me and try not to ask too many questions. Jace and Wolfe are outside, pulling the front porch furniture around to the back deck. There's seating out there, but we need more.

Because Artemis and Saint turned into Artemis, Saint,

Antonio, Vittoria, Daniel, and Malik. *Malik*. I thought my eyes were going to pop out of my skull when Wolfe sheepishly asked if he could invite him.

Oh, and my guests. Nate, Nadine, and Alex.

My *cousins*. That was a weird thing to come to terms with, too. I went from a foster kid with just adoptive parents—plus a few aunts and uncles out of state—to being surrounded by fragments of a past life.

I grab the beer Daniel had set in front of me a few minutes ago and take a few big gulps. Everyone is going to be arriving soon, and the creeping anxiety has fully taken hold of me.

Apollo glances over at me. "You okay?"

"Fine." I smile tightly at him.

He comes over and hugs me. The move is surprising, but I don't hesitate to hug him back.

"How about you go take a break?" he suggests. "I'm almost done anyway."

I smile and step back, nodding slowly. "Okay."

The doorbell rings. I jump.

Daniel chuckles from his spot at the kitchen island. He's been watching us work near-silently, typing on his laptop, but now it's all tucked away. He has a drink in front of him, and his arm slung over the chair beside him. "You look like you're about to meet your executioner."

I stick my tongue out at him. Jace and Wolfe are still out back, so I head to the front and yank the door open.

Tem has a bouquet of flowers in her hands. I grin at her and draw her into a hug, letting out a little breath when she squeezes me too tight. Jace casually mentioned that he'd asked Tem to keep an eye on Saint... full time.

I'm eager to ask her about how that's going, but from her pinched expression... not well.

Saint doesn't seem like he's faring so bad. Maybe because he's a better actor, or he's the one doing all the tormenting. He gives me a one-armed hug, and I gesture for them to go in ahead of me.

"Welcome to our house."

First time I've said those words.

Tem grins. "It's beautiful. Secluded, too."

I take her hand. "How has city living been treating you?"

She pulls me to a halt in the hall and steps closer. "Listen, don't get me started. Seriously. I'm going crazy, and I don't know whether to direct my rage at Saint, Nyx, or Jace for setting this up in the first place." She takes a breath. "Let's just pretend it isn't happening for tonight, okay?"

I frown. "Yeah, sure."

"Great." She heads down the hall.

Worry tugs at me, but I put it aside. *For now.* I'll give her the night, and then we're going to have a serious conversation about her mental health.

The doorbell rings again. I should just leave the door open as a silent invitation, but I also like being able to welcome people in.

Of course, until I open it and see not just Nate and Nadine, but their father, too. I hadn't invited him because... I don't know. It didn't feel right. He's my uncle, sure, but he's also done a lot of shitty stuff. Some good stuff, too, like saving me from a fire. Then bad, like knocking me out instead of explaining who he was.

See? It's confusing. I can't tell if he's the villain or a hero. Especially since he's the last remnant of my parents' generation of Sterlings.

Why did he manage to skate under the radar of the person who was killing my family off?

My family.

When did I take ownership of them?

I'm getting a headache. It pulses behind my eyes. I ignore it in favor of a plastic smile, welcoming the three of them in. Jeremy pauses beside me, his eyes sad. He doesn't say anything, though, and he continues inside.

The sound of chatter is reaching me, and it feels a world away.

Alex arrives next, his sleek car quiet as it rolls down the drive. I step out onto the porch and close the door behind me. Tonight, the wind is the perfect temperature. The breeze curls around me, lifting my hair.

Of all of us, Alex must've inherited more of his mother's genes. I haven't seen a photo of them together, but I imagine they must be nearly identical. He doesn't bear much resemblance to Jeremy, Nate, or Nadine. But he does seem every inch the part of interim mayor in his dark suit.

"Hi," he calls, closing the car door gently. He's got a box under his arm. "I brought you something."

My eyebrows rise. "You brought something for me?"

"Those pictures." He climbs the stairs and stops in front of me. "I figured it would be hard to get you over to my house with everything going on, and I wanted you to have them."

Real pictures. Not the newspaper-approved ones, blurred by time and the grainy library archive screens.

"Do you want to look now?"

I nod, unable to speak. There's a lump in my throat that blocks my voice. I swallow a few times, then glance up at him. "I think I'm going to need you to tell me who's who."

"Oh, right." He sets the box down on the only table remaining. The chairs have been pulled around back, so we remain standing.

347

He opens the box and pulls out a handful of photographs. He hands them to me, and I stare down at the first one. I'd bet anything that it's my mother. She's in a beautiful white dress, the train extending down behind her as she poses for the camera. Her hair is blonde, curled and pinned back. The gauzy veil is draped over her shoulders.

My chest cracks open.

"Your parents' wedding day," Alex says softly. "Your mom was a beautiful woman."

I nod, and embarrassingly enough, tears flood my eyes. I blink them away furiously, trying to discretely dab my sleeve in the corners of my eyes.

He continues narrating the photographs as I flip through them. The wedding party, my father and mother at the center. They seem so happy, it almost kills me. Some shots of Nadine and Alex as children, hoisted in their parents' arms. Jeremy is easy to recognize, as is Wilma Sterling. My other uncle, Mason, who has his arm around a woman's shoulders.

She and Alex do look alike.

"Isabella," he says. "My mother."

"She was beautiful," I whisper.

He doesn't have any of me, though. I hunt through the box for any baby photos and come up empty-handed.

"Sorry, Korinne—" He freezes.

I force myself to laugh it off, even though the discomfort twists my gut into nausea. "It's okay. I prefer Kora, though."

"It just slipped," he mutters.

"Kora?" The front door opens, and Jace steps through. He freezes when he spots me with Alex. "Sterling." His tone is suddenly guarded. "How are you?"

"Well, thank you." Alex puts the lid back on the box and nudges it in my direction. "I'll leave this with you?"

"Thanks."

Jace opens the door wider, allowing him entry. "We're getting ready to eat," he says to me. "You good?"

"Yeah." I swipe under my eyes again, checking the pads of my fingers to make sure I don't have makeup running everywhere. "It's just kind of strange to see people who look like me, and who appear... happy."

"I'd bet." His hands slide around my waist, to the small of my back. "Sometimes I try to see my features in Kronos. Like if there were signs we were actually related. He could've been bullshitting the whole thing."

My heart squeezes, and I rest my cheek on his chest. I wrap my arms around his neck. "Yeah, he could've been. Or maybe he was telling the truth. I guess the good thing is that you get to decide which version you want to accept."

He grunts. "Doesn't make the truth any less true."

Right.

"Come on, princess. Let's eat, drink, and be merry. Or whatever the fuck Apollo's apron says."

I giggle and let him pull me inside.

Everyone is getting along, and my heart has never been so damn full. We're all outside on the back porch, enjoying the evening sky show. The sun is setting on the other side of the house, but we have an amazing view of the water and the clouds to the east. They're blazing oranges and purples, mixed with the darker blues of twilight.

We've been talking about everything and anything, although the conversations have all been light. Mild, in some respects. No one touches on the gangs or politics or the Sterlings. But I'm learning things about my cousins and uncle, like what they do for fun—Alex is into archery, Nadine likes to run, Nate is part of a soccer club, and Jeremy is an avid fisherman. I offer to run with Nadine, remembering the freeing runs Ben and I used to take around the Isle of Paradise.

It's the first time I've noticed Alex and Nate acting more like cousins and less like professional colleagues, too. They share jokes, and Alex has no problem teasing Nadine.

Daniel and Jeremy get talking about the best fishing equipment. Jace and Apollo both seem curious about the soccer club.

In the back of my mind, I wonder if my parents would be proud of me. If they'd be glad that I'm taking the time to get to know my other family.

And it hurts that I'm not speaking with them.

My phone has remained off, mostly. I check it sometimes, when I have the patience, but the missed calls, voicemails, and text notifications are piling up. I haven't bothered to listen to any of them before I switch off the phone again.

I'm sitting between Tem and Wolfe on the outdoor couch. Jace is on the other side of him, and Apollo occupies one of the many chairs. The Bradshaws are reclined in their own chairs, too. Saint sits in the corner, keeping pretty quiet.

Not that I blame him.

My gaze is drawn to Saint more often as the evening progresses, and when he stands to refill his drink, I hop to my feet, too. I follow him to the kitchen. He rummages for the alcohol he wants, but he pauses to eye me.

It's hard to reconcile this version of him with the man we rescued out of Kronos' chapel. I look down at my hands, and my gaze catches on the hourglass.

He has a matching one.

"Does it bother you?"

I glance up, surprised to find him staring at my wrist, too.

"The brand?"

He nods.

I sit at one of the island's stools. I run my finger over the silvery scar tissue, which is barely raised anymore. "It used to," I confess. "It used to remind me of everything bad—all the stupid decisions I made, like trusting Kronos and staying in Sterling Falls. I hated that it was a symbol of my weakness."

He doesn't respond, but his jaw tics.

"I've accepted it now," I continue. "I know it wasn't my fault that those things happened to me, and nothing I did could've prevented him from pushing that iron into my skin."

He undoes the first few buttons of his shirt, revealing the top of his brand. It's still in its healing phase, ugly and raised and red. It seems infected, actually.

I hunt down the first-aid kit. He watches me take out antiseptic and bandages, and he doesn't say anything when I motion for him to undo the rest of the buttons. His shirt parts, hanging open, and I carefully smear the antiseptic over the wound. I press a bandage there, then grab his hand and have him hold it while I find the tape.

"Thank you," he says when I'm done.

I shake my head. "Don't."

"Elora..." His Adam's apple bobs as he swallows. "Nyx once mentioned that you might want to cover it. Any tattoo you want, just... let me know."

"Are you working again?"

He closes up his shirt and shrugs. "When I have clients, I try to force myself to be there for them and put my heart into it. It helps, actually, to focus on something other than..."

"Yeah," I whisper.

There's been so much loss, but Nyx has hit us the hardest.

"Artemis won't leave me the fuck alone," he adds. "But at least she waits in the office or the front room while I'm tattooing. Sometimes she even leaves the shop entirely, and I feel like I can breathe again."

His eyes lift over my shoulder.

I turn around and see Tem in the doorway. She's frozen, her expression... devastated. She shakes her head and storms through the kitchen, pausing only long enough to drill me with a fiery gaze. "Keep him here, since Jace seems to think he won't survive a night on his own. And he's not welcome back at my condo tonight."

She snatches her bag off one of the side tables, and a second later the front door slams.

I raise my eyebrows at Saint. I have no idea why he seems to hate her. Especially when she's all he really has. But he's not looking at me. He's glowering at the hallway Tem just disappeared down.

Fun.

I leave him in the kitchen and head back outside. I tell Jace what happened in a low voice, and he sighs. His lips brush my temple, and he rises.

"Sorry, guys, but if you'll excuse me..." He takes his drink with him.

"This is my cue to leave," Alex says. He smiles at me. "Give me a call if you have any questions, Kora."

I stand, meeting him halfway in the middle of our circle of chairs. I suddenly freeze, unsure if I should hug him or shake his hand or—

He pulls me into a hug, and I relax against him.

He pats my back, then withdraws. He gives Jeremy, Nadine, and Nate all handshakes, his smile wide. "It was good to catch up with you guys."

"I think it's time for this old man to get home, too," Jeremy says. "Thank you so much for inviting us over, K."

Oh, what the hell. I hug him, too. It might be the warmth from the beers Daniel and Wolfe have been keeping fresh in my hand, but he rubs my back in the same manner that my dad does, and a lump forms in my throat again.

"I'm really glad we're getting to know you," he says in my ear.

I nod my agreement and release him.

Nate puts his hand on my shoulder. "I'm still looking into those snakes," he says. "Things have been crazy with the Hell Hounds and Titans disintegrating, so our labs have been overwhelmed. But I promise I'll let you know as soon as I hear something."

I face Nadine, and she smiles. "Thanks for having us over, K."

The nickname doesn't bother me as much as it once did. They're trying to honor me as Korinne *and* Kora, and I can respect that.

Finally, it's just Daniel, Wolfe, Apollo, and me. Jace never returned with Saint.

I stretch. "I'm heading to bed," I say. "I can't keep my eyes open anymore."

Wolfe grabs my hand and pulls me down. His lips touch mine, and I brace my hand on his shoulder. His tongue strokes the seam of my lips, and I part them for him. The kiss sends little zaps of pleasure through me.

I turn and almost run into Apollo. His hand slides around the back of my neck, into my hair, and he tilts my head back. He kisses me hard.

"See you upstairs, baby," he whispers.

My cheeks heat. "Night, Daniel," I mutter on my way by.

His laugh follows me inside.

Upstairs, I find Jace sitting on the edge of our bed. His brows are furrowed, his lips twisted. I go to him and brush his hair off his forehead. He leans into my touch. My nails scratch his scalp, and I try to soothe away whatever's haunting his thoughts.

"Tired?" he asks.

I nod. He nods, too, and unbuttons my jean shorts. He pushes them off my hips, and I step out of them. He moves on to my shirt next, my hands leaving his head temporarily for him to lift it over my head. I pull his shirt off, then slide my fingers into his hair again.

He has the softest hair.

With a groan, he rises and shucks off his jeans. He tosses the covers back, and I climb into the center of the bed. He joins me, wearing only boxers. He doesn't stop crawling until he's hovering over me.

I pull him down, huffing a bit at his weight, and wrap my legs around his hips.

He nuzzles my cheek, then down lower. "Your family probably saw the bite marks," he says between kisses.

I cringe. "I forgot to cover them!"

He chuckles. His hand sneaks between us and under my panties. He runs his finger through my wet center and pushes it into me. "Horny little creature," he growls.

I sigh, my embarrassment forgotten. "For you? Always."

He adjusts and moves my panties aside, lining his dick up. He pushes forward, inching into my pussy with painstakingly slow movements. His blue eyes burn into mine. The sheets are pooled at the bottom of the bed, the lights on. He can see everything. And he lifts away from me to look at my body, and the way his cock is sliding in and out of me so fucking slow, then collapses back down on top of me.

This feels different.

He slides his arms around my back, hugging me tightly, and I mirror him. When our lips touch, it's sweet. Like I'm something precious.

I lift my hips, silently urging him to move faster. Chasing a high I want to reach with him, but he doesn't give it to me. Not until I dig my nails into his biceps and score his lower lip with my teeth.

"Impatient," he admonishes. He rocks into me harder.

Not faster, but with more force. All the way in, nearly all the way out. My muscles clench at the emptiness before he shoves back in.

"Fuck," I groan.

His lips move to my ear. "If I wasn't already married to you, I'd steal you away and marry you for real. I'd put a ring on your finger and a baby in your belly so you could never leave me."

Butterflies erupt in my chest.

"Olympus was one big call sign to the girl who loved Hades," he continues, stroking me in a way that makes my legs tremble.

But that confession is causing more than just my legs to tremble.

"To the girl who thought he wasn't just the Devil, but a defender."

My heart skips.

"You." He pulls back and stares down at me, and for a moment he drops his guard. The one that I hadn't even realized was still in place. But all of a sudden I can see everything he's feeling. The lust and desire, sure, but the passion and fury and *love*.

Then it shifts, and the love is all I can see.

All I can focus on.

Something inside me clicks back into place. A broken thing healing.

My eyes flood, and the tears overflow. They spill down my cheeks, running down past my temples, hair, and to the pillow under my head.

"Say it," I demand.

He touches my cheek, catching a tear, and raises his finger to his lips. He licks off the salty drop, and then he kisses my cheek. He tastes more of my tears.

And I can't stop fucking crying.

"I love you," he declares. "I love you so fucking much, I don't know how to handle it. I'm terrified and awed and—"

"I love you, too." I shake my head and try to banish the liquid in my eyes. "You get under my skin like no one else. You've hurt me, you've saved me. You protect me and defend me and—"

"And I waited for you. I can't tell you how much I wanted you to come to Olympus. But when you did, I destroyed you—"

I kiss him. I give him everything I have in me. My heart, my soul. My forgiveness and acceptance and peace.

He lets out a shuddering sigh.

"Now please," I whisper. "*Please* fuck me."

He does. His hand slips between us and strokes my clit, and his movements quicken. I wrap my legs around his hips, lifting mine to meet every slam. My eyes roll back, but he kisses and nips along my jaw until he finds my lips again.

I come with his name on my lips—and he swallows that sound, too.

He follows a few seconds later, stilling inside me as his release rocks through him. He pulls out and rolls off me, taking me with him. He nestles me into his side and adjusts the sheets and blankets back over us. I undo my bra and toss it to the floor. I tangle my legs with his and allow the smallest smile.

Then sleep takes us.

wolfe

I head upstairs ahead of Apollo. Kora was excited about the fact that he kissed me, that our feelings are evolving, but I'm just not sure I believe it. I don't know *how* to believe it. Because we've been friends since we were eleven, and I've never...

I don't know. Maybe I just thought all guys are close like we are.

Or maybe I'm fucking delusional.

It's already in my head that I'm going to sleep in the guest room. Except, when I get there, the door is shut. I curse softly. Saint is there, and I doubt he'd enjoy my intrusion.

Couch, then.

I trot back downstairs and almost crash into Apollo.

"Daniel's gone," he says, his brows coming together. "What are you doing?"

"Um..." I don't have a good excuse.

He glares at me.

"Sleeping on the couch, I think," I say. "Just to make things easier."

"Easier," he repeats. "Sure, you chicken."

I stiffen. "I'm not a chicken."

He pushes me against the wall and gets in my face. I stare at him, angry and shocked and more than a little hurt... and turned on.

He looks between us and smirks. "I had a thought," he says, still inching farther into my space. "About how it would feel to fuck your ass while you were balls-deep in our girl."

I close my eyes and fight the strong pulse of desire. I'm of half a mind to go drag her out of bed right this moment.

His thumb touches my lower lip, pressing on it. I open my eyes and find him inches away, his dark eyes boring into mine. My mouth opens, and his thumb trails down my chin, back to my throat. He leans in, and his lips ghost across mine.

I shove him away before we can do something reckless. Anything is reckless at this point. My heart hammers against my ribcage, and I struggle to keep my breathing even. But one look down his body reveals his hard-on standing proud against his jeans, tenting the fabric. He palms it, adjusting himself, and lifts a shoulder.

"I'm going to bed," he says. "And you're coming with me."

"Apollo." My voice is low. "I—"

"Easy, friend." He shakes his head. "To sleep." But then he's eyeing me again, his expression different. More serious. "The time we spent with the Hell Hounds almost destroyed us. Your father keeping us separated... keeping *you* isolated, was the worst thing he could've done to us. But the four of us are back together, and we're going to be okay. All of us."

It's easier to believe it when he says it. The words don't sound so fake when they're not coming from my mouth.

He prods me up the stairs ahead of him. We enter the bedroom, where Kora and Jace are asleep. The lights are still on and everything.

I tug off my jeans and shirt and climb in beside her. I poke them until they shift over, sleepily inching and groaning. Apollo turns out the lights and climbs in behind me.

True to his word, he doesn't touch me. Kora, though, tangles her legs with mine. Her hand reaches back under the blankets and latches on to mine. We stay like that until her breathing evens back out.

It's okay, I tell myself. *Just breathe.*

Something touches my leg over the blankets, and I roll over to look at Apollo. Except, he's facing me with his legs under the covers. His eyes are shut, his mouth parted as he breathes deeply.

I squint in the darkness. We didn't close the blinds, so the moon gives a little illumination. The weight continues moving across my legs. Jace, maybe? Stretching out and trying to keep cool?

But then I *see* it. The dark slithering thing coming up the bed toward us.

I yell and grip the comforter, flipping it off us. It slides off the bed in a heap.

Apollo's eyes shoot open, his hand reaching for my wrist. Kora and Jace bolt upright, their eyes wild.

"What happened?" Jace asks.

I scramble over Apollo and dive for the light switch. I point to the comforter just as a thick black snake slithers out.

Holy shit.

Kora screams.

I'm yelling, because I fucking *hate* snakes. I put on a brave face and put the one on our door out of its misery— but it was also pretty much all the way dead, and it wasn't slithering *at me.*

Apollo hops out of bed and scoops it into his hands.

I stare at him in shock, but he just lets the beast wrap its tail around his wrist.

"What the fuck?" I yell at him. "You can't just go picking up random snakes—"

"It's a rat snake." He shrugs. "They eat... rats."

"So?" My voice is still so loud, but I can't get over the fact that he just picked it up like it was nothing.

"I grew up on a farm." He looks down at it. "Plus, pretty sure this is the same kind of snake on our door a few weeks ago, right?"

"Yeah," Kora says. She snatches my t-shirt from the floor and slides it on. "Um, I think so anyway. Not that I'm an expert."

"Well, rat snakes aren't venomous. They kill smaller prey by strangulation." He holds it up. "So this wasn't about killing us either."

Kora's hand smacks over her open mouth.

Our bedroom door crashes open.

I whirl around, ready to pounce, but pause when I realize it's only Saint.

Well, I say *only*, like he isn't wielding a knife and has a wild look in his eyes.

"Saint," Kora says gently. "It's okay. It just... um, scared us." She approaches him and puts her hand on his forearm.

He flinches, then focuses on her. His chest rises and falls harshly.

Poor guy.

"It's okay," she repeats. "Can I..." She plucks the knife from his grip.

"Why the fuck are you holding a snake?" Saint asks Apollo.

I raise my eyebrows at Apollo. Telling him a silent, *See? Told you so.*

"Do we have a bucket?" Apollo stalks out of the room with the snake.

I eye Jace, trying to figure out how we even begin to determine who put a snake in our bedroom. Or if it was purely an accident. Maybe we have a rat problem.

Different kind of rat problem.

"Someone who was here," he says quietly.

Kora gasps. "You think someone here—"

"Has been sending threatening messages to you, wife?" He pulls her close, resting his chin on top of her head. "Yeah, I think so."

"Count Artemis and I out of your suspect list," Saint says. "She'd never hurt Kora. Neither would I."

"I believe you," she says automatically. "But..."

"That leaves a few other people. Of particular *Sterling* blood," I say.

She sighs. "Great."

"We'll figure it out in the morning," Jace says. He releases her. "Let's check the rest of the house just to be safe, then we need to get to sleep."

Kora smothers her yawn, nodding her agreement. I follow Saint down the hall, and we split up to check the remaining rooms. His bedroom is the only one currently with a bed, although I suppose we should furnish the remaining two. It wasn't exactly a priority when we bought it. There's a desk in one, although that sits mostly empty, too.

I check everything where a snake or human might be hiding. In drawers, under furniture, behind doors and in closets.

I meet Saint at the top of the steps, and he shakes his head.

"I don't think I can sleep," Kora says at the foot of the stairs. Her face is so freaking pale it makes me want to go on a rampage. "Maybe I'll just make some coffee..."

"You should try to sleep, flower," I argue. "We'll just keep watch in turns."

Apollo nods. "Everything down here looks okay, the doors are all locked, the windows intact. Let's just go back upstairs and try to rest."

She hugs him, and his hands slide down her back. He leans down and picks her up by the backs of her thighs, urging her to wrap her legs around him. He carries her upstairs like that, with her face buried in his chest.

A warmth I didn't know I possessed floods my chest.

"You should sleep," Apollo says to me. He reclines on the bed with Kora still wrapped around him like an octopus, but the look he gives me warns that I shouldn't argue.

I am tired. I feel it in my bones. It's been a long few days handling the Hell Hounds—but thankfully, my phone has stayed quiet.

"Malik never showed up," Kora mumbles, already fading back to sleep. She's so fucking cute with her cheek mashed to Apollo's chest.

But then I register her words, and I grimace. "I chickened out about inviting him."

Her eyes crack open. "Wolfe."

"I know." I settle on the pillows beside them, stretching out. Part of me is still jumpy at the idea of more snakes sneaking around, but I force myself to confront it. They're not venomous, Apollo said. So... unless it wraps itself around our throats while we sleep, we're probably fine.

She slides off Apollo and lands between us. She's still in my t-shirt. Her hair is messy, just-fucked. Which makes me think Jace and her were busy while Apollo and I continued our conversation with Daniel.

I slip my hand between her legs. Her inner thighs are wet with evidence of Jace's cum. She sighs, her legs falling farther open.

"You want an orgasm, flower?" I roll on my side to face her, tracing her inner thigh. "Will it help you sleep?"

"Maybe." Her eyes close. "But there's something I'd rather see..."

I swallow and lift on an elbow. "What's that?"

"Can you show me how he kissed you?" She peeks at me through her lashes. "And then we can go to sleep."

Apollo meets my gaze. "For her?"

I sit up, then move to my knees. On Kora's other side, he mirrors me. We stare at each other for a moment, but it isn't quite right. Not a recreation anyway, and it seems like that's what she wants.

I hop out of bed and stand next to the wall. Near it anyway. "We were in an alley," I explain to her, "coming back from scoping out the bikes."

Apollo helps Kora out of bed, too, positioning her near us. Because I know what he's going to do, my blood sings under my skin. I look from her to him.

He reacts faster than he did this afternoon. He lashes out like he's a goddamn striking snake, his hand wrapping around my throat and slamming me to the wall. I growl at him, and I immediately see the devilish delight in his eyes.

His kiss is hungry. I immediately lean into it, fighting back. His teeth graze my lips, nipping them. His fingers flex

367

on my throat, pressing into my pulse points, and a light-headedness hits me. He loosens his grip and sucks my tongue into his mouth. It's like a blow job for my fucking tongue, and I'm hard in an instant.

"Touch him," Kora whispers.

My hands, which had been glued to my sides, now unfreeze. I slide my palms under his shirt, over his abs and higher. Then lower. Not below his waistband. Neither of us acknowledge our raging hard-ons. His one hand lingers on my throat, the other on my waist.

Finally, we break apart. He takes several steps back, his chest heaving.

Kora grabs my face and pulls me down. Her kiss is no less fierce. I press into her, turning and putting her against the wall. My heart skips when I slip my tongue into her mouth, because she tastes like home. Her natural flavor is sweet. Her saliva, her cunt, her skin. I'll take it all.

I motion to Apollo, and he steps toward us. Close enough for me to fist my hand in his shirt and reel him in. I direct her mouth to his. Her body is still pressed to mine as she kisses him next. I wrap my hand around her waist, grounding myself.

"I need you both," she gasps, tearing her lips away. "I just—wow. That was beautiful. Thank you for sharing it with me. But I want both of you right this second."

Apollo pushes the t-shirt up over her head. It falls to the floor, and he palms her breasts. She arches back, her mouth opening.

Mindful that Saint could come upstairs, I go and close the door.

When I turn around, he has her on the edge of the bed —and his face between her legs.

I groan and bite my knuckles, watching as she braces

back on her elbows. Her head tilts back. I go to the foot of the bed, then nudge Apollo. "Shift her this way."

We position her across the corner of the bed, so he can still have access to her cunt, with her legs over his shoulders. The bed supports her upper body, and her head is hanging slightly off the edge of the bed.

I push my boxers down, and her mouth automatically opens. "Wolfe," she moans, her eyes closing. She reaches up and grips my thighs, pulling me closer. My cock bobs in front of her upside-down face, and she cranes her neck to lick me.

I inch into her mouth, but I hold myself back until she comes. She makes the prettiest noises, her eyes screwed shut. I push farther into her mouth, and she sucks at me. Her fingers dig into my legs, urging me to move. To take her face. But I wait.

Apollo rises and shifts her legs, meeting my gaze. He shoves his pants down and frees his cock. For the first time, I allow myself to be captivated by the sight of him. No fear of rejection or being improper. Yes, I've watched him fuck our girl before, but never with the mind-altering coexisting thought that I could have him, too.

Apollo smirks. "Like what you see?"

She groans when Apollo thrusts into her, and the sound sends vibrations down my dick. I bite back my own sound, but her moans of pleasure are nearly my undoing.

"Come for her," Apollo orders.

Fuck.

Kora's nails dig into my ass, and she drags me deeper into her mouth. I give in and take my pleasure from her, until my balls tighten and my cum spurts into her throat. My knees almost give out.

I slip out of her mouth and drop to the floor, pressing an

upside-down kiss to her lips. Her body jerks with Apollo's thrusts, and I look up. I raise her, too, so she can brace against me and see how he fucks her.

"You want that," Kora whispers, turning to kiss me again. She bites my lips, not expecting an answer. It seems like too fucking much, when prior... all I wanted was her.

But as I kiss her, and reach down and palm her tit, I realize I don't want her any less. There's just more room in my heart for Apollo, too.

I pinch her nipple, and she whimpers. The bite marks on her skin, a collection from the three of us, and the sinful noises she makes... She's the best thing that ever happened to us.

Apollo reaches up and takes her other nipple between his fingers, tugging and teasing at her skin. He leans down and kisses between her breasts, then inches higher. Collarbone, throat, jaw. He kisses the seam of our connected lips, and I automatically turn my head toward him.

The three-way kiss is sloppy, wet. Our tongues tangling and exploring. I taste her and me in their mouths.

I pull back and let him kiss her fully. She cups his face and peppers softer kisses down his jaw, all while his hips flex and his ass tenses with every thrust. His abdomen is tense. The scar from his gunshot wound stands in sharp relief to his golden skin.

His body tenses, and he stills inside her. His lips part. He comes, filling her cunt.

I lick my lips as he withdraws, but I don't do anything except help Kora sit up farther. She smiles at me and stands, shaking out her dark-red hair.

"I'm going to shower," she murmurs. She strides into the bathroom and closes the door behind her, and we're left staring at each other.

"Go to sleep," Apollo says, his voice unusually gruff. "I'll be downstairs."

I watch him tug his clothes back on and then stride out the door.

And the strangest thing of all?

I suddenly don't mind being left alone.

I refuse to let Jace win.

He's ahead of me on the trail, his jog steady but fast. Faster than any pace I usually keep up. Wolfe and Apollo are behind me, horsing around.

We're only out on this trail because I was going stir crazy in the house. Sure, it's pretty. Lovely, even. But when you're forced to stay inside it for days on end with only lingering fear and desperation to keep you company...

I rearranged all the cabinets in the kitchen, to Apollo's horror. Cleaned out the fridge and color coded everything. *I color coded shit in my own fridge.* And that was only on day two. My restless energy came in waves. Sometimes I wanted sex. Sometimes I wanted to eat everything in sight. Sometimes I just wanted to talk. Fast. About nothing.

The guys were getting frustrated, too.

It's been four days since the dinner party and the snake. Four days of radio silence.

Daniel's been pretty unhelpful.

Saint returned to Tem's condo.

A security system was installed, so we would know the

minute any door or window was open—or broken. Of course, Daniel didn't help matters by muttering about even the best security systems being hackable.

That put a damper on things.

I glance over my shoulder. Wolfe has lost the amused expression, and he's gaining ground on me.

We're about a quarter mile from the house.

So, fuck it. Right?

I stretch my stride until I'm sprinting down the narrow path. My footsteps are light, and I dodge loose rocks and stones. I catch up to Jace, and I barely spare him a glance as I shoot past him.

He shouts, and I grin. The wind snatches at my hair, my clothes. My lungs burn, and my calves immediately ache. Then my thighs, my ankles, my ribs.

Don't care.

Still, Jace is on my heels. It's only by a miracle that I find another gear and outrace him.

I break through the tree line and hold my arms up in victory, slowing slightly.

Arms band around my waist. I scream when Jace lifts me over his shoulder, grasping my ass. He's still running—except we go past the house.

"What are you doing—"

I let out another scream when we go airborne.

Off the edge of the cliff.

I catch sight of dark-blue water rushing up toward us and take a deep breath. We hit the water feetfirst, and the force nearly drives the air from my lungs. After that, though, we're weightless.

He loosens his grip on me, his hands sliding up to grasp my waist. I feel him propel us to the surface, and when we break above the gentle waves, I shove away from him.

"What the fuck was that?" I snarl.

He grins. "I'm a sore loser."

"Apparently." I spin in a slow circle.

The water has warmed up over the past week, and it's not entirely unpleasant. Especially since it washes the sweat from my skin. The cliffs here aren't nearly as bad as Olympus. Maybe half the height. There's a rope ladder embedded in the rock, giving us a way up.

There's a whoop from above, and then Wolfe is flying over the edge.

He tucks his knees to his chest and hits the water with a *crash*, creating a splash that nails Jace in the face. I tread water and giggle at the expression that crosses Jace's face, then search for Wolfe.

Apollo stands on the top of the cliff, watching over us.

Something wraps around my ankle. I gasp, and then I'm dragged under the surface.

I force my eyes to open, my vision blurry. I descend against my will and kick out at nothing. My heart hammers. But then Wolfe drifts up in front of me, and he reels me in closer. His lips press to mine.

I hit his chest, and we swim back to the surface.

Jace scowls. "Not funny."

"Not funny," Apollo echoes, louder, from above.

Wolfe laughs. "Are you coming down here or what?"

"Or what," I whisper. Not that I think he won't jump, but... he doesn't seem too keen.

Apollo hesitates.

"Come on," I call. "You can do it!" I float on my back and let my fingers run up my shirt. It's stuck to my skin, and it gives me a rush as I drag it higher. My nipples are pronounced, visible through my sports bra and the t-shirt.

Apollo glances over his shoulder, then gives us his back.

Jace tenses.

Apollo disappears.

"Where'd he go?" I ask Wolfe. I almost expect him to appear midair over the edge, flying down toward us. But when he doesn't, my stomach knots.

"I don't know." He exchanges a look with Jace and heads toward the ladder.

Apollo appears back on the edge a moment later. "Get your asses up here," he yells. "We have a visitor."

Jace and I follow Wolfe up the ladder. It's marginally easier to manage with sneakers on, even if they're sopping wet. Jace is right below me, almost on top of me, and I'd like to think that he's doing it so I don't accidentally plunge to my death and not so he can stare at my ass.

We reach the top, Wolfe and Apollo both taking my hands and helping me over the lip. Jace scrambles up next.

I wipe my wet hair away from my face. "That was exhilarating. Why didn't you jump?"

Apollo shrugs and tips his head back toward the house. "I heard the car."

"He was afraid," Wolfe says in my ear, smirking.

"I was not," Apollo grits out.

"You'll just have to prove it next time..."

We go up the steps and through the sliding glass door that leads into the kitchen. At the island, perched on one of the stools, is Nadine.

She frowns when she sees the state of us, and her brows come together. "I'm sorry. I didn't mean to—"

"It's okay." I hold up my hand to stop her apologies. "If you'll just give me a moment to get changed..."

"I'm not in a rush."

I eye her dress, her makeup, the perfectly coiffed hair. It seems like she's going to—or perhaps coming from—work.

But there will be time for questions later. I hurry upstairs and change, brushing out my hair and wrangling it into a braid that hangs over my shoulder.

Jeans and a black t-shirt are fine, I reassure myself.

When I get downstairs, she has a glass of water in front of her, and her fingers tap against it with an almost nervous quality. She stands when she spots me.

"I have to talk to you." She gestures to the door. "Do you mind if we go outside?"

"Not at all."

We go back down to the cliff edge, and she creeps closer and closer, leaning forward to peer over the edge.

"I could never jump," she says. "Even if it was supposedly safe. How do you do it?"

"Well, this time I didn't really have a choice in the matter."

Nadine gasps and clutches my arm. "Did they throw you over?"

I chuckle. "No. Jace picked me up and carried me with him."

She contains her horror admirably well, swallowing delicately and tucking an invisible strand of hair behind her ear. She steps back from the ledge rather fast, though, and glances behind her. Like someone will sneak up and shove her.

"Let's walk this way," I suggest.

We amble along the path in silence. I'm not bothered too much—more curious, waiting for her to speak. She seems nervous, though, and eventually pulls me to a stop.

"I would really appreciate if you could listen to my whole story." She eyes me. "It's going to sound... bad."

She winces.

I narrow my eyes. "Sure. But maybe we should return to the house?"

Once we're back on the porch, she sits opposite me and crosses her ankles. Even now, with worry flickering across her expression, she seems outwardly composed. She fiddles with a bracelet on her wrist, then clears her throat.

"I'm the one who blew up the bikes."

My mouth drops open. "What? Why?"

Nadine has the grace to look ashamed.

I hold up my hand again before she can proceed. "Wait. No. The guys need to hear this."

I rise and practically run inside, skidding to a halt in front of Jace. He's on the couch, arms slung over the back. Clearly giving us privacy that I *don't* want. Apollo sits next to him.

"I need you guys," I breathe.

Jace hops to his feet, searching my gaze.

Apollo rises, as well. "I'll get Wolfe."

While I wait, I pour myself a glass of water. My hand shakes, and suddenly Jace is gripping the handle of the pitcher. He lifts it away and sets it down beside my glass.

I lean back into him, and he wraps his arms around my waist.

"You okay?"

"Hardly." I shake my head and push off him. I'll take my comfort later, when Nadine is gone.

Wolfe and Apollo come downstairs, and they both seem... set. Like they know something bad is coming, and they're just bracing for it. I can't blame them for that. The one-sentence confession has my heart pumping faster, my need for answers burning brighter.

How? Why?

What could she want?

And why is she telling us?

I take Jace's hand and grab my water, leading them outside. The guys fan out, surrounding Nadine. She grows visibly more nervous, her eyes flicking around.

"They won't hurt you," I assure her. "Unless you came here with ill intentions."

"She's not so stupid," Jace murmurs.

Nadine pushes her shoulders back at that, her spine straightening. "I came here to clear the air at my father's urging."

"So he knows you blew up their bikes?" I ask.

They don't react. *Much.* Apollo's jaw clenches. Wolfe leans back in his chair, a pretense of calm. And Jace just sits there. But of them all, I can't tell who's madder. Wolfe? Having grown up in a motorcycle club, bikes are their babies. Hurting them is a serious affront. Jace? He gets prickly about certain things—and his property, his *bike*, is certainly one of them. Apollo, though... Apollo seems to be doing the poorest job of hiding his anger. He looks away from me, his teeth grinding together.

"I'm sorry," she whispers.

"Were you behind the first attempt, too?" Apollo spits, finally facing Nadine. Searing her with a look that could kill. "At the university?"

She nods. "I was."

"You almost killed us," he growls. "Kora—"

"I wouldn't have done it if you were on the bike," Nadine says. "My intention wasn't to permanently injure you."

"You still haven't said *why*," I point out.

She meets my gaze. We share similarities in our eyes, the red tint to our hair—mine darker, hers blonder—and even our face shape. Put us beside each other, and we may as well have been sisters.

My gut clenches.

"It's not the only thing I've done," she says softly. "I also sent you the photo."

My mind whirls, and I suddenly lock on to the damn *photograph* she must be talking about. The mysterious envelope that appeared at our door, and the horror it contained. "The one where my throat was slit? I don't suppose you snuck that outfit into my closet, too?"

Her brows furrow. "The outfit you wore that night?"

"I—" I press my lips together.

I can feel Jace's attention on the side of my face, crawling up and down my profile. I had almost let that damn outfit go, but now everything that stood out comes back in sharp relief. The way I felt after I realized it wasn't just an outfit the guys got me.

"No," she says. "The snakes weren't me either."

"Say we believe you," Jace says, leaning forward. He braces his elbows on his knees. "Say we accept that you destroyed our property and threatened our girl."

My heart thumps harder.

This is my cousin.

Once upon a time, we would've been close.

Once upon a time, if she's to be believed, we *were* close.

She sighs and uncrosses her ankles. Recrosses them, the left over right. She smooths her hand down her thighs. Nervous energy.

Which means there's more.

"I wanted you to leave Sterling Falls." Her eyes land on mine again, pleading. "You were in danger."

"How could you have possibly known that?" My throat

hurts, like I've been yelling. When in fact, my voice just keeps getting quieter.

"Because..." She closes her eyes briefly, and her nails dig into her legs. When she opens her eyes again, there's new resolve there. Determination. "I'm the one who saved you."

"Explain," Wolfe snaps. His patience is waning.

"Nearly seventeen years ago, my mother was murdered." She stares hard at me, willing me to believe her. "Uncle Brendon didn't want it splashed across the papers. He paid off everyone to keep it quiet. The sheriff's office, the coroner, the paper itself. They wrote that she was *slain*, when in reality she was stabbed."

I gasp. The article does come back to me. The questions I had. It only said she was slain in her home, and that her daughter...

"You found her?"

Nadine nods. "Dad was at work. Nate had some after school thing, probably sports. I walked in and saw her on the kitchen floor. There was so much blood... But after Uncle Brendon, your father, paid to keep it quiet, the investigation fizzled. There were no solid leads, no evidence to tie anyone to it. The case went cold."

I can't imagine that horror as a teenager.

"About six months later, Uncle Mason and his wife were killed."

"In a fire. Right?"

She shakes her head. "You have to understand, Kora. The Sterlings are powerful. If the town found out we were being slaughtered..." She swallows. "No one wanted to believe it, and your father least of all. I don't blame him. He was grieving, first for his baby sister, and then for his brother.

"But he refused to see that he was in danger, too." Her

eyes flash. "The police were on it, investigating more than ever, but nothing could be done. Alex was sent to live with his father—"

"What?" Shock ripples through us, and I lose the teth-ered-to-earth feeling that's been getting me through Nadine's confession.

She cocks her head. "What?"

"What do you mean, Alex was sent to live with his father?" I repeat. I reach out and grab Jace's hand. I just need something to ground me right now. "I mean, he had said he was out of town for a while..."

"With his father. James Russo."

I'm so fucking lost.

Nadine sees that, and it makes *her* confused. "I'm sorry, Kora, I thought you knew this. Alex's mother, Isabella, married Uncle Mason when we were kids. I think Alex was sixteen at the time? I was twelve. You were just a toddler, of course. Alex didn't mention that?"

"He goes by Sterling." My tone is hollow. "Why does he have the seat on the city council? I thought... I thought he held the Sterling spot."

She clears her throat. "Mason never officially adopted Alex, but it was clear to everyone who knew them that he loved the kid. So when they died, Alex changed his last name. He was eighteen. No one really made much of a fuss about it."

"But—" How could the town just collectively *forget* that Alex *Sterling* isn't an actual Sterling? That his mother married into the family?

"How did you survive?" Wolfe asks her. "If someone is killing the Sterlings like you thought, why aren't you and your brother dead? Or your father, for that matter?"

She shakes her head. "We kept the name Bradshaw.

That's the only reason I can think of. But that's not..." She takes a deep breath. "I'm getting off track. After Alex's mother and stepfather died, my father, brother, and I started to put it all together. You have to understand—this seemed like coincidences at the time. Awful, horrific coincidences. My mother stabbed, and six months later, a fire claimed Uncle Mason's life? Tragic, but not connected."

"But it was," Wolfe says.

"I knew it was only a matter of time before someone came for your parents, Kora." Her eyes fill with tears. "Dad and I kept an eye on them, but then... you turned five, and I could just feel this sense of evil building around your family."

I can't even fucking speak. I just wait as she pauses to collect herself.

"I waited until your parents were asleep, and I snuck into the house. I packed you a bag, some things that I thought might bring you comfort—"

Her words are echoing around in my head, but she doesn't stop.

Even as I desperately want her to *not*.

"And I took you out of Sterling Falls." She meets my gaze with unabashed tears. "I loved you so much, I knew that whoever was killing us would come for you, too. You were always going to lead. Your father talked about it all the time. It meant you were in danger just as much as your parents."

"Where did you bring her?" Jace asks.

He's gripping my hand just as hard as I'm holding his, except I'm doing it for comfort. He's trying not to lose his shit on her.

"I used to get therapy in Emerald Cove. Geraldine Wilcox met me at a church in the center of town. She was an art therapist, and she worked in the foster system. Before I arrived, she created a new entry. A fake name for you, a fake mother who abandoned you at the church." She wipes at the tears now falling from her eyes. "Handing you over to her was the worst thing I've ever had to do. But I was right. Because two days later, your parents were dead."

I was right, she said.

She saved me and destroyed me at the same time.

"For two days, did my parents wonder what happened to me?"

She flinches.

There it is.

"For two days, my parents lived in agony that their only child was missing?" I stand. "You took me from them, and then they died not knowing if I was safe—"

"My father told them," she blurts out. "That you were safe. And they were so furious with him." Her voice cracks. "I'm sorry, Kora. But I would absolutely do it again if it meant that you would live."

"Jeremy knows the Sinclairs." Apollo flips a knife between his fingers. The sharp edge glints in the light. "Did he arrange for them to adopt her?"

"It... it took some time for the paperwork to be arranged. For them to be approved. But, yes. Dad convinced me that if we were wrong, if nothing happened to your parents, we should be able to retrieve you. And that would never have happened if you actually got lost in the system."

I'm still on my feet, but now I drop Jace's hand. I don't have words. I don't know what the fuck is real anymore. There's a part of me that can picture that night. Of a teenage Nadine putting things in a bag for me: the music box, the pendant, some clothes. A stuffed animal that was stolen from me as soon as I got to St. Theresa's. The way she must've helped me get changed out of pajamas and into the overalls, then carried me down the stairs.

The most startling part is that I can vividly remember how my room looked. Where things were placed. The pale-pink walls, the white gauzy curtain that waved in the breeze. My bed, lined with stuffed animals. A dollhouse in the corner, a pile of other toys fanned out around it.

I don't want to do this with her anymore.

I don't want to *remember* anymore.

No one says a word when I slip back into the house.

I float up the stairs. I lock myself in the bathroom and twist the knob on the bathtub. I shed my clothes and step into it as it fills with hot water. When I sit, I draw my knees up and hug them to my chest. The water rises quickly, covering my feet, then my ankles. It gets all the way up to my chest before I uncurl long enough to turn off the water.

I sink beneath the surface. My hair, still wet from my earlier ocean experience, drifts in front of my face. It tickles my skin. My lungs ache after a minute, but I force myself to stay under.

My parents had to live with so many terrible things right before they died. They knew their fifteen-year-old niece betrayed them and kidnapped me. They knew that there was a high chance that they'd either die or I wouldn't be coming back. And they knew—and had to suffer for— the fact that my future was going to be a bleak one.

I open my eyes. I'm inches below the surface. I unfurl, letting my legs stretch toward the other end. But I'm too buoyant, so I blow the air from my lungs. Bubbles surge from my lips, and only then do I settle to the bottom of the tub.

The water is hot, caressing me. Lulling me to sleep.

I'm desperate to breathe.

But not as desperate as I am to undo everything in my life. To pull the thread and take myself back to five years old. To scream when Nadine tried to pick me up, to kick and wail and beg for my parents. To wake them up, to stop her.

A shadow crosses the water, and suddenly even warmer hands are wrapping around my wrists. I take a breath before I breach the surface, sucking in water.

I come up coughing and sputtering.

"Kora," Wolfe says, his voice so fucking gentle that I'm going to die from pity. He rubs my back, then pounds on it, forcing more water up. "Don't give up."

"There's nothing to give up," I rasp. "I knew I was an orphan. I've known my birth parents are dead. But someone shot them, Wolfe." I rise on my knees and fist the front of his shirt. The water sluices off my skin, my hair. "If she could save me, why wouldn't she save them?"

He shakes his head, and I know his heart is breaking for me all over again. "Their sacrifice kept you alive, flower."

"But it won't hold off my death forever," I whisper.

And there's the awful truth. The horrible reality staring me in my face. That no matter what happened in my past, no matter what tragedies we suffered, it has done *nothing* to stop someone from trying to kill the Sterlings.

Kill me, too.

The snakes seem like a warning. The murdered Hell Hounds seem like a bigger warning, a giant red flag over our heads.

A masked man leering at me from the depths of Olympus, his voice curling in my ears. *I got to these men, with their gang and their fighting skills and their training. I'll get to you, too.*

jace

"O pen." The man jabs a cotton swab in my mouth, running it along the inside of my cheek. He retreats quickly, putting it in a tube. He repeats the process with Kora, smiling tightly at her. "They think you're a Sterling, hmm? The Sterling?"

She eyes him and snaps her lips shut as soon as he's out of range.

"That's what we're finding out," I say.

Alex Russo is a fake and a fucking hypocrite. That's his real name. Not Sterling.

But no one seems to believe us. He's got no Sterling blood in him—and my girl is the real deal. So we're doing paternity testing to make it official, if she ever decides she wants to step into those shoes. To prove that Brendon Sterling is her father, and Wesley Graves, aka Kronos, is mine.

According to our lawyer, the previous Hell Hound scum who Wolfe happily dragged to our house one day last week, there's a sizable inheritance waiting for Kora. If she can prove her identity, of course. And Kronos left behind some stuff to his heir, too. He simply said *son* in his will, and it left me wondering if his last mission was to create chaos between brothers.

If Ben was still alive.

But he's not.

"You're all set," the doctor informs us, opening the door. "We'll give you both a call when the results are in, which should just take a few days."

"Thanks," Kora mumbles.

She reaches for my hand, her fingers automatically lacing with mine, and drags me out of the room. Her hair is in a braid around her head like a crown, the ends tucked in. I admire the slender curve of her neck, her shoulder.

It's unseasonably warm today, and she's in a flowy black tank top that shows off her shoulders. The black pendant necklace sits on top of her shirt for once, visible to the world.

My gaze runs down her back, lingering on the curve of her ass in her light-washed jean shorts. They're almost too short, hugging her thighs with little frayed white strings hanging down. I can even see the bottom edge of the front pockets.

We get through the maze of corridors and emerge into the waiting room of the doctor's practice. We went somewhere small, with a team that could be paid to keep their mouths shut. Although, with his comments, I'm doubting he's going to follow through.

I'll have Wolfe and Apollo pay him a visit later. To make sure he understands the importance of privacy. The choice to reveal whether or not Kora is actually Korinne Sterling will not be ripped from her.

I replaced the bikes, and now we head across the lot to my sleek new one. It doesn't make me feel any better knowing Nadine was the one trying to scare Kora off—

seemingly by any means necessary. It makes me feel worse knowing there's someone out there who scares Nadine and her father.

A car screams into the parking lot and skids to a halt in front of us.

I jerk Kora behind me.

Nate Bradshaw leaps from the driver's seat and circles around. "You two need to get somewhere safe. Immediately."

Kora squints at him. She doesn't trust him anymore. Not after what his sister revealed. Nadine told me on her way out that only her father knew what she had done, but I'm not sure I fully believe that.

"What happened?" she asks. "How did you find us?"

"Apollo told me where you were." He runs his hand through his hair.

He's once again off duty. No badge clipped to his hip, no visible gun—although I doubt he's *not* packing heat, and I'd guess there's one in a hidden holster under his shirt and another on his ankle—and no uniform.

"Nadine just found my father." He shakes his head. "Dead."

Kora gasps.

There's a rushing noise in my ears.

"You don't understand," the sheriff says. "Dad's been a hermit for years. He avoids being out in public, he's always watching for tails, sweeping for bugs... paranoid behavior. After my mom died, something in him cracked. And then his brothers-in-law. He thought someone would be after us, too. Or him. For knowing something."

"I'm so sorry," Kora manages. She reaches out and touches his forearm. "How...?"

"I don't know," he whispers. "She was inconsolable."

I pull Kora back into me. The last time we were in danger, we were ambushed. And quite frankly, I'm not convinced *this* isn't an ambush.

"Call me when you find out," I snap. I guide her around him, hurrying to the bike. We both feel the urgency, and I don't have to tell her to hurry. She's already on the bike, helmet in place, when I slide on in front of her.

The sheriff stands beside his car and watches us rip through the parking lot. We hit the road, and we both automatically lean forward. Into the wind, into the speed. I weave between cars, trying not to think about how this city has seen so much damage in the past twenty years.

The mental scars are worse than the physical ones.

We fly past the construction zone near Descend, where crews are still working to repair the road. Past Sterling Falls University. Kora's grip on me tightens, and she lifts one hand to point toward the steps into the administration building.

Alex Russo.

We need answers.

I turn into the lot sharply, drawing his gaze. He doesn't seem surprised when I park at the foot of the steps.

Kora is off the bike faster than me, hurrying toward him. He smiles, seeming happy to see her, but I know something is wrong. Besides the obvious. It's the set of her jaw, the tense way she strides.

Her hand balls into a fist, and I chase after her.

Too late.

She punches him in the mouth.

He rocks back, his eyes wide. For a split second, I see a monster. The pain dropped his guard, but faster than we can blink, it's gone. He's back to being a smooth-talking politician.

He rubs his jaw, eyes wide. "Wow. What did I do to deserve that?"

"You're a bastard," she hisses.

I grip her arm and tow her back.

"You're going to regret messing with my family." She points at him. "I promise you that."

He just shakes his head, his brows furrowing. "I think you're confused, cousin. Maybe someone gave you bad information? I'd hate for us to go to war over a misunderstanding."

She tenses, like she's preparing to hit him again. I loop my arm around her waist and haul her against my chest, and she kicks out. She's fucking furious, a wild cat that can't be contained. But Alex just eyes us, and he laughs.

The sound cuts through me, and I'm of half a mind to release her. Just to see her take him down a few fucking pegs.

He turns and jogs up the rest of the steps, his laughter not stopping until the heavy wooden door slams shut behind him.

The fight goes out of Kora like a flame extinguishing. She finds her feet and leans on me for another second, then straightens.

I nuzzle my face into her neck, inhaling her scent. "I love you," I whisper in her ear. Just in case she forgot that she has a way of reaching into me and tangling up my insides.

She turns in my arms.

But then she catches sight of something over my shoulder. Her mouth opens.

There's a prick of pain in my neck. Burning pain spreads down into my chest, my arms. I touch my neck. The world slants, and my knees go weak.

Kora grabs me before I fall. We both go down, but she's still staring over my shoulder.

"What the fuck are you doing?" she asks.

Someone grips the back of my shirt and rips me away from her.

My reaction time is not good. I try to get to my feet, but my legs don't listen. My view shifts. The sky is bright blue, almost searingly so. Someone looms over me, and my brain takes a second to put it together. To connect the face with the name.

"Revenge," Parker says evenly. He tosses her something. "Put that on."

"Fuck off."

"The hard way, then," he says. He puts something on my chest and presses.

My eyes are already heavy. I can't control them, can't make myself do anything. Even as my chest screams, and I can't seem to take in a breath.

The burning that started in my neck seems to be taking over my whole body. I try to rebel, to get my muscles to work, but all I can do is flop weakly against the object on my chest.

"Stop," Kora cries. "You're hurting him—"

"Good," Parker says. "This is just a taste."

I lose my grip on reality and force my eyes shut.

Their voices disappear, and then rough hands are lifting me. The people gripping me don't say anything, and I rage at my vulnerability. I float away from my body as they drag me, each bump sending ricochets through my skull. I'm coated in fire, surrounded by darkness, and I've never known such pain.

This is just a taste.

I will myself to lose consciousness, but it doesn't

happen. I'm awake, paralyzed, for every fucking second. Even though I can't so much as move my eyelids.

I'm tossed in what I assume is another trunk, my body stiff and unyielding. They fold my legs and arms in. The ride is pure hell. I'm unable to protect myself when we take fast corners, and my head knocks against the side more than once.

We stop. The trunk is popped, and cool air kisses my skin. The brightness of the sun is gone. Hands drag me out, gripping under my arms, and I'm carried between two or three of them for a few minutes. Doors bang shut.

I'm dropped to the floor, and my bones rattle from the impact. No one says anything, and another door closes. I hate the helplessness that floods me. It reminds me of life with my deadbeat father. The way he liked to hear the smack of fists on flesh, and I was too weak to stop it. I was too weak to protect my mother, too poor to do anything—I couldn't escape, I couldn't rebel. I just had to live in it.

Kora.

I focus on her face, try to conjure it up in the darkness inside my head. But instead of the woman I know, I see the five-year-old version of her. She's sitting in the closet, touching the carved words on the bottom of the music box without knowing what they say.

Then she's a teenager. A girl I don't know, but my heart lurches. She's got a bruise on her arm in the shape of a handprint. The fingers etched into her biceps. She stares at me with a look that just begs me to save her.

We shift again, and she's closer to the woman she is now. No nose ring, just a haunted expression. She sits in the forest in a cheap black dress. A crumpled gold mask in her hand. Her feet are bleeding.

That's how *we* treated her. That's what I did to her, even

after I heard her name. I left her there to find her way out of the darkness.

Now I understand.

I know the spark that was burning inside her, daring her not to leave Sterling Falls. The ties that bound her to us as surely as to the city.

That fire is in me, too.

We're running parallel. I'm lost in the woods with no way out. But if Kora could manage it, then that's what I must to do, too.

To save both of us.

kora

Parker sits across from me, a cane balanced across his knees. When he first came into the room, using it to walk, he gave me the ugliest glare.

Wolfe's damage to his knee was going to end his career, he informed me. The cane might be permanent. He was pissed about it, gripping the head of it so tightly, I thought he might snap it.

I don't know where we are, although that's not surprising. He blindfolded me the moment he got me into his car. The handcuffs are still locked around my wrists at my back.

At the moment, I can't bear the thought of dislocating my thumbs to slip free.

The room we're in isn't particularly large. It is dark, though, and damp. It smells like we're underground. There are no windows. Just pipes that run through the walls and along the ceiling.

For a moment, I wonder if they've taken over the Titans' chapel. If Ben might be alive and conspiring with my narcissistic, abusive ex-boyfriend.

That would just be the icing on the cake.

I open and close my mouth for the third time, biting back the urge to ask about Jace.

If there's one thing I know, it's how Parker's mind works. He's already told me what he wants: *me*. And having me means getting rid of Jace, Wolfe, and Apollo.

But does it mean killing them?

He's always been capable of violence. I know that first-hand. But his twisted love is a form of madness... and I fear I can't predict what he would do to an enemy.

"Thirsty?" he asks.

He's asked me a series of questions over the last hour. Questions ranging from innocent, like if I'm thirsty, or hungry, or comfortable, to dangerous. Like where Wolfe and Apollo are. Am I really a Sterling. How I could do this to him.

The dangerous questions are designed to trip me up. To keep me flayed open.

Because of that, I've kept my mouth shut. And each question that's met with silence is ramping up his anger a notch or two at a time. He's a ticking bomb waiting to explode in my face, but I just... I just need a little longer.

"Do you love Jace?" he asks. "Would you be heartbroken if he died?"

His eyes light up on the last word, and bile rises in my throat.

"Hypotheticals will get us nowhere." I curse myself as soon as the words leave my mouth. It's the first time I've spoken, and my voice is hoarse. Shaky. Not at all like the confident image I thought I was projecting.

The sick glint in his eyes grows, until it's taken over his whole face. He rises from his chair and runs his finger down the side of my face. I hold still, even as he lingers on the rising bruise on my jaw.

Not the first injury he's given me.

Won't be the last either.

He presses on it, and the dull pain intensifies.

I bite the inside of my cheek to keep from reacting. Instead, I glare at him until he's had enough.

"I forgot how much your suffering wakes me up." He smiles. "And there's no need to pretend here, is there? We can have fun, you and me. No pretenses."

My stomach churns, bringing back memories of being in an apartment with him. Nowhere to go but into the wall, to the floor. He didn't always hit me. Sometimes he took what I cared most about and made me watch it burn. Photos, memorabilia, childhood stuffed animals I held near to my heart.

Parker chuckles to himself and goes out one of the doors. His cane makes a dull thump with every step. The limp isn't so pronounced in his walk. If I didn't know... I would just assume he'd strained the muscle. There's more satisfaction there, on my end, knowing that Wolfe gave him lasting trauma. I do wish the cliffs had finished the job, though.

There are two men stationed outside, their backs to me. Parker says something to them in a low voice, and they leave their post. He waits, propping the door open with his hip.

The sound of scuffling reaches us.

A moment later, an unconscious Jace is dragged inside and dropped to the floor between Parker's chair and mine.

Jace is pale. There's sweat on his brow, and his eyes move behind his closed eyelids. His hair is damp, locks stuck to his forehead. His shirt is ripped. I wonder if they patted him down and removed all the weapons. The knife he keeps in his shoe, the two firearms. His cell phone.

His chest rises and falls, so shallow it almost tricks me for a moment.

"What did you do to him?"

I don't think I'll get an answer, but Jace doesn't look unconscious. He looks sick. And it's the worry, above any fear for myself, that keeps me rooted in place.

Parker takes his seat again, but he leans back and props his feet up on Jace's chest.

Fury spikes in me, and I lunge for him. The chain my handcuffs are attached to only allow me to half rise out of the chair. I fall backward abruptly, into my seat.

Parker laughs. "Snake venom. A paralytic." He makes a show of studying his boots, grinding his heels into Jace's shoulder. "I paid a pretty penny for it, but I must say... the effects are dazzling." He lifts his gaze. "Maybe I should test it out on you, too. When you wake up, you can explain it to me. Tell me how it felt to have me between your legs again."

I fight my shudder. "I can tell you right now if you get near me with your cock, I'll cut it off."

"Oh, Kora baby, when did you develop such fire?" He shakes his head and rises. "We have some time, I think. Would you like to play a game with me?"

"No," I spit.

He returns with a pair of handcuffs, which he deftly clicks on Jace's wrists, and a capped syringe. He shows it to me, smiling lightly all the while. "I'll save this for last, I think." He tucks it in his breast pocket and circles me.

I cry out when he yanks on my handcuffs. He forces me to my feet and drags me over to one of the metal support beams. He attaches me to it, then reveals what's now in his hand.

A small plastic bag—the size of a silver dollar, if that—

rests on his palm. It's filled with white powder. There's an angel stamped on the outside of it.

He opens the bag. "Do you know what this is?"

I shake my head.

"Angel dust." He shoves me to the floor.

My ass hits the concrete first, my legs out in front of me. I couldn't break my fall with my hands, and pain zips up my spine. Angel dust. It sounds vaguely familiar, a street name...

"A hallucinogenic." Parker smiles.

All at once, I'm lightheaded.

He wouldn't do that to me.

He leans forward, his face inches from mine. "I'm going to drag you into a nightmare, Kora. And I can't wait to hear you scream."

Before I can retort, he straddles my legs. He grips my jaw, his palm covering my mouth. I glare at him and try to shake him off—to no avail.

The helplessness that whispers through me is familiar. I wish it wasn't. I wish I had never known helplessness at his hands.

But then his fingers pinch my nose, cutting off my airway.

I fight harder. My legs kick, my whole body strains. The metal handcuffs bite into my wrists, tearing my skin, but I can only focus on my lack of oxygen. And the look in his eye... he's enjoying this. He watches in fascination as I struggle, as my face probably turns red, then purple.

My chest burns with the need to breathe, and I shake my head back and forth. My eyes fill with tears.

With his free hand, he opens the bag wider, holding it open. He jostles it a little, then carefully scoops some out on the back of his fingernail.

My lungs are going to burst. White spots flash in front of my eyes. It's hard to keep my eyes open at all, and I lose focus.

And then he releases my nostrils.

I suck in a deep breath, greedy for air—and inhale the drug.

My eyes flash, and I see his fingernail just below my nose. So close that I had no choice but to take it in. I don't know why the first emotion to hit me is betrayal. Because he had never used drugs on me? Never forced me to take anything I didn't want?

That's a lie.

My whole relationship was a goddamn travesty, and I don't know *what* the younger me was thinking. The villain of my story is standing in front of me in a nice suit, with perfectly gelled hair and a smile that flashes his straight, white teeth.

He'll torture me.

My gaze slips to Jace.

Parker doesn't tear his eyes away from me, though. He's still sitting on my thighs, and I don't have anything in me to buck him off. I don't know if I could.

"Did you like my gifts?"

I refocus on the monster in front of me. His palm leaves my mouth in a clear indication that he wants an answer.

I lick my lips. My heart is pounding, and I keep waiting for the drug to kick in like a gunshot wound. Whole one second, shattered the next.

Is that what it'll be like?

"What gifts?" I ask.

He frowns. "Don't tell me you didn't put it together?" He hops up and crosses the room. To his little workbench.

I lean back against the pole, my knuckles scraping the concrete. I'm so fucking tired, my eyes close for a minute.

When he calls my name again, it's distorted. Warbled, as if I were stuck underwater. I crack my eyes open and shriek at the snake in his hands. It opens its mouth in front of me, hissing, and strikes.

Never makes contact, though.

Parker's laugh echoes around me.

"How are you feeling?" His fingers scrape against my scalp, fisting my hair. He pulls my head back, forcing me to look up at him.

My tongue doesn't work.

Actually, my tongue is gone.

My heart thumps harder, and I try to swallow. I gasp and gag, and he releases my head. I lean to the side and vomit.

"Fucking hell."

As soon as I'm done, he hits me. It doesn't really register, though, and I sag against the pole. My cheek pulses, and Parker's carefully crafted image seems to be cracking.

Something lands in my lap.

I eye the black snake. It curls between my thighs and raises its head to stare at me. Its tongue flicks out, tasting the air.

I whimper. I can't take my eyes off it, although there's some part of me that says I shouldn't be afraid.

Why?

My memories slip away, as fragile as fog.

I *am* afraid. Especially as the snake inches up along my belly, moving up my body.

"Why snakes?" I manage. "Why did you chop one's head off and leave it in my bed?"

He crouches behind me and grips my hair again,

yanking my head back. He exposes my throat and hides the snake from my sight. I try to regulate my breathing, to force myself to inhale and exhale in counts.

But the numbers are jumbling in my head.

"I so enjoy your fear."

Something pricks my neck. His teeth, the snake, I don't know.

I squeeze my eyes shut.

"Like now." His voice is far away again.

The snake is curling around my wrist, then leaving me entirely. I let out a breath when it goes, but I think it took my body with it.

"Please." The word is out before I can stop it.

Before I can remember that I know better than to beg a monster for mercy.

"Please what, Kora baby?" Parker grips my jaw, turning my face this way and that. His hands move to the button of my jeans. "I think it's time for our little experiment, don't you think? Lock you in that pretty head of yours with all your nightmares."

I fight a shudder, pulling my legs up to kick at him, to do *something*.

"Don't worry." He leans in close, his hand on my shoulder. He lets me see the monster that he only let out at home. The monster I learned to live with—*fast*. The one who carved me up and spit me out, leaving me a broken hull. "I'll make sure you stop moving with your eyes open. So you can see every filthy thing I'm going to do to you."

I try not to tremble. But I know what Parker is capable of doing to me. It's more than six months on the Isle of Paradise would be able to fix, that's for sure.

This isn't part of the angel dust.

This is real.

He shoves my jeans open wider, tracing the edge of my black panties. "I expected more," he says on a sigh. "Lace, a thong, *something*. You manage to keep the attention of three men, don't you? It isn't because of your personality, that's for sure. Too fucking stubborn."

I growl at him and throw myself forward.

My forehead connects with his mouth, which isn't the best aim I've ever had.

He falls back on his ass. "You're going to pay for that." He touches his lip. "Fuck, that hurt. You bitch."

He uncaps the syringe and holds it up to the light.

This drug he gave me makes me feel like I'm floating, wrapped in fear and darkness. It's not a good float. It's a drag-you-to-the-bottom-of-the-ocean floating. *Sinking.* Drowning.

"Parker," a voice barks from the doorway.

My ex straightens, all the psychotic joy in his eyes going blank. Suddenly, he's back to being the charming Sterling Falls DEA agent. He recaps the syringe and replaces it in his breast pocket.

He faces the person who came in, but I can't see them. Their voice is distorted, too. I ignore their low conversation and focus on Jace.

He's still on the floor, unmoving. Except his eyes. They bore into mine, and I read the pain and misery there. It just compounds on mine, turning into an avalanche of hurt.

I did this.

It's my fault that we're in this mess, that Parker kidnapped us. He's always wanted me in his possession. A broken house pet to show off to his friends. A trophy for his mantel.

My eyes close.

"What were you going to do to her before I walked in?"

the newcomer asks Parker. His voice seems, for the most part, unruffled. Uncaring, even. Yet he strides over to me and presses his fingers into my throat. My pulse hammers against his touch. Not sluggish, like if I were drugged. Not like how I imagine Jace's is crawling right now.

My eyes won't open. My body is gone—it's a wonder I can feel the stranger's touch at all. I strain to put his voice to a person in my head. I've got to know them, right? But everything is underwater and so fucking muffled.

"She's mine," Parker says. "And I was just going to show her."

The stranger sighs. "You stupid fuck."

"Excuse me?" He's still relaxed, still charming, still trying to salvage this for himself. That comes through my drug haze loud and clear.

"What is it you wanted to do to her? Drug her? Rape her?"

Each word is another nail drilling into my heart. Parker instilled fear in me, yes. Helplessness. But this is almost worse. An unbearable rage that's trapped behind steel bars. I can't do a thing about it. I'm trapped in my own skin.

"It's not rape if she's asking for it," Parker finally answers.

I laugh at that. It bounces through my brain, and maybe it makes it out into the open, too. My eyes still won't work, and I mumble, "I'd never ask for your little dick near me ever again—"

He punches me. It's not the open-handed slap he used to deliver at our apartment, hard enough to send me into a wall. This is his fist, his knuckles cracking down. I crash to the floor. My face hits the cold concrete, and I stop moving. Stop breathing.

The floor is moving in waves.

I'm back in the ocean with Wolfe, his warm body pressed to mine.

And then he's gone, and I'm still drifting.

Parker nudges me with his foot. "If I can't have you, no one will."

He kicks me in the stomach. I'm not prepared for how much it fucking hurts, even masked by the drugs. My stomach cramps, and I automatically curl up. He gets another kick in, and I lose my breath. My fingers flex helplessly.

"Enough," the other one says.

Parker goes to kick me again. His leg draws back, the rounded toe of his fucking loafers.

A *crack* splits the air.

I flinch down, but I can't feel anything. I desperately try to open my eyes, and I get a blurry view of Parker in front of me. He's holding his chest, blood oozing over his fingers.

The stranger steps toward Parker. The only part visible is the back of him.

"Here's a life lesson," he says. "If you try to take what doesn't belong to you, in *this* city, something bigger and badder will always come along and put you in your place."

He presses the muzzle of his gun to Parker's forehead and pulls the trigger. The sound shatters me again, because I just know that this is my fate.

The sudden clarity almost bowls me over.

Whoever he is... he killed my parents.

This is the Sterling family murderer, and I can't even see his face. I can't recognize his voice. I only know that he's a *he*, and he just killed Parker.

My eyes close again, and I get another impression of someone bending over me.

"What did he do to you?"

407

"Angel dust," I whisper.

He sighs. And then he's straightening, leaving. The door closes behind him, and I'm left in silence. With my fear, with my horror. With Jace paralyzed, and Parker dead.

I open my mouth to scream for help, but the only sound that comes out is a weak huff. Barely a yell at all. Instead, I force my eyes open. I force myself to watch Parker and Jace.

But there are other things in this room with us. Moving shadows, creeping monsters. Spiders that crawl across my skin. The black snake, back again. I can't control the wild scream that escapes me. My muscles heave, and I twist on the floor. Trying to fight off those invisible demons. Parker may be dead—or maybe he's another hallucination, too— but his nightmares continue.

I'm helpless to stop them.

kora

I wake up slowly. My headache is the first thing to make itself known, the pounding behind my eyes almost unbearable.

"Kora," Jace whispers.

I groan. I'm lying on my side, my cheek mashed to the concrete. My hands are numb, arms constrained behind my back. I wiggle my fingers, trying to get some feeling back into them. Strands of my hair are stuck to my face.

If someone tells me I went to Hell and back, I wouldn't be surprised.

"Kora," Jace whispers again.

It takes me a moment to figure out how to sit up without using my arms. My abdomen screams when my muscles tense, but I manage to shove myself upright. Once up, I try to conceal how badly I'm panting. Sweat pricks my brow.

Jace is on his knees, his arms stretched over his head. I follow the lines of his arms up to the handcuffs on his wrists, then farther along the chain that connects to a pipe on the ceiling.

"I'm okay." I swallow and almost flinch at the pain. "Are you?"

Jace meets my gaze, and I suck in a shallow breath. His eyes are wide, bloodshot, and it dawns on me that he was put through the specific torture of watching someone you love in danger. He's bleeding. There's blood on the corner of his lips, and a new cut on his cheekbone. I grit my teeth and do a mental inventory of the rest of my body.

My mind, I don't want to even think about. Not when the horrors press so close behind my eyes, I almost see them overlaid on top of reality.

I can move both of my legs, but they tingle. Shots of stabbing pain course up my back, into my head. Everything else is manageable. Not broken—not irreparably anyway. I shift again, and my blood runs cold.

My jeans are unbuttoned.

I try to figure out when that happened. Before or after Parker drugged me, and if he managed to get his hands... I shudder, my jaw working. Bile rises up my burning throat, and tears prick my eyes.

Don't lose it, Kora.

But I need to know.

"Jace, did—"

"No." He forces himself to his feet, grimacing as he does. He steps forward as far as he can, shaking his head. "No, he didn't go there."

I nod carefully.

Part of my nightmares included his murder, but... was that real?

Was the snake real? I long to run my hands down my neck, to make sure the only bite marks still lingering there are from my guys. No spiders crawling through my hair, threatening to go into my mouth and nose.

If I look over my shoulder, I might see Parker's body. Or I might just see an empty floor.

And I don't know which would be worse.

"How long was I out?" I ask instead.

Jace shakes his head. "I don't know. A long fucking time."

I close my eyes and breathe through my nose. My chest aches, my stomach is in agony. The more I concentrate on my stomach, my abdomen, the more it hurts.

Fuck this.

I look over my shoulder.

There he is.

His blood is in a halo around his head, which is tilted in my direction. His cane is beside him, his fingers still curled around it. His eyes are open, but so, so fucking empty. Then there's the hole in his forehead.

He's dead.

Very, very dead this time.

"You okay?" I ask Jace.

"The paralytic wore off," he tells me.

That's not a yes. But it's not a no.

I nod at him.

Footsteps outside the room pull us into silence. We both stare at the door until it swings inward, revealing Parker's partner. The one who killed him without even hesitating.

Alex Sterling.

My heart beats faster. I'm pissed that he's taken the Sterling name for himself. Because of all the things Nadine told me, the one that sticks out the most is that he's an imposter. A pretender.

Alex *Russo.*

But I didn't realize that translated into more. Like... family killer more.

"Korinne," Alex greets me. He crouches beside me and unlocks the chain around the cuffs. He grips under my arms and puts me back on my feet. "I should've realized he had an unhealthy obsession with you."

His hands linger while I find my footing. My legs are weak, and I stumble back against support beam I was just chained to. He thinks Parker has an unhealthy obsession with me?

"And you don't?" I blurt out.

He chuckles. "I don't give a shit about you." He glances at Jace, stuck in the middle of the room. "Either of you."

"I..."

Alex fixes his suit. I thought he'd have blood on him after killing Parker. But his suit is pristine. There's a shadow of a bruise on his jaw, though, from where I decked him. Was that earlier today? Yesterday?

"Here's the thing, Korinne Sterling. I had what I wanted. I *succeeded* in taking this city. Until a few short weeks ago, when Cerberus James oh-so-delicately announced who you were."

I stare at him.

"You killed my parents." I just need to know if that much is true.

He cocks his head. "I knew what I wanted from a young age. And nothing was going to stop me."

"Why?" I whisper.

"Korinne." His voice is deep, mocking. "Power is a drug. When my mother married Mason Sterling, and we moved to this beautiful, corrupt town, I saw the truth. That everyone had their heads bowed, ready and willing to kiss the Sterlings' feet if any of them asked. Because they supposedly built Sterling Falls from the ground up. Because the businesses, the charity, the *philanthropy*." Now he's absolutely mocking. "As a boy, I had nothing but a poor mother and a father who would've chased his own tail for a dollar. As a kid, I fought for everything I had. And then they divorced. My mother found Mason."

"The Sterlings loved you, didn't they?"

He leans in closer. "I'm the unloveable one, Korinne. Mason, your parents. Even Wilma, as levelheaded and unassuming as she was, tiptoed around me. So, no. If not for my mother, I would've been sent packing. And I was. After I slipped sleeping pills into Mason's and my mother's drinks, I set their house on fire."

What a fucking lunatic.

I stare at him, trying not to show the hatred simmering through me.

He had tricked us. All of us. Maybe not Jace, who always seemed to regard him with a certain level of wariness. But... I would've gone to his house to look at those photos. I would've gotten into a car with him if he asked.

He had me *fooled*.

I need to drag myself back to reality. "What about Wilma Sterling? What did she do to you?"

"She caught me testing out her husband's guns." He sneers. "It backfired on her, though. And then on your parents."

"And you're going to kill me." My gaze goes over his shoulder, to Jace.

His expression is full of pain. For me, for this whole conversation.

"You weren't in danger until yesterday, Korinne."

My attention snaps back to him. Now, *that* I find hard to believe.

He raises his hands. "I never did a thing to harm you."

"What about the snakes?"

Nadine filled in the other blanks: the photo, the exploding motorcycles. I didn't get a chance to ask Parker if he was responsible for putting the outfit in my closet. It could've been just a mistake... forgotten tags in the plethora of clothes the guys got for me. Parker didn't know I was in Sterling Falls at that point. Not until Cerberus dragged me in front of the cameras.

"Parker." He frowns at the dead man. His blood is pooling around his head. Hell's version of a halo. "He wanted you, which means he wanted the men you were fucking to die. Thus the drugs in your glassware, the snake in your bed that was meant to dissuade you from getting naked in it... or some such idiocy. He rambled, and I listened sometimes. Not enough. Our partnership was rather new. Did he like torturing you when you were together?"

I swallow at the explanation, and then the rapid question. It knocks me off guard, and I can't help but answer truthfully. "Yes."

"I'm not the bad guy here, Korinne. I didn't touch a hair on your head."

"Until now," Jace grumbles.

It's not my head. It's everything else he's ruined. My chance at happiness with my birth parents. Growing up surrounded by family.

I had family, though. The Sinclairs have been good to me—the best, even. And if none of this had happened, I wouldn't have met Jace at St. Theresa's, wouldn't have set him on a path to join the Hell Hounds and then eventually start Olympus.

Alex shrugs, keeping his focus on me. "That wasn't even me. I didn't drag you down here. In fact, I'm fairly certain I saved you from Parker continuing to attack you. That's the way we can spin this, Korinne."

I hate when he calls me that. But he said that we can spin this, which means...

"You're not going to kill us?"

His smile is brilliant. He's got the winning hand at poker, and this is his big reveal. "Because I want your support. Come out as Korinne Sterling and give me your vote. Show this town that you're wise enough to go with the man who has been here for them for years. Live your life as you see fit. As I said... I don't really give a shit. I just care about what you can give me. And right now, with rumors flying around town, you're worth more alive than dead."

"I..." It would be so easy to agree, wouldn't it? To promise to give my support, to let him continue as interim mayor. And perhaps even the official mayor one day. To lord over Sterling Falls like *he* owns it.

Alex turns me around and unlocks my handcuffs. But then he pulls a gun from the small of his back, and I can't decide what's worse—to be restrained with an unarmed madman, or free with a firearm-wielding psycho.

He tips his head, analyzing me again. "I can see that you aren't fully convinced. How about this? You can walk out this door right now. Go home, make sure your precious boyfriends are still breathing. I don't know what happened to them. Truly. If Parker didn't outright kill them..."

I go for the door without thinking. I get almost all the way there when his voice stops me again.

"Oh, Korinne? I forgot to mention... the moment you leave, I'll be putting a bullet in Jace King's brain."

He raises the gun level with Jace's head, emphasizing his point.

"I wonder who's still alive." His smile is brittle, cold. An angry slash across his face. "You know, when I was corresponding with Parker, I chose an alias. He didn't know who the fuck he was talking to until we met in person a week ago. Do you know what I chose?"

I shake my head, fighting the urge to step forward and throttle him.

"Deicide. It means *god killer*, which is rather ironic, don't you think?" He keeps fucking smiling. "I chose it because the Sterlings were like gods in this town. But as it turns out, Jace is like a god, too, isn't he? *Hades*?"

I flinch. Jace doesn't.

"The only way you can save them is if you vow to help me. You help me, I help you."

My muscles ache. My attention lingers on Jace, but he just stares back at me. So fucking stoic, his fate already sealed in his mind. A certain resignation that comes with looking death in the eye.

He doesn't think I'll choose him.

And my heart breaks all over again.

"That's quite an offer." I step away from the door and instead go over to Parker. His perfectly gelled hair is messed up. The hole in his forehead puts a damper on his looks, too. I kneel beside him and rest my hands on his chest.

His body isn't warm anymore. The blood around his head is drying at the edges, the blood on his skin already dark brown.

We've been down here too long.

Alex probably left us down here to ride out my high. He wanted a coherent girl to convince, not an incapacitated one.

Incapacitated.

I dip my fingers into Parker's suit jacket and carefully remove the syringe. It's a miracle that it's still in one piece.

And then my fingers brush across a set of slim keys. For the handcuffs?

God, I hope he wasn't bluffing about the venom. But the keys are also worth their weight in gold, so I palm them.

"What are you doing?"

I close my eyes and take a deep breath. I remember every fucking lesson Ben taught me—including the last one. To fight for your life with every ounce of yourself. When your opponent has the upper hand, it's the only leverage you'll get.

I face Alex. He's a lot closer than I expected, suspicion clear in his gaze. He doesn't trust me. I wouldn't expect him to. I hide the syringe at my side, along my wrist, and clutch the keys in my other fist.

Jace steps forward. The chains rattle, and the movement draws Alex's attention. It nearly draws mine.

Instead, I take the opportunity to attack first. I toss the key in Jace's direction and crash into Alex. He's unsteady, unprepared, and we tumble to the floor. He hits hard on his back, his head cracking into the concrete. He loses his grip on his gun, and it goes sliding across the floor. But he comes alive with a viciousness I wasn't prepared for. He shoves me off and is immediately on top of me. He throws a punch into my stomach, and my breath leaves me in a sharp exhale.

His hands wrap around my throat. "Just because it would be easier to keep you alive doesn't mean I won't finish what I started."

I gasp and choke, trying to break his hold. I thrust my hips up to dislodge him, but it's not fucking working. Panic heightens in me as I try to get him off.

He's too big. Too strong.

My lungs burn and ache, but it's my throat, too. He could crush my windpipe like this.

I flick the cap off the syringe. The plastic piece goes skittering across the concrete. I flip the syringe in my hand and raise it fast, stabbing it into his thigh. I press the end, injecting the liquid venom. My hand slips off it, and I flicker at the edge of consciousness.

He roars and yanks it out. His grip momentarily loosens on me, and I suck in a breath. It isn't enough. I've gone too long without air, without blood flow to my brain.

Something crashes into Alex, knocking him off me.

I lie there and gasp, desperate for oxygen. Once the spots in my vision fade, I spot the empty syringe by my side. It has to work. If it was just a fear tactic Parker was going to use on me, then... I don't know what will happen.

Jace and Alex are trying to best each other on the floor. Jace's movements are jerky, and they lack his usual power. Alex gets in a few quick jabs, to his side—and the tender, healing stab wound—and to Jace's face.

My heart leaps into my throat.

They grapple and twist. I can't tell who's going to come out on top, who's going to win this particular fight. Finally, I rip my gaze away and search for the gun he dropped. I force myself up and stagger around like I'm drunk, but my damn headache threatens to upend me.

I continue my search, keeping one eye on the guys.

Jace takes Alex back to the floor. They struggle. All the while, I pray the venom works quickly. I keep waiting for it to happen, for the realization of what I poisoned him with to flicker across his face.

The gun is eluding me, and I fall to my knees. Bile surges up, and I barely manage to catch myself on my hands. I throw up, my stomach rolling and aching.

I inch away from it and wipe my mouth.

My attention is dragged back to the fight.

Alex's legs go out first. He goes from scrambling at the smooth concrete floor to them just lying there. He pushes at Jace's mouth, his head, and at first, it seems like he's drunk. He keeps missing, his hands sliding off. Unable to focus, with no coordination between his mind and his body.

After a minute, his arms fall to the floor. Jace shoves himself off, stumbling back. We watch Alex fall completely slack, his eyes even going still.

I cover my mouth. His chest barely rises and falls. Then that stops, too.

Silence.

We don't move for a long moment, and my pulse thunders in my ears.

"Did I just kill him?" I ask.

"I... fuck. I don't know." Jace kneels and checks his pulse. He rocks back on his heels and looks up at me. "Either he's dead or his pulse is slow enough that I can't feel it."

I'm suddenly on my unsteady legs, trembling. The fear that I've been suppressing since Parker's hired hands put him in yet another trunk flares up again, and I rush to Jace. I drop to my knees beside him and throw my arms around his shoulders. "I thought we were going to die."

He hugs me back, dragging me onto his lap. We cling to each other, trying to get closer than humanly possible. I press my face to his chest and inhale deeply. His scent, the spiced cologne he wears, calms me down. After a few minutes, my chest loosens enough to breathe deeply.

"I thought Parker was going to rape you," he admits into my ear.

He reaches between us and rebuttons my shorts, and I

squeeze my eyes shut. I hadn't realized they were still undone...

"He was already going to die for putting such fear in your eyes. And your screams. I never want to hear anything like that ever again." His voice cracks. "Can you forgive me?"

I pull back and cup his cheek. "There's nothing to forgive."

He traces my stomach. "The way you cried out for help... I felt so fucking useless. I haven't felt like that since I was a kid."

I kiss his forehead and smooth my hands through his hair. The action is soothing. Not just to me, but to both of us. "But I'm okay. *We're* okay."

He nods his affirmation, although the doubt still lingers in his eyes. I wonder what he sees in mine.

I bite my lip. "Do you think Wolfe and Apollo are okay? If they died—"

"I don't know how long we've been down here, princess. Wolfe was with the Hell Hounds. He could still be." Jace brushes my hair behind my ear. "And Apollo was at Bow & Arrow with Artemis and Saint. I'd bet that they're both okay, and Alex was just trying to bluff."

I close my eyes. Jace seems in no hurry to get out of here. Instead, he hugs me closer. I tuck my face into his neck again.

Somehow, we got through it.

Two more bodies on my ledger, though. Two more ghosts who will haunt my dreams.

"I won't let them haunt you, princess," Jace says on an exhale. "I can promise you that."

FORTY-FOUR

I stand beside Wolfe. A dozen bikers are behind us, idling on the road. They occasionally rev their engines, and the sound vibrates in my chest. Ahead of us, the sheriff and Nadine are arguing.

Another car pulls up, and Daniel hops out of the passenger seat. My sister joins him, leaving the driver's door open. It takes Saint a minute longer to join us, unfolding his tall frame from the backseat.

It's all hands on deck—if we can get the Bradshaw siblings on the same page.

"Jim Russo," Daniel calls, jogging over to us. "His father's name."

"We don't know Alex Sterling is involved," Nate snaps.

Wolfe laughs. I glance at him, because the sound is pure crazy.

Ever since Kora and Jace went missing—witnesses say a man injected Jace with something and then restrained both Kora and Jace and put them in a car—he's been in a foul mood.

Not that I've been better.

One sleepless night of dead ends, and now we're here.

Ready to search every fucking building in this godforsaken city until we uncover them. This will *not* be like the last time, when war broke out and we couldn't find them. If we don't find them, it won't just kill me. Wolfe will be lost to his demons.

They're right there now, skating under his skin.

"We know Alex is involved," Wolfe growls. "We know *Parker fucking Warton* is alive and involved. Your witnesses identified him, remember?"

I focus on Daniel again. "What about his father's name?"

"He owns a hotel, of all things." Daniel shows me the deed on his phone, then goes and lets the sheriff scan it.

I glance behind us, at the bikers who are ready to ride or die for Wolfe. They'll tear right through the sheriff—and the entire police force—if he commands it. In the last month, Wolfe has proved himself to them. Not the way his father has. Not through fear or intimidation.

The men respect Wolfe.

Recruitment interest is even back up, almost doubling... which hasn't happened in years.

"We'll take it," Wolfe says, motioning for Daniel to send him the information. "You just give us a ten-minute head start, Brad."

The sheriff plants his hands on his hips. Unlike the last few times we've seen him, he's decked out in full uniform. His hat shades his eyes, but he seems to be contemplating us.

"Let them," Nadine urges. "We owe them that much."

Their father died yesterday. Or sometime in the night prior. His face was hacked to pieces. Someone with a real temper did that to Kora's uncle. Not to mention over thirty stab wounds in his chest and neck.

And Nadine found him.

I don't particularly like this tug of sympathy. She found her mother, too.

"He was at work yesterday," the sheriff says. "All day."

It takes me a moment to work out why he's protesting.

He doesn't want to believe it.

"You let Alex Russo in, believing he was one of you." I step closer, shaking my head in disgust. "You know he's not a Sterling, but you say nothing while he wears *your family's name*. And you can't believe that he wouldn't have paid for that in Sterling blood?"

Nathan Bradshaw's jaw tics, and he contemplates the truth in my words.

He sighs. "There's no judge in this city who will grant me a warrant. So you better find something we can nail him with."

I smile. Anticipation and adrenaline sing through me, and I jerk my head at my sister. She comes forward, touching my arm.

I lean down to speak into her ear. "Stall the sheriff, would you? I don't trust him not to be there to arrest Alex right away."

She pulls back slightly, her eyes narrowed. "What are you going to do?"

I shrug, my eyes fixing on Wolfe's back. Sometimes, the only way to get demons out is through blood. This will help him. I have to believe that.

"Okay," she agrees. She heads toward Nathan and touches his arm, much the same as she touched mine.

"Come on," Wolfe yells at me.

I jerk around, trying to ignore that Nathan didn't retract

from my sister's touch. I get back on my bike, and we rumble past the sheriff's car. Nadine lifts her hand in a silent wave, and I nod at her.

As soon as we're past, we pick up our speed. I follow Wolfe's bike as he guides us through the financial district, to the edge of the downtown area. We sail past a classy hotel and around back, down a wide alley.

Even the alley is fucking spotless. Wolfe and I hop off our bikes and run to the metal door that most likely leads to the basement. Call it a hunch, but somehow I doubt Alex Sterling—*fuck, Alex Russo*—would put Kora and Jace up in a plush hotel room. Where guests or employees might see, or housekeeping might walk in. It would be too risky.

The door is chained shut. A thick padlock hangs down from it, taunting us.

Wolfe whistles sharply at the bikers who followed us. "Bolt cutters."

"Yes, sir," a Hell Hound responds.

A moment later, he rushes up with the tool in his grip. He doesn't hesitate to cut the chains. They unwind and fall to the ground with a hissing clank.

Wolfe yanks the door open, sparing a glance for the Hell Hound. "Stay up here. Don't let anyone leave if they come out this door."

I pull my weapon and follow him into a stairwell. The door slams shut behind us.

We descend into darkness. It takes too long for my eyes to adjust, even with the flashlight that Wolfe clicks on. We check the rooms that we pass by, our footsteps quiet on the grimy concrete. My fingers flex on the handle of the gun, ready to act in a split second. Muscle memory above anything else.

We get to a chain-link fence. Beyond it is more gloom, more darkness.

Wolfe shines his light on the floor, and I eye the scratch marks that cut through the dust. It's been moved. Recently.

We lift it together and drag it back wide enough for us to slip through, ignoring the god-awful noise it makes. Nothing comes rushing out at us from the dark, so we keep going.

Movement catches my eye, and I elbow Wolfe. I point.

Wolfe illuminates the corner, and I scowl at the rat that stares back at us. It chitters angrily, its tail lashing. Fucking gross. I don't care if we're in a basement—it has to be a bad sign that the hotel has rats.

He's about to continue on when something else moves in the shadows. I grab his wrist and direct the light back.

Farther back is a black snake, coiling along the dusty floor. Its eyes are locked on the prey.

"You've got to be fucking kidding me," Wolfe growls.

The snake's head lifts, preparing to strike.

In an instant, it has its teeth in the rat. It quickly wraps its body around the creature, immobilizing it.

I turn away.

We're in the right spot.

I march forward and clear the next room. But the one after *that* is shut, where everything else has been left open. The basement seems to be an abandoned storage space. At least, in this area, blocked off as it is.

There's light emanating from under this door. Wolfe and I stop on either side of it, our weapons drawn. It seems quiet on the other side, and I pray that we're not too late.

I move to kick the door in, but it swings inward before I can touch it.

Jace looks at me, his hand on the knob. Then at my stance. "Did you even check to see if it was unlocked?"

I gape at him. "You're here. You're okay."

"That was a no," Wolfe mutters. He steps inside and peers around. He lets out a low whistle. "You've been busy."

"That asshole isn't dead." Kora steps out of the shadows, and she steps immediately into Wolfe's embrace. Her arms wind around his waist, and she fits into him perfectly. Her head tucks in the crook of his neck.

He shudders at her touch. He went to a dark fucking place, and now she's dragging him back out. As she always does so easily.

I step into the room. Alex Russo is on the floor in an expensive suit. He sure looks dead.

Then I spot Parker, who *really* seems dead. Bullet between the eyes and everything. I can't help but let relief that he's gone—and a bit of anger that we didn't get to take care of it ourselves—seep through me.

As it is, he got the ending he deserved.

"Alex isn't dead?" I go over and nudge him with my foot. He doesn't react, doesn't even blink. "Could've fooled me."

"Kora injected him with a paralytic." Jace sighs. "She made me recheck his pulse, because we thought he really was dead the first time. But it's there. Very faint. He'll probably come out of it in the next few hours."

"Great. We're taking him with us, then?" I go back to Kora and press a kiss to the top of her head. Wolfe still hasn't released her, which is fine. I run my hand down her back, then up. I cup the back of her neck, and she shivers.

But when I step back, she reaches out and snags my hand. She squeezes twice, and I smile faintly.

"Yes," Jace says. "We're not done with him."

"We need to move," Wolfe says. "The sheriff..."

"He's on his way," I finish. "Tem's buying us a little time, but it probably won't be enough if we linger."

Wolfe and I go to Alex. He gets his legs, and I heave him up by his wrists. I don't care if his shoulders get dislocated in the process. We manhandle him out the door, Kora and Jace trailing us. There will be time to make sure they're really okay later.

Right now, we have a man to torture.

wolfe

I stare up at the man who calls himself a Sterling. In the last hour, he's got his feeling back in his face. He blinks, he moves his eyes around. His fingers twitch, like he's testing his limbs. But his arms and legs remain slack, even when I dig the tip of my knife into his skin.

You can't beat a pain reaction.

Well, unless you're paralyzed, I suppose.

He's back to breathing normally, too.

I glance at Jace, who lingers in the shadows. He was injected with the same venom. Not as much, because he says he was able to keep breathing. He went still with his eyes closed, too.

Kora sits on the floor at Jace's feet, resting her head on his leg.

Apollo is beside me, sharpening his knife. He alternates between rasping it against the whetstone—an old method, if you ask me—and flipping it across his knuckles.

I watch him for a moment. He's the one who had the idea to string our captive man up in Olympus. Right here in the center of the fight room.

We laid out a tarp beneath Alex's body. His arms and legs are stretched out with rope that crisscrosses the room. He's off the ground, supported by only another few ropes around his thighs that act as a harness of sorts.

When we cut those away, the true agony will begin. All his weight pulling at his wrists, his elbows, his shoulders.

Something will give out first.

Eventually, he's able to talk. He licks his lips and asks why he's here. What we plan on doing with him. Endless, *mindless* questions.

I glare at him until he falls silent again.

A hand slides into mine. Warm, small, soft.

I look down at Kora, who now curls into *me*. She wraps her arms around my one arm, hugging it into her, and rests her forehead against my biceps. Hiding her face from me.

"What is it?" I whisper into her hair.

She sighs. Her breath hits my bare arm. She has injuries that she hasn't yet unveiled to us, but I don't ask. If she's not complaining, if she's still breathing and moving and talking, then it can wait until we finish this.

"He killed my parents."

My gut swoops.

I figured as much, but the confirmation fucking stings.

"What do you want to do?"

She lifts her head and meets my gaze. She's not wearing any mask, and I openly see her misery. I can't imagine the horrors she faced with Parker *and* Alex. I want to know them, though. I want her to tell me every second, so I can take the pain and let it live in my chest instead of hers.

If only it worked like that.

"I want his pain," she says softly.

My lips curl into a smile of their own accord.

The beast that usually sleeps inside me, the one that,

when awakened, shades my vision in red, cracks an eye open. It stretches and slips through me, as easily as a cat extending its claws.

Kora curls her fingers over the handle of my knife, over my fingers, and I lift it between us.

"Do you want him to survive it?" My voice doesn't sound like my own. "For now."

She inclines her chin and takes the knife from me. I go with her, practically her shadow. I'm electrified, turned on, pissed off. I step up behind her, one hand pressing to her abdomen. She hisses out pain, but I don't ease my grip. If she wants to hurt him, the pain needs to come from her.

I slide my other hand down her arm, my fingertips light on her wrist, and hold the blade over her fist. Not doing it for her. But guiding.

Apollo and Jace watch. I lean down and lick the shell of her ear.

"You don't have to do this," Alex pleads. He struggles harder, his chest shining with sweat.

Our first cut severs the rope-harness that hold most of his weight. He drops a few inches, shrieking at the sudden pull on his arms. His artfully crafted mask cracks. "Please don't. Korinne. We have so much—"

I think it's the *Korinne* that breaks her.

We step forward, in sync, and slash across his stomach. I show her exactly where to dig the knife in, where to ease it out. He screams at first, watching the blood pour down his body. Watching my blade molest him. Sliding in and out without his permission.

It's fitting justice for everything that's happened to Kora.

Especially here, in this very room.

But then he stops screaming. He falls silent entirely and

just watches us with a dead look in his gaze. We don't step back until his abdomen is split open. Until his intestines threaten to fall free of his body and unravel on the floor.

Kora's breathing is hard, her back pressing into my chest with every heave.

"He doesn't care," Apollo says suddenly, breaking the silence. "And this isn't making her feel better."

I turn Kora in my arms, touching one blood-covered finger to her chin.

Apollo is right.

Her eyes are filled with tears, while Alex's are curiously blank.

Fuck.

Fuck.

I hate that I did that. I press her head into my chest and take the knife from her fingers. She lets it go easily, her grip slick.

I keep her against me, blocking her view, and stab him in the fucking heart. The blade cracks in its handle as I force it through his breast bone. His eyes widen, but I don't give a shit. I hit my mark.

And when I tear it out, an impossible amount of blood flows down his chest. Worse than from his stomach. It drips to the floor, puddling.

The life goes out in his eyes. Extinguishes.

I pull Kora back slightly and shake her shoulders. "He's gone. I killed him. Not you. Okay?"

Those beautiful tears of hers drip down her eyes, and her gaze burns into me. For a second, I can't read her. I don't know what she's thinking. It shatters me inside.

But then I realize it isn't me who shatters.

It's the beast that just wreaked havoc. The madness

that's lived under my skin dissipates like smoke, leaving me...

Free.

I can't explain it. I don't want to explain it.

Kora seems to notice, though, because she reaches out and grips my hand. She squeezes it again, as if to reassure both of us that we're still here. "Can we go home?"

"Yeah, flower." I kiss her forehead. "Let's get the fuck out of here."

Apollo and Jace grunt their affirmation.

Finally together. And finally safe.

kora

We leave Alex behind. I sit beside Apollo in the backseat of the car and lean my head on his shoulder. Now that the adrenaline is fading, my body aches. We get back to the house in record time, and Apollo helps me out of the car. We go straight upstairs, and the guys circle around me. Jace sits on the edge of the bed, his blue eyes locked on my face.

Apollo and Wolfe carefully peel my shirt off. I glance down at the patchwork bruises across my stomach. They're mostly dark purple and blue, fading to red at the edges. I didn't show them at Olympus. Apollo brought in cool bottles of water and granola bars, which Jace and I ate way too fast.

I threw it up in the bathroom immediately after, but I didn't have the heart to tell them.

But now they're staring at the bruises, and my stomach somersaults again.

"Parker kicked her." Jace's voice is hollow.

I shake my head at his tone. The way he's taking blame with three simple words. "It's not your fault."

It's mine.

"Baby." Apollo directs my attention back to him. "This is Parker's fault. Alex's fault. Not yours, not Jace's."

I nod carefully. Wolfe's hands are hovering over me, moving along my limbs as he catalogs every bruise, every scrape. He touches my cheekbone, and I hiss. I remember Parker hitting me, but... I thought I was hallucinating.

It suddenly occurs to me that I don't know which parts of what I experienced are real.

I pull free from Wolfe and Apollo and stop just in front of Jace. "My reality is warped."

His brows draw together.

"Did Parker put a snake on me?"

He hesitates.

I reach forward and brush my finger over his brow, trying to smooth away his scowl. "Please, Jace. I need to know."

"He did."

"Did it bite me?"

He shakes his head slowly. "Not that I could see."

I blow out a breath. I have evidence of the hit. The kick. And the stupid drug in my bloodstream...

"Spiders," I mutter, scratching at my arm.

"No spiders," Jace confirms. He catches my hand.

"Why are you asking what happened to you, flower?"

I turn back to Wolfe. He's rigid; his expression is terrifying. I'm glad Parker is dead—because I don't think I could handle more torture.

"He forced her to take angel dust." Jace slides his hands along my hips. Just at the fringe of pain. He pulls me back a step and nuzzles my neck, placing little kisses along my spine. "And took advantage of putting her in a nightmare."

I shiver. For once, I don't mind that he's talking about

me like I'm not here. I'd rather not associate his words with *me*.

Wolfe's hands open and close in fists, but Apollo puts his hand on his shoulder. His agitated movements stop, and he seems to remember that Parker met an ugly end. Even if it was a little too quick.

"I want you," Jace admits into my hair. "But I don't want to hurt you."

"Pain is grounding." I take his hand, sliding it across my stomach. "I want you. All of you. For-fucking-ever."

That draws a smile to their lips.

They seem to come to a silent agreement, and Jace rises. He drags my shorts and panties down, holding my hips while I step free. He undoes my bra. I drag it off my arms, tossing it to the floor. There's blood staining my skin, old sweat from the drugs and coming down from the high.

He kisses my uninjured cheek. I turn and catch his lips with my own, looping my arms around his neck and keeping him close.

He picks me up easily, walking us back until I'm pressed to the wall. He only releases my thigh long enough to shove his pants down and kick them off, and then his grip is back. Sure and steady.

"If you died, I'd die right along with you," he confesses.

The tip of his cock runs up my center, eliciting a shiver from me. I'm wet for him. I want him so fucking bad, because this feels right. It's assurance that we're okay. Our bodies meeting.

Wolfe and Apollo have backed off. They watch from across the room, their eyes dark with lust.

Jace notches his cock at my slit. Hovering there. My gaze goes back to his face. His ice-blue eyes, which I used to think were so cold, burn hotter than I've ever seen.

"Don't look away," he whispers.

I don't. Not when he pushes into me, filling me so slowly, I groan at the pleasure of it. Not when he moves, his hips thrusting forward. I lock my ankles around his back and let him fuck me as slow as he wants.

It's not so much fucking as lovemaking.

We've been here before.

I trace his jaw. The trimmed beard, his full lips. My memories flicker, showing me a ten-year-old-boy who sat at the foot of my bed to keep the nightmares away. To the adult version of him doing the same fucking thing.

The signs were there.

He was trying to tell me all along.

And I missed it.

My eyes fill with tears. He leans in and kisses the corner of my eye. His tongue flicks out, tasting the tears that do spill out, but then he's pulling back to look me in the face. One hand slips up my sore side, his thumb brushing my nipple.

"Why are you crying, my love?" he whispers.

"Because I love you, too," I answer. "And you gave me every indication that I should know who you are. I missed every single goddamned sign." The music. The nightmares. His *name*. I had blocked all of it out so thoroughly.

He lifts me away from the wall and carries me to the bed. It doesn't matter that we're both disgusting. He pulls out and helps me scoot back, until my head is on the pillows.

Apollo and Wolfe have disappeared.

I refocus on Jace as he lowers himself between my legs. He kisses my inner thigh, and my hands automatically find his head. I curl my fingers through his hair, guiding him to my hot center. He groans when he tastes me, and the sound rushes up and over me.

But the sound is nothing compared to the feeling of his lips and tongue on me.

"Jace," I pant. My nails dig into his scalp. "Oh my god."

He chuckles. "Husband," he corrects.

My thighs tense around him. "Husband," I whisper.

He sucks my clit into his mouth, and my back arches off the bed. He bands his arm over my abdomen, holding me down, and the throbbing pain mixes with the intense pleasure.

It's too much.

He pushes two fingers into my cunt and sucks hard.

I scream through my climax. I shove at his head, but he keeps lapping at me. Licking and thrusting his fingers in. He hums.

I groan, trying to crawl away from him. "Jace."

He growls and nips my thigh, then chuckles. "That made you wetter, my dear wife."

"Just please," I try. "Please fuck me."

"Once more." He continues until I'm writhing on the bed. My hands leave his head and grip the sheets instead, trying to control my insane reaction to him. He's got me right where he wants me, and pleasure bursts from me.

I'm boneless when he lifts and climbs over me. He trails kisses between my breasts, up my sternum. His teeth scrape my throat.

That feels bruised, too. Inside and out.

He lowers himself on top of me, his face right over mine.

"How much did I scream?"

His gaze shutters. "You don't want to know that."

I don't. But I need to know.

"You didn't stop screaming until you passed out." He dips down and kisses me. Stealing any more words or objections.

My heart breaks that he had to listen to that. To *me*.

I wrap my legs around him and urge him forward. He doesn't need much more beckoning to slip back inside me, and we both let out a breath.

He fucks me slowly, and I hear every single beat of his heart in my chest. His movements tell me he loves me. The way he stares into my eyes. My love and admiration for him is right there, too, on the tip of my tongue.

When our lips meet again, my heart skips. I inhale his scent and taste myself in his mouth. I slide my hands down his back, gripping his ass. Urging him faster.

He picks up his speed, soon slamming into me. Every push sends pain through my bruised muscles. Every stroke sets me on fire.

But I feel the orgasm building up anyway. In the way my nipples are brushing against his chest, bouncing with the power of his thrusts. In the deep spot he's hitting inside me.

He cups my jaw and forces me to look at him as I come for a third time, breaking to pieces around him. He follows soon after, stilling with a groan inside me.

He lowers his body weight on top of me, and I welcome it. I wrap around him and bury my face in his neck.

Apollo and Wolfe let us be, even though I almost expected them to be knocking down the door for their turns.

Impossibly, my eyes close. I don't mind his weight on me, crushing me into the mattress. But he turns us anyway, his cock slipping out as he rolls me onto my side. My back to his front. He loops his arm around my waist and holds me close. He lifts my thigh and slides back into me. I groan at the new angle, but he doesn't move. He just lowers my leg back down and stays there.

And that's how we fall asleep.

I WAKE up a hundred times more sore... and on the cusp of an orgasm. Jace rocks in and out of me, in the same position we fell asleep. His hand is on my clit, and I'm *right there*.

His lips touch the sensitive spot under my ear.

I fall over the edge.

He groans, then rolls us so I'm facedown. I don't even think we're both really awake. The room is dark, and my eyes can barely open. But the delicious feeling of him between my legs is too good to be a dream. His weight presses down on my back, and he hitches one of my legs up. Spreading me to get deeper.

I bite my lip and grip the top edge of the mattress, subtly pushing back against him. Not that I have any leverage to do so.

He bites my shoulder. I feel like a wild animal pinned in place, and the rush of heat that flashes through me only serves to spur him on. Until he comes with his teeth in my skin.

"Wow," I whisper.

"Sorry." He kisses the spot he bit, his tongue darting out and soothing it.

"I'm into it." I roll to face him, hissing in pain. But what's more important is that I immediately miss the warmth of him between my legs. "Where are Wolfe and Apollo?"

He lifts one shoulder. Concern draws his brows down. "I don't know. Do you want to go find out?"

I think about that. But I've already had four orgasms since we got home, and I'm not sure my body can take much more.

I need a bath. And to try not to puke again.

Wait.

Nope, I'm going to vomit.

I spring out of bed and rush to the toilet. Jace's alarmed voice follows me, but I manage to make it to the toilet and drop to my knees before it comes up. I close my eyes as I throw up, trying not to be freaked out by the metallic taste on my lips.

Jace gathers my hair from my face, pulling it back. He flicks on the light, and I gasp.

Blood in the toilet bowl. It coats the porcelain like I killed something in it.

"Fuck." He lifts me, wiping my mouth with the hem of his shirt. I don't miss that it comes away pink. "How do you feel?"

I try to focus on my body. "Nauseous. Achy. Thirsty. Cold."

He picks me up and carries me back to bed. Instead of laying me down, he just sets me on the edge. He disappears into the closet and reappears wearing jeans and a black t-shirt, holding more clothes for me.

I don't really understand what we're doing. He guides my foot into the panties, then leggings. Then the other foot. He has me hold on to his shoulder to stand and tugs the fabric up. He threads my arms through the button-up shirt he grabbed and deftly does the buttons.

"I'll be right back," he promises.

I stare at my bare feet, trying not to puke again. My vision flickers.

When Jace returns, he picks me up again. The room spins. A chill goes through me, and it occurs to me that I'm freezing. I lean into him, resting my head on his chest. Apollo and Wolfe both rush into the room, only pausing to look at me before yanking clothes out of the closet. They follow Jace and me downstairs, into one of the cars.

I don't know where all these vehicles came from. They just started appearing one day, and no one seemed inclined to return them.

I'm in the backseat of the SUV with Jace, in his lap. Wolfe slides in with us and takes my hand.

"You're clammy, flower." His voice is tight. "Apollo, turn on the heat."

There's a low purr as the heat kicks on. Apollo guns the car down the driveway, and I close my eyes.

When I open them, we're in front of bright, fluorescent lights. Wolfe holds the car door open for Jace, who slips past him and jogs inside. My breath leaves me with every jolting step. Automatic sliding doors *whoosh* open, admitting us, and my nose wrinkles. The smell is all antiseptic.

Hospital.

Why am I at a hospital?

"I'm fine," I mumble.

But Jace is already at the counter, with me cradled in his arms, and I can't seem to focus on his words. The urgent tone—then the angry tone. He shifts me, and cool air touches my stomach.

Even that hurts.

Someone gasps.

We're moving again. I curl my fists in Jace's shirt. I'm

shivering uncontrollably, and everything feels heavy. A deep-seated dread curls through me like shards of ice. The last time I was in a hospital, I woke up intubated and restrained.

Someone squeezes my leg.

Jace's arms leave me. I tighten my hold on his shirt, but not enough. The fabric slips through my fingers.

"Don't go," I try to say.

But I have a feeling I'm already gone.

jace

Internal bleeding.
   Emergency surgery.
   Doesn't look good.

Those words were all I heard before I take off. I burst free of the hospital and just start fucking running.

I end up at the twenty-four seven diner. Wolfe's cousin's head lifts from her spot behind the breakfast bar, smiling automatically—then severely frowning. I ignore her and go to the booth in the back, choosing the side that gives me the view of the rest of the diner.

It's the middle of the night. A fun little fact I didn't realize until I spotted the time glowing on the dashboard in the car. Three in the morning.

I fucked Kora while she internally bled.

While she got sicker and sicker.

I slam my hand on the table. At the end of it, the salt and pepper jumps.

The couple on the other end of the diner turn and stare at me.

"Coffee?" Wolfe's cousin appears at my side with a mug dangling from her finger. A carafe in the other.

I should know her name. I should read her nametag. I should respond.

When I don't, she sets the mug in front of me and fills it. She walks away, and I slump lower. The guilt is going to eat me up—but I don't know what I'll do if Kora dies.

I'm positive Wolfe and Apollo will leave. They'll never forgive me.

I was *there* when Parker kicked her repeatedly in the stomach. When she curled up in a ball. When she tackled Alex, when she saved *my* life, and he punched her in the stomach, too. Worsening a small injury, maybe? Making it a *bad* injury?

Then we waited it out. Sat at Olympus for who the fuck knows how long, while her blood pooled in her belly.

My thoughts consume me, and I don't realize someone is approaching until they're sliding into the seat across from me.

I glower. "What are you doing here?"

Saint sighs. "Saving you, apparently."

Fuck that.

"She'll be okay." He reaches out for the packets of sugar, the little cup of cream that Wolfe's cousin left behind with the coffee. He pulls my mug toward him and doctors it, then takes a sip. "This is surprisingly good coffee."

"It's middle-of-the-night coffee." I lift my gaze and meet his. "They go through it too fast to burn it."

What a pair we make.

"How's Tem?" I ask. To poke a wound other than my own.

"She's with Apollo and Wolfe at the hospital." He raises

a brow. "I told her that I wasn't fucking going in there. So she sent me to find you."

"Errand boy."

He glares at me.

I smile, though. And a second later, he does, too.

"I'm not going to kill myself," he says. "I think I'm good to move out. Reestablish myself... somewhere else."

"No."

His brow lowers. "No?"

"No," I repeat. "It's been six weeks since Elora died. You still look like a miserable jackass."

"You look like a miserable jackass, too," he mutters.

I cough. "Yeah. I deserve to look like this. You don't."

Saint shakes his head. "You're full of bullshit, man. Did you do that to Kora? Kick her until her organs shredded up on the inside?"

"Fuck off." I glower at him. "You know what I mean."

"Don't think I do." He leans back and slings his arm over the top of the seat.

I stay silent. Huffing and seething at myself. He doesn't say anything else either. Not to me. He asks the waitress for another cup of coffee and nudges it in my direction when it comes. Then he orders pie. A slice of apple, pumpkin, and chocolate cream.

He eats half of all of them, smiling at me as he licks his spoon clean.

I shake my head and drag the chocolate cream one closer. I take a bite. The flavor blesses my tastebuds, and I swallow it quickly. I'd rather it tasted like ash. But my stomach rumbles. We haven't eaten since the dry granola bar Apollo shoved at us in Olympus. Prior to that, it was before Kora and I were...

I don't know what to call it. Kidnapped? Abducted? Stolen off the street by a fucking madman? *Taken.*

Before I can stop myself, I'm shoveling the pie into my mouth. The sugar boosts my system, reviving me a little. I go through one after another. By the time I push the empty plates to the center of the table, Saint is grinning openly at me.

"Fuck off," I sigh.

Eventually, his phone goes off. He eyes the text from Tem, then pulls his wallet out. He tosses a few bills on the table and gestures at me to get up.

"Kora's out of surgery."

I rise quickly, almost tripping over my feet in my hurry to follow him. We walk the few blocks back to the hospital, and my stomach cramps.

What if she's mad at me?

"Don't be ridiculous," Saint says. He stops just shy of the doors. "She loves you, doesn't she?"

"Yeah." I clear my throat. "She does."

"Then you'll survive seeing her... like that." He swallows. "Okay. Go. I'm not going in there."

"Where will you go?" I eye him.

"Managed to snag a late-night client." He hooks his thumb in the vague direction of his tattoo shop. "Tem can find me there."

We all handle our worries differently, I suppose.

I go inside, following the receptionist's directions to the third-floor waiting room. When I step inside, Apollo shoots to his feet. He comes over and hugs me. Not the usual back-slapping hug, but a real one. I grip him back just as tightly.

"She's okay," he says in my ear.

My gaze lands on Wolfe. He's almost doubled over, his

elbows on his knees and his head in his hands. He doesn't look like he knows she's okay.

"He'll be better once he sees her." Apollo appraises me. "And you, too."

"When can we?" I clear my throat. "See her, I mean?"

Tem joins us. "I just talked to the nurse. She said give them about ten minutes to get her back into a real room, then we can go in one at a time."

I take the seat next to Wolfe.

We wait.

After the time is up, Tem goes first. She reappears only a few minutes later, smiling. "She's asking for all of you."

"Saint went to his shop," I tell her. I should've told her before, but...

"Thanks." She hitches her purse higher up her shoulder. "I'll see you guys."

Apollo stands. "One at a time, or should we just—"

"Yeah, let's go." Wolfe shoots to his feet. He grabs my wrist and tugs me up, too. "We're not waiting."

"Okay." I follow them down the hall. Better that I didn't try to find her room on my own, because I missed when we got directions.

Apollo locates it and steps in. He murmurs a hello to her, and I hear her answering rasp.

My heart kicks up double-time.

Wolfe practically shoves me into the room, and I freeze when I see her.

It isn't so different to how I probably was, waking up in the hospital after my surgery.

"Welcome to the Injured Torsos Anonymous club." Wolfe shakes his head. "Part of me wants to go out and get stabbed in the stomach so I can be included, but—"

"No," Apollo and Kora both say.

She smiles and reaches out both her hands. Her left has an IV taped to the back. She has a blood oxygen reader attached to her earlobe. And so many wires come out of her gown, attached to a million monitors.

I take her right side, and Wolfe goes left.

She looks to him first. "Please don't go out seeking trouble. I'm sure it'll find you without any help."

He grins, then leans down and kisses her forehead. I don't miss the way his fingers tremble as he brushes her hair behind her ear. "You scared us."

She squeezes my hand before I can pull away. "I'm sorry."

"*I'm* sorry," I say. "It's—"

"Don't you dare blame yourself." She yanks me forward with surprising strength, releasing my hand and cupping the back of my neck. My forehead touches hers, and I breathe her in. She doesn't have the same scent. Instead, she just smells like the hospital.

"We're okay," she repeats.

Eventually, she releases me. Apollo and I find chairs, while Wolfe perches at the foot of her bed.

"So." She grips the blanket. "Now what?"

We all exchange looks. Her question hangs over us. Now what, indeed?

I think the answer is pretty obvious. And judging from Wolfe and Apollo's expressions, they're in agreement.

Apollo is the first to crack, a grin splitting his face. "Now, baby, we get to *live*."

kora

TWO MONTHS LATER

I stand in front of the Chosen. The ten fighters who surpassed our expectations and made it into Olympus. They're immobile, although I can sense the energy surging through them.

A smile pulls at my lips when I reach those I recognize, and I offer the first his choice of cards. He draws the ace of spades. *He'll go last.*

I continue down the line until everyone has their match. "You know who you're fighting," I say. "And you know the legacy of Olympus. Our traditions."

They all nod along.

"Get going, then. And wait for your call."

They file by wordlessly, disappearing back into the fighters' hall. They each have rooms where they can warm up and prepare, and one of our boar-masked men will make sure things run smoothly in this hall. I catch sight of him down toward the end, sitting on a stool and reading a book. He has to hold it up to see through the holes of his mask.

Someone snags my wrist and tugs.

Apollo spins me into him, and I catch myself with a hand to his chest. He's yet to put on his gold paint, although I would bet anything that he'll be doing that next.

One day, I'll fuck you in this gold paint. I shiver at the reminder of his words from over a year ago.

Only if you win, I had responded.

Now he's fighting, the ace of spades in his grip and a cocky smile on his lips.

I haven't forgotten our promise, but he still thinks I'm on activity restriction. In reality, I got the all-clear from my doctor this morning.

It'll be one hell of a surprise.

I trail my finger down the center of his chest, smiling brightly. "Break a leg."

He leans down to kiss me, and I give him my cheek. I've been driving him crazy all day, avoiding his mouth, his cock... Amping him up for what I hope is a great night under the guise of innocence.

He growls lightly, his grip on my wrist tightening.

I tsk and push him away. "Go get ready. The doors are opening soon."

"Fine," he whispers. "We'll discuss this later."

He strides away, and I watch his back muscles flex with every step.

I'm in more trouble than him, I think. Especially since I'm now impossibly turned on and left aching between my thighs.

Worth it.

"Ready?"

Jace comes out of the front atrium. He and I seem to be the first ones ready. His skull mask is secured over his face, the smears of charcoal visible on his pale skin under the open suit jacket. He looks every inch the malevolent leader.

And yet... *I* lead, too.

Soon after my surgery, the paternity tests came back for me and Jace. I am related to Brendon Sterling, and the doctor confirmed him to be my father. They ran additional tests, just for the hell of it, to confirm that Leisl Sterling is my mother. *She is.*

With that confirmation came a visit with our lawyer and a hefty stack of paperwork. My inheritance is on its way in the form of an enormous check and property. Stakes in businesses. It was way too overwhelming at first, but I've managed to wrap my head around it now.

And Jace...

Jace is not the son of Kronos.

In a way, I think that released the last few chains on his soul. He had made peace with the fact that his father was a deadbeat—his words, of course—who made questionable choices. Who terrorized his family when Jace was a child.

Thinking he had actually come from Kronos... that was a harder pill to swallow. The elephant in the room that we had put on the back burner, especially after Saint killed him. It wasn't a priority.

But it's obvious how much this news has lightened Jace.

He holds out a slim white box for me. "This mask instead."

I slip off the plain gold mask that I found buried in a drawer in Jace's room here at Olympus. It was a bit crumpled, and I smiled inexplicably when I found it. I didn't ask whether he found it in the forest or stole it from my apartment after I went to live with them. It just made my heart go all weird that he kept it at all.

In the white box is a mask of flowers. Real ones, judging

from the floral scent that wafts up. Gold, black, and red flowers. Some are pressed, making the mask flat. Others are still vibrantly alive. The red-stained peonies at the temple explode outward.

"It's beautiful," I murmur. Flowers for all of them.

I hold it up to my face and turn around, letting him tie the black silk laces behind my head. He moves my hair over one shoulder, and his lips brush my neck.

I shiver.

"It's time," one of our employees calls.

Jace straightens, his fingers skating over the spot his lips just were.

Goosebumps rise on my arms. "Ready?"

"Yes."

I take a deep breath and eye the boar-masked man. "Let them in."

Jace and I go to the stairs, winding our way up to the second floor, and sweep down the hall. We stop in the shadows, and he stands just behind me to watch the people filing in. I wanted to catch their reactions. The flowers, the candles, the darkness. It's ethereal and perfect.

It's a sign that Olympus is back in the rightful hands.

We had a statue made. A new stone throne. The statue sits overlooking the landing of the staircase and the atrium, in general. It's a woman with long flowing hair and a crown of flowers on her head. One hand is curled around a staff not unlike Apollo's, but flowers bloom around a skull at the top. In her other hand, resting against her thigh, is a dagger.

I say *we* had a statue made—but in reality, it was the brainchild of Jace, Apollo, and Wolfe. A surprise for me.

Did I cry when I saw it?

Maybe.

Wolfe comes out of the shadows and stops at my shoulder. He leans down and kisses my jaw—the only part of my face that's accessible. He's dressed the wicked part, with his blood-red mask and contacts, the open white shirt spattered with blood. Fake blood, I think. I never found out, never wanted to know. His chest is speckled with red, too, and it takes everything I have not to slide my palm along his abs... or lower.

"Are you sure you want to do this?" he asks.

I smooth my hands down the pale-yellow dress. The bodice is fitted, and the skirt flares delicately from my hips. When I spin, the skirt fans out around my legs. I chose strappy black heels that click against the stone when I walk. My hair is long and loose.

Tonight, I'm hosting.

"I do," I say evenly. I smile at them. "Stop worrying so much—I'm fine."

We get a signal from one of our men, and the doors swing closed. The atrium is packed. Far denser than I'd ever seen it before.

Reopening night.

It took far too long for us to get it ready. There were changes we wanted to make. And we wanted to give Sterling Falls time to forget the madness that reigned Olympus when Cerberus held it captive.

"We had to turn people away." One of our men appears through a trick door, pausing just shy of us. "There are more outside."

I grin. Our marketing plan worked, then. "That just means they'll come earlier next time. Right? Let them hear the roar of the crowd, then have them move along."

Jace nods, agreeing with my plan.

I take a deep breath and step out into the open. Wolfe

hands me a staff. It's pitch-black with a skull on top. Similar to the statue's, minus the flowers. It takes me by surprise, and I cast a glance over my shoulder. Jace, with his skull mask and the twisting horns, the same one I stole from him so long ago, grins at me.

Okay.

I stride down the stairs and stop at the top of the landing. The lights are on me.

"Welcome to Olympus," I call, slamming the bottom of the staff into the marble. The sound is impressive, a perfect punctuation for my words.

Suddenly, all the eyes are on me. Silence falls. I grin, knowing it probably seems demonic to some. How could a girl in flowers and pastels command an entire room? *I don't know—but I'm ready to find out.*

"I'm your host for the evening. You can call me Persephone."

kora

I slip into our room at Olympus. Apollo paces in front of the couches, his energy high.

He *demolished* his opponent. This was one of the only fights I've watched where my heart was in my throat in a good way. In an adrenaline-fueled haze, I screamed and cheered with Jace at my back, his hands on my hips. He was my own personal bodyguard, his twisted mask and reputation enough to keep us from being jostled at the edge of the platform.

It was my pleasure to step up and take his hand, raising it high. Well, as high as I could manage, seeing as how he still towers over me. Even in heels.

I close the door harder than necessary to draw his attention.

He goes completely still. He's removed the plain brown mask he fought in, but he's still shirtless. The gold paint is streaked down his chest, his neck, into the waistband of his brown pants...

My mouth waters.

"Congratulations," I whisper, stepping closer.

His jaw works.

I remove my mask, setting it on the floor. It's too beautiful to ruin by dropping it. My hands go to the back of my dress, and I unclasp it and tug the zipper down.

"What are you doing?" His voice is strangled.

"Did you forget your promise?" I smile coyly. I let the dress slide off my shoulders, revealing the lace lingerie. I can't even call it a bra—it's just a lacy strip across my nipples and an underwire pushing them up. It doesn't leave anything to the imagination. My panties are pretty much the same—the thong not much more than string.

The fabric pools at my feet, and I step out of it. I leave the heels on.

His eyes rove over me, but they pause at the scar on my stomach. It's the only remnant of the surgery I had. The only thing left to remind us that I almost died at the hands of Parker and Alex. It's not big, but it draws his eye all the same. "You can't—"

"Doctor cleared me this morning." I smirk. "Unless you'd rather I go find satisfaction elsewhere..."

He clears his throat, his expression suddenly a lot more hungry. "You sure?"

"I've been dying for this." I finally get within reach of him.

No sex for two months has almost killed us—but all of them were adamant that my health came first.

Bastards.

They didn't even let me get myself off. Because apparently orgasms would've tensed my abdomen and potentially caused harm.

Let me just tell you, trying to get myself to come and having them pull my hands away... *not fun.* I pouted. A lot. And eventually took to sleeping in one of the guest bedrooms, because being surrounded by all that male energy and unable to do anything was driving me insane.

But now we're on the other side of it, and I want to jump all of their bones. Many, many times. Starting with Apollo.

"I want you to cover me in this paint." I reach out and run my finger down the largest streak across his chest. I rub the gold between my fingers. "Can you do that?"

He groans. "You don't have to even ask, baby."

Something in my chest flutters. More excitement, anxiety. I don't know. He pulls me closer and dips his head down, pressing a kiss to my lips. It goes from soft to scorching in an instant, and I grip his biceps. I taste the blood on him from one of the few hits he took. His bare chest moves against mine, and my nipples stiffen through the lingerie. He lifts me and carries me to the couch. But he doesn't put me on it. He puts me back on my feet—on the heels—and steps back.

"Turn around," he orders.

I do. My body zings with electricity.

He puts a hand on my spine and pushes me over the back of the couch. He widens my stance, his hands lingering on my hips. But then he's kneeling, and I moan at the first hot breath that touches my center.

"This has been neglected," he says, tracing a pattern up and down the inside of my thigh. "So as much as I want to fuck you until we both can't stand, you need to come first."

"Please," I beg. "God, please touch me, Apollo."

He chuckles. "Eager?"

"Aren't you?" I snap.

But then his tongue is there, running along my slit, tasting me. He sucks and nips everywhere except my clit, until I'm writhing against the back of the couch and nearly incoherent. Only then does he suck my clit into his mouth.

I shatter.

Immediately.

I grip the couch hard, my legs shaking with the force of my orgasm. When I float back down to earth, it takes me a moment to realize he's still got his face between my legs. He pulls my hips back, then thrusts two fingers inside me.

I clench and groan. "Apollo. Please just fuck me."

He strokes the inside my walls. Again, so teasing. His other hand goes down my leg, cupping my calf, then my ankle. "You look so fucking hot in these heels."

"Great." I shudder as he builds me back up. "I just—"

"I know what you want, Kora. I know what you need, too." His teeth latch on to my ass cheek.

I yelp, startled, but there's nowhere to go. The pain of his bite radiates out, mixing with the pleasure in my pussy.

I'm going to come again.

I wiggle against him, but he just licks and nips my ass cheek until my face is red. Then he spreads my cheeks and tongues my asshole.

"Holy—"

He eats my ass until I'm coming on his fingers again, my face smashed into the couch. My legs are jelly. But he just flips me around and plants my ass on the back of the couch. He's lost his pants, and my eyes go to his dick.

His *pierced dick*.

"When did you do that?" I rasp.

Dear. Lord.

Three horizontally placed bars on the underside of his shaft.

"When we were on a sex ban." He smirks. "You like?"

I nod wordlessly.

"These are supposed to stimulate my partner..." His gaze darkens. "Let's see if that's correct, hmm?"

Without another word, he spreads my thighs and thrusts into me.

I arch my back and grip his biceps hard. He doesn't hold back, pounding into me with a ferocity that stokes a fire inside me. He wraps his arms around my back, pressing me closer, and kisses me. His tongue slides into my mouth, tasting me.

I missed this.

My body aches in the most delicious way, but it's my heart that pounds like I haven't actually been with them for two months.

Which is ridiculous. Because they've been right there, living with me, talking to me.

I guess I just like to connect during sex.

I tear my lips from Apollo's and trail kisses down his jaw. He tastes like sweat and chalk and blood. He pumps harder into me when I nip his neck. Harder still when I suck on his flesh, alternating between licking, biting, and sucking on the same place.

I want to mark him like he's marked my soul.

"Kora," he groans. He tilts his head to give me more room.

My hand slides into his hair, and I tug him back as I move down lower. I repeat, driving him nuts, until he pulls my hair to lift my head. Then he's leaning me back and ducking lower. He captures my nipple through the lace of the bra we never got around to taking off. I groan and shiver, holding his head to my chest.

Another orgasm builds deep inside me.

I rake my nails down his back, scratching his skin. He trembles against me, holding off his climax by sheer force of will. The piercings are an added bonus, hitting just the right spots every time he moves in and out of me.

"Hold it," he orders, nipping my earlobe.

I shudder.

He catches my clit between his thumb and finger, rubbing and sliding across my sensitive nub.

"*Now*, Kora," he growls.

It's not hard to fall to pieces again. I let loose and come with a gasp, and Apollo thrusts into me twice more before emptying inside me. We go still, holding each other close until we catch our breath.

Then he presses another kiss to my lips. Sweet, lingering.

My heart skips.

"I love you," he says, his mouth still on mine. "So fucking much."

I kiss him, then pull back. I stare into his dark eyes so he can see how serious I am when I say back, "I love you, too."

When he withdraws, I feel the evidence of him between my thighs. He chuckles, eyes sweeping my body, and I realize... he was successful. I'm covered in gold paint. Some of it dried flecks, stuck to my arms and thighs. Other are smears, where our sweat rewet the paint and made the transfer easier.

It's all over my chest, my stomach, my bra.

"It goes well with your dress," he murmurs. He pulls his pants back on, then retrieves the dress. His eyes gleam.

I laugh. "Well, I planned this outfit on purpose..."

"Naturally."

I make my way into the bathroom on unsteady legs. I eye myself, truly looking for the first time. I went with light makeup, just a winged eyeliner and mascara. Any trace of the pale-pink tint I had on my lips is gone. And my hair...

Jeez, he didn't touch my hair that much, but it's still wild. It's just-fucked hair, and no matter how many times I run my fingers through it, nothing calms it down.

Apollo waits for me just outside the door. He helps me zip up my dress.

"Ready to party?"

I grin. He hands me my mask. He helps me tie it on, and then he turns around, and I do the same for his deer skull mask. He's only missing the staff that he carried in the beginning. He takes my hand, threading his fingers with mine, and we go down the fighter hallway to the main room.

We have a gathering waiting for us.

On the platform stands Jace as Hades, Wolfe as Ares. Saint in his Hermes outfit. There are some familiar masked people gathered around the platform, too. Everyone has drinks in their hands—Jace and Wolfe each have two.

I take the offered one from Jace, smiling sweetly. His hot gaze travels up and down my body. No doubt imagining what filth Apollo and I got up to while they lingered out here. The evidence is right there on my skin.

"To our fighters," Jace says, raising his glass.

We cheers. I clink my glass against the guys', while the people on the floor do the same to the people around us. We all sip.

The familiar burn of whiskey fills my mouth and coats my throat.

I capture Jace's face and pull him toward me, careful of the horns, and kiss him. Our mouths open, and more whiskey floods into my mouth.

I swallow it, biting back a groan.

The taste... well, if Jace gives me shots like that, it might grow on me. He releases the hold on my hip that I hadn't realized he had.

Wolfe snickers, then turns and faces the small crowd. It's made up of our employees—past and present, because apparently the guys had enough interest to put everyone on a revolving schedule—and tonight's fighters.

"Ready to party?" he asks them.

They let out whoops and shouts.

Wolfe waves his hand, and someone must hit a button. The lights dim, and music pours out of invisible speakers. He immediately comes to me, taking my glass and passing it off to someone else. He tugs me close, his hot palms burning into my waist.

I tip my head back and smile lazily at him.

Three orgasms will do that.

He leans in close, our masks brushing as he puts his lips next to my ear. "If I kiss Apollo, will I taste you on his lips?"

I shiver, and my grip on his shirt tightens. "I think you might, if the whiskey didn't rinse it away."

His laugh is dark, and he takes my hand. He guides me down from the platform, which is already being mobbed with dancing people, and catches Apollo's eye.

Apollo follows us down a hall and into an alcove.

We kissed in this particular alcove, I think. Hiding from the patrolling Hell Hounds and trying to get me out of Olympus undetected...

Wolfe winks at me, then shoves Apollo against the wall.

God.

In an instant, desire floods through me.

Wolfe grips the front of Apollo's pants. He unbuttons them with slow deliberateness, then leans forward and steals a kiss from his lips.

My heart picks up speed. I shift to see them better,

even as they move deeper into the shadows. I block more of the light. Their own personal protector. Guardian of moments.

Apollo pushes off the wall, deepening their kiss. I can feel the lust and love pouring off them in waves.

Over the last two months, they've gotten closer. Emotionally anyway. Because they both swore up and down that they weren't going to cheat and get each other off if I couldn't.

Nice thought, even though the guilt about that was almost unbearable.

They never complained, though. None of them did. If anything, they did more of the rule enforcing... because I sure as hell didn't want to follow those directions.

But I guess seeing me as they did, weak and shivering and bleeding in my abdomen and stomach at an alarming rate, would make anyone a rule follower.

Wolfe pushes Apollo back, separating from his lips. He scowls at Apollo, and I don't miss that his hands are still curled in the waistband of Apollo's pants.

With deft fingers, he undoes the button and drags it down. Apollo lets out a breath when Wolfe goes to his knees.

Oh my word.

I lean against the wall and try to control my breathing, because my heart is now slamming against my ribcage. There's new wetness between my thighs, and I press them together.

This is their time, and I'm honored to be given the chance to witness it.

Wolfe opens his mouth and licks Apollo's cock. His tongue flicks around the piercing, his eyes only going wide for a moment before he suppresses his surprise. He plants his hands on Apollo's thighs and takes him all the way into his mouth.

God, it's beautiful.

I cover my mouth to muffle the groan that wants to escape again.

Apollo's back hits the wall, putting more of his weight on it. His eyes, behind the mask, close. He lets Wolfe bob up and down.

But at some point, Wolfe's patience snaps. He rocks back to sit on his heels and stares up at his best friend. "You want me to keep kissing your cock, Apollo? Or do you want to fuck my face?"

A thrill goes through me.

Apollo's eyes fly open, narrowing with the twist of his lips. Without a word, he grabs Wolfe's head and shoves his cock in his mouth.

"Yesss," I whisper. I cup my breasts, desperate for any relief.

I literally just came three times in a row, and now I want more.

Insatiable.

"Our girl is getting off on this," Apollo grunts, leaning over Wolfe as he slams his dick down his throat. "*Fuck.*"

Wolfe reaches up and cups his balls, squeezing and tugging lightly. His eyes are wide open and fixated on Apollo's face. His head is tipped back slightly. He seems to be daring Apollo to come—and he does. He grits his teeth and stills in Wolfe's mouth.

A few drops of his cum spill out Wolfe's mouth and drip down his chin. As soon as Apollo has stopped moving, stopped trembling with his release, Wolfe rises.

I lick my lips. He comes for me, and I have a feeling this is payback.

He catches the back of my neck and reels me in, kissing me hard. Open-mouthed, sloppy. I taste Apollo, I taste Wolfe.

And I fucking love it—but it's not doing anything for the ache between my legs.

He backs me up against the wall and lifts my leg in one motion. My dress shifts, Apollo gathering the skirt out of the way. He lines up with my pussy, his lips never leaving mine, and slides inside.

I whimper. He fucks me fast, probably turned on out of his mind. Apollo's hand drifts between us, brushing my clit. Over and over in small circles.

I love their hands on me. Wolfe's tongue in my mouth, delivering the salted, musky taste of Apollo. I love that they love each other, too.

Wolfe's thrusts get harder, more frantic. I chase his climax with my own, and Apollo presses firmer on my clit, rubbing faster. I come suddenly, my scream swallowed by Wolfe's mouth, and clench around him.

He lets out a groan that rumbles through his chest and stills in me, his cock pulsing and jerking.

"Wow," I finally say when our lips break apart. "That was one hell of a kiss."

Wolfe laughs. It's warm and low, and I don't think I've ever heard a more perfect sound. Of all of us, he laughs the least. Or the quietest—it's hard to tell sometimes. It's in his nature to be quiet. Nearly silent. Dragging him out of that mind frame has been a goal of mine in the past few weeks. I cup his cheek and lean in, stealing another quick kiss.

Then one from Apollo. Just because.

I smile, and I let them escort me back, one guy on each arm.

My heart is so fucking full.

I f Saint is surprised to see me, he doesn't show it. He just looks up from the guy he's tattooing, then continues on with his work.

While he's distracted, I examine his shop. It's surprisingly cool. The walls are black, but there are a million brass-framed pieces of art hanging, mostly on white paper. The contrast is edgy. He has some plants around, one on the counter with creeping vines that trail toward the floor, another standing in the corner.

There's a white couch with a wooden coffee table in front of it. Someone had laid out a collection of tattoo magazines—including one that immediately captures my attention.

I flip to the middle spread, more than a little shocked to see *Saint*. Standing in front of his shop with his familiar scowl in place. His white button-down shirt hides most of his tattoos, except the few creeping up his neck and down his hands.

Making waves with Saint Hart and his tattoo shop, Starlight, reads the headline.

A lump forms in my throat as I scan the write-up about him. Apparently, he tattooed someone who then went on to be a reality TV star. They mentioned him, word picked up, and business has been steadily increasing ever since.

The buzzing of his tattoo machine stops, and I glance over my shoulder to find him striding toward me. The guy he was working on is heading in the opposite direction.

Saint snaps off his gloves and raises one eyebrow.

"Hi."

"Did Artemis send you?" he asks.

"No. Why didn't you mention this?"

He glances at the open article and shakes his head. "I just got it in today."

"It's impressive." I close it and face him. "What's your schedule look like today?"

"Just going to finish up this guy, then go get drunk." He smiles, and it's not a particularly nice one. Which doesn't really make sense because he's been kind to me up until right this moment.

But... ah. He thinks I'm a spy for Artemis.

When Jace told me he was making them live together, I think I choked. But apparently, it's not going as well as Jace thinks it might.

"Well, maybe we can delay getting drunk and you can give me a tattoo?" I narrow my eyes. "Or I guess I could go to that shop by SFU..."

To his credit, he immediately realizes that I'm serious. And that he *offered* to tattoo me.

"Fuck." He pinches the bridge of his nose, his eyes squeezing shut. "You want a tattoo?"

"Yep."

"Artemis really didn't send you?"

I punch his shoulder. He sways back, more out of

surprise than anything else, and I scowl. "No, Tem didn't send me. I haven't talked to her in a few days, actually. I was sort of expecting her to be here."

He rubs the spot I hit. "I banned her from the shop."

Interesting.

"Ready, man," his client calls, returning to the chair.

"Can you come back in an hour?" Saint asks me. "Sorry, Kora. I don't really know what's gotten into me lately."

I roll my eyes. "I'll be back."

An hour later, I return equipped with a bottle of tequila, margarita mixer, and a small pack of plastic cups. Also, tacos from a street vendor. Because we may as well fully embrace the theme. The door is locked, but an interior light is still on. Saint comes to open it when I knock, and he smiles faintly at my supplies.

We take seats on the white couch. He unwraps one of the tacos and eats like he hasn't all day.

Maybe he hasn't.

I frown at that, but I'm definitely not one to be on yet another rescue mission. We eat in companionable silence, then finally I crunch up the foil and toss it in his bin.

"Okay," I say. "I want a tattoo. Two, actually."

He watches me with interest. "What're you thinking?"

I detail what I had in mind, and he nods thoughtfully.

"Let me draw up those two designs. We can tweak them until you're satisfied."

I sit back, pulling my legs up. "I doubt we'll need to make many changes. I trust you."

I close my eyes while he draws, thinking about how the guys are going to react. I may have told them a little white lie and said Tem and I needed a girls' night. Which is why, when I left Starlight, I texted her and asked her to cover for me.

She didn't ask any questions, which was nice. But she did agree.

He clears his throat, and I crack my eyes open. I follow him back to his tattoo space, and he shows me the first design. My chest tightens. I take the paper from him to look at it closer.

I wanted something to represent me and my family.

My official decision about being a Sterling was to do... nothing. Not yet anyway. Maybe one day I'll want the alderman seat that my father occupied. But until then, I made a formal statement that my dear cousin, Nadine Bradshaw, has my full support. Which shocked her at first, seeing as she admitted to trying to scare me out of Sterling Falls.

Another thing came to light shortly after. The murders.

Parker fucking Warton.

After his body was discovered in the basement of the hotel—alone, of course, and scrubbed free of any evidence of Jace, Alex, and me—police searched his apartment. They found a shit ton of photographs of me. A deputy told me Nate nearly lost his damn mind. But they also found photographs of the decapitated Hell Hounds, pre-beheading. Surveillance photos of the three who accompanied me to that stupid press event. And then more photos of the man I fought being dragged out of Olympus. He wasn't just stalking me, but his victims, too.

Then there was the giant butcher knife.

Anyway. Even if Parker wasn't dead—which he really, *really* is this time—there would be enough evidence to convict.

Meanwhile, Alex Sterling is missing.

Missing as in, fully dead and at the bottom of the ocean. But, you know. We couldn't turn a whole town against him and reveal all his dirty secrets. He was loved. There would've definitely been a riot. People have an interesting habit of ignoring the truth.

But it's okay, seeing as how he openly shared with the world how happy he was to have another Sterling back, alive and well. That helped make my transition with the public... smooth. Ish.

It's weird. Sometimes I get recognized on the street by my red hair, or the photos that appeared in the paper. They were candids, me walking alongside grumpy Jace or smiling Apollo.

The only one who has managed to avoid getting photographed is Wolfe.

Because Wolfe has a biker club to run, and getting his face blasted across the papers would just be too much publicity for him. They're keeping some of their illegal businesses in practice, like boosting cars and stripping them for parts—which I didn't even know they did, but I suppose that's beside the point. He's also taken over West Falls, previously Titan territory. They've been remodeling Descend as another club with a lighter vibe.

Sometimes we accompany Wolfe and the Hell Hounds on rides. Nadine replaced the bikes she destroyed, along with another lengthy apology. But I've forgiven her. I just want family, and I've gotten closer to her and Nate.

After their father's funeral...

We think Alex killed him. But that's a mystery we'll never solve.

"Do you like it?" Saint asks.

I push away the memories and blink hard. The tattoo in front of me is a flower encompassed in a mandala—a circular geometric shape. It flows with the simple pattern on the inside. He took my rather vague description of wanting something to represent being surrounded by family and made it perfect.

"It's exactly right," I say.

He smiles.

Then he extends the other paper, with the second tattoo design, and my breath catches.

"Saint," I whisper. "This is even better."

His smile widens. "Let's get to work, then."

wolfe

"Why am I so fucking nervous?" I bounce on my heels, trying to work off some of this extra energy. I'm not usually the *bounce around* type, but this is different. This is like I have electricity pouring into me and just ricocheting around without an outlet.

"We're all nervous," Apollo mutters.

I glance at him and sigh. *He's* not fidgeting.

Tem is bringing Kora to us. Jace, Apollo, me.

We're in our best clothes—white collared shirts, black slacks, dress shoes. There are a million lights around us, set up with help from our Olympus employees.

When we told them our plan, they freaked out. That made me freak out a little. Because Jace is Kora's actual husband. We went to City Hall and looked it up, to confirm that the paperwork had been filed. What a trip that would've been if we discovered Cerberus never finalized their agreement.

I shake out my arms. I never stopped freaking out.

"Please stop moving." Jace glowers at me.

I turn away from them. "I can't."

"Oh my god," Apollo groans.

Kora slept over Tem's house last night. We haven't seen our girl in more than *twenty-four hours*, and it's getting to me. Maybe more than this insane, harebrained idea.

Apollo's phone chimes, and I practically leap across the clearing to read over his shoulder.

He elbows me, then lets me see the screen.

We're here, Tem said.

Fuck. Shit.

There's a path of glowing lights through the trees, and I can hear Kora's voice slipping through the darkness toward us. Questioning Tem, a slight tremble in her voice.

And then she must see the lights, and everything goes quiet.

It goes quiet in me, too, like all the electricity has been yanked out.

Jace, Apollo, and I move to stand in a line at the end of the path. It's too perfect that this clearing is on our property, that it's the right size, that it isn't too far from the house...

My heart is beating so fucking loud, rushing in my ears, I almost miss the hitch in Apollo's breath. The way Jace is curling his hands into fists, then relaxing them.

I smile. They're nervous, too. Sure, Apollo just told me as much. But it's hard to believe him without evidence. And now I have it, I relax further.

Kora comes down along the path, her brows drawn together.

My heart skips.

She's the most beautiful girl I've ever laid eyes on. Tem must've told her some lie to get her dressed up. She wears a pink, high-waisted skirt that swishes when she walks and a black cropped top. A sliver of her stomach is visible. The lights reflect off the delicate gold chains draped around her neck, in her ears, the little ring in her nose.

Her hair is pinned out of her face, but it flows down her back.

"What's going on?" she asks, her gaze moving from me to Jace to Apollo.

We agreed to do this one at a time.

Starting with me.

To be fair—we drew straws.

I step forward, leaving my brothers behind, and meet her in the middle of the clearing. It's where I chased her that day, when I was on the verge of absolutely fucking breaking. *She* pulled me back from that ledge. I hold on to that now.

"Wolfe," Kora says in an even voice, her nostrils flaring. "Are you going to tell me what's happening?"

I take her hands and press a sweet kiss to her lips. She leans into me, automatically wanting more, but I draw back. I can't help but smirk at her narrowed eyes. But then my smirk is gone, vanishing in front of the serious words I'm about to tell her. Words that shake me to my core, that I can't take back once they're out in the open.

"I want to spend the rest of my life with you, flower."

Her eyes widen.

I grip her hands tighter, hoping and praying she doesn't say something to devastate me. Like, *no*, or, *I can't*.

"I love you so much, I wonder how I ever existed without you in my soul." I lean in and touch my forehead to hers as her chin wobbles and her body trembles. "You are ingrained in my soul, Kora Sterling."

The name she's been going by—for now anyway.

Maybe one day she'll decide she wants to be a Sinclair again. Or she'll take one of our last names.

Kora James. Kora King. Kora Madden.

Kora James-King-Madden. That would be a bit much.

Focus.

She lets go of my hands and slides hers up my arms, to my shoulders. "I love you," she whispers. "You're in my soul, too."

I glance at the bandage on her wrist, then back at her face. I'm curious, but it can wait.

Then, as planned, I go down on one knee. I pull the ring from my pocket and offer it to her. "Will you marry me, Kora? Under the stars?" It doesn't matter that it won't be a legal marriage. It'll be real in our hearts.

"Yes," she whispers.

I slide the ring on her finger and rise swiftly, kissing her with every ounce of love I possess. She hugs me tightly, her fingers digging into my back. Her tongue slips into my mouth, and I groan at the taste of her.

Too soon, though, I pull away. I release her and step back.

Apollo strides forward, taking my spot. I stand next to Jace, who eyes me with a wide smile. Joy belatedly fills my chest. She said yes. She didn't run screaming, or argue about semantics, or *any* of that. She wants me as much as she wants my best friends.

"Light of my life," Apollo rumbles. "I've discovered a love I never knew I could feel. You're deep in my bones."

"I love you," she whispers to him. "Every side of you, every piece of you. Light and dark."

He goes down on one knee. "Will you marry me, baby?"

"I will." She grins.

He slips it on her finger. It will sit snugly against the one

I already put there, the diamonds overlapping and hooking together.

Awaiting the third.

They kiss. He tips her back as he tastes her, and I suppress my groan of need.

Then it's Jace's turn.

FIFTY-TWO

jace

I swallow around the lump in my throat as I walk toward Kora. Memories flicker in the back of my head. Meeting her for the first time. Holding her hand. Deciding to climb into her bed and fight off her nightmares.

Then later, choosing to be something that nightmares should fear.

For her.

Taking away her hope for a future. Taking away her choice. Taking and taking and taking until there was nothing left—but she still stayed strong. She still smiled.

How can she forgive that?

How can she forgive *me*?

"Jace." Her hands tremble at her sides, and she looks up at me with such amazement. The rings glitter on her finger. Her blue eyes stare into mine, and I see into her soul. She shows me her love.

It's hard to reconcile that emotion with how I think she *should* feel.

She said yes to Wolfe and Apollo.

"It's okay," she whispers, stepping into me. Her cheek presses to my chest, her arms wrapping around my waist. She hugs me until my lungs unlock, and I suck in a breath I didn't know I needed.

"I took away your choices," I admit to the top of her head.

She doesn't respond for a long moment, but then she's stepping back and nodding.

Agreeing with me.

"I'm so sorry." I drop to my knees. Both of them. Because I'm not proposing—I'm begging for forgiveness. "I thought I'd never apologize. I thought I'd be able to keep you as mine, and we'd just..."

She cups my cheek. "Jace. Stop."

I shake my head.

This is not how I thought it would go. Coming apart at the seams like this. But seeing her happy with Wolfe's and Apollo's proposals has undone some insecure part of me.

"It's always been you," she whispers. She drops to her knees, too, right there on the ground in front of me. Her hand is still on my cheek. "It has *always* been you."

I stare at her.

"From the beginning," she continues. "Every moment I spent in your presence shattered me more and more, and I didn't understand that you were helping me uncover lost memories. Of my parents, of the music box, of *you*." Her lips pull down. "I don't know how I buried you in my mind so deep, I didn't even recognize your name. Or your eyes."

Her words echo in my soul.

"I love you," I tell her honestly. The second time, maybe third, that I've ever voiced those words to her. "All I ever wanted to do was save you, but I fell in love with you instead."

Damning us both.

Her eyes fill with tears. "Love sets us free." Her voice is rasping, containing all the emotions she's feeling. "Love is what saved us."

"I don't have any right to ask this," I say, "but will you marry me?"

She grins and dashes away a stray tear. "With every fiber in my soul. *Yes.*"

I retrieve the last ring from my pocket and catch her hand. I eye the bandage with curiosity, my thumb brushing over the tape. She winks at me, then stills as I slide the ring on her finger.

It makes one whole ring. Three solitaire diamonds on their own bands. In the light, she'll be able to see the subtle variations. But here, in the darkness, with only hanging lanterns around us, they shine the same.

I offer her my hand, and she rises gracefully. I take a moment to brush the bits of dirt and grass stuck to her skirt, then stand, too. She doesn't let go of my hand as I lean down to kiss her. It's quick, though, because suddenly Wolfe and Apollo are surrounding us, cheering and yelling. I break away from Kora and mirror her grin.

"I wish we could make it official." She sighs.

I knew she was going to say that. I whistle, and Saint comes striding down the path. He's in a black suit, black shirt. He needed a job for tonight. Tem got her here—but I wanted him involved, too.

In his hand is a small book.

Kora stares at him, then narrows her eyes at me. I give her a smug smile.

Saint stops in front of us, his grin infectious. "I got ordained online," he offers. "I know it's not real... but I wanted it to count, if you want it to."

Kora freezes. "Are you going to marry us?"

He inclines his chin. "If you're okay with that."

She grins, then leaps forward and hugs him. I'm not the only one mildly surprised by her reaction. She whispers something in his ear, which causes his hand to tighten on her back. I almost step forward—a ridiculous instinct, seeing as how it's *Saint*—but he's already releasing her.

We arrange in a half-circle around him, and he cracks open the book. He reads through a short introduction, then asks us the important questions. Will we be there for each other in sickness and in health? Until death do us part?

Kora shakes her head at that, her hand tightening on mine and Wolfe's. "Even death won't tear us apart," she vows.

My face hurts from smiling so hard.

"You may kiss the bride," Saint says. He steps back.

I kiss her first, then spin her into Wolfe's arms. She clutches his arms as his lips press into hers, and then she's moving into Apollo's embrace. Their kiss lingers, and he tastes her. My heart thuds harder.

The four of us. Together forever.

I'm good with that.

kora

Jace carries me into the house and up the stairs. Apollo and Wolfe follow, their eyes on me. I let my hand wander along the back of Jace's neck, flashing my ring at them. Jace's grip on me tightens at the sensation.

He places me on my feet in the bedroom.

"I missed you," I breathe, stepping into his arms and rising to kiss him. I lick his lower lip, sucking it between my teeth. Our mouths open, the kiss deepening by the second. I hold his arms.

Fingers at my back undo the zipper of my skirt and drag it down. They go to my cropped top next. Jace and I separate long enough for them to get it off, and someone trails a finger down my bare spine.

"No bra," Apollo murmurs.

There's a *rip*, and my panties fall away.

I glance over my shoulder, surprised to see Wolfe holding up the remains with a dark smile.

Jace pulls my face back around and kisses me again. His tongue slides into my mouth, and I moan at the full possession. Apollo kisses along my shoulder, down my back. I gasp into Jace's mouth when he widens my stance and pushes a single finger inside me.

"Wet," he announces. "Positively soaked."

"You have a bite mark on your ass, flower," Wolfe says.

Jace growls. He grips my waist, his fingers digging in. Apollo withdraws from my pussy, his fingers leaving tingling trails where he touches my inner thighs.

I break free from Jace's lips and wink at Wolfe. "Apollo likes to mark his territory, I guess..."

"Fuck," Wolfe breathes.

My eyes drop to his pants. His cock presses against his slacks. Actually, they're all still clothed, while I'm completely naked. I start undoing the buttons of Jace's shirt, my fingers moving fast. But not fast enough, because the frustration surges halfway down. I grip the sides and rip them apart.

Buttons go flying.

Jace's eyes widen, then he laughs. "Fuck, I like this side of you."

"Good," I snap. I push him back on the bed and undo his belt. He helps me shove his pants and boxers down, his shoes already long gone. His dick springs free, saluting me, and I drop to my knees before him. His lips part when I take him in my mouth.

Fuck. I don't know why giving him a blow job turns me on.

But then a hot breath draws my attention between my legs.

I draw back and look down. Shock flickers through me that Apollo is lying under me.

"Sit," he urges, his hands wrapping around my thighs. "Don't try to fucking hover either, beautiful."

Oh my god.

My face flames, and I slowly lower myself. Well, I try to do it slowly. Apollo pulls me down, and his mouth meets my pussy. He licks me, then plunges his tongue into my cunt.

I cry out.

Jace fists my hair and guides my mouth back down to his cock. I take it and roll my hips, grinding myself on Apollo's mouth.

It's too much.

It's not enough.

I can easily spend forever with these three.

Jace groans above me, his fingers tightening. "Your mouth is magic. Fuck, keep doing that—"

I reach up and cup his balls. I feel them tighten, and I take his cock deeper. I suck harder. It's a race to get him to climax first, because Apollo's working wonders on my pussy. My legs tremble.

"I'm coming," Jace warns a second before his hot seed spills into my mouth.

I swallow eagerly, my jaw aching from the delicious stretch. He pulls out, and I glance over my shoulder again. Wolfe has been suspiciously quiet...

And it's because his lips are latched around Apollo's cock.

Apollo groans under me, adding a finger to my pussy while he licks and sucks my clit. I hold Jace's thighs and rock against Apollo's face, but I can't take my eyes off Wolfe. He's the only one with pants still on, his dick clearly straining the fabric. His hips rock slightly, fucking the air as he sucks and teases Apollo.

Jace cups my breasts. He leans down and sucks my nipple into his mouth.

The stimulation between what I'm seeing and what I'm feeling is too much.

I come with a sharp cry, falling forward over Jace. He grips me tightly, and I rise off of Apollo's mouth.

Apollo quickly sits up and yanks Wolfe off him.

Jace pulls me onto his lap, facing outward and sliding his semi-hard cock inside me. My walls clench at him, but he doesn't move. He just bands his arms around my waist, one hand on my breast and the other going to my clit.

His strokes are light, and he kisses along my neck as I stare at Wolfe and Apollo.

Apollo tears off Wolfe's pants, his movements urgent. Wolfe watches him and lets him manhandle him. Apollo parts Wolfe's legs roughly, gripping his cock.

Wolfe tips his head back, his eyes closing. Apollo's hand squeezes and strokes him.

"Look at me," Apollo groans.

Wolfe slants his eyes open, glaring at Apollo. With his other hand, Apollo lines up his wet cock at Wolfe's ass and pushes into him.

They both let out moans.

I clench around Jace and shift a bit. Jace is right there waiting for me, his hips thrusting up into me. He pinches my clit.

Apollo fucks Wolfe's ass brutally, thrusting in and out with powerful strokes. Wolfe braces on his forearms, his eyes locked on Apollo's the whole time. And at the same time, Apollo jacks Wolfe off.

Jace's fingers are moving faster on me. He pinches and pulls at my nipple. His lips slide along my neck, with the occasional nip of his teeth.

I let out a breath. An orgasm builds inside me. Slow.

"Fuck," Wolfe moans.

Apollo growls again. He moves harder, faster, until Wolfe lets out a groan. He comes, his cock spurting. He covers his stomach, chest, and Apollo's fist in ropes of cum. He sits up and grabs the back of Apollo's neck, dragging him toward him. Their lips meet, and I see Wolfe's teeth dig into Apollo's lower lip.

My own climax takes me by surprise, so fixated on them that I barely noticed my body's building sensations. The orgasm sweeps through me, and my head falls back on Jace's shoulder. I try to keep my eyes fixed on them, though.

Apollo stills, fully buried in Wolfe, a moment later. His ass flexes as he comes.

Their kiss turns slow, languid, and my heart skips a beat. Or a few.

Hottest.

Thing.

Ever.

They finally break apart, and Apollo helps Wolfe to his feet.

"Wow," I whisper.

Wolfe drops to his knees in front of me, looking up at me. "You like that kind of thing?"

"If you're happy, then I'm happy." I lean forward and kiss him.

Jace is getting harder inside me again. He never really lost it—he has the stamina of an endurance racer—but now it's getting thick. Every move I make draws my attention back to it.

To him.

A shiver rushes through me, but then he pulls out. Lifts me and off him, more like. He rises, too, and puts me on my back. He climbs between my legs, giving me a smirk as he slides back into me.

He grips my wrists and holds them up over my head. "We're going to get you ready."

"For what?" My voice trembles, and I clear my throat. I'm not afraid of whatever they have planned—and being stretched out beneath Jace is one of my favorite places.

"For Apollo and Wolfe to take your sweet little cunt together."

Oh. God.

He chuckles, kissing the corner of my lips. "I think she's into that idea."

Wolfe reclines next to me. Apollo on the other side. They both let their hands rove over my chest, my pinned arms, as Jace fucks me. Each slow thrust into me makes my eyes flutter. But then Wolfe's hand is slipping down to where Jace and I are joined.

He doesn't touch my clit as I thought he might. He goes lower and pushes a finger into me. Right alongside Jace's cock.

I hiss, the feeling of being fuller almost too much.

One finger becomes two, and he curls them inside me, hitting my G-spot. Plus Jace's thick length. It's almost unbearable.

"This is nothing," Apollo whispers in my ear. "But a few more orgasms will relax you."

I shiver.

True to their word, they fuck and finger me into oblivion. I come hard. At some point, Wolfe pulls his fingers free and Jace picks up speed, until he's slamming into me. I lock my legs around his hips and raise mine to meet him.

We're slick with sweat, our bodies sliding together. Wolfe and Apollo are hard, but they ignore their erections. I'd fist them both if I could, but Jace still holds my wrists hostage above my head.

Finally, his pace hits a frantic note, and he buries himself all the way inside me. He comes hard, his lips touching down on mine.

Before I can catch my breath, he's helping me up stand with him. Apollo takes my spot on the bed and motions for me to join him. Jace sets me down until my back meets Apollo's chest.

I can't stop the shiver that races through me.

"We'll go slow," Apollo says in my ear. His tongue touches my earlobe, and I sigh.

He slips into me easily, thrusting up from behind a few times. Jace's cum slicked the way for him. *For them.*

Wolfe crawls on the bed, between my legs and Apollo's. He eyes my pussy with a wicked glint in his eyes, and my breath catches for the fifth damn time when he lowers his head between my legs.

"Fuck," Apollo groans.

Wolfe must be touching him, even as he's impaled inside me. His tongue flicks at my slit, and I jump. He's licking both of us...

I almost come from the thought alone.

His lips close over my clit.

I make an indecent noise. Apollo shifts his hips, rocking in and out of me slowly. Just micro-movements.

My gaze lifts, locking on Jace. He sits in a chair that was in the corner but is now a hell of a lot closer. His eyes burn into mine.

Wolfe stops just shy of bringing me to orgasm. Instead, he kisses his way up my body and puts his cock at my opening.

He kisses me. His fingers find my clit again, and I come instantly. Wound up, left hanging. I come hard, my vision going white. His lips stroke mine, his mouth swallowing my noises, and as I'm on my way back down to reality, he pushes into me.

My lips pop open.

Pain and pleasure spar inside me. The pressure...

"Relax, baby," Apollo whispers in my ear.

Wolfe's hips meet mine, and we share a look.

They're both inside me.

Oh. My. God.

Suddenly we're moving—rolling onto our sides. Wolfe in front of me, Apollo at my back. But now Wolfe doesn't have to try to stay off both of us, I guess.

We lay there, our legs tangled and my breathing ragged. They stay still for a moment, letting me adjust. But I need movement. Right now.

"Please," I whisper.

Wolfe kisses me. I turn back and catch Apollo's lips.

They rock in and out of me, and it's pain and bliss wrapped up together. I've never felt anything like it—and judging from their expressions, neither have they.

"Your piercing is going to be the death of me," Wolfe groans.

Apollo chuckles.

"Guys." I can't control the wobble in my voice.

"Yes, wife?" Wolfe asks, kissing my throat.

"Mm, wife," Apollo agrees. He fists my hair and tips my head back, giving Wolfe more room to explore my skin.

All the while, they thrust in and out of me. They alternate, they move in sync and then opposite. But after the first few minutes, something breaks in all of us. Their speed increases. I try to keep a stranglehold on the pleasure that's blooming through me in waves, but it's useless. Desperate noises come from my mouth. They both take what they need from me—

"Wait for me," Apollo orders Wolfe. He reaches over me and puts his hand on Wolfe's throat, his grip tight.

Wolfe eyes him, his mouth opening and closing. Fire flashes in his gaze.

But somehow, he holds off until Apollo releases him.

They come within seconds of each other, both filling me up and exploding. I let go of my control, too. Pushed over the edge, my cunt clenches and pulses around them.

Wolfe slips free first. Then Apollo.

I try to catch my breath, but it's gone. My lungs have taken a vacation.

Jace leans over Wolfe and kisses my jaw. "That was worth watching," he says in my ear. "You okay?"

I nod. My eyes are already closing. Vaguely, I'm aware of Apollo getting up. Jace takes his place—his scent is unmistakable. He loops his arm over my waist and tangles our legs together.

The light goes off.

On the other side of Wolfe, the bed dips. Apollo rejoins us.

My heart is so fucking full, I can't wipe the smile from my lips. Even as I drift off to sleep.

"Y ou going to explain the bandage, princess?"

Jace's sleep-tinged voice—which may be my new favorite sound—curls in my ear. His lips follow, touching my earlobe. His hand drifts down my arm, landing on the bandage still taped to the inside of my wrist.

I smile and crack my eyes open. Apollo is curled around Wolfe, their bodies glued together. Wolfe's face is only a few inches from mine, half on my pillow, and his hand holds mine. I shift a little, and Jace moves my hair off my shoulder.

He sucks in another breath, and I smile wider.

He's found the second of the two tattoos.

"To represent us," I whisper, glancing back at him. It's up high, just under the base of my neck in the center of my back. It wasn't the most pleasant thing I've experienced, Saint's needle passing over my spine multiple times. "How I'm not alone, you know?"

He brushes his finger over it.

My hair did a good job hiding it last night—and after

their proposal in the woods, we didn't really have time to examine the white bandage covering my wrist.

Now we do, though.

Wolfe stirs, and his grip on my hand tightens. He pulls it up to his mouth, and his lips skate across my knuckles. "Round two? Or... fuck. Five?"

"Kora was going to show us her new ink," Jace says.

Wolfe sits up suddenly, jostling Apollo awake. He rolls me onto my stomach, and Jace moves my hair.

"Wow." Wolfe leans in closer. "That's Saint's work, for sure."

I smile. "Yeah."

"Her wrist," Jace says roughly.

Wolfe lifts it from where I had moved it under my pillow, frowning at the bandage. I know what they're thinking—the hourglass scar is on this wrist.

I sit back against the headboard. Apollo watches me from the other side of Wolfe, his expression curious.

They're *all* curious.

With a sigh, I pull the bandage off and show them.

Saint didn't hide the hourglass. No—he made it stand out. Flowers from the top and out from behind it. The flowers are the pretty part. Some red, some black, some gold. He shaded inside the hourglass to give it a rounded look, and then added cracks to the surface.

He turned something ugly, something I was ashamed of, into a piece of art. It's me.

I think of the girl I used to be. The stubborn girl who refused to leave Sterling Falls because she thought bigger monsters were behind her. The one who made a deal with a devil and got caught in his trap, who faced being branded, who starved, who refused to ask for help...

My skin is sore, but I insisted that I could do it in one

session. Afterward, Saint and I drank our cheap, homemade margaritas and talked. I asked him if he was going to cover his brand, and he contemplated it.

But then he said that if I had the courage to keep mine —albeit altering it—he'll hold on to his for a while.

Better to accept it than cover it up.

When Tem showed up, we were properly drunk. She drove both of us back to her condo. Saint slept on the couch while I took his room. And then the shopping spree, the outfit she pushed on me, the hair appointment...

It makes sense why she did those things. She wanted me to be ready to marry my best friends.

My heart swells.

I'm not sure when they became not only the guys I fell in love with, but my friends, too. But it's absolutely, one hundred percent true.

And I'm so fucking lucky to have married them.

"We should tell your parents about this." Apollo snags my left hand and running his thumb over the ring.

I frown. The Sinclairs... we're okay. I mean, as well as we can be. One good thing about having too much downtime in the last two months was coming to terms with what they did. The guys urged me to forgive them—not their actions, but as people. Not for them, but for me.

So I did.

But I'm not sure they know the full truth of my relationship with these three. They know Jace and I are close. We didn't mention the whole married thing, for obvious reasons. One of which being my dad very nearly had Jace killed by Jeremy Bradshaw.

Of course, Jeremy wasn't going to *kill* Jace. But he could've. He had us vulnerable.

"Maybe invite them for dinner," Wolfe adds. His hand slides up my ribcage, stopping just below my breast.

My stomach somersaults. Although more at his words or his touch, I can't say.

"Or maybe we already did," Jace whispers, kissing my neck.

I groan. "You didn't."

"And Nate, Nadine, Saint, Artemis, Malik... it's going to be a party." Wolfe grins. "A good one, this time, with no evil murderers allowed."

"A wedding party?" I tilt my head to give Jace better access. "What if I had said no?"

Apollo kisses my knuckles. "Then it would've been a pretty depressing party. Thank god you chose well."

Wolfe pushes me back into the pillows and climbs on top of me. A chill runs up my spine, and I trail my hands along Wolfe's abdomen, up his chest. Jace and Apollo pull my thighs aside, and Wolfe wordlessly slides into me. I sigh at the blissful, full feeling.

It almost drowns out the worry of hoping my parents accept my relationship with them.

And then it fully erases it when Wolfe rocks into me harder, stoking a fire under my skin. With Apollo and Jace right beside me.

Perfect.

THE END

acknowledgments

This series has been a journey of epic proportions. I've been through major highs and lows while writing it. I fell in love with Kora and her guys, with the glamour of Olympus and the darkness of Sterling Falls.

I hope you enjoyed it as much as I did.

I hope it felt as real to you as it did for me.

BIG thank you to the readers who sent me messages while reading, who loved Wolfe and Jace and Apollo, who helped share this series with their book friends. Y'all are the best.

Thank you also to my incredible team: Najla & co at Qamber Designs for creating the beautiful covers and alternate paperback covers, Wander Aguiar for his photography. Emmy at Studio ENP for edits, and Paige Sayer Proofreading. Erin Spencer and her crew at One Night Stand Studios, plus the narrators Addison Barnes and Tyler Darby for their hard work in the fantastic audiobook production. (Seriously, have you listened? The duet narration is just extra perfect.) To my early readers, Rebecca, Ari, Jolie, Erica, Brandy, Shawna, Clarissa—I am so grateful for your feedback and cheerleading (and on occasion, your tears. #sorrynotsorry).

And lastly... I'm not closing the door on the world of Sterling Falls. I can't leave Artemis without love (and her fair share of heartbreak). Stay tuned for her story in 2023.

also by s. massery

about the author

S. Massery is a dark romance author who loves injecting a good dose of suspense into her stories. She lives in Western Massachusetts with her dog, Alice.

Before adventuring into the world of writing, she went to college in Boston and held a wide variety of jobs—including working on a dude ranch in Wyoming (a personal highlight). She has a love affair with coffee and chocolate. When S. Massery isn't writing, she can be found devouring books, playing outside with her dog, or trying to make people smile.

Join her newsletter to stay up to date on new releases: http://smassery.com/newsletter

Printed in Great Britain
by Amazon

16981428R00310